milly
johnson

Here Come
the Girls

SIMON &
SCHUSTER

London · New York · Sydney · Toronto

A CBS COMPANY

First published in Great Britain by Simon & Schuster UK Ltd, 2011
A CBS COMPANY

16

Simon & Schuster UK Ltd
1st Floor
222 Gray's Inn Road
London WC1X 8HB

www.simonandschuster.co.uk

Simon & Schuster Australia
Sydney

A CIP catalogue record for this book is available
from the British Library

ISBN 978-1-84983-205-2

Typeset in Bembo by M Rules
Printed and bound by CPI Group (UK) Ltd, Croydon, CR0 4YY

This book is dedicated to the wonderful people of Yorkshire. The ones who have taught me, healed me, employed me, supported me, laughed with me, lent me tissues, scoffed cake, broken bread and drunk wine with me, represented me legally, tucked me in at night, cooked for me, delivered my babies, read my books, called me 'friend', called me 'mum', liked me – and loved me.

On the third day out I get it, the sea
Is not one thing, it constantly transforms
Itself, and in unthinking majesty
Tapestries horizons with sun or storms.
So then lying now, rocking to and fro
On its soothing and gentle amniotic swell
I loosen thoughts of home, and let them go,
And my shipwrecked heart can start to heal.
What promise for me, what spirit salve
When unanchored here I find at last,
Something has shifted, giving me resolve
To let hope aboard, jettison the past.
The sea has given me a chance to live,
And leads us maybe to a safe harbour, love.

'The Voyage Out' by James Nash

'Twenty years from now you will be more disappointed by the things that you didn't do than by the ones you did do. So throw off the bowlines. Sail away from the safe harbour. Catch the trade winds in your sails. Explore. Dream. Discover.'

Mark Twain

Here Come the Girls

Prologue

People always remember the winters of their childhood as being as white as iced Christmas-cake tops. They recall their journeys to school as being trapped inside a giant snow-globe, recently shaken. Likewise they remember their long-ago summers as hotter and brighter and longer than they ever were. The sun switched on its light in May – all 950 watts of it – and didn't even begin to fade until all the rusty, crispy leaves had dropped from the trees in late September. Indeed, whenever four women thought back to a certain afternoon twenty-five years ago, they pictured the shapes in the clouds as more defined, the sky impossibly blue and the sun the colour of a massive sherbet lemon. The grass they lay on was more velvet than itchy, and no one remembered sneezing because their hay fever had been triggered off.

Full of Cornish pasty and lumpy school gravy, four fourteen-year-old girls reposed on the grassy bank in their red and grey regulation uniforms and looked lazily up at the sky.

'That one looks like a squirrel,' said Ven, pointing to a white mass of cloud.

'Eh? Where the hell are you looking?' replied Frankie.

'There.' Ven stabbed upwards with her finger. 'That bit there is its tail and the big round thing is its head.'

'Oh yeah,' said Roz. 'I sort of see what you mean, but you

have to admit that it does look more like a squirrel which has just been run over by a tractor. Aw, look – there's a heart.' She sighed, making the others groan.

'Has it got "I love Jez Jackson by Roz Lynch" written across the middle of it, by any chance?' laughed Olive.

'It might have,' said Roz bashfully, or as bashfully as she could manage as the thought of Jez Jackson glided into her brain. Three years older than her, he lived across the street and was skinny and lithe and never acknowledged her. He was the 'Boy from Ipanema' and made her heartbeat rev up whenever she spotted his Marc Bolan perm.

'That one looks like a cloud,' said Olive.

'Oh, very funny!' snorted Roz.

'No, I mean like a proper cloud in a cartoon. Flat at the bottom but bobbly on top. By the way, did you know that Zeus was the God of Clouds?'

'Ooh, who's been paying extra attention in Classics,' said Frankie, poking Olive in the ribs. 'Swotty Olive Lyon, that's who.'

'Give over!' chuckled Olive.

'I'm surprised she pays any attention in Classics,' said Roz. 'She's always too busy looking into Mr Metaxas's eyes.'

'That's a big lie. I am not!' refuted Olive, but laughing too because it was true and her friends knew it was.

'I reckon you're going to move to Athens, Ol, and become a Greek bride. You'll change your name to Aphrodite and live off vine leaves. They love blondes out there, apparently. You're worth at least a couple of camels,' said Frankie.

'They don't use camels as currency in the Med, dafty,' said Roz.

'Oh whatever,' Frankie returned with a sniff. She sat up and swished her long black sheet of hair behind her. 'Olive, the most-a bellissima fruit in the world-a,' she said, affecting an accent very similar to Mr Metaxas's sexy Greek one. 'How juicy the olive is. I just want to eat her ... er ... *it* all up in-a one-a bite.'

Olive was giggling and blushing and trying not to think of snogging Mr Metaxas. His Mediterranean tan, black hair and huge brown eyes had done their fair share in helping to kick-start her adult hormones. She often went to sleep thinking of him calling her 'Olive' in the same way he did in class. Out of all the crap names her parents could have called her, 'Olive' had always seemed by far the worst. If only her parents had called her 'Olivia' which was far more posh and acceptable. But Olive! It was the name of the frumpiest woman ever in *On the Buses*. Mr Metaxas always managed to make it sound so romantic and rich, though.

'That one looks like a ship,' said Frankie.

'Ooh yes, it does,' Roz said, agreeing with her for once. 'God, I wish I were on a ship now having a nice holiday. I've got double Classics this affy.'

'So have I,' smiled Olive wistfully. She was the only girl in the school who looked forward to it, apart from a couple of spotty, brainbox types in the year above who were aiming for Oxbridge. 'Paraclausithyron,' she added with a sigh, making it sound more like a sexual act than a Greek motif.

'What's that when it's at home?' asked Frankie, who had double Spanish and wouldn't have liked to have swapped. She had a natural flair for languages. Her family were Italian and she was already bi-lingual and on course for being tri-lingual.

'An entreaty at a closed door,' said Olive, still in her half-dreamlike state. 'When a lover is outside appealing to be let in.'

Ven chuckled. 'What do you know about not letting randy Greeks in the door? You'd let them all in, you romantic saddo.'

'It costs thousands of pounds to go on a ship for your holiday, I heard,' said Olive, trying to wean her thoughts away from Mr Metaxas. At least that's what class show-off Colette Hudd had told her when she was queening it with her holiday photos aboard a Cunard ship. Her dad owned a secondhand car lot and was absolutely loaded. She got dropped off at school every morning in a Rolls-Royce and out of school wore proper jeans with labels on them like 'Brutus Gold'. Not like Olive, whose mother bought all her clothes from Littlewoods. Olive and her parents had never holidayed further than Skegness in a caravan. Hot water and an indoor toilet would have been a luxury, never mind a flaming cabin with a porthole.

'We'll all have to go on a cruise one day and pick Ol up a husband with brown eyes and garlic-stinky breath,' said Roz, flicking the grass off her long legs. 'When we're all old and rich.'

'Not too old,' said Olive. 'I won't get a husband if I'm all hunched up and wrinkled with a stick.'

Frankie thought of the beautiful English teacher at school, Miss Tanner. She was everything Frankie hoped she would grow into one day – curvy, husky-voiced and confident. Thanks to all the secret fags she smoked, she was almost there with the voice. And she knew Miss Tanner had just turned forty because Frankie had been asked by Mr Firth (French) to stay in at break and make a birthday card for her because Frankie was pretty good at Art too. It was obvious to everyone in the school that English and French were having an 'entente cordiale'. And him not even thirty yet. Way to go, Miss Tanner!

'Forty would be a good age. We'll all be rich and gorgeous by then. We'll have to go on Ven's birthday though because she's the only summer baby,' decided Frankie.

'Okay, let's do that then,' said Olive. She held her hand out for the others to put theirs on top of it and seal the deal. They did, and it was now set in stone that on 24th August, Venice Smith's fortieth birthday, they would be on the sort of ship that made the one Colette Hudd showed off about look like a blow-up dinghy.

The ship-shape cloud had morphed into a big white mess

now. The end of dinner bell sounded and Roz, Frankie and Ven grimaced at each other. Only Olive had a spring in her step as she headed back towards the school building, her heart full of dreams of being a bride carried away to a lush, sunny island in the middle of a wine-dark sea.

Chapter 1

Twenty-five years later

'What about this one then?' Roz said, holding up birthday card number eighteen.

Olive took the card and read the outside of it aloud. '"What do you call a forty-year-old woman who is single?"' She turned to the inside for the punchline. '"A lucky bitch".' What a surprise – another man-bashing joke from Roz. She handed it back with a pained expression. 'It's quite funny, I suppose. But I can't say I'm rolling around on the floor laughing.'

'It's only a card – you don't need to wet your pants with hysteria,' tutted Roz. 'It's relevant on the age forty and the single-status front though, don't you think?'

As well as relevant to you on the 'I hate men' front, thought Olive, though she wasn't snipey enough to say that. Instead she decided, 'I'm going for a sentimental one. Something like this,' and she held up a sweet flowery card with a nice 'friend' verse.

'Huh. Ideal if you like slop. Don't get me a card like that for my fortieth, I'll throw up.'

'Oh, I shall,' teased Olive. 'I'll get one with little kittens on the front and a long verse about what a wonderful person you are.'

'You'd better buy me an accompanying bucket as well then,'

said Roz. 'Oh sod it, I'm getting this one otherwise I'll be here all day. What are you going to buy her as a present?'

'I haven't even thought about it yet,' replied Olive. 'I'm not as organised as you. I bet you've got your Christmas presents bought and wrapped already.'

'Not all of them,' sniffed Roz. Olive knew she wasn't joking. She'd probably have all their fiftieth birthday cards bought and written by this November.

'Maybe I'll get her a hamper,' mused Olive.

'A hamper? What sort of hamper?'

'One with TENA Ladys, Werther's Originals and a nasal hair-trimmer in it.'

Roz tutted. 'I thought you were being serious.'

'I am,' twinkled Olive, leaning in to impart her secret. 'Actually it's not that much of a joke these days. Don't tell anyone, but I stuck the trimmer that David's cousin got him for Christmas up my nose and it started making all sorts of zzz-ing noises. Scared me to death. I never thought the day would come when I'd have to trim nasal hair or wax my face.'

'Don't talk to me about facial hair,' said Roz. 'If I didn't get mine ripped off at the salon every couple of months I'd be walking around like Rolf Harris.'

Olive chuckled as they made their way to the till. She knew Roz would wake up out of a coma to put her make-up on. She wouldn't pull the wheelie bin out unless she was wearing mascara, even though she didn't need to. Roz had a gorgeous face with slicing cheekbones like the top models in magazines.

'Ol, do you fancy clubbing together and getting Ven some-thing between us for her birthday?' Roz suddenly asked.

'Yes, I'm up for that. Thirty quid each – is that enough?'

'It's more than enough. Are you sure that's okay with you, though?' Roz didn't say 'can you afford that amount?' although that's what she meant. It was no secret that Olive was perma-nently skint. She had cleaning jobs all over the place but a nest full of big cuckoos with ever-hungry mouths ready to devour the wages she earned.

'It's my mate's fortieth birthday and it's important she has a nice present,' said Olive firmly. 'Especially one who's had such a crap couple of years.' Losing both a mother and a father within thirteen months had really brought Ven very low. Then, if that wasn't enough, her rotten stinking husband declared he was off with a floozy, divorced her and was awarded half of everything she had – including the money her mum and dad had been putting away for her all their lives. And just to kick her whilst she was at her lowest, a few weeks after her Decree Absolute came through, she was made redundant from her job. Bad luck always came in such big chunks, unlike good luck, Olive thought.

They walked up the hill and down into the shopping arcade, throwing ideas for suitable fortieth-birthday presents at each other until they reached the Edwardian Tea Room. Already sitting at a table inside, Ven waved heartily at them through the window.

'Wotcher, girls,' she called as they joined her. Ven's face had always fallen naturally into a big dimply smile, but today she was grinning like a loon and her dimples were as deep as Grand Canyons.

'What's up with you?' said Roz, noting it. 'Lost a Ryvita and found a cheesecake?'

'Nope. I'm just happy to see you. Let's order straight away 'cos I'm parched.'

'My usual,' said Roz.

'Ditto,' added Olive.

'Three nutty honey lattes, two pieces of cappuccino cake and one slice of lemon drizzle, please,' Ven said to the waitress who came over. Smiles seemed to be oozing out of her.

'What's the matter? Have you been on laughing gas?' asked Roz.

'Nope,' Ven said. 'Nothing's up with me. Absolutely nothing at all.'

'Okay,' conceded Roz. 'So, have you made up your mind where you fancy going for your fortieth-birthday celebrations? Shall I book us a Chinese banquet at the Silver Moon, an Italian at Bella Noche or a curry at the Raj?'

'Flaming heck, Roz, I've got five weeks until then,' laughed Ven.

'She's obsessed,' tutted Olive, shaking her head in exasperation. 'Anal, totally anal.'

'I want to get it booked,' Roz explained. 'Honestly! What's wrong with that?'

'So my choices are egg fried rice, korma or spag bol. How our plans have shrunk over the years,' laughed Ven. 'Remember being on the school playing-fields and planning that cruise we were all going to have when we got to forty?'

'Aye, well, we were young and daft then,' said Roz. 'If you remember, I was going to be a PA for an international businessman and travel the world on private jets, not work for an old sow in a boring bank.' It was no secret that Roz hated her administration job in a town centre bank, and despised her pernickety, frumpy boss – Mrs Hutchinson – even more.

'Aye, and we were all convinced we were going to be multi-millionaires by the time we were twenty-five,' added Olive. Oh, if only she still had all those dreams packed tight in her heart like buds ready to flower into giant blossoms. She had managed to live out only the one – spending a single summer on a Greek island – but the rest had rotted from neglect. 'God, it seems another lifetime away – the four of us lying on the grass in our grey, white and red uniforms, looking at shapes in the clouds.'

She felt Roz bristle at the memory of them being 'a four'. However much she had reconstructed history and reclassified them as a 'three', to Olive and Ven they would always be a quartet. *The Fabulous Four.*

'Would you still go on a cruise if you could?' Ven asked.

'Course I would,' said Roz with a humph. 'In fact, I've got a spare five grand in my purse. Why don't I nip into Thomas Cook's right this minute.'

'But if you did have a spare five grand ...'

'I'd get a new bathroom,' Roz counter-interrupted. 'But I haven't, so that's the end of that one.'

'I'd go on one,' sighed Olive. 'I haven't been abroad for twenty years.' She thought back to *that* summer, swimming in water that was as blue as Paul Newman's eyes, harvesting olives, tasting fruits that had been kissed by the sun.

'Yes, well, we aren't fourteen any more with heads full of stupid dreams,' said Roz, with that bitter tone they were so used to hearing in her voice these days, but it still had the effect of a cold shower on the conversation for a while.

Eventually Olive broke the silence. 'Do you fancy a surprise party?' she piped up, which made Ven laugh and Roz roll her eyes and say, 'That's a grand idea, Olive. But let's not mention it to Ven. We wouldn't want her to GUESS WHAT WE'D GOT PLANNED.'

'No, I don't fancy a surprise party, thank you,' Ven told them. 'I have an idea what I would like, but I need to do a bit of arranging first.'

'Like what?' asked Olive. Conversation broke off for a minute whilst the coffee and cakes arrived.

'Never you mind,' said Ven, tapping the side of her nose and picking up her fork. 'But let me just say that my money's on an Italian meal.'

Chapter 2

On the bus home, Olive was all wrapped up in that revisit to a precious memory of them all at school on the playing-field, lying in the sun, Frankie pointing to the sky and saying, '*That one looks like a ship.*'

And Roz saying that she wished she were on a ship instead of psyching herself up for double Classics with Mr Metaxas.

Mr Metaxas. Olive smiled to herself as she thought how she always turned to mush whenever he said her name. He made it sound like something earthy and desirable. Then five years later she was to meet a man with the same smouldering Greek accent who didn't only make her name sound beautiful and succulent as sunshine embodied into fruit, but he made *her* feel beautiful and ripe and ready for the plucking.

Her smile grew a little wider when she remembered herself aged fourteen. Then, she'd thought anyone over twenty-four was ancient. And people at forty were only fit for sitting on deckchairs reading books about jam-making, if their cataracts allowed them to. Her younger self had never considered that at thirty-nine her spirit wouldn't have aged a day, even if her body had. In her head she was still that same skinny, leggy lass who loved rounders and had posters of the Police up on her wall. Olive, Ven, Roz, Frankie. *The Fabulous Four.* They had even nicked their thumbs with Ven's dad's razor-blade and sealed their friendship in blood after seeing it on a film because apparently it would bind them together for life. Well, that obviously hadn't worked. Everything was a right old mess now.

Olive got off the bus at her stop, crossed the road and walked down the back alley opposite to the house where she lived. She never thought of it as 'home', because it wasn't. It was her mother-in-law Doreen's home. Home was a place for which she would choose the carpets and the wallpaper. She was a lodger at number 15, Land Lane. It was not her home and she suspected it never would be.

She pushed open the front door and stepped inside.

'Olive, is that you?' That screechy female voice dragged her kicking and screaming back from warm memories of girlhood into the dull chilly present.

'Yes, it's me,' Olive said, slipping off her eight-year-old raincoat and hanging it up next to David's work jacket. Although the word 'work' was pushing it a lot. She couldn't remember the last time he'd done a full day's labour. She wasn't sure he ever had, come to think of it.

'Did you get my corn pads?'

'Yes, Doreen.'

Doreen Hardcastle shifted her bulk in her specially wide wheelchair so she could straighten all the gold cushions around her. She looked like a very fat queen on a reinforced sturdy throne. Except instead of a crown on her head there was a helmet of tight curls, thanks to over-zealous perming by the mobile hairdresser who came once every eight weeks with a bag full of rollers and some stinky setting chemicals.

'I've been sat here for ages watching the same channel. The batteries have conked out in the remote.' Doreen Hardcastle huffed with some annoyance. 'And I've run out of pop.'

'Where's David?' asked Olive, falling into automatic 'sorting-Doreen-out' mode and going to the drawer for a pack of AA batteries.

'He's having a lie-down – his back's been playing up again.' Doreen's voice softened, as it always did when she was referring to 'her boys' – David, her only child, and Kevin, the nephew who came to live with her at fifteen when Doreen's unmarried sister died. Butter wouldn't have melted in either of their mouths.

'Ooh, our poor David. He does suffer with his back.'

Marvellous, thought Olive. Not only would she have to pander to her mother-in-law's whims, but she foresaw an afternoon of running up and downstairs as well after David, who would no doubt be groaning like a baby with croup. Then in four hours she would be off to yet another cleaning job when the rest of the world was getting dressed up to go out and celebrate their Saturday nights.

'Is that you, Olive?' Olive heard a limp voice float down the stairs.

'Yes, I'm back.' She checked her watch.

'Can you give my back a rub, love? I'm in agony.'

'I've a toenail that's digging into my slipper as well,' said Doreen. 'When you've sorted our David out, nip it off for me, would you?'

Please, added Olive to herself. Not that anyone in the house ever used the word to her. That would have dangerously elevated her from slave status.

'Anything else before I go up and sort David out?' she asked, turning on the bottom step.

'Aye,' said Doreen Hardcastle. 'Cup of tea. Make it three sugars, but don't stir because I don't like it too sweet.'

Olive back-tracked to the kitchen and nearly tripped over a huge black binliner spewing out smelly jeans and pungent men's pants.

'Doreen, what are all these clothes?' Olive called.

'Oh, our Kevin's stopping here for a bit. He's split up from Wendy for good this time. Can you make sure the spare room is all right for him when you go upstairs? He's just gone back to get the rest of his stuff.'

Olive opened her mouth to protest, but what could she say? After all, it was Doreen's house and she was just the skivvy who did the laundry, the cooking and all the cleaning.

Sunshine seemed even more than a few million light years ago from Olive's life.

'Hello, love. How were the girls?' Manus gave Roz a kiss in greeting as she walked through the door. He noticed, as always, that her neck twisted in reflex so that his kiss would land firmly on the edge of her lips, not full onto them. He tried not to let his spirits dip, but these constant subtle rejections from Roz never got any easier to bear.

'They're good,' said Roz. 'And send their love.'

'Fancy getting a DVD out of Blockbusters and having a curry delivered tonight?'

'Oh, er, which film?' said Roz.

'Anything you want.'

Damn, thought Roz. He was making it hard to refuse. She knew he was being nice but she couldn't help being annoyed, because she was good at being annoyed with him – and pushing his boundaries.

'Not sure I'm in the mood for a film. I might do the ironing and then get an early night.' Whoops, thought Roz then. Not the ideal thing to say after a month without sex. She imagined Manus's brain starting to tick. But for the first time he didn't pick it up and run with it. He didn't say, 'Ooh, early night. Can I join you?' Because if you kick a dog enough, eventually it learns. Instead he gave a conceding nod and said, 'Ah, no worries. It was just an idea.'

Roz felt the hard impact of a turning-point in their relationship.

Chapter 3

The following Monday morning, Ven drummed her fingernails on the table as she prepared to ring that number. The notepad next to her was full of a weekend's scribbles and crossings out. She had no doubt in her mind that what she was about to commit herself to was the right thing, so what was stopping her? The logistics of her grand plan were a nightmare; there were just so many points where it could all go horribly wrong. Really, she shouldn't think about it too much. Her head was already on the verge of exploding.

She sipped at her coffee and noticed a chip in the edge of the mug. She should get herself some new ones. The kettle was on its last legs too. In the time it took to boil, she could fly over to Iceland, fill up a jug with water from one of those hot springs, and fly back home again. Replacing all the old and broken things around the house hadn't been a priority though, since being made redundant from her deputy-managerial position at Furniture for You when it fell into receivership eight months ago. It hadn't been the most scintillating of positions but the people she worked with had been lovely. She'd been doing a bit of rubbishy temp work since, until a permanent job came up, but it didn't exactly bring in enough money to go mad and splash out. Still, things weren't that bad that she couldn't go and buy herself a few new badly needed cups, she smiled to herself.

She herded her thoughts away from the state of her crockery and towards the job in hand. It was now or never. Ergo, it had to be now. Her hand reached out for the phone then shot back to her side.

Oh sod it and just do it. Her dad's favourite saying blasted into her brain. He'd used it when she was prevaricating about buying her first car, having her waist-length hair cut off, getting a kitten, buying her first house ... She heard his gentle voice say the words again to her, then she heard her own voice repeat them aloud.

Sod it and just do it.

She picked up the phone and pressed in the number written down on her pad. Apparently Roz's boss at the bank was a right old bat but very active in the WI and always on the lookout for donations, which was a good bargaining point. A woman's plummy voice answered after three burrs: 'South Yorkshire Banking Services, Margaret Hutchinson speaking.'

'Hello, Mrs Hutchinson,' began Ven. 'I understand you are Rosalind Lynch's boss. I wonder if I might have a word with you about her.'

Chapter 4

The alarm went off and after seven shrill beeps, a barely conscious David kicked his wife in the calf, his long toenail digging uncomfortably into her skin.

'Olive, wake up. Your alarm's going!'

His voice dragged Olive from her sleep. She had been swirling in a bright blue sparkly sea, which she didn't want to leave. Her hand came out and connected with the snooze button, not that she would be able to find her way back into that dream in the nine minutes she had until the beeps went off again. As soon as her eyes had opened, it had disappeared for ever.

She was no longer swimming with dolphins, but in bed with a whale. In jokes, wasn't it the woman who was supposed to make the major claim on the space? David slept like a man on a crucifix, arms spread out leaving barely a sliver of bedspace for his wife. Olive tried to stretch. Her back was playing up at the moment which was probably caused by vacuuming all the stairs in Mr Tidy's five-storey house. She was half-crippled by the end of her Monday, Tuesday and Friday hours there. She hated that house; it had a horrible cold feel to it – a permanent Monday-morning feel. She kneaded hard at her lower back and wished she could just pull the duvet over herself and stay in bed and rest. She fantasised about

David not being there and having the whole five-foot width available to starfish her limbs.

David snored so loudly he woke himself up fully and rolled over onto Olive.

'Ow!' she shrieked. A few more degrees and he would have squashed her flat as a pancake.

'Ow,' he echoed, rubbing his spine. 'Are you still here? Have you overslept?'

'No, I'm just psyching myself up to get out of bed,' replied Olive. 'My back's hurting a bit.'

'Hmmm, I know that feeling well,' yawned David. 'I hardly slept a wink last night, mine was so bad.'

Olive fought down the retort rising inside her. *Hardly slept? You were snoring like a machine for at least eight hours.* And no doubt, he would go back to sleep for another eight, as soon as she was up and out of the house. But then he shifted position and groaned and sounded in such genuine pain that she fell instantly into dutiful-wife mode.

'Would you like me to give you a bit of a rub before I go to work?' she asked.

'Oh yes,' he said, flipping quickly over onto his front and sighing with anticipation.

Olive reached for the tub on his bedside cabinet and scooped the cold gel out, warming it up between her own hands before applying it to David's back. He shivered with delight as she worked her thumbs into his skin, trying to find the muscle under the fat as he fired instructions at her. 'Higher, lower, shoulders, left a bit, right a bit . . .' and all the while, her own aching back groaned in protest.

'There,' she said eventually as the snooze button went off again and called an end to her ministrations. 'That'll have to be it for now. I've got to be at Mr Tidy's by eight.'

'Hang on,' squealed David. 'You can't leave me like this!' He rolled over with the agility of a man whose back had just been dipped in the water at Lourdes. Then he pointed to his very stiff erection.

'Come on, Olive.' He tried pulling her on top of him. 'Sort me out.'

'I can't,' she protested through her teeth as the bed gave an almighty creak. 'Your mother will hear.'

'Give me a blow job then. I'm only a couple of sucks away.'

And afterwards he had the cheek to ask her to bring him up a cup of tea before she went for her bus.

Chapter 5

'The usual for me.'

'Ditto.'

'Three nutty honey lattes, two pieces of cappuccino cake and one slice . . .'

'. . . of lemon drizzle.' The waitress finished off Ven's sentence. She had taken the same order so many times she could have reeled it off in her sleep.

'Thank you,' laughed Ven.

They were sitting in their usual Saturday-afternoon fortnightly haunt, the Edwardian Tea Room. For once they'd got the coveted table in the corner. When the waitress had gone, Ven turned to Olive. She looked to have aged five years in the two weeks since she had last seen her.

'Sure you don't want another shot of espresso in yours, Ol? You look knackered.'

'I am knackered,' said Olive, unable to stop the yawn that followed her words.

Even though the friends only met for coffee once a fortnight, they kept in regular contact by phone and text, so they knew that David's cousin Kevin had now moved in and was as dependent on her cooking/washing/arse-wiping duties as the other members of the Hardcastle clan. Kevin usually managed to migrate from one woman's flat to another's when his transient sexually-fuelled relationships ran out of steam, but for the first time he had been unsuccessful and needed a place to lay his head and stink the house out with his dirty underwear.

'I can't understand why you put up with all of them,' said Roz. 'I'd tell them where to go.'

'It's not my house though, is it? I've got no say in who stays.'

'I've been telling you for years to put yourself down on a list for your own council house,' snapped Roz.

'David wouldn't leave his mum alone in her state.'

Roz bit back the retort. She was convinced, as was Ven because they'd talked about it on many occasions, that Doreen Hardcastle's 'poor crippled bad legs' were, in fact, 'capable fat lazy legs'. She was far too happy to let Olive run ragged after her and charge her rent for the privilege. Roz wanted to shake some sense into Olive every time she saw her. There was being soft, then there was being Olive. Try and let Manus treat her like that and see what happened!

Ven gave Olive a kind smile. She was too selfless by half, was Olive. She didn't have it in her to say the word 'no'. She couldn't wait to put her plan into operation and give Olive the break of a lifetime.

By the time the cake and coffee had arrived, Ven had started to do that deep-dimple grin thing again. Her mouth was curved upwards so much, the ends were nearly joined at the top of her head.

'Are you on drugs?' Roz commented.

'I'm high on life,' winked Ven.

'I knew it. What is it? Heroin?'

'Cappuccino cake is all the drug I need,' Ven said, and she took a big forkful as if to prove it.

'Three weeks to your fortieth,' sniffed Roz, ignoring her frivolity. 'Have you booked that Italian for your birthday like you said you were going to? Or do I have to do it?'

'You are so anal,' said Ven. 'A total control freak.'

'One of us has to be,' said Roz. 'If it wasn't for me, we'd end up having a few bags of chips at home for your big milestone. Anyway, I'm guessing you haven't done anything about it yet, so I will, when I get home.'

'Actually, there's no need. I have booked my "do", so there.' Ven nodded imperiously.

'Where? The Bella Noche?'

'Nope.'

'So, come on – where then?' huffed Roz. 'Honestly, it's like pulling teeth with you sometimes.'

Ven put down her fork. This was her moment. She was centre stage with a captive audience and the full spotlight of its gaze upon her. She was bubbling so much with anticipation she could barely get the word out.

'Venice,' she grinned.

'Oh, for God's sake!' Roz's fork clattered down. 'Right – I give up. I'm trying to sort out your big day and you're playing silly buggers . . .'

'I'm not joking,' cut in Ven. 'I'm going to the place of my conception – Venice – for my fortieth birthday.'

She looked at the two blank faces across the table and giggled inwardly at their expression, which said, 'The woman's mad.' Then she took a breath and delivered the best bit.

'And you're both coming with me.'

'Very funny,' said Olive, through a mouthful of lemon drizzle sponge.

'Hang on and listen,' Ven continued. 'I did a competition ages back and the company rang me a couple of weeks ago to say I'd won a holiday.'

'Get away!' said Olive.

'I fully intend to,' said Ven.

'What competition? What did you have to do for it?' demanded Roz.

'I had to think of a slogan for Figurehead Cruises.'

'What did you send in?'

'"We are The Sail of the Century",' beamed Ven proudly.

'And you won a holiday for that?' scoffed Roz. 'Bugger off.'

'Honest. I won a sixteen-day cruise for . . . three. On their new ship – the *Mermaidia*.' She dragged her handbag off the floor, opened it and scooped out a folded brochure. 'Look, three thousand one hundred passengers, swimming pools, bars, cinema, restaurants, ice-cream parlour, outdoor cinema, a spa . . .'

'A cruise? For sixteen days?' gasped Roz.

'Flaming heck,' said Olive breathlessly as she looked at the pictures of the opulent interior to the ship. It looked like a five-star hotel. Six even. Possibly ten.

'We leave two weeks tomorrow – the sixteenth of August. We've got five hundred pounds each spending money up front to get kitted out, and all our onboard credit will be paid for – providing we don't go mad and buy some Van Goghs at the onboard art auctions.'

'Is this for real?' gulped Roz.

'One hundred per cent for really real,' replied Ven. She reached into her bag, pulled out two folded-up cheques and handed them to her dumbstruck friends.

'This is a cheque from you!' said Olive.

'Durr,' tutted Ven. 'I've banked the cheque they sent me and this is your share.'

'I'm not sure I would get time off at such short notice,' said Roz, more quietly now that she was actually starting to believe Ven wasn't pulling a strange, sick joke on them. 'That old bitch Hutchinson wouldn't let me off work if I'd died in the night.'

'Well, that's where you are wrong because yes, she would. I conspired with Manus then rang her up and booked it as holidays for you.'

Roz's eyes opened so far her eyeballs nearly rolled out. 'You. Are. Kidding?'

'No, I wanted to make sure this went without a hitch. Sorry, Ol, I couldn't do the same for you.' Conspiring behind Olive's back with David would have been a no-goer. He wouldn't have let her off the lead. Plus, Olive was self-employed and so 'permission' wasn't really an issue to get past.

'Well, Manus certainly can keep a secret,' mused Roz aloud. 'Which is surprising, given his past history of blurting them out.'

'I love Manus,' said Ven, ignoring the caustic jibe. 'I wish I had a man like him at home.'

'He's a sweetie,' added Olive, thinking of his lean muscle and comparing it with David's big wobbly beer belly.

Roz just shrugged. She knew that Manus was a good-looking man, even if she didn't outwardly acknowledge it. She also knew that she was blessed to have found someone who was so kind and patient, whom her friends loved, who worked hard, who ticked all the boxes. Rough and ready, no airs or graces, rocker-blond hair, kind eyes and a very fit athletic frame. She often wished she were one of those wild creatures who could just dive on their man and take them there and then on the staircase. *Like Frankie would.* That thought sent a bucket of cold water splashing down on any rising sexy thoughts of Manus.

'You'll have to cancel your cleaning jobs for that fortnight,' said Ven, turning to Olive.

'I wish,' said Olive with a frustrated exhalation of breath. 'It would be lovely, but you know I'm going to have to let you down, don't you?'

'You can't,' said Ven. 'We always wanted to do this and now we've been given the perfect chance to. It's fate. I knew that if I won, the dates would be tight – it warned you about that in the rules, that there wouldn't exactly be a lot of lead-up time – but you can't turn this down, Olive. I won't let you.'

'I'll have a think,' said Olive. But it was obvious to them all that it was something she was just saying to get Ven off her back.

'Where does the ship go to?' said Roz, still in shock. Manus never mentioned a word about planning this behind her back. Was he trying to get her out of the way? She didn't let the possibility that he might be doing this for her sneak past her more negative deductions.

'Malaga, Corfu, Venice, Dubrovnik, Korcula, Cephalonia . . .' Ven left a long gap after that port and looked expectantly at Olive. Olive's head snapped upwards as Ven knew it would. 'Then on to Gibraltar for the last port.'

'Where does the ship leave from?' said Roz.

'Southampton.'

'Southampton!'

'Yes, but don't worry, it's effortless. We pick up a bus in Barnsley that takes us directly to the shipside – it's all included in the prize. Once our cases are loaded onto the bus, we don't see them again until they're outside our cabins. And if the bus gets held up for any reason, the ship waits for us. Simple and stress free.'

'Bloody hell,' said Roz. 'You're deadly serious, aren't you? I need a wee before I wet myself.'

'Go on and get one then,' said Ven.

'I'm going.' Roz got up and wandered off to the back of the café where the toilets were.

'What if I said to you, take Frankie instead of me,' whispered Olive, when Roz was out of sight and earshot. 'Much as I would love to come with you, how can I leave David and Doreen for a fortnight? They wouldn't cope. They fall to bits when I go shopping to Morrisons for an hour.'

'Frankie and Roz on holiday together – without you to help me stand between them? Are you serious?' Ven raised her eyebrows to their maximum height.

'Don't you think it's all such a shame?' said Olive. 'One stupid snog and so much ruined. And we could put it all right, if we just told—'

Ven held her finger up and said sternly, 'No, it was up to Frankie how she played it, not us. Whatever you or I might have thought.'

'She made a very wrong call,' said Olive. 'And I've told her that on many an occasion.'

'And you think I haven't?' Ven replied. 'But at the time, what else could we do but agree to what she asked?'

'I wish I'd said something,' sighed Olive. 'I know what Frankie was trying to do, but it wasn't fair on any of us to keep quiet. It was a first-class cock-up.'

'Yes, well, hindsight is a wonderful thing, but we're stuck with it, Ol. Things have been left far too late to change,' said Ven. 'Can you imagine the fallout if the truth came out now?'

'Yeah, I suppose you're right,' Olive conceded with a slow, sad nod of the head.

A lifetime of friendship smashed up because Frankie and Manus had once kissed. Guilt-ridden, he had confessed to Roz and it had destroyed her already fragile trust in men. The others knew that Manus had been trying for four years to put things right, but good luck to him, because he was fighting an army of ghosts from her days of being married to the serial adulterer Robert Clegg.

'I wish something would happen to make everything okay,' Olive went on. 'That's what I'd wish for your fortieth birthday. The four of us all together again with our heads full of nothing but laughs. Like we were when we were kids.'

'Me too,' said Ven. She opened her mouth to go on, but shut it at the last. This had all been in the lap of the gods from day one. She had to keep her trust in them to carry on the good work.

Chapter 6

On the bus home, Olive studied the cheque for five hundred pounds. Not that she would put it in the bank. Ven had given her this money to buy some cruise-worthy clothes and she had taken it home with her to shut her enthusiastic friend up, but she wouldn't be going with her on holiday. How could she go? Even if by some miracle she found herself on board, she would be haunted by pictures of Doreen struggling to cope. Doreen wasn't paralysed, she could walk a little, but it was so hard for her that a wheelchair was necessary. Who would wash her mother-in-law and put her to bed? She couldn't have her own son doing it, even if his bad back allowed him to lift her. She would spend a fortnight away from them not sleeping for worry, and be scared stiff what she would come home to. A dead old lady in a wheelchair, who had reached in vain for a glass of water that might have saved her before tumbling to the ground? And a man at death's door in his bed, spine contorted in agony, unable to rise, even to answer the dying pleas of his mother? No, she wouldn't be going.

And how could she go back to Cephalonia? How could she return to that island and risk losing the perfect picture of it that she carried with her always? Tanos would no longer be the tiny unspoiled village she recalled. It would be a disco and karaoke-bar-filled horror story by now, because it was too pretty not to be commercialised. Going back there would remind her too painfully of the one dream she had managed to live out – flying off and working in a bar one hot summer twenty years ago. When she was young and brave and free to go where she wanted in that small window of opportunity – when she was Lyon by name and Lion by nature. Then the guilty feelings had set in, taunting her that she shouldn't be gallivanting about having a good time when she had aged parents to look after. So she had torn herself away from the island, back to her familiar life of drudgery, to be charmed by David Hardcastle and his fancy ambitious talk. No, she couldn't bear to go back. Although her heart had never left.

As Olive stepped into her mother-in-law's fag-smoky house and saw the mountain of ironing awaiting her before her shift cleaning the offices up the road, she felt the weight of duty on her shoulders and her eyes filled up with tears. Talk of this cruise had stirred up too many muddy waters inside her. Or rather, azure-blue waters with gentle waves, little fishes and a salty Greek tang.

Chapter 7

Manus dragged his hands down his face in despair. He couldn't believe he'd got it wrong again. But here was his partner bollocking him for helping to arrange for her to go on a free cruise with her mates.

'I didn't suspect a thing,' Roz had thrown at him.

'But that was the idea, love!'

'Quite the little secret-keeper, aren't you?' she sniped.

Manus shook his head slowly and resignedly. He didn't want to fight again. He'd had four years of fighting with this woman whom he loved so much. It crushed him that he couldn't get through to her. They rarely made love these days, and even when they did he felt that she was just going through the motions so she had an excuse not to 'do it' again for another few weeks. Her orgasms were mechanical, a bodily response to stimulation. He could make her come, but he couldn't reach her mind – he knew that. He'd prayed that the walls around her heart would start to crumble, but they just got stronger, more impenetrable. Still though – like a fool – he kept on trying, but he was so tired. He didn't know how much more he could be pushed away, but he daren't say that because she would take it and run with it. He could hear her now: *Yes, I knew you'd end up leaving me like that first prick. You're all the same.* The first prick being her ex-husband, who ran off with Roz's pregnant cousin. She had idolised him and their deceit had crippled her. It had been a hard slog to get her to trust men again, but Manus had been hooked from the first sight of this tall, slim woman struggling with an iced-up lock on her car outside a supermarket, seven long years ago. He had moved in on her like a white knight and made her promise to come out to dinner with him as his fee.

Yes, she had softened towards him through his intense courtship, because he had battered down her defences with his romantic offensive on her, determined to show her that men could be faithful, but my God, it was hard work. Then he'd stupidly had to fall from grace and kiss her best mate. Years of building up her trust undone by a three-second weak moment of weakness when, after yet another row with Roz, his own hunger for warmth and comfort had met with the same from Frankie. And if that hadn't been idiotic enough, he had thought it best to confess it to her because he had promised never to lie to her. Oh boy, she'd never let him forget it. He couldn't have been more vilified if he'd had an orgy with her whole office, her two stepsisters and her mother's Standard Poodle. Not once had he made any excuse for his action that night. He wouldn't have tried to hurt Roz by telling her how desperate he sometimes felt for a crumb of kindness, love or affection from her. The fault was his and he would have to bear the consequences.

Now, for the first time, Manus Howard felt the hopelessness of his situation. Nothing he did could thaw Roz. She wouldn't talk to him openly about what happened that night with Frankie but would refer to it constantly in sarcastic asides. He stepped around her on eggshells, not even daring to mention if someone on the TV was pretty. And if his eye happened to stray unconsciously towards a female, especially a dark-haired one, when they were out together – all hell was released. He didn't feel they had moved one single step forwards in the past four years. And listening to Roz now, levelling at him that he might want her out of the way for a fortnight, when he just wanted her to have the holiday of a lifetime with her friends, well, he wasn't sure this was healthy for either of them any more. The sad truth was that it was killing him, and if the sight of him was still making her hate him so much, how could it be good for her either?

Manus Howard was a big, hard man but there were tears threatening outwards now. He came from a dysfunctional family in Ketherwood, the roughest part of the town, and had fought his way out of the rut he was destined for – the dole and drinking too much. He'd worked hard all his life, had a profitable garage business and a bit of money in the bank. He had everything he wanted, but his bed was so cold – even with his woman in it. When he touched her, he felt like a client who had rented her body for an hour. Not that he dared say that either. He could imagine what argument she would make from that one.

He sighed and his shoulders fell with the weight of despair on them.

'Roz, I'm not sure how much more of this I can take. Maybe,' his voice cracked and he coughed before continuing, 'maybe you should think about what you really want when you're on holiday.'

'Maybe I should,' said Roz, her clipped delivery masking the panic his words had kicked off inside her. Attack was the best form of defence. 'Maybe it's a good thing that I'm going away. I think . . . I think it might do us both good to have a complete break.'

Once the words were out, she wished she could pull them back into her mouth and swallow them. She didn't want to hear that Manus might agree with her. But he did.

'Aye,' he said wearily. 'Maybe it's for the best, Roz.' The way he said her name was painful to hear; the word died in his throat.

'We shouldn't contact each other whilst I'm away. At all,' she pushed.

Manus's head snapped up. 'Is that what you really want to happen?'

'Don't you?' said Roz, again with that defensive hard edge to her voice. 'You've just agreed that we should go on a break!'

Manus opened up his mouth to stop this now and say that he didn't want to see the holiday as a break at all, but for once, his anger flared up and made a matching contestant for her own.

'Do you know, Roz, I think you're right. No contact, as we *both* agree then – how's that? It's fine by me. I think you need to seriously consider what you want in life and so do I, because this is crap. You're not happy and it's clear to me that I can't make you as happy as Robert obviously made you! Now, do you want me for anything because I'm going back to the garage for an hour or so. I promised a customer that I'd finish his van as soon as I could, and I need to do an oil change on it.'

For once Roz didn't give him a smart-mouthed reply. She watched him go, and hot, self-loathing tears rose up in her eyes and felt like spikes there. She wanted to fling herself at his back and tell him that she was sorry she was such a cow to him and really she knew it was that bitch Frankie's fault anyway. Frankie had always been a forward piece. Manus wasn't. She suddenly wanted to feel her man's arms around her, his lips on hers, showing her once again that he loved her. But she had got so used to over-protecting herself.

Once upon a time, she had laid herself wide open to Robert and he had trampled all over her. She couldn't go through pain like that again. However much she might want to open up to Manus, she had lost the keys to the door that was so tightly shut around her heart.

Hearing Manus's car engine start up, Roz slumped down

onto the chair behind her. She had finally managed to do it – push her sweet, loving, long-suffering man to breaking-point after four long years of trying. So why didn't she feel in the slightest bit victorious?

Chapter 8

Ven and Roz drove over to Meadowhall after work the following Monday. The sales were on and the shops were buzzing – a bit like they were inside. If only Olive had been there with them picking out holiday clothes, they both thought, with more than a little sadness.

'Aw, I hope Ol does come,' said Ven.

'She won't, the silly, soft sod,' replied Roz, picking up a blue bikini. She wasn't sure if she dared bare that much flesh in public though. Her stomach was as flat as an ironing board but she carried all the insecurities of a middle-aged woman whose first husband had run off with a skinny minx, even if that was over nine years ago and she was now living with a guy who would have savoured her whatever size she was, given half the chance. She put it back and plumped for a black all-in-one with a plunging neckline. She was proud of her bosom and would rather show some of that off than her stomach anyway. Out of the four of them, she had been first in the chest queue when God was giving them out. Ven, a close second, Olive just behind and Frankie way, way at the back of the same queue, with flat-as-a-fart AA cups. 'Froz' as they used to call themselves, long before Jedward segued their names (or had even been born), could never swap clothes the way that Ven and Olive could, being of similar heights and builds. Roz was leggy, slim and tall, Frankie was short and on the plump side. Although Roz did once catch Frankie trying on one of her bras, having stuffed the cups with loo paper.

'Must be nice having tits,' she had said, admiring her new pronounced profile in the bedroom mirror.

'It is – not that you'll ever know!' Roz had laughed. They'd laughed a lot once, the pair of them. Froz.

Roz shook her head and dragged her thoughts into the here and now. *Why the hell am I thinking about* her *so much again, after all this time?*

'I am sure they'd all cope without Ol for sixteen days,' said Ven. 'I know for a fact that Doreen isn't as disabled as she makes out because I once saw her waddling from the shop on Warren Street with a packet of fags in her hand. She didn't look like a woman who couldn't get off her backside without assistance then. And David's so-called bad back hasn't stopped him doing some sly pointing work on my neighbour's gable end for some cash in hand. He didn't know I saw him, but I did. He was halfway up a ladder with a cap on but I would recognise that flabby bum hanging out of those jeans anywhere.'

'Crafty buggers!' tutted Roz. 'Have you told Olive?'

Ven nodded. 'She thought I was mistaken on both counts. She *knows* that David couldn't get up a ladder without the aid of a winch. He's too good an actor. Takes after his mother,' she added with a sniff.

Roz shook her head. 'Who in their right mind turns down a free cruise?'

'She's not going to turn it down,' said Ven decisively, fire in her sea-blue eyes. She didn't know how she was going to get Olive on that ship, but she was; even if she had to play dirty tricks to secure it. Though in the end it wasn't *her* dirty tricks that made it happen.

Chapter 9

'Did you get some nice clothes then when you went shopping?' asked Olive at their last Saturday meet before the cruise.

'I got a few bits in the sales, yes. By the way, I noticed when I did my banking online yesterday that you still haven't put your cheque in,' said Ven, slapping Olive on the hand. 'It's still not too late, you know.'

'How can I bank that five hundred quid?' replied Olive. 'That money is for holiday clothes, you said it yourself. And seeing as I won't be going on holiday with you tomorrow, I can't take the money.'

'You are going, you know,' replied Ven, shovelling in a huge piece of cappuccino cake. 'Whether you like it or not.'

'I wish!' laughed Olive. Not that she had much to laugh about, even less so with yet another lazy mouth to feed. David and his mother and smelly Kevin were slouched in front of the television all day arguing over what to watch. If it wasn't for having to get up to go to the toilet occasionally, they would atrophy. David did manage to struggle to go out and sign on though, but it was Kevin who was really doing Olive's head in at the moment. He was like a locust in the fridge. He bit off chunks of cheese and drank milk straight from the carton, and no one would want those custard teeth near any food they were going to touch. And he never flushed the toilet. And someone had raided Olive's savings pot. It was a fiver light and no one was owning up to it. She was saving for her friends' fortieth-birthday presents in that pot. Olive was only glad she'd taken out the thirty pounds to give to Roz for the locket they'd bought between them for Ven. Roz was going to take it on the cruise with her and give it to her on her birthday with her cards. They'd be in Venice that day. Another place Olive had always wanted to go. One of her cleaning clients had been and described it as 'so beautifully unreal, you'd think you were on a film set'. She wondered if anything could be as hauntingly idyllic as Tanos though. She envied her two friends calling at Cephalonia more than she envied them anything else.

'Have you spent up, Roz?' asked Olive, ignoring Ven.

'Not quite,' said Roz. She'd taken her five hundred pounds and hit the shops big time, trying to drive the picture of Manus's watering eyes out of her head with every purchase. 'Ven says there are shops on the ship though, so I might buy something on there.'

'There is everything you want on the ship,' nodded Ven. 'From tampons to tuxedos, so don't fret about forgetting anything because you can buy it on board.'

'It sounds perfect,' sighed Olive.

Ven suddenly grabbed her hands.

'Please, Olive, please come. They can all cope for a couple of weeks without you. Sixteen days out of your life – that's all. There's a ticket in my safe with your name on it. In nineteen hours' time, Roz and I will be getting on a bus and going down to Southampton and it won't be the same if you don't come with us. I am begging you. You know what a crap few years I've had with Mum and Dad dying and losing my job and Ian doing the dirty on me . . .' Ven was deliberately curling up her lip and tilting her eyebrows to gain sympathy.

'No emotional pressure then,' smiled Olive. 'Honestly, if there were any way, I would. But I'd feel too guilty.'

'Sod them!' said Ven, releasing a bit of red-head anger that Olive had been so fooled by them. 'They'd all fend for themselves if they had to.'

'Who'd look after them if you dropped dead now?' added Roz, maybe a bit heavy on the point.

'I know you think I'm stupid. I *am* stupid,' said Olive, sadly. 'I know they rely on me too much and are probably a little bit more able than they make out they are, but I couldn't just up and go, even if I wanted to – and trust me, I do. Plus, I'm out cleaning tomorrow afternoon. I can't let my clients down. Double-plus I haven't got a stitch of summer clothing. I haven't got a stitch of any decent clothing, come to think of it.'

'The taxi is booked for twenty to eight tomorrow morning,' said Ven adamantly. 'It'll be at yours by five to. You don't need spending money because it's taken care of by the competition people and you can borrow stuff from me and Roz.'

'Don't call for me, Ven,' Olive said quietly. 'I won't be coming.' She checked her watch. She needed to be heading off soon to attend to the first of her two cleaning jobs of the day.

'Please, Olive,' Ven begged, squeezing Olive's hand. Oh God, she just wished she had more artillery. She had pleaded, even tried emotional blackmail, but Olive was too honourable, too caring, too last-in-her-own-queue, too bloody soft.

Roz drained her cup and looked at her watch too. Her parking time was nearly up. She needed to get a move on and finish packing. She stood, then pushed her wild blonde hair back over her shoulders as she bent to Olive.

'You're a very daft woman, Olive Hardcastle,' she said, giving her a sad hug.

'I know I am,' said Olive.

Chapter 10

Olive had had a bit of a headache all day, but after saying good-bye to Ven and Roz, it revved up with a vengeance. She managed to struggle through her first cleaning job, but sitting on the bus heading off to job two, she knew there was no way she could work through it. It was obviously caused by the stress at having to turn down a free holiday with two of her dearest friends. What was she doing? Like Ven said, it was sixteen days out of her life and she would never have another chance like this again. She realised she was sat in a prison but holding the key to the door herself. Kevin might have been a lazy blighter, but he was able-bodied with no back or leg problems and could hold the fort for a couple of weeks. And, like Roz intimated, if she dropped down dead, they would all cope, because they'd have to.

Olive rang Janice, her fellow office cleaner on her cheap pay-as-you-go mobile – there was just enough credit left for that call, but not enough to let David know that she'd be back early. She was suddenly struck by the irony that she worked all hours, including now on a Saturday night, and all she could afford was a fifteen-pound phone from Asda – and yet there was Kevin scamming off the state but able to afford a fancy iPhone and twelve million downloaded apps. She stared out of the bus window and caught her reflection. She looked years older than her age, with her long blonde hair tied back so harshly in a cleaning-practical ponytail. Her clothes were drab and frumpy, piling on even more years. It was the image of a woman tired of life. And she realised that was because she *was* tired of it. If it wasn't for her olive-green eyes, she wouldn't have recognised herself as the same person who was once so fresh and smiley and full of dreams.

Olive couldn't remember a time when she wasn't caring for people. Her dad was lame and she was always fetching and carrying for him; her mum, constantly in her bed with some ailment or other. At the time of her conception, Olive's mum was in her mid-forties, her dad in his late fifties, and both seemed even older in their outlook. They never came to see her in school shows or prize-giving events. It was Ven's mum and dad who were there to cheer her on and in whose house she found some semblance of the loving parent/child relationship for which she longed: Mrs Smith busying around them making sure they were fed and watered, Mr Smith slipping them secret money to go to the pictures with. Home for Olive was more of a workhouse than a sanctuary. To her shame, sometimes she felt like one of those 'designer babies' conceived only to look after her parents in their dotage.

It would probably have been better had she *not* gone away to Cephalonia that summer, because it made her realise there was a lot of world and life out there to be enjoyed. But one day, when she rang home from the phone in the Lemon Tree, the feeble voice of her mother reprimanded her for leaving them to cope alone, and the guilt drove her instantly back to Barnsley where she found her parents in a right old state of not looking after themselves, which scarred her deeply to see. And yet, on his many call-out visits, the doctor intimated, quite impatiently sometimes, that there was nothing much wrong with either of them.

Olive's dad died of a stroke when she was twenty-four. She

was grieving for him when the big, cocky David Hardcastle stood up on the bus to let her sit down. That simple act of giving to someone who wasn't used to it secured him a whole-hearted yes, when he asked her out for a date. He was something to take her mind away from her mother's increasing mental confusion. When she became a danger to herself and Olive couldn't handle her any more, she was put into a lovely home in Penistone, although Olive had to sell their house to pay for the bills. Being in David's arms and listening to the plans he had for them took her away from all the drudgery of form-filling-in and visits to a mum who didn't recognise her any more. Doreen, she recalled, was always friendly to her and Olive felt flattered that the woman would ask her to 'stick the kettle on', a sign that she was welcome in her home. It made sense for David and Olive to get married and move in with Doreen when the house sale was completed. The money was all gone by the time Olive's mum died. There was nothing left for a deposit for her own home. But by then, she had slipped into a routine of caring again – different home, same rules. And the idiot that she was had been so blinded by a bit of love-light shining in her direction that she hadn't seen it coming.

A surprise of tears pricked at her olive-green eyes. She never cried – she had no time for the luxury – but she realised, sitting on that bus and looking at the reflection of the sad-faced woman in the window, how totally worn out she was. When one job ended, another started; she only rested when she was asleep in the sliver of bedspace which David allowed her. There was no break in her routine, no meals out or trips to the pic-tures or holidays to look forward to like normal people in normal marriages. She had blinked and her whole life had somehow gone by and she had nothing to show for it.

She was just too weary to do all the bending and cleaning with this pain thrumming persistently in her temple. Janice would do her share of the work for her share of the pay, but it would be worth it tonight. Olive got off at the next bus stop. It was winter-cold for August and the rain was lashing down, but she for one was glad of it. It was just what her headache would have prescribed. The cool drops on her forehead were like a medicine.

She walked slowly down the narrow alley towards Land Lane and pictured what it must be like for Ven and Roz, looking forward to going off on holiday tomorrow morning – on a luxurious vessel that would have taken her eventually to Cephalonia with its white beaches and blue, blue sea. How would it feel, being single figures of miles away from Tanos and the Lemon Tree? And Atho Petrakis. How would he look now, twenty years on? Would the grey have rampaged through his thick black wavy hair? Would his eyes still be as big and bear-brown? Would his skin still smell of wood and coffee and herbs? *Would his lips still be as full and soft?* Olive cut off those thoughts. They weren't exactly helping her headache.

She was nearly at the end of the alley now and wondering instead if anyone had lifted a finger since she went out of the house that afternoon or, by some miracle, someone had washed up or vacuumed the carpet, or splashed some bleach in the toilet. Then, just as she was about to cross the road, she saw the front door of Doreen's house open – and what she witnessed was to jerk the course of her slow life off its track in favour of a far more perilous and unpredictable one.

Roz was just struggling to close her suitcase when Manus came in, his overalls scented with oil and petrol. The smell of him prodded an old responsive part within her that was hidden under her pettiness and stubbornness. And there was she, telling Olive that she was weak, when she wasn't strong enough to say to this kind hunk of a man in front of her that she should be going for some sort of medical psychiatric help because she loved him and couldn't tell him. In the past fortnight, since agreeing to the break, they had been living like virtual strangers, civilly talking to each other when it was needed but no more than that. Manus had moved into the spare room.

He didn't attempt to kiss her in greeting. Instead, he pushed down on her suitcase so she could close it more easily.

'Packed then?' he said. 'Got the kitchen sink in there?'

'More or less,' she said with a small smile.

'I've got a little something for Ven myself,' he said, reaching in his pocket and handing over a black pouch. 'It's only because it's a special birthday. Forty, like.'

She watched him stumble over his words, expecting her to make some smart-arse comment about buying presents for other women, and realised what a nervous wreck she'd made him. It was easier to rebuff that fact than accept it as the truth, and she heard herself say tightly, 'I'll pack it and give it to her for you.'

'I haven't had time to wrap it, as you can see.'

'Doesn't matter. You're a bloke – she'll understand.'

Once again she lumped him with a bunch of useless men. She wanted to backtrack and say that she didn't mean how that came out, but her stupidly galvanised pride wouldn't let her.

She watched him walk out of the bedroom, his expression stone. She had not thought it possible he could look so cold.

Chapter 11

'Bugger,' said Doreen Hardcastle to herself as she opened up her packet of Black Superkings to find it totally empty. David or Kevin must have sneaked her last one when she was napping, the little monkeys. Neither of them were at home to send to the shop for her, and Olive was working and not due back for at least two hours. There was no way Doreen could wait that long for a nicotine fix.

Because she was alone in the house, she didn't have to go through the pretence of struggling to her ailing legs. She stood up fairly effortlessly, despite her bulk, and crossed the room for her purse. She double-checked the clock. Nope, no one would be around for ages yet. She had plenty of time to nip out to the newsagent on Warren Street and replenish her stocks.

She opened the front door cautiously and poked her head left and then right. The street was totally clear. Doreen stepped out, walking stick under her arm, and closed the door quickly behind her. She moved so nippily down the street, there was smoke coming off her slippers.

Just as Doreen had turned the corner from Land Lane into Warren Street, a scruffy yellow Volvo pulled up doors short of the Hardcastle home.

'Drop me off here, will you, Gary mate,' said David to the

driver. He didn't want anyone peering out of the window and seeing him carrying his bag of tools. 'Have you got my money?'

'I have,' said Gary, levering on the hand-brake then fishing deep in his pocket for a brown envelope. 'Cash in hand as agreed.' He tapped the side of his nose. 'I've got a couple of soffit jobs for you next week – I'll ring you on the moby. Probably Wednesday or Thursday, providing it's not pissing down.'

'Smashing,' said David. Fixing soffits onto the roofs of houses was a good little earner and he was loaded at the moment because of all the work Gary had put his way. But he didn't want to overdo it or risk the benefits people rumbling that he wasn't incapacitated, after all. Or worse – Olive finding out that he was fit and well enough to run after himself. He couldn't do without her molly-coddling him, or his mum mothering him; he had got far too used to that.

David climbed out of the car and swung his huge bag of tools onto his strong back, giving Gary a friendly wave as he drove off. Slyly, he opened the door to the garage at the side of the house and threw in his bag. Then he began his preparation for entering the house. His shoulders slumped and a hang-dog look of back pain crept over his features. He hobbled the few steps to the front of the house and took out his key, fully – and safely – back in character. He was so chuffed with himself, he didn't see the figure across the street hiding in the alley.

Ven's mobile rang just as she was checking her 'money, tickets, passport' for the zillionth time. She didn't recognise the Barnsley number on the caller display so answered it tentatively. 'Hello.'

'It's me,' said Olive, her voice shaking.

'Hiya, Ol. You okay?'

'Oh Ven, I don't know what to do.'

'Whatever's the matter, love?' said Ven. 'What's upset you?'

'Upset? Ha!' said Olive in a suddenly very strong voice. 'I'm not upset, I'm bloody livid. You were both right. I am stupid and I deserve the biggest slap . . .'

'Ol, calm down and talk slower,' said Ven firmly. 'Where are you?'

'The phone box just outside the post office on Ketherwood Street,' said Olive, breathing in and out so hard, it was as if she was revving herself up for a fight with Muhammad Ali.

'Don't move. I'm driving round for you now.'

Olive was in a terrible state. One second she looked as if she was going to burst into tears, then her mood suddenly segued into homicidal mania.

'Blimey, what on earth's up?' said Ven, as Olive threw herself into the passenger seat of her car and buckled herself in.

'I believe you. I believe David has been swinging the lead and claiming benefits for a bad back when there's bugger all wrong with him, and I believe that Doreen can get up off her fat lumpy arse and tottle down to the shops. I also believe that the whole bloody Hardcastle family thinks I'm a doormat and I've been pathetic enough to let them treat me like that. Will I ever learn?'

'Wow,' said Ven, with her eyebrows raised so high they needed oxygen. 'What's brought this on?'

'I saw them,' said Olive, the tears pushing through now and making themselves an exit. Hot, angry tears that Olive couldn't wipe away fast enough. 'I had a headache and didn't go to my second cleaning job and I didn't have enough credit on my phone to ring David and say I'd be home early. Anyway, I was just in the alley opposite and I saw our door open. Then I saw Doreen peep out to check the coast was clear. Then . . . then – she *ran* down the road like Sebastian Coe and was back, presumably from Warren Street newsagents, with a packet of cigarettes before I had a chance to blink.'

'Oh crikey,' said Ven, really clamping down on the urge to say, 'Told you so.' Any joy she felt in seeing the scales ripped from Olive's eyes was offset by her friend's distress, which she didn't want to see.

'Oh, hang on, there's more!' laughed Olive in a very dry, humourless way. 'In between Doreen leaving the house and coming back, a car pulls up at the other end of the street and out springs – like Wayne Bloody Sleep – my husband with a massive bag of tools over his sore delicate shoulder. Then, when the car drove off, I watched him hide the bag in the garage, flop into his usual "ooh, me back's killing me" shape and drag himself into the house. It was like watching a Jesus miracle in reverse.'

'Oh heck,' said Ven.

'So I left it five minutes,' Olive went on, 'then I did a really slow walk in to give them all a chance to rearrange themselves in their usual tableau, and sure enough upon my entrance I found that David was "in agony" leaning over the sink, and Doreen was hobbling on her zimmer frame to the kitchen to get a "slice of dry bread" to see her poor starving twenty-stone stomach through till I got home to make their tea.'

Ven opened her mouth to sympathise, but Olive still hadn't finished.

'Wait, there's even more. Then lovely Kevin appears at my back with a plastic basket full of rancid clothes. How that man manages to get that many stains on a pair of underpants is beyond me! "Any chance of getting these ironed for tomorrow?" he says. "They aren't washed!" I say back. "Well, I meant, washed and dried and ironed," he says. "I'd do them myself but I've got a date." "Sorry, but I can't stop now, I'm working," I say, and grab a bottle of bleach and pretend I'd just called home for that. And then I rang you from the phone box.'

For the first time Olive felt the boil of anger bubble through to the forefront of her feelings. She really had been a first-class idiot. She had washed Doreen and hauled her over to the toilet and pandered to her every whim, she had supported her lazy sod of a husband who hadn't put a penny in the housekeeping pot for years, and all the time Doreen was probably more able-bodied than she was. And if David was back-pocketing money on sly jobs, he wasn't declaring any of it – to her or the taxman.

'Do you know, if I could come with you on holiday, I bloody well would,' said Olive, wiping away the fat drops which were now spurting from her eyes.

'Then do. Come with us,' said Ven, seizing on the delicious moment.

'Yes, well, if I had anything decent to wear I'd throw it in a suitcase. But I haven't. Come to that, I haven't even got a bloody suitcase.'

'You've got a passport, that's enough.'

'Aye, I'll sew a couple of straps to it and use it as a thong.'

Ven checked her watch. 'Look, Meadowhall doesn't shut until ten this week because the sales are on.'

'I didn't put the cheque in the bank . . .'

'Never mind that, we'll sort it out later. I'll stick what you buy on my Visa. We've got about two hours to get you a holiday wardrobe.'

'It can't be done,' said Olive.

'Oh yes, it sodding well can,' said Ven. The miracle was that Olive was coming with her. Anything else was child's play.

Chapter 12

Fifteen minutes later, they were in Meadowhall hurtling towards Marks & Spencer. Ven was grabbing clothes off rails and shoving Olive into changing rooms. By nine o'clock, Olive had a basic capsule cruise wardrobe: trousers, shorts, new undies, T-shirts, two posh blouses, two skirts, sundresses, a sarong and a couple of little black cocktail dresses, which Ven assured her could be tarted up with the loads of scarves and costume jewellery she was taking. Oh – and a big pink suitcase. Anything else she could buy on the ship or in a port. Olive packed it all at Ven's house, then rang all her clients from Ven's phone and left messages on their voicemails to say that she wouldn't be able to come for at least a fortnight because she had caught a contagious virus and had to be quarantined. If she returned home to find they had dispensed with her services, well, so be it. Because nothing was going to stop Olive from getting on that ship now. She was riding on the crest of a wave of anger that refused to bring her back to a sensible shore.

Ven's ancient tabby cat jumped on Olive's case and scared her to death.

'Ethel, you made me jump!' she said, giving the purring cat a scratch under her chin. Ven had got Ethel from a rescue centre when the cat was nine, and that was well over thirteen years ago. Ethel had no teeth now and cloudy sleepy eyes. Ethel spent her life journeying from Ven's rocking chair to the food bowl, fitting in a couple of loo visits in the garden along the way, and was always on the lookout for a visitor to scratch her head. Flaming cat has a better life than me, Olive thought suddenly.

'My Cousin Jen is picking Ethel up in the morning. She has the life of luxury on their farm – gets petted to death by the kids.'

'She's a lovely lass, is Jen,' agreed Olive.

'She is, bless her. Poor as a church mouse but a heart of gold.' Ven smiled fondly at her friend. 'I can't tell you how glad I am that you're coming with us, Olive. You're going to have such a great time.'

God, I hope so, thought Olive. She had a feeling she would be facing hell when she got back. So she'd better make it worth the punishment.

As Ven dropped Olive and her bag of cleaning stuff off at the end of Land Lane, she was thrilled to bits that the gods had been looking out for Olive, after all. As Ven said, 'Goodbye, see you in the morning,' she almost went on to tell Olive her secret. But at the last second, she shut up. If everything went tits up, she alone would take the blame.

Chapter 13

When Olive got home, Doreen had a face like a vinegar-sucking Shar Pei.

'Where've you been till this time? I've been waiting for you to put me to bed.'

'I'm sorry,' said Olive in her usual meek way, but she was sorely tempted to give her mother-in-law a mouthful. Dutifully, she helped Doreen change into her voluminous nightie and bore her weight as she helped her onto the toilet, nursing the thought that she wouldn't be doing this again for another two and a half glorious weeks. Then she pulled the lounge sofa out into a double bed – the same routine she had done for nearly eight years now, when Doreen decided it was too much for her to go up the stairs to sleep. She put Doreen's teeth in a glass to soak, made her a Horlicks with the usual six teaspoons of powder and full fat milk, then she switched off the big light leaving the small lamp on next to the sofa bed so Doreen could read a few pages of her latest Mills & Boon. As she went into the kitchen, she tried not to look at Kevin's washing basket, which he'd asked her to sort out for tomorrow. She also tried not to breathe in the cheese and vinegar sock smell which was heavy in the air. The washing machine was ancient but easy enough to use. Even an idiot could load it and press the button that said either 'On – quick wash' or

'On – long wash'. Then again, maybe it was still a bit high-brow for Kevin.

She'd only had the slice of lemon drizzle cake to eat all day and decided she'd better get something to fortify herself before she collapsed. She had made a huge shepherd's pie that morning to be heated up for tea. True to form they hadn't left her any. The dish was scraped empty on the work surface. She picked it up to soak it in the sink, then had a rethink and put it down. *No, let them do it.* She smiled to herself as she toasted two slices of bread and spooned some coffee into a cup. There was no point in having decaff – she wasn't going to sleep much anyway.

Olive then had a quick bath and packed some underwear, toiletries, her best shoes, a couple of nice tops, her only decent dress and passport into one of the bags she used for her cleaning stuff. David was snoring like a pig whilst she crept around their bedroom. He always said that medication didn't help his back pain so it wasn't worth taking; however, beer knocked him out and at least allowed him to get some well-needed sleep. She had always accepted that as a feasible argument. How the Hardcastles must have laughed at her. Well, they wouldn't be laughing again for a while.

She took her bag back downstairs into the kitchen and then got a writing pad and pen out from the drawer and wrote:

Dear All

I'm going on holiday and will be back on Tuesday 2nd September.

Olive

Then she ripped out the sheet, stuck it in an envelope and propped it up against Doreen's fag supply next to the kettle. That way, she knew it would be found first thing.

Olive checked the clock; in less than seven hours' time a taxi would be calling for her. She didn't think she would nod off in the easy chair in the never-used dining room, but she did – and dreamed of being naked on the ship and that Cephalonia had turned into a seedy seaside town.

DAY 1: AT SEA

Dress Code: Smart Casual

Chapter 14

Manus was standing at the side of Roz's bed with a cuppa as her alarm went off and she jerked awake.

'Wakey, wakey, Penelope,' he said, then immediately clarified that before she broke into: 'Penelope? Can't even get my name right nowadays. Who's Penelope? Not one of my friends, for a change.'

'Penelope Cruz as in *cruise*, I meant – you know.' Manus coughed, wishing he had never made the joke. 'Anyway, here's a caffeine shot for you. Thought you might need it. ' He was dressed only in boxer shorts; he suited them. He had strong muscular thighs that her eyes settled on until she ripped them away and took the coffee, thanking him politely.

'I'll get some clothes on,' he said, thumbing to the spare room in the manner of someone suddenly realising he was inappropriately attired. Another sign of the ever-increasing divide between them that he could be embarrassed to be half-naked in front of her after seven years.

When Roz came downstairs, showered and dressed, it was to the smell of hot buttered toast which he had made for her. 'I could have taken you and Ven myself to the bus station, you know, instead of you having to get a taxi,' said Manus.

'The competition people are paying for it,' replied Roz, taking a half slice of the toast. She was far too stirred up to eat any more.

'Do you want me to come and see you off?' Manus asked. Had she imagined it, or was there a little note of hope in his voice that she would say, 'Yes, please come'?

'No, don't worry,' she said. 'I grew out of waving through windows when I was twelve.' Her insides were at war with themselves. Why didn't she just say 'Come and wave me off,' like she wanted to? It hurt her that he didn't press it.

'Fair enough,' was all he said with flat emotion. She deserved nothing more than his indifference, she knew.

Roz was halfway through brushing her teeth when a taxi horn sounded in the street.

'Jesus, they're early!' she flapped, drying her mouth, expertly applying two smooth lines of lippy and dragging an afro comb through her wild, wavy hair as she ran down the stairs.

Manus had already taken her suitcases out and was hugging Ven and wishing her a happy birthday for next week.

Roz grabbed her handbag from the hall-stand and checked inside for her money and passport again. She didn't know how to say goodbye to Manus appropriately. He wasn't giving any impression to Ven that they were hanging on by a thread as he helped the taxi driver load the cases into the boot. Nor did he allow Roz time to stage their parting because he bent to her cheek and laid a soft kiss there.

'Have a lovely time,' he said. He was scared to give her more, she knew, and she momentarily hated herself for it. Then she hated him for not fighting back. Hate, hate, hate. She felt full of it and it exhausted her.

'I will,' she said with a dry smile. Then she climbed into the back seat of the taxi and kept her head facing forward, and defied those tears that were rising within her to make a show.

Olive switched her alarm off after the first ring, panicking in case it alerted anyone else in the house, but she needn't have worried. The shrill ring would have more luck waking the dead on Cemetery Road. It was like an awful choir as she tiptoed to the bathroom: Doreen snoring contralto in the lounge, Kevin – alto from the spare room, and the mighty bass – David, in their bedroom. They would have turned to dust, getting up at six on a Sunday morning. She wondered how they would feel, rising after eleven and finding there was no comforting smell of bacon and eggs drifting from the kitchen. They'd combust! Dutiful feelings started to creep in and poison Olive with guilt and she galvanised her resolve and batted them away. They needed this wake-up call. For all their sakes, they needed to realise that Olive wasn't a slave. It wasn't good for Doreen to be immobile for such long periods of time either, she reasoned. Obviously nipping out for fags was the most exercise she was getting, if that wasn't ironic. And Kevin might be a more attractive prospect if he could clean his own clothes, though brushing his teeth might help a bit as well. The tortoiseshell-glaze look would never be in vogue, although by the number of women he'd pulled in his time, maybe he knew something the dental world didn't. As for David – well, having to do what Olive did for the family day in, day out might just make him learn to have some respect for her. Yes, they would all benefit from her being away, and she needed to keep that thought fully in focus, especially when those guilty feelings started gathering again, as she knew they were bound to.

At seven forty-five, she crept down the hallway with her bag and was just about to open the door and go out into the street so that the taxi didn't beep its horn on arrival, when Kevin's voice hit her from behind and scared her half to death.

'Where are you off to at this time, Olive?'

Olive turned to see Kevin, yawning and looking like an anorexic xylophone with his skinny bare chest. He was clutching the pink toilet roll he had just come downstairs to fetch and wearing only a red thong with a porn-star bulge pushing at the material, which was drawing Olive's attention where she didn't want to give it. Ah, so it wasn't the tortoiseshell teeth that was the hook, after all.

Flustered, she was about to reply that she had an early-morning cleaning job, but then an imp took over her mouth.

'I'm clearing off,' she said cockily. 'To Greece. See you later, Kevin.'

The taxi was just drawing up when she went into the street. And just like Roz, after climbing into it, Olive didn't look back at the house which she had just left.

Chapter 15

'I can't believe you are here,' said Roz, smiling and hugging her. Ven had already filled her in on what had happened the previous night to make Olive change her mind. 'What a brilliant surprise. I am thrilled you made it.'

'Trust me, it was eleventh-hour. Fate stepped in,' said Olive. 'And Ven. And Meadowhall's late-night opening hours.'

'I don't care what stepped in, I'm just chuffed to bits and pieces. Oh Olive, we are going to have such a fantastic time – the three of us.'

'You've remembered my swanky pink suitcase, haven't you, Ven?' Olive asked in a sudden moment of panic.

Ven feigned forgetfulness and shrieked, 'Oh my God – no! It's still on the kitchen table!' Then she quickly nudged Olive and grinned. 'As if.'

'Oh, this is going to be so good,' said Roz. She looked like her old self, light and smiley, as in the old days, before Robert the Brute took over her life and squashed all the joy out of her.

Oh God, I hope so, thought Ven. Because she knew that all wasn't quite as it appeared on the surface.

It was less than a ten-minute journey to the bus station, during which the three of them twittered like an excited dawn chorus on the back seat.

'I'll pay the driver,' said Olive, getting out her purse, as the taxi pulled up.

'Ah, ah – no, you won't.' Ven slapped her hand. 'I have been sent the cash to pay for all these peripheries like fares and coffees when we stop at the motorway services, so don't you dare.'

'Are you sure?' said Roz.

'Yes,' growled Ven. They were always having this sort of 'generous argument'. It infuriated her.

'Bloody hell. Who donated the prize? Rockerfeller?' laughed Roz.

'Oy, it's big business getting the right slogan. I could make them millions,' sniffed Ven proudly.

They arrived at Barnsley Interchange where a crowd of people with similar tags on their suitcases were waiting, so at least they knew they were in the right place. The tags were all different colours, denoting which deck the suitcase was destined for.

'Didn't think there would be this many going from Barnsley,' said Olive. 'Half the ship will be full of Yorkshiremen.'

'Don't be daft,' laughed Ven. 'The ship holds more than three thousand passengers.'

'Do you reckon B deck is more expensive than our C deck?' whispered Roz, as the elderly owner of a suitcase with a B deck tag, in a blazer and tie, was asking an E deck man, 'Is it your first time on the *Mermaidia*?'

'It's our first cruise full stop,' said E Deck Man.

'It's our thirtieth,' said Mr B Deck, puffing out his chest. 'Our eighth on the *Mermaidia*, isn't it, Irene?'

'Big-headed sod,' said Ven. 'If—' She bit off what she was going to say. *If Frankie were here, she'd have had him like a hungry Jack Russell with a rat!*

'Think I'll nip to the loo,' said Olive. 'Oh heck, are you sure I can buy things on the ship? I had a nightmare last night that I didn't have any clothes and was walking around naked.'

'Olive, look at my suitcases.' Ven gestured to her heaving luggage. 'I've over-bought so much stuff. Share my wardrobe. You've been doing it since we were twelve anyway.'

Olive and Ven always were the same dress size. Olive never had a lot of money to spend on clothes but Ven had a real eye for fashion and was happy to let Olive loose in her wardrobe when they were teenagers. She used to think that loads of her clothes better suited her blonde friend. Greens and reds and violets always looked more stunning against Olive's lovely long golden hair than her own auburn locks.

'Thanks,' smiled Olive. 'I think I might have to take you up on that. Apart from the stuff you bought me last night, I've only got a couple of tatty rags. Oh God – I didn't buy a swimsuit, did I?'

'No worries, I've packed five,' said Ven. 'Or was it six?'

'Trust you,' said Roz.

'And three trankinis.'

'Trankinis?' Roz burst into laughter. 'Sounds like a cocktail for drag artists. It's tankini, you twerp.'

In the toilet, Olive wished the bus would hurry up. She kept imagining a truck full of Hardcastles arriving at the bus station to hijack her and force her home where they would chain her back to the sink. Then again it was a Sunday morning at just past eight o'clock, and that was tantamount to midnight for them. Kevin would have thought she was a hallucination when he saw her by the door and she had no doubt he had gone back upstairs without her parting words sinking properly into his little brain.

'Bet Manus will miss you, Roz,' said Ven.

'Well, he's got a lot of work on so he'll be too busy to miss me,' replied Roz with a shrug. Ven frowned. So many times she wanted to butt into Roz's business and say, 'Stop being a cow to him,' but she didn't. She wasn't like Frankie who said things straight up – with one notable exception, of course.

Olive returned and then went straight back to the loo again. 'I know it's only nerves, but I'm just making sure I'm empty,' she explained.

'There will be a toilet on the bus, you know,' said Roz to her back. She turned to Ven. 'I hope she's going to let herself go and enjoy this.'

'She will, because I'll *make* her enjoy herself,' said Ven. 'Ooh, is this it?' A fancy white bus with blue waves painted on it and the name *Easy Rider* in bold red lettering manoeuvred skilfully towards them.

Olive bounced out of the loo and came running over in a panic.

'Chill,' said Ven. 'There's no rush.' Although she would have been better telling Mr B Deck that one because he was hurrying to the front, wheeling his fancy suitcase and making sure his timid-looking snow-haired little wife was following behind. He must have been in his early seventies, but was advancing with youthful determination to make sure he was first on that bus.

Roz was surprised to see such an age mix of passengers. She'd presumed cruises were just for rich old people. But waiting to get on the bus there were two families with small children and one with a babe in arms. And a young hand-holding couple obviously on their honeymoon from the *Just Married* stickers on their luggage. And also a very jolly party of seven adults and a little boy with his own WWE suitcase.

The bus driver was the widest bloke Ven had ever seen. He had a neck like a tree trunk, carried himself as if he had forgotten to take the coat hanger out of his shirt, and a tsunami of belly flowed over the top of his trouser belt, but he lifted the hefty suitcases as if they were featherweight and slotted them in his luggage hold like Tetris bricks.

Olive, Ven and Roz climbed on the bus, passing old Mr B Deck who was telling some other poor sod, 'Yes, Irene and I have been on thirty cruises. This is actually our eighth on the *Mermaidia* . . .'

'I pity whoever gets stuck on his dinner table,' mocked Roz, making them laugh with her whispering impersonation of him. '"*This will be the forty-eighth time I've had lobster in the Gobshite restaurant. And this will be the seven-hundredth crap I've had on board*".'

The bus engine shuddered awake and Olive breathed a sigh of relief. She wouldn't be truly happy until it was moving and she had escaped any chance of David and her in-laws catching up with her. The bus slowly turned out of the interchange and headed uptown.

'Well, good morning, everyone,' said a cheery Peter-Kay-Lancashire bus-driver voice. 'Are we all in a holiday mood?'

'Yes,' came a jolly chorus. Although Olive looked more as if she was going to throw up. She was scanning for Hardcastles wheeling or running lumpily towards the bus sides like hungry zombies.

'Well, I'm Clive your bus d*r-ah-ver* for the journey. Just have a few *likkle* legal obligations to tell you *a-bow-t* . . .'

Clive went on to tell everyone about the safety features on the bus, that they should use the seatbelts but he couldn't enforce it if they preferred to ignore him. And how to break the window with the secreted hammer in an emergency. And that he got home late last night because he'd had to wash the bus down and then had to heat up his tea in the microwave; he'd had liver and onions and peas. Not 'gorden' peas but marrowfat ones out of a tin.

'Blimey, I bet the time just flies by on a date with him,' said Roz, then she called across the aisle to Olive, fidgeting in her seat. 'Ol, will you calm down. You're safe.'

'Yes, I'll be calm in a moment or two,' said Olive as the bus gained speed and headed down the slip road of the M1. She held out her hand, steadily posed to prove her nerves were intact. 'Look, now I'm calm – see?'

Clive thrilled them some more with talk about where he was going to stop on the motorway to pick up some more passengers, and to inform them that there was a toilet at the back of the bus and how to flush it (by standing on the button on the floor). But he was stopping in ten minutes for a toilet break anyway.

'Crikey, I know my pelvic floor is knackered but I'm sure I can last longer than that,' said Ven.

'How can it be knackered – you've had no kids!' said Olive. None of them had. Ven, because she had never found Mr Right to have them with, Olive because she had never fallen pregnant naturally with David. Roz had never been that maternal. Manus hadn't been that bothered either; he was happy enough just as a couple. At least, that's what he used to say. As for Frankie, well, Frankie was a different case entirely. Once upon a time they were going to have four kids each and all sixteen children would be best friends – like they were.

'Does *she* know we're going on your birthday cruise?' asked Roz suddenly, as yet another annoying thought of Frankie Carnevale popped into her brain.

'Frankie, you mean?' Ven asked, though she knew who Roz meant because she reserved a special tone of voice for the rare occasions when she referred to her once best friend.

'Yes, *her.*'

'Yes, I told Frankie,' replied Ven, opening up a bag of Cadbury's Eclairs.

'Wasn't she pissed off that she was left out?'

'I'll make it up to her,' replied Ven.

'What, by bringing her a bottle of wine back?' laughed Roz. 'Anyway, I don't know why I'm asking about *her.*'

'Give it a rest, Roz,' said Ven quietly but firmly.

Roz shut up. Slagging Frankie off was now a long habit and really didn't have any place on a journey towards a luxury cruise. Especially when dissing her to a mutual friend who had

chosen her above Frankie to fill the third place. Roz played
with the thought of putting herself in Frankie's shoes and being
told that she wouldn't be going on a cruise because someone
else took priority. Frankie would have taken it better than Roz
would, had the situation been reversed.

'Have you seen her recently?' she asked, trying to sound a bit
less negative.

'A couple of weeks ago. I went down to see her.'

Roz was about to rear up at the thought of Ven going down
to Derbyshire and not telling her. Then she remembered she
had said ages ago that she didn't want to know anything about
Frankie. As usual with Roz, there was no pleasing her these
days. She was suddenly curious, though.

'Is she single?'

'Yeah, she's been single for ages.'

'What happened to that bloke she moved down to be with?'

'Bloke? Oh yes, well, they ... they split up not long after.'

Oh dear, Ros sniggered to herself.

'Is she still in Bakewell – where the tarts come from?'

'Yes,' said Ven, ignoring the barb tagged on at the end. 'She's
got a little cottage.'

'Thought she had a big house!'

'She sold it and found a smaller place to rent.'

'What the heck did she do that for?'

'She wanted to free up some capital when she lost her translating job,' said Ven, being careful what she said.

'Oh, so she's not working now,' said Roz with more than a
touch of smugness.

'She's doing some freelance work, here and there,' said Ven,
chomping down on her toffee. 'She's having a ... a career
break,' she worded carefully.

'Career break?' scoffed Roz. *How the mighty fall*, she added to
herself. Then she was suddenly shocked at how mean that made
her feel. *What sort of person have you become?* said a disgusted little

voice inside her. She didn't like the sound of that voice at all. She grabbed a magazine out of her handbag. It fell open at the page about *Putting the zing back into your love-life*. As if she needed to have it rubbed in.

Within fifteen minutes they had stopped at a service station and picked up some more passengers, and before Clive had repeated his scintillating safety information to the newcomers and told them about his infatuation with tinned peas, Olive had fallen asleep. She jerked awake a few minutes later with a falling sensation, but as she had barely had any sleep the night before, it wasn't long before she had drifted back to the Land of Nod. Roz wasn't far behind her and eventually Ven's eyes shuttered down too.

They awoke as the bus jerked to a halt outside another service station. Clive was announcing that they would have an hour's lunch here because he was legally obligated to eat something himself.

'Amazing what you can make yourself believe when you want to,' laughed Ven.

'He's hardly going to wither away,' whispered Roz, with a long stretch and a yawn. 'He could digest himself and live on the meat for years. I wonder if he'd eat himself with peas or without.'

'Well, I don't want him fainting through starvation whilst he's driving,' said Olive, wondering if he was really 'legally obligated' to eat and if any militant food police would be around to make sure he cleared his plate of meat and twelve veg.

People were getting off the bus. B Deck Man was first off, Roz noted, strutting towards the café with his missus a dutiful three paces behind him.

'Let's go and have a coffee,' said Olive. 'If I don't get some caffeine in my system, I'll go into a coma.'

She looked at her watch. The Hardcastles would be stirring from their crypt now. Doreen would be screaming for Olive to help her go to the toilet. She felt a pounce of guilt that David would have to step in. Then she remembered that Doreen was quite capable of getting to the toilet by herself if she could skip down the road for fags as she did. She thought of all the years she had tended to her, without a word of thanks. The big, bossy, idle so-and-so. She'd always known her parents could have done a lot more for themselves than they let on, and yet she'd gone and fallen straight in the same trap with the Hardcastles. What a first-class chump she was.

'Oy, stop thinking about that lot,' said Ven, nudging her as they queued up for coffee. 'I know you, lady.'

'I was just thinking they'll be getting up now. They'll have read my note and be in a state of chaos.'

'Good,' said Roz. 'I bloody hope they are.'

Chapter 16

At exactly the same time as the bus driver slid into first gear for the final leg of the journey, David Hardcastle was woken up by his mother hollering for Olive.

'Olive. *Olive!* Get up. I need the toilet. I'll wet myself if you don't hurry up.'

'Olive, get up, my mother wants you.' He farted on his wife and laughed because it was a hot smelly one, and if that didn't get her jumping out of bed, nothing would. Olive hated anything to do with farting and would be up in a flash now. Getting no reaction, David rolled over in bed, disappointed that he hadn't hit the target. Her side of the bed was cold and empty. More than that, it looked unslept in.

He swung his feet out from under the duvet and had a good scratch as he lumbered out of the bedroom to shout down the staircase.

'Olive, where are you? My mother wants you.'

'She went out,' called Kevin's yawning voice from behind the spare-room door. 'Said she was going to clear off some grease.'

'Clear off some grease?'

'That's what she said.'

Funny, thought David. She never said she was working this morning. He hoped that didn't affect the Sunday dinner being made.

'Olive!' screeched Doreen.

'Oh shut up, Mam, I'm coming.'

'Fetch my fags, David. And my lighter. They're by the kettle.'

'Hang on.' David plodded down the stairs and into the kitchen and there he found the envelope propped up against Doreen's Black Superkings. He ripped it open and read it.

'She's gone on holiday,' he said to himself. 'What does she mean, she's gone on holiday?'

'If you don't hurry up, Olive, I'll wet myself, I will,' called Doreen.

'Shurrup a minute, Mam.' Again David read the note. What drug was Olive on? She didn't have the money to go on holiday. Or any decent clothes to take with her. What was she on about, 'going on holiday'?

'I warned you, Olive!' called Doreen. 'I couldn't wait. I've wet myself. You'll have to get a cloth and clean me up. You should have come when I called.'

David's lips pulled back over his teeth. He didn't know what little stunt Olive was playing, but when she eventually got tired of it and came home, they were going to have serious words.

Chapter 17

The bus crossed the border into Southampton. Olive was in raptures looking at all the lovely posh houses that lined the main road into the city. She knew she would never live in anything that big, but she'd hoped for something better than a grotty terrace house full of cigarette smoke, nicotine-stained walls and kitchen appliances snatched from the Ark. David had promised her the world when they were courting. He certainly had the gift of the gab in those days. He walked tall and straight, not weighed down by a paunch, and had a round, smiley, cheeky face. He kissed her a lot too and cuddled her, which she loved, because her parents had never been demonstrative.

Olive tried to remember when he'd stopped putting his arm around her and telling her he loved her, but couldn't. These days it was only when he wanted sex that David touched her. And, funnily enough, when she thought about it, his back seemed perfectly okay when they were doing that! But in their courting days, he was full of ambitious, exciting plans. He was going to build them a big house to their own design, and Olive was going to grow vegetables in their massive garden and sell them to top-quality farm shops. She loved being outside in the open air and growing things. There was only a yard at the back of Doreen's house, just big enough for a few pots of tomatoes and the wheelie bins. They were only supposed to be living with her mother-in-law for a few months when they married thirteen years ago.

Ven nudged Roz awake. 'Oy, sleeping beauty. We're nearly there.'

Roz stretched the sleep out of her long limbs. 'What time is it?'

'Half past one.'

Clive, the bus driver, had started on another tack now. He was telling everyone to feel sorry for him because he had to go back and pick up another load of passengers tomorrow, but after that he was off for a few days. He had never been on a cruise and didn't think he ever would either, because he would only want one of the posh suites with a balcony and he couldn't afford that.

'He wants to stop eating takeaways then,' sniffed Roz. 'He could afford to charter a ship after a week with all the money he'd save. The big fat get.'

'You are rotten,' laughed Ven. Roz's wit always did have a caustic edge to it, more so these past few years, but she could also be very funny. She started to do a heavily accented and wicked impression of Clive that had Ven in fits.

'On Tuesdays, Mother and I like to share a plate of crispy pancakes and a big tin of marrowfat peas whilst watching re-runs of *Crossroads* on Saddo TV. Well, when I say *shur* I eat them all because Mother has been dead for two *yurs* and so she doesn't eat much. She's just happy sitting in her rocking chair, decomposing whilst she watches what Benny's up to.'

'If you look to your left you'll catch the first glimpse of your ship,' said the real Clive, as they edged closer to the dock. There in the near distance was a white ship with a yellow crest. It was approximately fifty times the size of the vessel that they all expected to see.

'Bloody hellfire, that's enormous!' gasped Roz. It was more like a floating multi-storey town than a boat.

Olive didn't say anything because she was so open-mouthed with astonishment that her jaw felt dislocated.

Big Clive asked everyone to wait a few minutes when they eventually pulled up, so that he could get the suitcases out first. Old Mr B Deck ignored him, of course.

Up close, the ship was even more massive. Olive was still gobsmacked. And to think, had she not had a headache last night and come home early she would have been halfway through cooking Sunday lunch now and trying not to retch as she loaded Kevin's washing into the machine. *What's going on between the walls of 15, Land Lane now?* she allowed herself to wonder until Clive boomed in loud Lancastrian, 'Okay, ladies and *jeng-kel-men*. You can come out now. Have a smashing holiday, and don't forget to send me a post-*cord*.'

'Come on, Olive,' smiled Ven. 'Your holiday's about to begin.'

They filed out and said goodbye to poor Clive. Ven hoped the fiver tip she gave him might soften the blow of him not going on a sixteen-day cruise. He could buy lots of tins of peas now. Especially if they were on a BOGOF.

'I can't believe I am actually going on *that*,' said Olive, pointing up at the ship and feeling the same sort of excitement she had experienced on seeing Blackpool Tower for the first time, when Ven's mum and dad took her there for a twelfth-birthday treat.

'You won't be going on it if you don't come with me and get in that queue,' said Ven. 'I've got your ticket. You concentrate on getting your passport out ready.'

'Is the competition bloke coming to meet you?' asked Olive. 'What's he called?'

'Er . . . Andrew something or other. No, nothing was said,' Ven replied. 'He'll no doubt catch up with us on board.'

'Thought he'd be here with a photographer to capture the moment for max publicity purposes. I mean, it's not exactly a tea-towel they're giving away, is it?'

Ven didn't answer, she just looked around at the pictures of the Figurehead fleet on the walls of the terminal building and stepped forward as the long snake of the queue began to shorten.

Olive had checked that her passport was in her bag at least sixty times but still had a panic when she couldn't locate it because it had fallen between the pages of her magazine. She reckoned since seeing Doreen skipping down the road last night, her heart must have done more racing beats than it had in the whole of her life so far.

They saw that Mr B Deck and his little missus were in a special queue of four passengers with an ELITE MEMBER sign above it. But then he was a hard-line cruiser, as everyone on the bus would surely know by now. He probably had his own bloke at Liverpool waiting to renew his passport every ten years.

'Look at that hunk over there with the dolly bird.' Ven pointed to a tall, impossibly handsome man with jet-black hair behind Mr B Deck in the queue. He was standing with a stunning, leggy woman with a pouty mouth, gravity-defying breasts and tumbles of long dark hair. Both were sporting shades of skin that couldn't possibly have been achieved naturally. It was more like woodstain than tan. 'He looks like Dom Donaldson.' Ven sighed, as she always did at the name of her idol, the soap star rough-diamond-with-a-heart character.

'So it is!' said Roz. 'And over there is Brad Pitt, and wait – David Beckham is bringing up the rear.'

'Okay, sarky beggar,' Ven said with a disappointed sigh. 'Aw well, it would have been nice to think that I was trapped on a ship with Dom Donaldson for sixteen days.'

Then Roz did a double-take of her own, for there passing quickly by was a drop-dead gorgeous man she could have sworn was Raul Cruz, the Spanish Michelin-starred chef on the television. He disappeared through a door marked Staff. Roz would never have admitted to the others that she had a crush on him; it would have been far too childish at her age and not 'Roz-like' at all. They would have teased her rotten about it. They didn't think she had a heart these days, never mind one that actually might beat fast with desire for a man. It wasn't her imagination playing tricks on her, though. According to the brochure he had a restaurant on board the *Mermaidia*, so chances were it was really him. Roz gulped.

There was a bank of check-in personnel so the queue went down pretty quickly and very soon Ven, Olive and Roz were standing in front of a desk, declaring that they hadn't had diarrhoea or vomited in the last twenty-four hours. Although Olive had come pretty close after discovering the truth about Doreen and David the previous night, but decided to keep quiet about that. Then they were all individually photographed with a camera that looked like a giant eyeball and presented with little plastic cards which they duly signed.

'These act as your passport and your key card, as well as allowing you to charge expenses to your account,' explained the lady at the desk.

Ven then produced her Visa. All expenses would be loaded onto that, and then Figurehead Cruises would reimburse her, apparently.

'I hope they do,' said Roz. 'Wouldn't like to think you'd be landed with all the champagne bills I'm going to run up.'

'They won't let me down,' replied Ven. 'Everything has gone smoothly enough so far.' *Oh boy, you really shouldn't have said that*, a sudden voice chided inside her head. If ever there was a passport to disaster on a plan it was to say that everything had gone smoothly so far.

'Bloody hell, what a competition prize. I've only ever won some shampoo on a tombola. And it was for brunettes,' said Olive, flying into a panic as her chain bracelet set off the metal detectors and she had to be frisked by a female security guard who looked as if she had come directly from *Prisoner Cell Block H*.

They were given a boarding card with the letter L on it as they filtered into a large waiting lounge, but seeing as passengers with letter K had just been called to the ship, it wasn't going to be a long wait. Then, immediately before they went on board, they posed quickly as a group in front of a photographer to capture the start of their holiday.

Olive was full of nervous excitement as they passed up the gently sloping and winding tunnel into the ship's body. Now it was Roz's turn to be struck dumb as they walked through the door and into a cavernous reception area which was opulent to the point of palatial and open-plan to five storeys. Two great glass elevators were carrying passengers upwards and downwards, and a line of apparently all Indian men in white suits were waiting to escort guests to their cabins.

'This way, ma'am,' said one, after Ven told him her cabin number. His name badge read *Benzir*. He gallantly took Roz's giant handbag from her and led them down a carpeted hallway, the walls studded with huge pieces of artwork, and then up in an enclosed lift to the ninth floor.

Their rooms were next to each other. Olive's pink suitcase had already arrived and was parked outside her door. She had assumed the pictures in the brochure Ven showed them were exaggerated or Photoshopped, and in real life her cabin would be a poky, bare space with a creaky hammock, but the photo didn't even do it justice when she pushed open the door. To her immediate right was a huge open wardrobe space, a tower of shelves and an inbuilt safe, and layers of thick snow-white towels lined more shelves in the pretty mirrored ensuite with the full-size bath in it; there was also a tray full of beautiful complimentary toiletries next to the sink. Straight ahead was a double bed with big fat pillows on it, two TVs – one angled to the bed, one to the sitting area where there was a large sofa and coffee table. Floor-to-ceiling glass doors led out onto a balcony furnished with an outside table and two chairs. Wow. Sixteen days wouldn't be enough, she knew that immediately. Already she was working out plans to stow away on the next cruise.

She had just started to unpack when Roz and Ven knocked.

'Glad you came?' grinned Ven. 'Or do you want me to get Clive to take you back home on his bus with him? You can pick up some peas and have a wild ride.'

'I'll force myself to stay for a while,' sniffed Olive. 'Might be a struggle, though.'

'You won't properly relax until we've set off, will you?' said Roz. 'I know how your brain works.'

'Probably not,' replied Olive. 'I know I'm a saddo, you don't have to tell me.'

'Well, you've less than three hours to wait now. We sail off at quarter past five.'

There was a timid knock at the door.

'Who's that?' asked Olive, in a panic.

'How the hell do I know?' returned Roz. 'I left my X-ray specs at home!'

'It'll be Doreen,' said Ven in a very sinister voice and forming her hands into creepy claws. 'She'll have free-wheeled all the way down from junction thirty-seven.'

'Don't joke,' laughed Roz. 'She'll believe you.'

Olive opened the door to a beaming-faced, dark-skinned man in an immaculate white tunic.

'Hello, ma'am, my name is Jesus and I am the cabin steward for the rooms in this section.'

'Flaming heck,' said Roz, raising her perfectly arched eyebrows. 'There's the height of luxury – having Jesus as your cabin steward.'

Jesus laughed heartily, then he proceeded to show the ladies the hairdryer secreted in the drawer and explained how to set the combination on the cabin safe and where the fridge, the kettle and the air-conditioning/heating controls were. He directed their attention to the big blue folder on the dressing-table which had details of all the holiday's entertainment, what was showing on the in-cabin TVs, the room service menu, stationery, the spa facilities and the card that told them which of the three restaurants, and sittings, they would be dining in that evening: the Olympia at 6.30, as it happened. Then he informed them that they had to attend a lifeboat drill meeting at 4.15.

'That's comforting,' said Roz, as Jesus showed them where the life-jackets were kept.

'It's the law, ma'am,' said Jesus. 'Everyone has to go. But I have never had an emergency in the twelve years I have been with the company.'

'There's always a first time,' sighed Roz, before Ven tutted at her. Roz's glass was always half-empty.

Jesus poked his head out of the cabin and announced that more of their cases had arrived, then he left them to introduce himself to other passengers whom he was also looking after.

'Right, we'll leave you to carry on unpacking, Ol. Have you rung Manus to say you've arrived, Roz?' asked Ven.

Roz pulled a pained face and Ven's smile instantly dried up.

'What?' she queried, not liking that expression at all.

'Look, you may as well know,' Roz began. 'Manus and I are on a trial separation.'

'Oh Roz!' said Olive and Ven in unison.

'Please.' Roz held up her hand to stem their flow. 'Let us just get on with it. It's been coming for a long time, you probably know that. Anyway, it's just a trial. Everything is in the air so I'd rather not talk about it. I want to forget home for sixteen days, so . . . let me do just that, will you both? Please.'

She was right, it wasn't all that unexpected, but it was still very sad because Ven and Olive thought Manus was a total catch and wished Roz could see him through their eyes. But their friend was so stubborn and unbendable where he was concerned. Olive cast a glance at Ven that spoke volumes: *Someone has to say something now. Before she and Manus split up for good. We can't let that happen, not knowing what we know.* But for now, all they could do was nod.

Roz unzipped the suitcase which sprang open with a sigh of relief. She thought of Manus pressing down on it with all his might so she could close it. She really should ring him and say she had arrived in Southampton, then she remembered her own rules of no contact and switched off her phone. She wouldn't miss the constant voice in her head berating her for how badly she treated Manus. Every time she sniped at him, she heard it pleading with her to grow up and stop pushing him because one day she would drive him too far – and she had now, hadn't she? She put the phone in the built-in safe until the end of the holiday. She would check it every few days just in case of emergency, but she had no reason to expect any calls; her mother wouldn't ring an 'expensive mobile number' even if she was dying. And then she would turn to one of Roz's step-sisters first.

Roz had never had an easy relationship with her mother. Her father left – and disappeared into the ether – when Roz was nine and her mother found solace in bitter tears and cheap white wine. For her first nine years, Roz had grown up with her ears constantly ringing from the sound of marital arguments. For the next nine, all she heard were drunken diatribes about how twisted men were. Any small step Roz put wrong was greeted with the criticism that she was 'stupid/wicked/selfish – just like your father'. And when she was low in spirits – which was often – Frankie would drag her over to the wonderful, warm and crazy Carnevale household for Lucia's home-cooked food and Salvatore's murdering of operatic numbers. Then Roz's mother met and married a total twerp with two daughters in a whirlwind romance and suddenly didn't hate men any more, but the poison she had dripped into her own daughter's heart sat in a dark pool and waited its time to burst its banks.

Roz moved in with her new step-family but it was clear from the off that she wasn't welcome and there were no objections from any of them when she said she was going to stay with the Carnevales instead. And not long after, the lean, beautiful young woman she had become managed to attract Jez Jackson's eye at long last and he moved her willingly into his bed and his home. He was to be the first of many men who would break her heart and reinforce everything her mother had said.

Roz tried to shake the thought of that all-encompassing, generous, wonderful family out of her head, like an annoying fly that was buzzing in her ear. She didn't want to remember how Lucia Carnevale would send over enormous dishes of lasagne and home-made ciabatta loaves as big as sheds to make sure she was eating all right. It was painful to think of how she'd had to cut herself off from them because of what had happened between Manus and Frankie. Something else to hate her for.

When Ven and Roz had finished unpacking and called for Olive to go up to the life-jacket meeting, she was sitting on her sofa having a cup of tea like Lady Muck.

'Made yourself at home, I see?' chuckled Ven.

'Yes, I most certainly have,' replied Olive. 'I just need a servant to pour me a refill and I'm sorted.'

'You should have asked for the room with the butler in it,' said Ven.

'Yeah, right!'

'Honest,' Ven went on. 'You can get rooms on here with your own butler. Costs an arm and a leg though, because they're the top suites.'

'No!' Olive gasped. How the other half live, eh? She grabbed her life-jacket and followed the others out, remembering to take the cruise card with her. People were bustling around, everyone carrying orange life-jackets, even children with smaller ones. They were marshalled by the ship's personnel down a beautifully wide staircase to a nightclubby-type place called Cinnabar where they commandeered a sofa between them.

'What are you wearing for dinner tonight?' asked Olive. It looked as if some people had changed already for the evening unless they had travelled down in very smart clothing, like Mr B Deck in his blazer and Mrs B Deck in her twinset and pearls.

'Just go as you are,' replied Ven. 'I think most people do that on the first night. Ultra-casual. You look okay as you are with your trousers. I'm going to change though, because I don't think jeans would be right.'

The life-jacket drill was straightforward enough. They all learned how to wear one and that they needed to step off a ship in an emergency and not jump. Some people were obviously a bit dense because when the order came to watch the demonstration by a crew member, they put the life-jackets on as well despite being clearly told not to. Roz wanted to slap them. She could hardly hear the instructions being given out on the Tannoy for the rasp of illegal Velcro.

'I don't think you'd sink anyway with those knockers,' said Ven to Roz.

'Good, because I doubt I'll be able to fit the bloody life-jacket over them. Where's my strap?' Roz replied grumpily, unable to locate it. 'And I'll never be able to get to the whistle!'

When it was over, the girls headed back to the cabin to put their life-jackets away, hoping they wouldn't see them again – and went out on deck for the leaving party.

There was a band playing jazz outside the terminal. They must have been freezing because the weather was rubbish for August and there was a bitter breeze in the air. Plastic Union Jack flags on sticks were being distributed and waiters were scurrying around with expertly-balanced trays full of champagne.

'Come on, we've got to have some bubbly,' said Ven and signed a chitty for three glasses.

'Wish we'd hurry up and leave,' said Olive, checking her watch and finding it was twenty past five. She wasn't sure if it was fear or excitement that was coursing through her system. She wondered what state the Hardcastles would be in by now, and whether David had known that his mother was about as much an invalid as Anton du Beke. Or whether Doreen knew that her 'darling boy' was just a lying, idle loafer with a perfectly functioning, if manufactured from jelly, spine. Well, they'd find out in the next couple of weeks, that was for sure.

There was a wonderful atmosphere building. Olive looked over the side of the ship and saw the waters being churned up, so something was starting to happen. She started mouthing the lyrics to 'Goodby-ee' which the band were now playing. People were leaning on the rails waving their flags towards the crowds over in the terminal who were waving back just as madly – friends and relatives come to see them off, presumably. The ship's horn blasted out.

'I think we're moving,' said Roz. 'Yes, we're definitely off. Oh no, look at that man running to stop the ship! It's David.'

Olive's heart bounced into her mouth.

'Joke!' said Roz. 'Sorry, Olive.' She laughed at the sight of Olive patting her chest, then that smile pinged shut like a snapped elastic band. Because walking towards her, bolder and brassier than ever, with a glass of champagne in her hand, was none other than Frankie Carnevale.

Chapter 18

'What the frig . . .?' Roz spun around to Ven, questions filling her expression.

'Okay, I'm sorry, but if I'd told you, you wouldn't have come, would you? And I wanted all four of us to be here. Like we always said we would.'

Meanwhile Olive had bounced over to Frankie and was hugging her like mad, and was being hugged back with the same ferocity.

'Oh my God, you're here. Last I heard, you weren't coming!' shrieked Frankie in her familiar smoky voice.

Roz's face was as sour as a rotting lemon.

'How are you doing, Roz?' said Frankie, warmly but cautiously. 'Long time no see.'

'I feel like jumping off the side,' growled Roz. 'That's how I'm doing.' She felt herself shaking with rage. She daren't look at Ven because she wanted to strangle her too much.

'Oh come on, Roz,' said Ven. 'Please. For me. Bury the hatchet for sixteen days.'

I'll bury it in her back, said Roz to herself. *Where she stabbed me.* She took a deep breath, nodded stiffly at Frankie and managed dryly, 'You've changed.' Which was putting it mildly. Once a plump girl with a flat chest, Frankie was now skinny-thin with a very generous bosom – surgically enhanced, obviously. It didn't take an idiot to work out that was where a big lump of the money from her house sale must have gone. Or rather two big lumps. Frankie's once long black sheet of hair was now very short, spiky and platinum-white. Only her diminutive height, her big dark Italian eyes and her curved and generous lips remained the same. She was wearing a two-piece trouser ensemble in beige. Frankie used to say she'd know she'd got old when she started wearing beige trouser suits, Roz suddenly recalled.

'Well, it's been a few years,' said Frankie. She knocked her champagne glass against Ven's. 'Cheers, buddy. Am I ready for this holiday or am I ready for it?'

Roz was sulky-silent as the other three chattered on excitedly and the ship started to head towards the open sea. Ven didn't drag her into their conversation. Roz would come round if she wasn't pushed. She hadn't tried to throttle Frankie yet or fling herself into the sea, so there was hope.

'Where's your room?' asked Olive.

'C162,' said Frankie, tipping the last of her champagne into her mouth.

'Next to me then,' said Olive with a grin. 'I'm C160.'

Roz was the only one not smiling. She should have questioned Ven more closely about Frankie not coming. *All for one and one for all*, that's what they always used to say. Ven wouldn't have left Frankie out, she should have known that. Ven wouldn't have left any of them out because she was too frigging nice. And Roz had to hold herself back from killing her for it.

Behind them, people were swigging champagne and leaving their jobs and woes at the dock. Roz felt as if she were on the outside looking into the scene through a thick layer of glass now. She didn't want to be here any more making small talk with this beige-wearing bitch, but what could she do about it? She roughly put her glass down on a nearby table and said, 'Right, I'll see you later. I'm going to finish off my unpacking.'

And with that she turned and headed off through the nearest door to the inside of the ship.

'Phew, that went well,' said Frankie with enforced jollity. 'I thought she might have been a bit off with me.'

'Aw, Frankie, she'll snap out of it,' said Ven. A reconciliation was long overdue and she was determined that bridges would be built on this trip. It was a miracle that she had managed to get all of them on board at all – and now they were, it was going to be bloody good. She would make sure it was – somehow! She just hoped she hadn't made the biggest mistake of her life playing God. But then, the situation couldn't get much worse than it already was – the only way was up!

Frankie put her arms around Ven and Olive and gave them a big squeeze.

'Fate gave us this holiday,' she began, mirroring what was going on in Ven's head, 'so it must have something nice in store for us. Bloody hell, Ven, I can't believe we're all here, can you?'

Ven tried to muster a smile. She almost pulled off a convincing one.

Roz stomped around in her room for a bit then realised, as those do who have cut off their noses to spite their faces, that she was alone whilst the other three were in the midst of gaiety and champagne. The reality hit her that she was on a cruise ship having a tantrum. And the friend who was giving her this free luxurious holiday had had a rotten time over the past couple of years. Ven still managed to keep that smile alight despite losing both her parents, her job, a load of money, her house and her husband, even if he was a prick. As sulky and annoyed as Roz felt, this was one of those times when she must look outside her own wants and needs and swallow it because this trip was all about Ven. She didn't know how she'd keep her hands off Frankie's throat, but she'd try; for a one-time offer of sixteen days only. So when Ven tentatively knocked on her door at twenty past six and asked if she was ready to come down to dinner with them, she made sure she was, complete with smile pinned to her face.

A few passengers had changed into posh frocks and suits, but most were very casual. Frankie was in a plain grey dress. Blimey – Frankie never used to dress in anything that didn't require sunglasses to view it. She was a lot thinner than Roz could remember her ever being, which made her look even smaller than her five foot two height. She'd obviously been on a huge diet before her boob job.

They followed the complimentary maps they'd all been given of the ship and joined a stream of people heading to the Olympia restaurant on the sixth floor.

'God, it's like the Ritz,' said Olive, feeling very underdressed in her black trousers and plain blouse. There was a sea of white tablecloths and waiters in crisp white shirts and black waist-coats, and greeting the guests were three smiling and beautifully dressed Indian head waiters with chocolate eyes-to-die-for.

Roz waited for Frankie to do a customary low growl of lust and say something lecherous like, 'I want one of those buttered.' She was disappointed, though. Frankie didn't say a word.

They were led to a table for eight and were the first arrivals.

'I'm loving this "ma'am" business,' said Olive, as their waiters Elvis and Aldrin pulled out the chairs and draped serviettes across their laps. Their table was next to a huge window affording a picture of a very grey sea and some bobbing fishing boats.

'Mr B Deck alert.' Ven nudged Olive. To their horror the dapper old man seemed to be heading their way, with Mrs B Deck close behind.

'I don't believe it, he's heading for our table,' hissed Roz.

'Evening, all,' said Mr B Deck, holding out a hand to be shaken. 'My name's Eric and this is Irene. We're from Barnsley. Weren't you on our bus coming down?'

They were all in the process of shaking hands and making introductions when another couple joined them. Fifty-something Royston and Stella were Cockneys who now lived in Essex. It was obvious from the first that Royston was a barrow boy made good and wanted everyone to know about it. They'd not even opened their menus before they had learned he had driven to Southampton in his brand new BMW. Quite a bit of his money looked as if it had gone on operations on his wife. Ash-blonde Stella had a slightly tight, wrinkle-free face with a waxy sheen and an artificially smooth neck for someone her age. Underneath her very clingy silky blouse, her boobs were high and round as a pair of best grapefruits, and when she smiled she showed off ultra-white and too-perfect teeth. But the overall effect was of a very good-looking woman, if a little Barbie-plastic.

'I reckon this could be fun,' Ven whispered to Roz. 'Wonder when the "how many times have you been on the ship?" questions will start.'

They didn't have to wait long.

'This will be our twenty-first cruise,' said Royston, puffing out his chest.

'Thirtieth for us,' said Eric proudly.

'Thirtieth?' echoed Frankie, genuinely impressed.

Roz waited for her to carry on. She always was a master-bluffer. She used to have them in stitches.

Thirtieth? You're like me then – once you find a good thing, you stick to it. This will be our fortieth. It's such a nice change not to sit with the Captain either. He wanted our company so much last time that I thought we were being stalked. Do you have the room with the butler? My, not to be recommended – they get in the way awfully. Although they do make a fabulous Wallbanger. If you get my drift – fnar fnar.

But instead Frankie said, 'Thirtieth? That's amazing. This is our first. We've been planning it since we were at school together.'

Roz was gobsmacked. Boy, Francesca Carnevale *had* changed!

'Evening, everyone,' came the chirpy voice of a beautiful Filipino woman with cascading black hair tied back in a pony-tail, very much like Frankie's used to be. 'I'm Angel, your wine steward for this cruise. Would you like to order some drinks or something from the wine list?'

'Blimey,' said Olive. 'We've got Jesus cleaning the room and an Angel bringing us drinks.'

'I'm just waiting to see Saint Peter on port security,' giggled Roz.

It turned out that it was Royston and Stella's first cruise on the *Mermaidia*, so Eric looked pleased that he was the leading authority on the ship.

Ven took some almond and pistachio bread from the basket and buttered it liberally. The menu looked fabulous. So far she had narrowed her choice of main courses down to four.

'If you don't like what's on the menu,' said Irene, reaching a talon-nailed finger over the top of Ven's menu and pointing to the lefthand side, 'there's always chicken, steak and salmon available.'

'That's me then, a sirloin,' said Roz, snapping her menu shut.

'You always have steak when we go for a meal!' said Ven.

'That's because I like it,' explained Roz with strained patience. 'Soup, steak and a coffee, that'll do me just fine. I'm a plain eater, as you know. At the end of the day, it's only fuel.'

'You never used to think like that,' said Frankie. 'You used to love your food.'

'People change,' replied Roz, trying to bat away the images attacking her brain of sitting at the Carnevales' dinner-table and stuffing herself daft on pasta.

'Well, I'm being adventurous,' Olive decided. 'I've never had John Dory so I'm trying that.'

'If you don't like it, they'll bring you something else, you know,' Royston jumped in. 'You can afford to experiment on a ship, that's what I always say.'

'That sounds far too good to be true,' said Frankie. 'In that case then, I'll have John Dory too.'

Roz bit back the snide comment about to rise in her throat that John Dory was a fish, not a man – was Frankie aware of that?

'Going to the show this evening?' asked Eric. 'First one is usually a very jolly affair. Lovely theatre on this ship, but I advise you to get there by half past eight for a good seat.'

'They've got a theatre on the ship?' gasped Olive.

'They've got two, actually. Broadway and Flamenco – which admittedly is half-nightclub, half-theatre. And there will be some sort of a show at each one every night,' said Eric. 'Didn't you see the *Mermaidia Today* brochure in the post-slot outside your cabin door? It'll tell you everything that's happening on the ship tonight, and you'll get another one before you go to bed about what's going on tomorrow. Oh, and in case you didn't know, the dress code for dinner is always formal on the second night. So if you ladies want to get your hair done, you'd better book up early because they'll be busy in the salon.'

Two theatres! Olive was open-mouthed with astonishment for the three-hundredth time since she came aboard. Three-hundredth-and-one, when Ven clicked her fingers as she announced to her friends, 'Ah well, I might as well tell you, we're all booked in at the spa tomorrow. Massage and then a hairdo and make-up.' She tagged on a whisper for the other three alone. 'Part of the package,' and tapped the side of her nose.

'You should get some highlights, Olive. Go platinum like me.' Frankie picked up a shank of Olive's hair and thought that with a good sharp cut and a splash of peroxide she could lose years.

'Yes, you should. Go for it, Olive!' said Ven. 'I'll ring up and speak to the spa people and amend the booking.'

Olive leaned back in her seat as her Moules Marinières starter arrived and felt that she was in a dream. Mussels, massages and make-up. How far away was this from her normal life?

'What the hell. I just might,' she said.

Chapter 19

Back in Land Lane, Kevin was putting fish and chips from Turbot's shop onto three plates. They always got whopping servings from there – enough to feed even them twice over. David was trying to pull a big cushion out of the washing machine. It was the one his mother had soiled. Funnily enough, when she realised that Olive really had disappeared and wasn't going to sort her out with a bowl of water and a flannel she managed to struggle not only to her feet, but into the downstairs bath by herself – albeit with a lot of groaning, huffing and puffing.

The cushion had split, and very lumpy filling was all over the drum. Doreen noticed that David seemed to be having no trouble bending down to scoop it all out. She was thinking that his back was very flexible when his wife wasn't around.

'Do you think she's got another bloke?' Kevin called to his cousin.

'Olive? Give over!' said David. 'When does she have time?'

'Where's she gone then?' Kevin dropped a fish piece on the floor and whipped it back on the plate before any germs leaped on it. He had always believed that it took ten seconds before it became 'dirty'. Still, he wasn't having that one.

'How do I know? She's playing silly buggers. She'll get bored after a couple of days and come home and then we'll find out why she's gone doolally. But I know two things for sure: she hasn't run off with another fella and she hasn't gone on bloody holiday!' Boy, would his wife get a mouthful and a half for having him run round like a blue-arsed fly after his mother.

'I bet it's the menopause,' decided Kevin. 'It's always something to do with periods either stopping or starting when they go weird. Have you rung her mobile?'

'Of course I have, I'm not thick,' snapped David. 'The bloody thing is switched off, isn't it?'

'Why don't you ring that mate of hers? Venice. The one with the gorgeous bum.' Kevin's tongue snaked out lustily.

'I'm not ringing and chasing her,' David grumbled. 'She'll be home soon enough with her tail between her legs. She knows which side her bread is buttered best.'

'David! Fetch me some clean pants!' came a screech from the bathroom.

David thought that his resolve not to chase Olive and bring her back might crumble sooner, rather than later.

Chapter 20

After a magnificent three-course menu and then coffees, the four ladies excused themselves from the table, to bag some good seats in the theatre, leaving Eric, Irene, Royston and Stella comparing past cruises.

'I feel like I've had a crash course in ship-life,' laughed Ven. 'How much information did those four cram into us?'

'Quite interesting information in some cases, though,' said Olive. 'As in which trips to book. And to turn our clocks forward one hour tonight.'

'We'll have a look at the trips tomorrow,' said Ven.

'Formal night tomorrow, according to the knowledgeable ones. Long frocks at the ready, ladies,' grinned Frankie.

'Oh heck, I haven't got a long one,' said Olive. There was no way she had enough clothes for this holiday. That nightmare was going to come true and she would be walking around the decks starkers.

'Olive, we'll go shopping tomorrow. Before your hairdo – and your massage,' said Ven, giving her hand a comforting squeeze.

'I've never had a massage before,' said Olive. She was a bit nervous about it, though she didn't want to make herself out to be a wimp and say as much.

'Scared you'll get turned on?' joked Frankie. 'It'll be a bit different to having your David rub you down with chip fat.'

David. Olive wondered what he would be doing now, then she threw him out of her head. There was no point being on a ship if her thoughts were going to be stuck back in Barnsley. She had promised herself that she would try very hard not to think about what was happening in Land Lane. She wouldn't see the Hardcastles again until after she had been to Cephalonia.

The *Mermaidia* had its own theatre company and they were very good. The six boys and six girls, all with perfect figures and beautiful faces, performed a musical tribute play to the 'Rock Around the Clock' era. Olive looked at one of the dancers, a long-haired blonde girl who was around the age she herself had been when she took off to work in Cephalonia for the summer. That girl had her whole life in front of her like a field full of freshly fallen snow on which to make her mark. Olive's memories of those months were flavoured with the fragrance of lemons and slow-cooked lamb. And Atho Petrakis's kisses.

Ven looked around at the eclectic mix of passengers. Lots of children, confidently strutting teenagers who seemed to have linked into friendship groups already, old couples, and a shaggy-haired, bearded and tattooed man, looking at odds with the rest of his conventional party. He appeared more as if he had been searching for the Southampton Hell's Angel Chapter and taken a wrong turning at the docks. Or was he a wild Viking – with something like 'Bloodaxe' in his name? Frankie was thinking on exactly the same wavelength.

'He looks wrong here,' she said.

'Maybe he's part of the security team. Wouldn't tangle with him, would you, Frank?'

'Oh, I don't know. Shave off that beard and tidy up the hair a bit and I bet he'd be quite handsome. Are we exploring?'

'I'm knackered,' said Olive. 'Do you mind if I turn in?'

'Don't be daft,' said Ven. 'This is your holiday, you do what you want.'

'I'm going as well,' said Roz, affecting a yawn. She wasn't that tired, but she didn't relish the idea of trotting around the ship with Frankie pretending they were bosom buddies again. Bosom being the operative word now with Frankie's new tits. No, there was only so much play-acting she could do in one day. So Roz and Olive said goodnight and headed back to their cabins.

They both made contented gasps when they went inside them. Jesus had switched on some subdued lighting, closed the curtains, turned down their quilts and placed a chocolate on their pillow.

Olive was too tired even to have a bath or a shower; she stripped off to her underwear then went to the drawer for her nightie. She was just about to put it on when she remembered she didn't need to. If she got up in the middle of the night to go to the toilet, she wasn't likely to bump into Kevin and his appendage-filled thong. She crawled between the starched white sheets stark naked, an extreme act of wantonness from her, and tried to remember the last time she had slept in the nude between sheets as crisp and cool as these. Her mind flew back twenty years and she saw herself rolling around naked with Atho Petrakis in his bed above the café, and though she was alone, Olive felt herself blushing. The ship barcaroled gently and made her feel as if she were in a giant cradle. Or Atho's double hammock, strung between the olive trees behind his parents' tiny villa. She slipped into sleep before she had a chance to savour her memories for long.

Next door, Roz lay on her bed staring up at the ceiling and thinking about Frankie. She wouldn't have recognised her if they had passed in the street, with her hair and her weight loss and her enlarged knockers. She could almost have been a different person but for those big sloe eyes of hers. But she wasn't. She was still the same Frankie Carnevale who had tried to seduce her man . . . then distorted and exaggerated pictures of

Frankie and Manus passionately locked in each other's arms loomed large and colourful in Roz's head. Her mother was right, after all. Anything with a dick should never be given the benefit of the doubt.

Frankie and Ven caught the lift up to the seventeenth floor as they had decided to explore the ship from the top down, but once they had flopped onto a comfortable sofa in the beautiful Vista lounge on the sixteenth, they knew it would be their last port of call for the evening.

'I'm so full, I don't think I could even fit a drink in,' said Frankie, feeling the curve of her stomach.

'Drink, ma'am?' came a waiter's voice at her side.

'A Classic Champagne Cocktail, please,' said Frankie.

'What happened to "I'm so full"?' Ven grinned and ordered the same.

'I am full, I'm just being a pig,' said Frankie. 'It's not every day you get up from a dinner-table and swan off without paying the bill, is it? I could get used to this life very quickly.'

'We're right at the very back of the ship,' said Ven, looking out to sea. 'I bet this is gorgeous during the day.'

'No doubt we'll find out tomorrow.'

'Sorry about Roz,' said Ven, suddenly changing the subject. 'I knew she'd be pissed off at seeing you. Not sure it was fair to risk it for your sake.'

'Oh, don't you worry about me.' Frankie tapped her on the hand. 'The ship's big enough for her to get out of my way if she chooses. I shall make no such detours, though. How's Manus? Still as lovely as ever?'

'He's wonderful,' sighed Ven. 'I wish I could find someone as nice as he is. But they're having a rough time, Frankie. They're on a temporary break.'

'Aw, that's a shame,' said Frankie, with quiet sorrow. 'I'm really sorry to hear that.'

'We don't know what to do,' said Ven. 'If she knew—'

Frankie held up a hand to stop Ven speaking further. 'You can't. It wouldn't be fair to tell her now. You just can't.'

'That's just it – I can't tell her and I can't not tell her, so I'm well and truly stuck,' sighed Ven. 'Things should never have got this far. You shouldn't have made us promise.'

'I know,' said Frankie, shaking her head sadly. 'I'm sorry, but I thought I was doing the right thing. I should have listened to you but I didn't.'

They paused to thank the waiter for the newly delivered champagne and for Ven to sign the chitty.

'I could murder you when I think about the mess,' said Ven through impatiently gritted teeth. 'But I could equally as easily murder Roz. She's been punishing Manus for Robert's antics ever since they met. She's not blameless in all this, so don't think I'm saying she is, but she's like a pit bull with a bone when she gets going.'

'And I didn't help.' Frankie's fist crashed into her thigh. 'I just wish I could turn the clock back to that night. He loves her so much. She's blessed – if she could but see it. He's fab, you can't help but love Manus, but not in *that* way. He didn't fancy me and I didn't fancy him.'

'I know you didn't.'

Once upon a time Ven had ventured to tell Roz that, hoping to smooth some waves . . . it had only made matters worse. Sometimes, she and Olive felt that Roz was more comfortable with Manus's mistake than with forgiving him.

'*She nearly broke up my relationship and she didn't even fancy him!*' Roz had railed, and Ven knew she had inflamed the situation whilst meaning to do the opposite. She was expert at getting things wrong when her heart was full of the best intentions, which was why she was worrying now that this trip was a disaster in the making.

'I hate all this,' said Ven, coughing back the tremor in her voice. 'I hate the way Roz hates you, because I know she does-n't really. She hates herself more than she could ever loathe anyone else, and it breaks my heart to see it. She gets herself into these ruts and can't get out of them. That fecking mother of hers did a great job at warping her brain.'

Frankie knew Ven was really upset because she rarely used hard expletives. 'Well, Ven, she's just going to have to carry on hating me. Because if you boil it down to the basic facts, I crossed the line ...'

'But ...'

Frankie wouldn't let Ven interrupt her. 'But nothing, Ven. I can cope with her hating me. And she never needs to know now, does she? Does she?'

Ven shook her head. She wasn't sure if she agreed, but when in between a rock and a hard place, it was as well to cling on to the more familiar of the two and hope for the best.

Frankie plastered on a smile. 'Okay, now for a bit of light relief. I suppose your ex hasn't been back on the scene?'

'Not since I signed the cheque for fifty grand,' said Ven.

'I bet your mum and dad are spinning in their graves,' said Frankie.

'I don't let my mind go down that road,' said Ven. It was bad enough that her husband Ian had been sleeping with another woman behind her back for two years, but to divorce her straight after her father had died and take half her inheritance in the settlement was cruel. Her parents had worked their whole lives to leave her a decent lump sum, even though Ven had told them to blow the lot. And now Ian and his squeeze Shannon were living it up in her former home and on her parents' money. What hurt most of all was that, with hindsight, she could see that Ian had been hanging on, waiting for her poorly father to die so he could make his monetary claim. She never thought he could be that cold – but people change over the years. Roz was testament to that.

'I hope your mum and dad's money chokes him,' said Frankie.

'Please,' sighed Ven, holding up an open palm to halt any more mentions of her perfidious ex. 'He's moved on, I've moved on. And there is nothing I can do about the money.' Ven had even returned to her maiden name of Miss Smith. She couldn't bear to see the name 'Venice Walsh' on any of her chequebooks and documents.

'I wish that thing of Olive's would move on,' said Frankie, closing her mouth before a huge gassy burp escaped. 'Sorry, that's the bubbles. You know, the other week, I asked her if she loved David and she said "I don't have bloody time to love anyone".'

'I know,' said Ven, glad of a change of focus in the conversation.

'Why does she stay with him?' asked Frankie, who had never thought David was good enough for her friend. And she despised Doreen and that layabout Cousin Kevin with his wandering eyes. How anyone who dressed like a hippy living in a skip with teak-coloured teeth could believe he was God's gift was anyone's guess. She only wished she had his powers of self-delusion.

'Because she wouldn't know how to leave, is my guess,' replied Ven sadly.

'I thought she would have had kids, you know,' said Frankie. Out of all of them, Olive would have made the best mother.

'It never happened for her,' said Ven. 'And I don't think they – you know, *do it* much anyway.'

'Perish the thought!' Frankie shuddered again. A hideous picture of a sweaty David puffing away above her nearly brought her John Dory back up. She took another quick glug of alcohol to quell her stomach.

'I was never passionate about wanting kids, the way some people are . . .' Ven's voice trailed off. 'Sorry, Frank.'

'Don't be daft,' said Frankie. 'I'm long over it.'

'I don't think I've ever found anything to be truly passionate about,' Ven confessed wistfully.

'This from the woman who was going to be Barbara Taylor Bradford when she grew up?' said Frankie. 'What happened?'

'I wanted to write but I couldn't find anything to write about,' Ven told her. 'Plus Ian said it was really rude of me to be tapping away on a laptop when he'd come in from work and hadn't seen me all day.'

'The bastard cock! Not as rude as him shagging about,' huffed Frankie. Then: 'Sorry, Ven. You know what I mean.'

Ven gave a little laugh. 'Yes, don't worry, I know what you mean.'

'Never too late though,' said Frankie. 'Catherine Cookson was into her forties when she got her first book published.'

'She wasn't, was she?'

'She was, you know. Look it up on your laptop. You can be as rude as you like on it now.'

'I wish I were like you, Frank. You were always throwing yourself into things: salsa, art classes, singing, belly dancing, scuba diving . . .'

'There's a belly-dancing course on board. I saw a poster in the reception area.'

'Are you going?'

'I doubt it,' laughed Frankie. 'It's great fun, but I want to chill – in the sun, if it's possible to chill in the sun.'

They sipped their champagne, suddenly too tired to talk any more. Then Ven yawned and Frankie grabbed her by the shoulders and lifted her up.

'Come on, before we fall asleep up here like two old farts.'

'I was going to look around the shops,' said Ven, 'but I'm far too knackered. It's just come over me all of a sudden.'

Frankie noticed the big hairy biker man again as they went out towards the stairs. He didn't look the type to be having a gin and tonic whilst listening to lounge music. Something about the incongruity of him here made her smile as he joined a bubbly group of people cheering as he approached them.

The ship was buzzing with activity as they walked back down to deck nine. A bar had big TV screens above it and men were baying at the football match being shown. There was a harpist (or harpoonist as Ven called her) playing soft mellow music in another dimly lit bar. The shops below were full of people checking out goods and squirting perfume testers, and there was a team quiz in a bar next to the library. People were flooding out of the theatre after the Mermaidia Theatre Company's second show of the evening.

'It's been a long day,' said Ven, fishing her cruise card out of her bag. 'So we're all meeting for lunch at Café Parisienne on the floor below? That still okay with you? Gives us all a chance to have a good kip.'

Café Parisienne had looked beautiful when they passed it. Quietly elegant without being stuffy.

'Sounds good to me.'

'Oh, and don't forget to follow Eric's instructions and put that card thing in your door slot. It says Do Not Disturb, then you turn it the other way when you leave your cabin tomorrow so the steward can do whatever he has to.'

'This is just too nice,' yawned Frankie. She gave Ven a big hug and went into her cabin, drawing the same sharp intake of breath that the others had at the sight of the cosy lighting and the pillow-chocolate and the bed just crying out for her to slip into.

Ven too snuggled between the snow-white sheets and savoured the feel of them against her skin. She squeezed her eyes shut and hoped with all her heart that they would have the best holiday ever, because real life was waiting for them back at the docks. And they all needed a break from it – just for a little while.

DAY 2: AT SEA

Dress Code: Formal

Chapter 21

'Olive? Olive, wake up! I need the toilet. If you don't hurry up, I'll wet myself!'

Olive sprang out of bed, crashed into a coffee table, which shouldn't be there, then realised she wasn't in her bedroom after all and that Doreen's voice was only in her head. She was shaking. For a moment, there she was back in Land Lane with David, her sleep continually disturbed by his farting and snoring, or rolling his bulk onto her side, forcing her to nearly break her back in hoisting him over again. She looked at the clock. Five past ten! She couldn't remember the last time she had slept past eight o'clock. In fact, six-thirty was a lie-in.

She opened the curtains to a picture of grey waves and sky. Boring, some might have said, but she thought it was lovely. Far nicer than the rooftops of the roughest council houses in town and the ubiquitous litter outside the kebab shop which was the view from her bedroom window. She stopped herself thinking about home by forcing her brain to remember the lyrics of 'I Am Sailing' as she went for a shower.

Twenty minutes later, she emerged tentatively from her cabin, and turned over the card in the door so that Jesus knew she had vacated her room just as Ven's door cracked open.

'Good morning,' her friend greeted her cheerfully. 'Sleep well?'

'Like a big fat log,' said Olive.

'Would you like to join me for breakfast, Lady Olive, then onward for some shopping?'

'This is unreal,' said Olive. 'I should have just finished at Mr Tidy's and be heading off to do Mrs Crowther's front room at this time.'

Ven shoved her arm through her friend's. 'But this Monday morning, Olive Hardcastle, you are going to be scoffing brekky with moi in the Buttery.'

Roz vacated her room about half an hour later and turned over the card in her door slot so Jesus could do his thing in her room. She called down to Reception first to get a brochure about the excursions they could take. Luck wasn't on her side as the first person she bumped into near the reception area lift was Frankie.

'Bugger,' she said to herself.

'Morning,' tried Frankie. 'Going up for some breakfast?'

'Er no,' said Roz. 'I don't take breakfast. I was heading up to the . . .' From the corner of her eye, she saw a woman in harem pants, a tinkly coin belt and a veil, standing with a group of ladies – none of them under sixty, by the looks of it – by a sign that read: *Belly Dancing for Beginners class meet here.*

'. . . belly-dancing class,' finished Roz.

'Ah,' said Frankie, with an understanding smile. 'Right, well, I'll see you later then.'

'Are you joining us?' asked Harem Woman, spotting Roz striding towards her. 'Brilliant, another member.' Then she set off with very wiggly hips up the grand staircase which led from the reception area up to the shops.

'Come on, ladies – to the Flamenco Room two decks up. You'll all be walking like me before the end of the cruise!'

Roz followed on, unable to sneak off. There was nothing for it. She would have to endure an hour of belly dancing just to avoid looking at Frankie over a breakfast-table. As if she didn't despise Frankie enough already.

Frankie bumped into Olive and Ven outside the Buttery, one of two huge self-service restaurants on deck sixteen. They'd gone up for a slice of toast and ended up marvelling at the spread of breakfast available and had almond croissants filled with crème patissière instead.

'I was just coming up for a coffee,' said Frankie, 'but I'll tag along with you instead if you're going shopping. I'm not that hungry in the mornings.'

There were four huge shops mid-ship on decks six and seven, ranging respectively from posh to less-posh: Gallery Mermaidia, the Boulevard, Pall Mall and Market Avenue. Outside them today were racks of tuxedos and evening gowns and stalls of costume jewellery being raked over by interested passengers, including Royston, dressed in a pink vest, flowery shorts and lime-green Crocs. He was surprisingly lean and toned for a man of his age and because of that didn't look half as daft as he should have done.

'Morning, girls,' he said chirpily when he spotted them.

'Morning,' they returned.

'Tried sunbathing, but it's *bladdy* freezin'. I'm just going to warm up with an Irish coffee instead. See you at dinner if not before. Remember the posh frocks!'

'We will. Have a nice day,' Frankie returned.

'Come on, you,' said Ven, pulling Olive into the shop and towards the beautiful long gowns in sumptuous colours.

'Wonder if Roz is up yet?' said Olive.

'She's gone belly dancing,' smirked Frankie.

'Get stuffed!'

'She has, I tell you no lies. I bumped into her in Reception this morning. It was either come to breakfast with me or pretend she was interested in the belly-dancing class. I suspect she might have tried to sneak off had I not kept staring at her to make sure she went in with them all.'

'You evil sod,' laughed Ven.

'Not at all,' grinned Frankie. 'I've done a bit of belly dancing myself. It'll do her the world of good. Might even start to defrost her knickers.' And with that she gave her friends a big knowing wink.

Chapter 22

'Good morning, ladies,' said Harem Woman in a very Welsh Wales voice. She then introduced herself as Gwen and went on to amaze everyone by telling them all she was sixty-seven. She had a figure like a nineteen-year-old. Flat-stomached, small-waisted, good legs and not a hint of a bingo wing on her arms.

'I'm warning you now, just in case anyone tells you that belly dancing is a lot of fat women wobbling their stomachs – you'll be crawling out of here, ladies,' promised Gwen.

Great, thought Roz. This could possibly be the longest hour of her life then.

'Let's begin with a nice warm-up,' said Gwen, switching on a CD behind her. Jangly music started up and Gwen began to gyrate her hips in a figure of eight, encouraging the class to follow suit. Grudgingly, Roz started to move. Then Gwen shifted to rotating her hips first one way, then the other whilst keeping the top half of her body still.

'Belly dancing is about learning to isolate parts of your body,' she explained as her hips undulated easily and hypnotically.

It was a lot harder than Gwen made it look. That's what hooked Roz in, because she hated to be beaten on anything. Then Gwen thrust her hips forward and back.

'You're doing great, girls!' she smiled.

Crikey, haven't done this movement for a while, thought

Roz, as the pensioners giggled at either side of her. She was quite puffed when the music stopped. And, though she wouldn't admit it to herself, strangely exhilarated.

'Right, now,' Gwen went on. 'Who wants to tighten up some thighs?'

Roz was quite interested to find that by vibrating the muscles of her thighs, her bum trembled in classic belly-dancer fashion. After a track-length of that, she felt like her quadriceps had quadrupled in size.

'I feel like I've done an hour on the leg press,' said a pink-faced passenger in Roz's ear. But she was euphoric at the same time.

'Okay, ladies, that's all for today,' called Gwen after some snakey arm dancing. 'We've got a lesson tomorrow here at eleven, so I hope you come again.'

'That's never an hour gone already,' said Pink Face.

Roz checked her watch and found, to her surprise also, that an hour had indeed passed.

Even more surprisingly, Roz knew that she would be here for that second lesson and that she'd be practising in front of the mirror before then. She would nail that isolation move if it killed her.

Olive felt like a shoplifter as she paid for three beautiful gowns, a pair of pink cropped trousers, some blingy paste jewellery and a pashmina with a mere flourish of the pen.

'You sure this is all on account?' she asked Ven. 'I'm having real problems believing that.'

'Yep,' said Ven, 'and I have a signed agreement to say so.'

'So what's to stop us buying everything in the shop then?' said Frankie, who was equally reluctant to believe any firm would be so stupid as to let four women loose with a free budget. Especially in shops with jewellery and clothes and handbags.

'I'm presuming that they trust we won't go barmy and start buying all the Swarovski we can lay our hands on,' said Ven.

'You'd better let me have a look at that agreement,' said Frankie, 'before we get into trouble.'

'No need,' trilled Ven. 'It's really all above board 'cos I've checked all the small print. Plus I'll go over it yet again if I must with the Figurehead rep when I see him. Even though I know there is no point. They made it perfectly clear we had carte blanche to spend.'

'I would have thought he might have been in contact by now,' said Frankie. 'Didn't he leave you a note or a message on the cabin phone answering machine?'

'Oh, never mind how they do or don't organise things,' said Ven confidently. 'He'll be in touch, no doubt. Right – I'm going on ahead to the Café Parisienne to grab a table, so see you in five. I can't believe I'm saying this after only having breakfast an hour and a half ago, but I'm peckish. It must be the sea air.'

'Sea air?' joked Frankie. 'Don't use that as an excuse. You're just a piglet!'

Chapter 23

Doreen was in the toilet when David got up. He'd never seen his mother move as much as she had done in the past twenty-four hours. It hadn't taken her long to dispense with the pretence of needing a mighty effort to rouse herself when she realised that Olive wasn't around to fetch and carry for her. David thought back to all the times when she'd been 'caught short' and Olive had had to clean her up. It appeared she had a lot more control over her bodily functions than she had let on, and it suddenly came to him how hard life must have been for his wife with such a demanding and devious mother-in-law. But a thought like that was far too near to the bone, and he shut the door on it quickly.

Kevin was buttering toast in the kitchen. He had fancied a fry-up but there was only one egg left, no bacon, two squidgy tomatoes and no sausages. Someone would have to go food shopping today. David needed to stop being so stubborn and find out where Olive really was, drag her home and let them all get back to normal life, thought Kevin. He was built for love and pleasure, not skivvying.

'So why has Olive left you, Dave?' he asked, sloppily chewing the toast. 'Haven't you been looking after her properly?' He winked.

'What's "looking after her properly" and a wink supposed to

mean?' David replied with more than a touch of impatience. That toast smelled gorgeous and it was the last bloody slice of bread in the house. And Kevin had put the only remaining Dairylea cheese slice on it as well.

'In the bedroom, of course. At "sausage o'clock" time,' said Kevin, crunching down again onto the toast and making David's stomach howl with hunger. 'I find that women who are looked after in the bedroom don't usually run away.'

'Of course I look after her in the bedroom!' snapped David.

'Well, I haven't witnessed much action since I moved in,' said Kevin. 'The only noise I've heard through your walls is you farting.'

'You've been listening?' David's jaw dropped open.

'No – listening and hearing are very different things,' mused Kevin, with the air of a great philosopher.

'We do ... all sorts,' grumbled David, very unconvincingly. 'We just don't make a noise about it. I don't want my mother hearing.'

'All sorts? You and Olive?' Somehow Kevin found that a bit hard to believe, and he mischievously pressed on with his line of questioning. 'What, different positions and toys and role play?'

'We weren't supposed to have positions in my day,' called Doreen from the downstairs bathroom. 'It was lights off and nightie up only.'

'Chuffing hell, she's got the ears of a bat!' called David, trying to knock the picture out of his head of his mother and father having sex in the bedroom upstairs.

'Although,' Doreen went on, 'my Auntie Maud always used to say, "You'll never be truly happy, married to a man who doesn't want to explore all your orifices".'

'Mam!' screamed David, slapping his palms to his ears.

'You give her lots of foreplay then?' Kevin probed even deeper. 'You don't just tell her to brace herself and then jump on, do you? Women have to be teased for ages and ages to get them truly going. They should be dripping wet and begging for it by the time you climb on.'

'Of course I— hang on, why the hell am I giving you details of my sex-life? I don't exactly see your ex-birds lining up outside for your attentions!'

'Oh, don't you worry about me,' smirked Kevin. 'I don't go short. Now I'm unattached, I can give a lot of ladies a good old service without having all the hassle of having to stay overnight or be tied to one person. Although that's okay sometimes, if you know what I mean.' He gave a smutty laugh.

David thought of a few of Kevin's harem and shuddered. Julie Two-Teeth; Ketherwood Kathleen – the footie-mad one who couldn't get to see any of the matches because her arse was too big to fit through the turnstile; Caroline with the cauliflower ear – and nose; fishy-smelling Diane who had just been up in court for shoplifting from the local Rhythm and Booze off-licence, and his latest ex Wicked Wendy who was actually quite a good-looking woman, give or take the Nigel Mansell moustache. Ugh. He couldn't go on. Pictures of them were worse than the ones of his mum and dad in a clinch.

'Your dad, God rest him, was a lovely man but he didn't know what foreplay was until he was in a home,' called Doreen again, after a far from ladylike parp. 'He saw it on a film where a couple were eating loads of things out of a fridge. Before that, he thought it meant "extra thick tissues".'

'Someone needs to go and get some shopping done,' said Kevin, popping the last of the toast into his mouth.

'I'll go,' David quickly volunteered. Anything to get away from this line of talk. And before his stud-cousin with his fancy bedroom tricks cottoned on to the fact that he knew even less than his father did about pleasuring a woman.

Chapter 24

Olive returned to her cabin to find her bed had been made, the sink and shower washed down, and fresh folded towels had appeared. Jesus must have flown around the room like Will-o'-the-Wisp. And to add to the magic of the day, she was now the owner of three new beautiful evening gowns which she took out of the bag and hung up: a long red one with shoestring straps and a matching shrug, a silver and black one with floaty cap sleeves, and the most gorgeous dark green one that cost as much as the other two put together.

Olive allowed herself a single thought of home and then cast it out, to be replaced with the quandary of whether she dare have a wanton lunchtime glass of wine or not in Café Parisienne?

When Roz joined Ven at the table in Café Parisienne, she was actually smiling.

'Crikey,' said Ven, at the rare phenomenon. 'What have *you* been up to?'

'Can you believe belly dancing?' said Roz.

'Was it good then?'

'To be honest ...' Roz was about to confess that she had only gone along to avoid Frankie, but she didn't want to see a look of disapproval on Ven's face so she tempered what she was going to say. 'Yes, it was great.'

'Wouldn't have put you and belly dancing together,' said Ven.

'Me neither, but it was like an aerobic workout. I wasn't much good but I'm going for the second lesson tomorrow.'

'Well done!' Ven waved as she spotted Frankie. She expected Roz's smile to wither then. She was right.

'Hi, girls,' said Frankie cheerfully, throwing herself into the seat next to Roz. 'Plenty of toilets on this ship, thank goodness. How was the belly dancing?'

'It was okay, thank you,' replied Roz with lukewarm politeness. 'Where's Olive?'

'She bought some frocks in the shops and has gone to hang them up,' Ven explained.

'Sea feels a bit rougher today than it did last night,' said Frankie. 'I noticed some of the stewards hanging sick bags on the staircases.'

'We're going through the Bay of Biscay,' said Roz. 'Apparently it can get a bit choppy.'

The happy face of Olive appeared and she bounced over to join them. She looked five years younger for a good night's sleep and a morning doing something for herself for a change.

'So you have posh frocks?' enquired Roz.

'Oh Roz, they are gorgeous. I'm just a bit worried that the competition people will say, "You can't spend that much, you cheeky cow".'

'Relax,' soothed Ven. 'Let's eat.' She picked up the lunch menu and scanned it.

'I had croissants for breakfast. I shouldn't really eat lunch as well,' whispered Olive. 'I'll be the size of a house.'

'You're on holiday,' winked Frankie. 'Live a bit. Besides which your massage will burn up all your excess calories.'

Olive's face dropped. 'I'm still not sure about having one of those.'

'Oh Olive, they're gorgeous – you have to,' Frankie gushed. At that moment, she saw the long-haired Viking passing by. He had jeans on and a rock 'n' roll T-shirt with big angel wings on the back. His arms were heavily tattooed, the biceps big and solid. He was studying a map of the ship and obviously going the wrong way because he doubled back, then turned around again and walked off, scratching his head.

'What you grinning at?' asked Olive.

'It's that bloke again.' Frankie pointed discreetly over. 'I bet it's his first cruise. He's making me look like a seasoned traveller by comparison.'

Roz muttered something which sounded like 'might have known it would be a man that she was looking at', but Frankie graciously ignored it.

'I'm having scallops, followed by the pasta,' announced Ven. 'And pass me that wine list, will you?'

'What's that? What did you say you're having?' asked Olive.

'Scallops,' said Ven. 'Not the Barnsley scallops, shellfish scallops.' In Yorkshire the fish shops sold 'scallops' which were a mashed-potato patty with a layer of fish in the centre.

'I do know,' tutted Olive with a mock-insulted smile. 'I *have* been out of Yorkshire.'

'Hmmm. I never understood why you came back home to Barnsley, saying you'd had the best summer of your life in Cephalonia, you mad bag,' said Roz. 'Roast-beef salad for me.'

'Well, Mum rang and didn't sound too good, and ...' Olive shrugged her shoulders.

'And?' pressed Roz.

Olive took a deep breath. 'And girls like me don't do mad things like marry Greek men.'

Then the waiter arrived at their table and cut the conversation off.

'Hello, Aldrin,' said Frankie, recognising him from last night in the Olympia. 'Working again?'

'We are always working, ma'am,' he said with a fresh-faced smile.

The wines in Café Parisienne had, apparently, been chosen by St John Hite, who was the sexiest, most floppy-haired, best wine buff on the TV. He had a weekly page in one of the Sunday newspapers and Ven found the descriptions of his featured wines so charged that she almost had to have a lie-down and a cigarette after reading it. The wine list was on par with his column: *a glug-fest of sticky black fruits . . . citrus oomph . . . a spank of raspberries . . .* Ven always imagined that St John Hite would be very good in bed.

'This looks interesting,' Ven said. She had intended to buy some champagne for them all, but her eyes were drawn to a Canadian ice wine. According to the description, the grapes were only picked when they were frozen on the vine, resulting in *a honey-smooth mouthful of ping*.

'Goes well with fruitcakes, apparently,' said Ven, reading from the menu.

'It's a must for us four then,' giggled Frankie.

So the ladies ordered food and ice wine when the wine waiter, ironically called 'Sober', came over.

'I prefer his twin brother "Pissed",' said Roz dryly, making them spurt with laughter.

Roz, Ven and Olive people-watched for a few minutes, while Frankie read her *Mermaidia Today*. She hadn't realised there was so much to do on a ship. There were lectures, classes, a gym, an indoor pool as well as the outdoor ones, art sales, private parties – indeed, someone obviously important enough to be known by merely her first name 'Dorothy' was inviting her friends to meet up at the Planet room, at the side of the Vista lounge for coffee. There was even a club for single passengers.

A troupe of little kids holding hands passed by on their way to their club, led by one of the smiley 'Youth Brigade'. Olive found herself smiling at them. She'd never have kids now, she knew, and accepted that. But occasionally a pang came from nowhere and scored a bull's-eye right in her heart. Women in their fifties were getting pregnant naturally these days, so it wasn't that, at thirty-nine, she was too old – but she suspected that something might be wrong in that department with either her or David. There had been more than a few occasions when they hadn't used protection during sex, but it had never resulted in anything. So many times, in fact, that they didn't use it any more. Still, it was probably just as well because she wouldn't have been able to afford children – time or money-wise.

The food arrived quickly. Everyone had a mouthful of Ven's scallops, which were divine. Olive had gone for pasta, Frankie for Croque Monsieur.

The puddings looked delicious in the glass display cabinet, but none of them could fit one in. In fact, Frankie was already regretting eating all that ham and cheese. She felt very full. Too stuffed even for a coffee.

'Ready for your rub-down?' Ven teased Olive.

'Oh, give up,' said Olive, growing pale before their eyes.

'You'll love it, you silly bugger,' said Frankie. 'And I can't wait to see your new highlights. You haven't chickened out, I hope.'

'No, sir!' said Olive, saluting, as Frankie laughingly pulled her to her feet and they set off for the spa.

The Sanctuary Spa was situated at the front of deck sixteen or *forward* as it was in ship's parlance. As soon as the four entered, the relaxed perfumed air stole into them and their shoulders dropped six inches. Well, three sets of shoulders dropped anyway. Olive was still nervous about the prospect of being fon-dled by a complete stranger, as she saw it. Her shoulders were so high they had clouds on.

They announced their arrival to the receptionist and took a seat for a few minutes.

Then to Olive's horror, a young, broad-shouldered man with Slavic eyes and a white uniform with strange flappy trousers called out her name, introduced himself as Leo and asked her to please follow him.

'Oh shit, not a man. I can't have a man!' she whispered to her friends. But she found no sympathy. Frankie pushed her forwards with a chuckle. Olive found herself, as always, unable to make a fuss and followed Leo into a white room with a central narrow bed.

'If you will take everything off to your pants, then lie on your front with the towel over your legs. I will be back in a little time,' said Leo, after warmly introducing himself and telling Olive that she was going to have a lovely massage and feel wonderfully relaxed afterwards. She doubted that. Her nerves were stretched to snapping point.

Olive quickly took off and folded up her clothes and put them in a neat pile on the top of a cabinet. She had just climbed onto the bed and covered herself up to the back of her neck when there was a knock at the door and Leo entered.

'Do you have anywhere you wish me to concentrate on?' he asked, as he pulled down the towel and tucked it in the back of her pants, and Olive just knew the crack of her backside was smiling up at him.

'Er no,' she said. *Just get this over with.*

She heard Leo's hands rubbing together and a flood of lavender perfume drifted towards her. Then his fingers started to work on her shoulders and back.

'You are very tense,' he noted. Which was a bit of an understatement. But that only made him knead her muscles more. 'Let me know if I am too hard.'

Olive could imagine what Roz or Frankie would have said to that and stifled a giggle.

It took her a good five minutes to slowly let her muscles start to relax. Flaming heck. No wonder David wanted her to rub his 'poor aching back' so much. Leo had very strong hands. She felt the impact of his massaging all the way down to her bones.

'You work hard,' said Leo after ten minutes. 'Much lifting, I think. Your back is in need of a lot of er . . . loosening up.'

'Urrr . . .' nodded Olive. At this stage she was not capable of intelligent speech. She was tempted to let herself drift off, but she didn't want to miss anything. Then Leo started on her legs and her feet, and Olive thought that if this was a taste of heaven, she would go and jump off the top deck and do away with herself now. No one had ever touched her feet before, give or take the woman measuring them up in the Clark's shoe shop when she was little. But she had lost track of the countless times when David would stick his rough size tens on her lap for a bit of attention. She was going to ask Leo to marry her in a minute.

Then she thought, how sad it was that she had been married for thirteen years and her husband had never once rubbed her feet or her legs or her shoulders.

After not long enough at all, Leo left her to get dressed and drink a glass of water. Olive was totally cabbaged. She struggled off the bed like Doreen did out of her chair. Her limbs wouldn't function properly. And she felt more light-headed than the lunchtime ice wine had managed to make her.

She veered out of the treatment room like an alcoholic with a gammy leg who had just discovered a bottle of cooking sherry in his pocket.

Ven emerged from the next room. 'Enjoy that?' she grinned.

'Urrr,' said Olive.

'I'll take that as a yes, shall I?'

'Urrr.'

'Now for your hairdo. The others will be out in a minute. We'll meet them in the salon, okay? You'd better go in 'cos you're going to take the longest.'

'Urrr.'

Ven linked Olive's arm and pulled her along. They'd use the lift to the next floor down, she decided. She wasn't sure that Olive's legs could carry her that far.

Chapter 25

David Hardcastle huffed off the bus with three bags full of shopping. How Olive managed five or six was anyone's guess. Mind you, she didn't have a bad back like he did. Then he remembered that he didn't actually have a bad back and came full circle to wondering how Olive carried so much shopping home.

Doreen was dozing in her chair when he went in. Kevin was out – probably servicing one of his women. Though 'women' was pushing it a bit. Most of them belonged in the zoo behind very strong fencing. This was bloody ridiculous. Where was his wife?

He threw the shopping down on the table and heard the crack of eggs from within one of the carrier bags. That really was the last straw. He picked up Olive's address book, which she kept by the house telephone, and flicked through it for Ven's number. He rang it, but all he got was an answering machine and he didn't leave a message. Then he rang Roz's number and got yet another answering machine. Didn't anyone ever pick up the bloody phone these days?

Then David had a brainwave. He got out the *Yellow Pages* and looked up Manus Howard's garage. If this was another answering machine, he was going to smash the phone against the wall.

But it wasn't. Manus picked up after two rings.

'Oh hello,' said David. 'I'm wondering if your Roz is about. It's Dave . . . Hardcastle. Olive's husband.'

Crikey, thought Manus. He didn't know that David had enough gumption to use a phone. He felt himself smiling mischievously.

'Er no, mate. She's gone on holiday. With Olive.'

'Has she?' gasped David, in a voice higher than Joe Pasquale's. 'Oh, er . . . Olive never said Roz was going as well.'

'And Ven,' added Manus. He wondered from David's tone if he even knew anything about the cruise at all. *Well, well, well.* So Olive had managed to escape her drudgery and think about herself for once. Go Olive, he thought.

'So . . . have you heard from them?' asked David tentatively. He didn't want Manus to think that he didn't know where they had gone.

'Well, they'll be in the middle of the sea, I expect, and so I doubt they'll get phone reception.'

'The middle of the sea?' squeaked David.

'Yes. They've gone on a cruise, didn't you know? For sixteen days.'

'Oh, er . . . Oh sorry, I've got to go. Mother's calling me. Be right there, Mum.' And David put the phone down quickly and let out a long double lungful of breath.

'What's up with you?' said Kevin, suddenly appearing in the kitchen doorway and grinning beatifically after a nice little lunchtime session with Julie Two-Teeth and her performing knockers. His cousin's face was the colour of uncooked pastry.

David slumped onto the kitchen chair. 'Olive's gone on a cruise. For sixteen days.'

'Eh?'

'You heard.'

'You are joking!' said Kevin.

'Do I look like I'm joking?' snapped David. 'Do I look like

a man who wants to chortle about his wife leaving him to cook, clean, shop and care for an infirm old lady?'

'Where's she got the money from, to go on a cruise?' asked Kevin.

Then both men jumped as they heard feet thunder up the stairs. Doreen was in a panic, crying out as she raced to her bedroom, 'I need to check ... oh my God, she hasn't, has she?'

'Auntie Doreen, what's up? You all right?'

'Mum?'

There was a big thump from above and then silence – then Doreen laughed, almost hysterically.

'Yes, I'm fine – no need to worry. I'm fine now.'

'So, you were about to tell me how she'd got her hands on that sort of money,' said Kevin.

'How the hell do I know?' growled David. Cruises cost thousands. Olive cleaned for peanuts. People like Olive didn't go on ships for their holidays. People like Olive didn't go on holiday. None of this was making sense at all. And just to add to the surreality of the situation, he reached for a can of beer from the shopping bag and plunged his hand into the tip-tilted eggbox instead. Immediately after yet another cracking sound, a fat yellow yolk slid out and landed on his lap.

Chapter 26

Olive looked in the mirror but it wasn't her reflection that was staring back at her. This Olive had trendy poker-straight hair and was infinitely blonder than Olive Hardcastle was. Many platinum streaks were woven in between her natural gold, and that, plus a good cut, made her green eyes shine out.

Her hairdresser was a Romanian girl called Ulga. She was going out with one of the waiters on the ship, but it wasn't very serious because he was going home to Mumbai at the end of the summer and she was going back to Romania to open up a coffee shop. Coffee was where her heart was at, apparently. Olive thought she was a borderline idiot to give up hairdressing, if she could make other women feel as if they had just been given fifteen hours of intensive plastic surgery just for a bit of colour and some sweet scissor action.

'So you have a gown ready for tonight?' asked Ulga, as she razored in some layers at the back.

'I don't know what colour to wear – I have a red, a green and a black.' Olive felt quite good saying that. It was a first, saying she had a choice of posh frocks to choose from.

'There is a black-and-white dinner in the second week of the cruise,' said Ulga. 'Maybe is good to wear your black dress both at the very beginning and the very end of the cruise.'

'A black-and-white night sounds lovely,' smiled Olive.

'It is,' said Ulga. 'All the formal nights are very much loveliness.'

From the corner of her eye, Olive saw Frankie bolt from the hairdresser's chair. Next to her, having a blow-dry, Ven mimed a sickie action to explain where she had gone. The ship was rocking quite a bit today.

'Your poor friend is sea-sick, I think,' said Ulga. 'It's very awfuls feeling. I was very sick when I first came on the ships.'

'I wonder why I'm not ill though,' said Olive, who had been expecting she would be very sea-sick but wasn't at all.

'It's about being out of rhythm with ship movement,' explained Ulga. 'It's really awfuls.'

In the spa toilet, Frankie was wondering how she could get off this ship and die somewhere on a quiet shore, because she couldn't escape the rocking motion. And it didn't help that the salon was at one end of the ship and high up and not in the more stable lower-middle.

There was a gentle tap on the door and Ven's voice filtered through.

'Frankie, are you okay in there?'

'No,' was all Frankie managed before retching and groaning with the pain of her stomach muscles trying to throw something up from a now empty stomach.

'Shall I go and get you some sea-sickness tablets from the shop?'

'I've had some and thrown them back up,' said Frankie. 'I took them as a precaution earlier. Cock lot of good they did me.'

'My hair lady said that you can go to the medical bay and get a sea-sickness injection. Apparently they're very good.'

Frankie was just about to say that she would curl up in bed and miss the formal night when her stomach lurched again with the ship. It might be worth trying to get an injection because she couldn't sit back and wait for this hellish feeling to subside naturally. She opened the cubicle door.

'Where's the bloody sick bay?' she croaked.

There were two middle-aged men seated and waiting to see the doctor in the medical centre on deck four, also with sea-sickness if their grey faces were anything to go by. They smiled sympathetically at Frankie and tried to look composed as she sat down on the opposite side of the waiting area. At least the bay was mid-ship and low down, the best place to be for sea-sickness sufferers.

Outside the medical bay a female voice was heard saying, 'Dad, get in there.'

'I just need a lie-down and I'll be fine,' returned a male voice.

'Dad, you have been lying down and it hasn't worked. Get in there now or you'll spoil the evening for yourself.'

'You're far too bossy for your own good.'

'Get in!'

The Viking man appeared in the doorway as a pretty younger woman pushed him in.

'Do you want me to stay with you?' she asked.

'Who's the parent and who's the child here?'

'I sometimes wonder,' sighed the woman. She turned to Frankie. 'Would you do me a favour and make sure my dad doesn't escape before he gets a sea-sickness jab?' she asked with a twinkle in her eye.

Frankie nodded. 'I'll do my best,' she replied.

The Viking had just sat down next to her when the first patient was called in.

'Bit rough out there, isn't it?' the Viking said; his voice had a surprisingly soft West Country burr to it. 'I'd never have let anyone drag me on a ship if I thought I was going to feel like this.'

'You're doing the best thing getting an injection,' called the man on the opposite side of the room. 'They work like magic. I've tried wrist bands and every tablet ever invented and nothing does the trick like that injection.'

'I hope you're right. Someone told me to get some ginger biscuits from the shop, but they didn't have any,' the Viking replied. 'I found out that Highland Shortbread doesn't work as well.' A fresh wave of nausea hit him and he groaned. 'Don't think I can stand much more of this.'

'Me neither,' said Frankie. 'I've just had a makeover and a hairdo. What a waste of money that was.'

'The white corpse look was very fashionable in the Elizabethan era. I'm sure it's only a matter of time before it comes back,' said the Viking, which made Frankie laugh – something she didn't think she would be doing in her state.

'Is this your first cruise?' called the man opposite.

'Yes,' replied Frankie and the Viking together, unaware as to whom the question was directed as the man had a bit of a turn in his eye.

'It's my ninth,' he replied. 'I'm going again next month to New York on the *Queen Mary*. That'll be my tenth.'

The Viking gave Frankie a sideways look that seemed to say, 'Does everyone on this ship brag about how many times they've cruised?' She wanted to giggle, despite feeling awful.

The doctor's door opened and the patient emerged rubbing the top of his bottom.

'Oh, it's not in your arm then?' deduced Frankie.

'Well, I can't lose any more dignity,' said the Viking. 'I've just thrown up on the staircase.'

'Oh no!'

'Well, into a bag on the staircase, but I had an audience of little kids going to their club who found it fascinating. I think they're going to employ me as a variety act.' He held out his hand then. 'Vaughan,' he said. 'Or The Incredible Vomiting Vaughan, as I'll be billed on the posters.'

'Francesca – Frankie to friends,' said Frankie, smiling and shaking his hand.

'Italian?'

'Three-quarters. Full Italian on Dad's side. Mum's mum came from Rome and Mum's dad came from Barnsley.'

'Barnsley and Italy, that's quite a mix,' mused Vaughan. 'Although I'm half-Norwegian, half-Cornish, so I can't really say too much.'

Ooh, Norwegian! thought Frankie. The Viking tag wasn't so far off target then.

Mr Nine Cruises was called into the surgery leaving Frankie and Vaughan alone together.

'First cruise for you too?' asked Frankie, with a mischievous glint in her eye.

'Can't you tell?' replied Vaughan with a grin. 'My daughter married into a family who are hardline cruisers. She got the bug and dragged me along with her in-laws. She said I needed "to chillax". Don't know how relaxed I'll be in a suit. I didn't own one until a month ago. I've had the in-laws sending me lists of what I need and my girl's father-in-law donating some of his wardrobe to help me out.'

He had nice smiley eyes, Frankie noticed. Blue. Although she couldn't see much more of his face under all that hair.

They sat in silence for a while after the ship gave a big jiggle.

'You okay?' asked Vaughan, passing her a creased sick bag from his pocket.

'No,' said Frankie, breathing through her nausea. 'I want to go home and be in my nice stable house which doesn't move. How can anyone think this is a fun way to holiday?'

'Is your . . . er . . . other half not affected then?'

'I'm here with three friends,' said Frankie. 'We've been planning it since we were at school. We didn't bank on this though.'

'I'll be glad to get to Malaga,' said Vaughan. 'I'd kill for some dry land under my feet.'

To Frankie's relief, the doctor's door opened and out came Mr Nine Cruises. She was next. But she doubted anything but a trip home could quell the rising and falling of her stomach.

'Good luck,' called Vaughan, as she followed the doctor into his surgery. Frankie nodded, because if she had opened her mouth to speak, more than words would have come out.

The doctor had the sexiest French accent Frankie had ever heard. He should have been doing voice-overs on porn films. Dr Floren was pudgy-faced with a paunch pushing at his uniform, but he could still have made knickers melt all over the world with his purr.

Satisfied that the best course available for Frankie was an injection, Dr Floren positioned the needle in her buttock.

'You may feel a little tired shortly,' warned the doctor. 'But this is very effective at removing the nauseous feelings. It will last for about eight hours.'

'Great,' said Frankie as the needle went in and she tried not to jerk. Why hadn't Ven won a holiday to Torquay instead? She hoped she would fall into a coma and wake up just as the ship was docking back into Southampton.

She made a comical show of rubbing her bottom as if in agony when she left the surgery.

'Does it hurt?' asked Vaughan.

'It's murder,' she grimaced. 'I don't think I've ever seen a bigger needle in my life!'

Vaughan's pallor faded another notch towards bleached snow. 'I hate needles,' he said.

'I'm joking,' said Frankie. 'Really, it was just a little prick.'

'What – the needle or the doctor?' said Vaughan, as the door opened and Dr Floren appeared, making Frankie giggle. She was feeling slightly better already.

'Hope it works for you,' said Vaughan, raising his hand in a man-wave as he followed the doctor in. 'Have a nice holiday.'

'Same to you,' said Frankie, passing the young newlyweds on

the stairs, who had also been on the Easy Rider bus from Barnsley. It looked as if they too were heading for the sick bay.

'Why did your bloody mother tell us we'd enjoy a honeymoon on a ship?' the young woman was saying. 'I knew she didn't like me!'

Olive knocked gently at Frankie's door to see how she was doing after taking her nap and to ask if she felt well enough to venture out with them for a small bite and a swank around in her evening dress. She didn't expect Frankie to open it with a flourish, dressed in a long black frock and looking the picture of health, complete with pink cheeks.

'Worked like a treat,' she explained to her delighted friend. 'I had an hour's kip and now I'm ravenous. Show me the way to the nosebag!'

Roz and Ven had gone on ahead, up to the Vista lounge where the 'Welcome Aboard' party for diners in the Olympia restaurant was being held. There the Captain was greeting guests and posing for photos with them. There were two entrances into the Vista, one for people who wanted a photograph taken with him and one for those who would rather get straight to the free booze and canapés.

'Are you bothered about getting your photo taken with the Captain?' asked Ven.

'Not really,' said Frankie. 'I think I might feel a bit daft posing,' which seemed to answer for them all. So they went in the quick way, noticing Eric in a tuxedo and Irene in a pale pink evening gown waiting in the queue for photographs.

Roz spotted Royston and Stella across the room and waved. Stella had on the most beautiful silver sequinned to-the-floor evening dress, which made the best of her lovely figure and accentuated her breasts. Must have cost a fortune, thought Roz. She wondered how rich some of the people in this room were. Lucky buggers. Must be nice to have a lot of disposable income to come on holidays like this, she mused. The first thing she would do if she found out she was rich was to tell old Sour-Tits Hutchinson to stick her job up her arse. To be fair, the job was okay if a bit boring, but Margaret Hutchinson was a one-woman PMT machine – always nit-picking, never happy. If she smiled, her face would crack like an ancient vase. She'd never need Botox, that was for sure. Compared with Miss Hutchinson, even Roz would look like the laughing police-man. The second thing Roz knew she would do would be to buy Manus the empty building next door to his garage so he could extend it, and she would work with him, doing all the paperwork he hated to do because he was a hands-on man who liked nothing better than to tinker with machinery. He was so good at it too – a genius with cars and vans. Then Roz snapped back to reality. There was no point in thinking about stupid stuff like that which was never likely to happen. Dreaming was a waste of time. And, God knows, she had wasted enough time dreaming about Robert Clegg in the past – and where had that got her?

Frankie caught the attention of a waiter carrying a tray of drinks. She swept a glass of red wine from him, raised it in the direction of her friends and said, 'Cheers.' 'Cheers,' returned the others with their gin and tonics; Roz said hers through gritted teeth, Frankie noticed. She swivelled around to take in the frocks and suits. There were some gorgeous dresses and lots of bling. She wondered if the flashy stones in Stella's ears were paste or real. They were massive.

'Have you had a look at the menu? It's posted outside the restaurant,' Ven said. 'I fancy . . .'

'No, shush!' said Olive. 'Don't tell me. I don't want to know in advance what there is.'

'Why?' said Roz.

'Because it's a nice surprise for me then,' Olive explained. 'I want to sit at the table and decide.'

'Okay, I'll shut up,' said Ven, with fond amusement. She was quite the opposite. There were so many lovely things on the menu, she needed half the day to decide what she was having.

'I'm a bit disappointed with the Captain,' sniffed Olive, looking at the smart, but quite short and square man in the gorgeous white jacket with four gold stripes on his black shoulder epaulettes, black trousers and black bow tie. 'Thought he'd be a bit more "Captainy" than that.'

'What, have a big beard and look like Cap'n Birdseye?' scoffed Roz. 'Carrying a tray of fish fingers with a parrot on his shoulder?'

'No, just … just …' Olive struggled to clarify what she meant until Ven rescued her.

'I know what you mean. You envisaged someone tall and handsome, big-shouldered and just mature enough to have a flash of grey at the temples. A sexy commanding-type with a Superman-type chest and a butt to die for.'

'Yes, that's it exactly,' Olive nodded.

'I'm not bothered what he looks like as long as he can spot an iceberg and avoid it,' said Frankie. 'You always did like a man in uniform, didn't you, Ven? Remember when we all went round to yours to watch *An Officer and a Gentleman* on your dad's video? I never realised your tongue could loll out that far.'

Ven slid into a recollection of Richard Gere scooping Debra Winger up in his whites and sighed.

'Were there many people in the sick bay, Frankie?' asked Olive, choosing a smoked salmon canapé from the waiter's tray. She hadn't had a canapé before. After tasting her first, she believed that she could very easily live off them.

'Four of us,' said Frankie. 'I can't believe I feel so good after that jab in my bum. It was miraculous.'

Roz swept her eyes over Frankie, whilst Frankie was sweeping her eyes over the room. No brash jewellery, a plain-cut dress . . . where was the Frankie Carnevale of old? This Frankie in front of her was a second-class Doppelgänger for sure.

'Shall we head off on a slow walk down to dinner?' said Frankie, watching the Captain take up position on the stage and dab on the top of a microphone to check that it was working.

'Aye, come on,' said Ven. 'I'm not bothered about listening to any speeches.'

'Great,' said Frankie. 'That sea-sickness jab has made me cocking starving.'

Frankie had eaten a full bread roll and two slices of speciality of the day bread – raisin and walnut – before she had even opened the menu.

'Soup and then steak,' said Roz, deciding quickly.

'You had that yesterday,' said Ven.

'So? I'm happy with that.'

'Well, now's the time to be wanton,' smiled Frankie. As soon as the words were out, she expected a backlash, but surprisingly didn't get one. Roz, for Ven's sake, was trying to throttle back on rising to any of Frankie's baiting and she just hoped that Ven appreciated it because it was killing her.

'Evening all,' said Eric, as he and Irene came to the table. 'Sorry we're late but we've been hobnobbing with the officers.'

'We saw you waiting to have your pictures taken,' said Ven.

'Oh yes, with Philip – such a lovely man. He's been on at least five other cruises with us.'

'Did he recognise you?' asked Olive.

'He did,' said Eric, puffing out his chest proudly.

'Once seen, never forgotten,' whispered Frankie behind her menu.

'Evening all,' said Royston, holding out the chair for Stella. 'My, don't you ladies look the bees' knees tonight.'

'Don't they just!' added Eric.

'Not looking so bad yourselves, boys,' beamed Frankie.

'So what have you girls done today then? Did you get ashore?' laughed Eric, after giving Elvis his order.

Behind him Irene was rolling her eyes.

'He always says that on sea-days,' she explained in her whispery voice. 'It's his little joke.'

'You see, you can't get off, can you?' Eric went into joke-explanation-overkill.

'Ah.' Ven nodded and prepared to play the game. 'No, we thought we'd stay on board. We just lounged about and drank coffee and then went up to the spa.'

'Your hair looks very nice,' said Stella to Olive.

'Oh thank you,' said Olive, embarrassed to be centre of attention as a wave of agreement rippled around the table.

'Did you go up to the salon? I always go on formal nights.' Stella patted the back of her heavy lacquered ash-blonde hairdo. It wouldn't have budged out of place in a hurricane. 'I'm always up for a bit of self-improvement,' she winked.

'None of you were sea-sick then?' asked Eric.

'Frankie was,' said Ven.

'Bay of Biscay,' nodded Eric. 'It can be a bit of a bugger. Although this is nothing to one crossing we made in the Atlantic – do you remember, Irene? In that force twelve cross wind? Even I had to have a lie-down that day!' He smiled fondly as if he was remembering something sweet and wonderful as he recounted how the waves reached as high as deck twelve and three million glasses whizzed off shelves in bars.

Their head waiter was doing his rounds – a huge wardrobe of a man with an ear-to-ear smile and a thick black quiff. He looked like a benign military dictator. The girls never did learn his real name because Eric leaped up and greeted him with a vigorous handshake and introduced him to the table.

'This is my friend Supremo. He's the big man on this ship,' beamed Eric. 'If you have any problem in any restaurant, this is the man to come to.' Supremo laughed with a mix of pride and bashfulness – but mainly pride.

After a brief chat and his announcement that tomorrow night there would be a Mexican buffet in the Buttery, Supremo distributed the red carnations he was carrying to each of the ladies before moving on to the next table. There were quite a few empty places on tables that evening, Frankie noticed as she looked around. People who hadn't done the sensible thing and sought medical help for their queasy tums. She felt fantastic, even though the ship was still lurching quite a bit. She wondered how Vaughan felt. She was curious to see how well he would scrub up in a suit too.

Her wish came true as they filtered into the theatre to watch the vocalist/impressionist after dinner. She caught a fleeting glance of his ponytail against the back of his tuxedo. He was fingering his collar as if it was trying to cut his head off. Frankie smiled at the sight of him trying to conform and not having a cat in hell's chance. He looked like one of those men who are happiest covered in oil and grease, like Manus.

After the act had finished, they went to the Vista lounge for an Irish coffee, but by half past ten the four of them were almost nodding off and decided to call it a day. Never had doing nothing been so tiring.

DAY 3: AT SEA

Dress Code: Semi-Formal

Chapter 27

Frankie was up and dressed by nine-thirty the next morning. She opened the thick curtains on a cloudy but calm sea, thank goodness. There was no sign of life from her friends' cabins, so she took herself down to the Samovar, the coffee shop on deck five, and picked up one of the ship's daily newspaper leaflets – the *Mermaidia Times* – to read with an espresso. It gave a précis of world and UK news, international city temperatures, sports results and share prices. It made for miserable reading – another soldier killed in Afghanistan, a teenager stabbed, the death of a famous actor ... Frankie put it back down. She didn't want to know what was going on in the world outside the ship. She didn't want to hear any bad news on here.

She was determined, however, to find out who 'Dorothy' was. The third copy of *Mermaidia Today* had announced that there was yet another meeting in the Planet room for 'Friends of Dorothy' at ten-thirty. She would just go up, take a quick look to satisfy her curiosity, then have a late breakfast, or a brunch – or possibly hang on for lunch.

Frankie walked up the stairs to deck sixteen, vowing to get at least some exercise whilst she was on holiday. There was a buzz of people inside the Planet room. Frankie walked past, tried to look casually inquisitive rather than downright nosy, but she couldn't see much of what was going on, apart from the 'Friends' holding cups of tea and one or two of them eating pastries. Pretending to be looking for someone in the Vista, she walked through the bar and full circle back to the Planet room, just as a familiar figure in jeans and a denim jacket was walking up the stairs.

'Good morning,' said Frankie with a ready smile. 'And how are you today?'

'Oh, good morning,' said Vaughan, mirroring her expression. 'I'm very well, thank you. That sea-sickness injection worked wonders, didn't it? It gave me the munchies a bit though. And yourself?'

'I'm great, thank you.' Someone laughed in the Planet room and Vaughan rubber-necked inside.

'So, are you a friend of Dorothy?' asked Frankie.

'Me?' Vaughan's eyes twinkled. 'Do I look like a friend of Dorothy?'

What an odd question, thought Frankie. What did friends of Dorothy look like? Did they have some kind of distinguishing costume?

'I don't know if you do or not.'

'Are *you* a friend of Dorothy?' Vaughan then asked.

'Me? No.' Frankie beckoned him closer and whispered, 'Who is she?'

A light seemed to switch on in Vaughan's head. 'Ah,' he said in a low, conspiratorial voice. 'Didn't you know? She's a girl with a dog.'

Frankie's eyebrows arched in confusion. 'I didn't know you could have dogs on board. How come she's had a party up here for the past two days?'

Vaughan studied Frankie to see if she was winding him up. It amused him to see that she was deadly serious.

'She's a popular girl,' he said.

'Is she very rich? Or famous?' Frankie bent her head around

the door but could only see a mingling group of men and two elderly women.

Vaughan opened his mouth to say something, then closed it. 'No, I can't do this to you,' he said. 'It's so tempting, but I won't.'

Frankie hadn't a clue what he was talking about. He pushed her gently into the Vista, away from the Planet-room doorway.

'Friends of Dorothy. As in Dorothy in *The Wizard of Oz*. Judy Garland.'

'Judy Garland's dead though, isn't she?' puzzled Frankie, still no wiser. What was he talking about? Judy Garland couldn't be hosting a party. Not unless it was via a Ouija board.

Vaughan shook his head and laughed.

'Judy Garland, *gay icon*?' he went on.

'Yes, I know she was ...' Then the penny dropped. 'Oh, there's no Dorothy!'

Vaughan clapped his hands. 'It's a meet-up for gay people.'

'I am so thick!' said Frankie. 'And a bit deflated actually. I was hoping for a Hollywood actress or someone really grand dripping in diamonds and holding one of those big cigarette-holders.'

'Sorry to disappoint,' said Vaughan.

'Curiosity killed the cat,' sighed Frankie. 'I should have left myself in blissful ignorance, believing that someone looking like Barbara Cartland was on board. Shouldn't have been so nosy, should I?'

Vaughan chuckled again. He had a nice friendly laugh, which was quite at odds with his angry Viking-like appearance.

'Well, I hope it hasn't spoiled your holiday too much,' he said.

'I'll try not to let it get in the way,' smiled Frankie, betting that Vaughan was really a looker under all that facial hair.

'Bye,' they said together. Vaughan went off into the Vista, and Frankie noticed he was still chortling as he walked off.

*

Roz arrived at the belly-dancing class to see that a few had dropped out, but there were still enough there to constitute a fair-sized class. Gwen had brought along a case of scarves with tinkly metal coins sewed onto them, and little finger cymbals. Some of the women were rifling through the things and playing with them.

'I thought we'd have a dressing-up session today,' Gwen said. 'I find it helps when your hips jingle. So, take a scarf, ladies, and tie it around yourself like this.' She demonstrated how to put it on and broke into a hip wiggle. The coins rippled beautifully. The room was suddenly full of jangling metal sounds. It was amazing how the addition of a simple scarf moved their efforts up a notch.

Roz had beads of sweat on her brow at the end of the session. And her thigh muscles told of a good workout. There wouldn't be a class the next day because they were landing at their first port – Malaga. She wondered if Manus had tried to ring her or sent her a text. She went back to her cabin after class and switched on her mobile phone only to find that he hadn't.

Frankie bumped into Olive looking at books in Market Avenue.

'Buy yourself a sexy blockbuster,' said Frankie, coming up behind her and making her jump. 'Find out what you've been missing.'

'Oh don't,' said Olive.

'Have you been for anything to eat yet?' Frankie picked up the bonkbuster that she had been encouraging Olive to buy. She hadn't been a great reader until she had to give up her job and ended up with too much time on her hands.

'I've only just got up,' Olive confessed guiltily. 'I can't believe it. How could I have slept so long? I haven't done anything except sit around and eat and drink.'

'It's called relaxing, Olive. Your body is telling you it needs to chill.'

'Talking of chill, it's a bit nippy outside, isn't it? I thought it would be warmer than this. We must be well past France by now.'

'Dunno where we are,' said Frankie. 'Fancy going for some nosebag?'

'If I must,' smiled Olive. 'Although I think I'm still digesting my meal from last night.'

They went up to the Buttery where brunch was being served on one half, and lunch on the other. A man in brown shorts walked past with enough food on his plate to stuff a Blue Whale and a portion of cheesecake on the side to finish it off, and trotting at his heels was his missus, with an equally loaded tray.

'A full English *and* cake?' Olive was nearly sick at the thought of eating all that food at once.

Frankie tutted. 'I'm sure some people are determined to eat their whole body weight in one sitting because it's "free".'

'How can you say that after those evenings we used to have in the "all you can eat for a fiver" Chinese buffet?' laughed Olive. 'I've never seen anyone shift more egg fried rice than you.'

'Oops, I'd forgotten about that,' giggled Frankie.

They plumped for baked potatoes with salad, which were delicious. Then, as Frankie got two coffees from the machine she spotted Vaughan leaving and felt a pleasant little tremor wriggle through her when he smiled and waved. She had just started to imagine him bare-chested in shorts when Olive nudged her.

'Look, those greedy buggers have gone back up and are getting yet another tray full of food.'

'They must be the Tray Twins,' smirked Frankie.

'Ronnie and Reggie,' Olive laughed back. Then she waved

at Ven and Roz as she spotted them wandering through the Buttery.

'Been dancing?' asked Frankie.

'Yes, thank you,' said Roz, not quite managing to keep the clipped tone out of her voice.

'Guess what, I found out who Dorothy is,' said Frankie, and went on to tell them the tale. Even Roz had a smile at that.

'Fancy a swim this afternoon?' asked Ven. 'In the ...' she referred to her pocket map of the ship '... Topaz pool?'

'Isn't it a bit chilly for a swim?' asked Olive.

'Maybe it would be in the open-air pools, but that's the one with the big glass roof over it. Apparently when it gets hotter they pull it back.'

'Not for me,' said Roz. 'Because I'm going to do something I haven't done in ages.'

'What's that then?' replied Ven. 'Have a potato?' Roz's fixation with the Atkins diet was a standing joke amongst them.

'No, I'm going to have a nap,' announced Roz. 'Like a pensioner. I think it must be the sea air, but I am absolutely pooped.'

'I'll come swimming with you, Ven,' announced Frankie.

'Can I borrow a cossy?' asked Olive.

'No, you can't. You'll have to go skinny-dipping,' said Ven. 'Course you can. Come down to my cabin and pick one out.'

By the time Olive had chosen a costume from Ven's huge wardrobe of clothes, Roz was already asleep, snoring softly on top of her newly made bed, courtesy of Jesus. Frankie had gone straight to the Topaz pool on deck fifteen but couldn't find three sunbeds all together. There were quite a few around the lip of the pool with towels spread over them in a 'reserving' gesture. Frankie was annoyed and told the others as much when they arrived.

'I've been here twenty minutes and no one has been to those

sunbeds. I reckon the cheeky beggars come down first thing, chuck a towel on and then don't bother to come back. Anyway, I'm giving it ten more minutes then I'm going to shift some and we're moving onto them. They tell you not to reserve chairs like that in the ship's newspaper thingy. It's just selfish.'

True to her word, after ten minutes precisely Frankie strode over to three sunbeds, scrunched up the towels that were covering them and rudely deposited them in the nearby towel bin. 'Come on, Olive, Ven!'

'Do you think we should, really?' Olive hovered nervously by.

'Sit down, you coward!' Frankie ordered.

Blimey, she hadn't been as forthright as this for a while, thought Olive. It was strangely nice to see a bit of fire back in Frankie's belly. She spread her own towel over the bed, lay back and looked at the glass ceiling above the pool. She could see that the sun had broken through the cloud, which was a good sign. And the clouds that remained in the sky were feathery and white and not grey and dumpling-thick any more. She was just closing her eyes when a waiter arrived with three tall fizzing flutes.

'I took the liberty of ordering you a Champagne Cocktail,' said Frankie in a pseudo-posh voice.

'Drinking champagne at this hour?' said Olive, taking a delighted sip and relaxing back. She calculated that, had she been at home now, she would be doing Mr Tidy's upstairs. What a misnomer that was – Mr Tidy. He was a scruffy blighter, especially in the bathroom. She thought of scrubbing his toilet week after week and how he seemed unable to grasp the concept of peeing into the pan. And he always made her feel as if she was exacting monies by menace when he paid her from the little girly purse which he held up to his chest. He never opened it very far in case the moths made a bid for freedom. But today Olive Hardcastle was not scrubbing at stains on his Armitage Shanks, she was here, sipping champagne at half past one in the afternoon and doing bugger all but that and breathe. She dreaded to think what Mr Tidy's bog would be like after nearly three weeks of not seeing any Toilet Duck.

'Cream tea in two hours,' said Ven, making them laugh.

'You are the third Tray Twin, you pig,' giggled Frankie, then had to fill Ven in on the gluttony she and Olive had witnessed in the Buttery. She adjusted her breasts inside her costume and caught the teenage lad a couple of beds down giving them a surreptitious look. She grinned.

'I'm going for a dip,' she said, stepping down the ladder at the side of the pool into the warm water.

'No sly weeing,' said Ven. 'Remember where you are.'

'As if,' tutted Frankie. Her shoulders sank beneath the water and she gasped with delight. If this wasn't bliss, what was? She did a couple of lengths, skirting round a little girl with arm-bands on. How lucky was she, going on a cruise ship at that young age? She was a lovely child, with dark curls and thick black eyelashes, just like Frankie had been when she was a baby. Like *her* baby might have been if she'd ever had one. Frankie ducked her head under the water to shock away thoughts like that.

'We were just saying it's semi-formal dress code tonight,' said Olive, when Frankie climbed out of the pool and flopped on her sunbed.

'What's that?'

'Not as dressy-uppy as formal but more dressy-uppy than smart casual,' Olive replied.

'Surprisingly, that makes sense,' smiled Frankie. 'What's the after-dinner entertainment?'

Olive referred to her *Mermaidia Today*. 'It's the theatre company doing a celebration of Motown music in Broadway. Or we could go and see a film in the cinema or watch a cabaret double act. Or go to the casino, or—'

'Flaming heck,' said Frankie. 'And there was me thinking I might be bored rigid cooped up on a ship for two and a half weeks. No brainer: Broadway for me again. I love Motown.'

A good half-hour passed before a shadow fell across Frankie's face and a man's irritated voice stirred her from a light doze.

'Excuse me,' he said. 'I think you'll find these three are our sunloungers.'

Frankie stretched and opened up her eyes to see a stunningly good-looking couple: a leggy pouty woman and the man who Ven thought was an actor from the telly. But all Frankie saw now was a couple of cheeky bleeders. And why had he reserved three beds when there were only two of them? So he wouldn't have the inconvenience of a mere mortal lying next to him perhaps?

'Nope, I don't think they *are* yours,' Frankie said, like a calm, confident John Wayne squaring up to an irate Jack Palance.

Had Olive been a snail, she would have retreated as far into her shell as it was possible to go. Ven's eyes just opened so wide that her eyeballs were in danger of popping out.

The woman, in very short shorts, a bikini top that barely covered her nipples and a fully made-up face, stood behind her man, hand on slim hip making annoyed supportive faces.

'I remember quite specifically which sunbeds were ours, thank you!' The man stabbed his finger at the sunbeds. It was a very refined finger too. Long and arty with a weighty gold ring on it. But then it did belong to a very attractive rest of him – thick black hair sleeked back, a young Sean Connery-type face, rugged arms leading from a vest that showed his chest area was very well defined. Deffo a six-pack in existence under the material too.

Frankie felt that stirring again inside her that had visited earlier when she first saw the earmarked unoccupied sunbeds. She felt possessed by the spirit of a confrontational imp – an echo of the old gutsy self that she had lost somewhere in the past few years.

'You can't stick a towel on a sunbed and walk off for hours, love,' she told him. 'There are over three thousand people on this boat and we all have an equal right to them.'

'Do you know who …' the man began, but the woman pulled him away before he started spitting feathers everywhere. Frankie watched him muttering angrily to her as they left, he blowing off steam like a giant's kettle, she patting his shoulder to calm him down.

'Who the hell was that knob?' said Frankie.

'That, I believe,' said Ven with a voice shaking like an opera singer on a vibrating plate, 'was Dom Donaldson.'

Chapter 28

'. . . And can you believe Frankie told Dom Donaldson off – *the* Dom Donaldson!' Olive was telling Roz in the Vista as they waited for the waiter to bring their pre-dinner cocktails.

'Not in so many words,' said Frankie. 'I didn't swear. I just told him he didn't have any right to reserve a sunbed and not use it. And I'm sure he was just about to say those words which immediately mark anyone out as a total cock: "*Do you know who I am?*"' She wondered what she would have said to him if he had.

They had commandeered four chairs around a table by the window. The sun was lowering into the sea, feathery clouds bobbing in a sky that seemed to be growing bluer by the hour.

'I'm sure he wouldn't have said that,' Ven defended her hero. 'Maybe he didn't realise how things work on a ship.'

'Absolutely, Ven. And maybe he's half-German,' said Frankie with smiling sarcasm. 'It wouldn't be his fault then. Just his natural impulse coming out to chuck towels on loungers.'

'You'll never win,' said Olive to Frankie. 'Dom Donaldson can do no wrong in Venice Smith's eyes.'

'His girlfriend looks very like Angelina Jolie, don't you think?' said Ven.

'Tangerina Orange Jelly, more like,' sniffed Frankie. 'She's about as much like old Angie as I am. Where the hell did they get those tans? They look like the colour of my fence.'

'Oh, shut up talking about them and look at that view. What a gorgeous evening.' Olive was wearing her new floral sundress and matching shrug and feeling not at all out of place amongst the other passengers.

Suddenly Dom Donaldson was forgotten as a tall hunk of a man in a pristine white uniform walked through the lounge and said, 'Good evening,' to everyone he passed. Ven's eyes rounded.

'Who. Is. That?' she said, her jaw dropping to deck six. 'Now he *is* my idea of what the Captain should look like.'

'Could you say that just a bit louder?' said Frankie. 'Only they didn't quite hear you in Hong Kong.'

'They don't pick the Captains on their looks, you know,' tutted Roz.

'Well, they should,' said Ven. 'I would if I worked for Figurehead.'

'I think I have to agree with you on this one, Ven. He's a bit gorgeous,' said Frankie, as Ven continued to study the officer who had set her all a-tremble. Tall with short, salt and pepper hair, very sexy light-grey eyes and a Robin Hood's bow for a mouth. She put him slightly older than them – early-mid forties – the age where men either became full fruit or withered on the vine. This man was, in the words of St John Hite: *a tang-tastic zingy partnership of chilled class and yummy body.*

'And sadly so out of my league it's untrue,' sighed Ven, getting ready to sign her name on the chitty for the three Tequila Sunrises and a Chocolate Banana cocktail.

Half an hour later, as the four ladies approached the dinner-table, they noticed there were weighted balloons floating over the middle of it.

'Ooh, is this something to do with your competition people?' Roz asked.

'No, can't be,' replied Ven, before adding quickly, 'at least, I don't think so.'

'Evening, all,' said Eric and Irene, also spotting the balloons. 'Someone got a birthday?'

'Not me,' said Ven. 'Not this week, anyway.'

The mystery was solved a few minutes later when Royston and Stella joined them. They'd ignored the dress code and were in full formal ensemble. The reason for that would become clear in Royston's first breath.

'It's our anniversary,' he explained. 'We were thinking about going to Cruz but we changed our minds.'

'Cruz, what's that?' said Ven.

'It's the celebrity chef restaurant on the seventeenth floor,' Eric jumped in, always at his happiest when imparting ship info. 'You know, Raul Cruz has given his name to it. You pay a small supplement to eat there but it's apparently superb. I do believe he's on board too.'

Wow, thought Roz. So it definitely was him she had seen at Southampton.

'But we thought it might be nicer to spend the big day itself with some company,' said Royston. 'It would be a bit boring with just the pair of us at a table.'

'Oy, cheeky.' Stella nudged him sharply.

'Wish we'd known, we'd have got you a card,' said Ven.

'Oh, don't worry about that,' said Royston and laughed. 'You can buy us a present in Spain instead.'

'So you're going to be serenaded then,' Eric nodded. 'I don't know, whatever ship you go on, whatever waiters you have, it always sounds the same.'

'Bloody awful,' grinned Royston.

Must be some in-joke, thought the girls. They hadn't a clue what Eric and Royston were talking about.

'Did you book any trips, ladies?' asked Royston, after giving Aldrin, who Royston had now renamed 'Buzz', his order for venison.

'Blimey, we forgot,' said Ven. 'We were too busy doing absolutely nothing.'

'Do we have to pay to get off the ship?' asked Roz.

'No,' Eric told her. 'You just check out with your cruise card. Depending on how far the towns are away from the port, there will be a complimentary shuttle bus to take you in. Irene and I don't tend to bother going on the organised trips these days. We've been on most of them and prefer to do our own thing.'

'We're off to Marbella,' said Royston. 'We've got friends who have a villa there and they're doing a lobster lunch for us.'

'Lovely, Marbella,' said Eric. 'Terribly expensive though. Anyway, we're only going to stretch our legs on land for an hour. We've been to Malaga several times now so there's nothing much we want to see. When everyone gets off, the ship is lovely and quiet. We'll get the pool to ourselves.'

He turned to the girls then. 'You really ought to look at the trips though, brilliant for first-time cruisers. Some of them are a bit pricey but there's a lovely one at Cephalonia. Melissani – a once-underground lake. Beautiful.'

Olive felt her cheeks heat up as if Eric could see the picture inside her head of herself in a boat drifting on the lake. With Atho Petrakis. And what they did in that boat.

'And what did you do today?' Eric asked Stella. 'Did you get ashore?' He chortled to himself as seven out of the eight people on that table wondered how many more times he would make his silly joke during the holiday.

'Actually I went to bingo and won twenty-three pounds on the very first house,' said Stella.

'There's bingo as well?' asked Ven.

'Every day, twice a day, but I just go to the four o'clock one in Flamenco. It's just a bit of fun, although it does get very serious at the end of the cruise if the snowball hasn't been won.'

She looked too posh for bingo, thought Ven, imagining those perfectly manicured hands holding a bingo dabber.

Angel arrived at the table with two bottles of pink champagne.

'Please join us in a glass,' said Royston.

'There's not enough room for all of us in a glass,' said Eric, giggling away at yet another poor joke.

'That's very kind of you,' said Irene.

'Well, it's not often you find yourself married for thirty-nine years,' said Royston, giving Stella a big wink.

'Goodness me,' said Eric, although it was noted that he didn't dive in and try and pip them by saying something on the lines of, 'Well, Irene and I have been married fifty-one years.' For once, the girls thought, Eric must have been outdone.

When eight glasses had been poured out, Eric led the toast.

'Many more to come for you both,' he said, tipping his glass their way. 'Happy Anniversary, Royston and Stella.' The others echoed that and sipped whilst they chose from yet another gorgeous menu, although Roz still plumped for soup and sirloin steak.

After dessert, the waiters began to gravitate towards their table.

'Oh here we go!' laughed Eric. 'The choir.'

After a signal from Supremo, the waiters launched into the worst rendition of 'Congratulations' the girls had ever heard. It was so bad it was brilliant. People from surrounding tables were clapping along – cruisers who had seen it all before, presumably, and knew the drill. Royston basked in the attention, Stella endured it with a tortured smile on her face and intermittent jangling from her many glittery bangles.

They went as an eight to the Motown show in Broadway and thoroughly enjoyed it. Then Royston insisted they all join him and Stella for a nightcap in the champagne bar Beluga. They parted company just after eleven o'clock; everyone went back to their cabins, full of fizz and good food, except for Ven who walked up the stairs and out onto the top deck. It was dark but the air was warm and soft. She looked out and, though there was nothing to see but a fingernail-snip of moon, dots of stars in the sky, and waves sprinkled with silver, she thought it was beautiful. The ship rocked gently on the shushing sea, the breeze tumbled through her hair and she smiled to herself. For the first time in ages she felt calm and rested and thought she might have *got it*, what people found so wonderful about such a simple thing as water, when it looked as if it could have gone on and down for ever.

Day 4: Malaga

Dress Code: Smart Casual

Chapter 29

Olive awoke first the next morning and realised the ship wasn't moving. They were in port. She threw back the curtains and, to her disappointment, the day looked dull again. She had been looking forward to wearing her new shorts and one of her swanky T-shirts. But it seemed as if it was going to be another cardigan day.

She had just put on her slacks and long-sleeved top when there was a sharp rap at the door and Ven's accompanying voice.

'Ol, are you up? It's me, Ven.'

Olive opened the door to Ven in skimpy shorts and a vest with shoelace shoulder straps.

'You'll catch your death in that,' Olive commented.

'You're joking,' said Ven, grinning a wide arc. 'It's gorgeous. Seventy degrees according to the announcement some Irish officer has just given out over the Tannoy, and it's not even nine o'clock yet. The sun is at the other side of the ship, but trust me it is out there and blazing for us. So take those thermals off whilst I get the other two lazy arses up and then we can go up for a nice sunny breakfast.'

And sure enough, when the four of them walked up to the Buttery, they passed the Topaz area and found that the great glass ceiling over the pool had been pulled back and the sun was streaming down through it. It was gorgeous. They were in Spain. Hot, bright, beautiful Spain.

'What shall we do? Just have a plod about on land?' asked Frankie, mid-toast-bite. She was wearing a lovely pale-blue top with a matching bolero and white shorts.

'Yeah, why not. Let's stretch our legs,' said Olive. 'When are we off next?'

'We've got a couple of days at sea then we're in Corfu,' said Roz. 'So it will be nice to have a walk about, won't it?'

'How's the weather back home?' asked Ven. 'Anyone know?'

'According to the *Mermaidia Times*, it's chilly with thunderstorms expected,' said Olive with glee.

'How awful!' exclaimed Frankie, with fake sympathy for all the people in the UK.

Ven popped the last of her almond croissant into her mouth. She dreaded to think how many calories it contained. But sod it, it was delicious and she was on holiday. 'Come on, then. Let's go and sample España!'

Getting off the ship was an easy enough experience. They went down to deck four, presented their cruise cards to a guy at a machine, which recorded they had left the ship and said a robotic 'goodbye' to them, and then they walked down a long tunnel and into a huge enclosed building with a small selection of shops promising better prices than Gibraltar. Once they had left the building and walked outside, the heat of the day hit them full on. Frankie stripped off her bolero and Roz caught her first glimpse of the angel motif on her shoulder.

'Bloody hell, she's got a tattoo!' she hissed in Ven's ear. 'Mind you, as if I'm surprised.' She hated tattoos. She thought they were common enough on men, but on women they were something else! Manus had a tiger on his arm, something he'd had since he was eighteen. She'd told him on more than one occasion that only idiots wanted to brand themselves.

Ven didn't reply. She wasn't that keen on tattoos on women

either, but she knew the angel meant something special to Frankie and the reason why she'd had it done. She definitely wasn't going to spoil the day and start taking sides on the matter though.

They joined the queue for the shuttle bus and enjoyed the short ride from the port with all its extensive building work going on, past a replica of a pirate ship with the magnificent figurehead of a crowned lion and a few moored multi-millionaires' yachts. Fifteen minutes later they were in the throng of Malaga shops.

'I'm tired out already,' said Ven. 'I'm not used to this heat. Let's go and get a coffee.'

'I'm all for that,' said Olive as they approached a square by the Cathedral. She gestured at one of the cafés there. 'What about this place?'

'No,' said Frankie, pointing to a tank full of live lobsters. 'Not here. It upsets me seeing them.'

'Blimey, you've changed,' scoffed Roz. Frankie was never that sensitive in her youth. She'd have delighted in picking out the fattest one and having it boiled for her lunch.

'Haven't we all changed?' said Olive, partly in Frankie's defence. It wasn't as if Roz was the same as she used to be years ago either. If only. These days, Roz's emotions were all wrapped up tightly in barbed wire, forbidden to escape. Even her choice of food was ridiculously rigid. It was as if she was compensating for feeling lost and adrift by grabbing at control over herself where she could.

'That's a nice-looking café,' said Ven, spotting one across the other corner of the square. 'Look at the desserts in there. Always the best sign of a quality place.' The twirling sweet cabinet was bursting with huge cakes.

'Just a coffee for me. Isn't it too early for cake?' grumbled Roz.

'I'm not looking at the clock on this holiday,' said Ven, turning to the waiter who arrived at their side as they chose a shaded table. '*Cuatro cafés con leche y er . . . tres gateau?*' She looked at the waiter but she had lost him after the coffee order.

'*Gato* is a cat in Spanish,' laughed Frankie. 'You've just ordered four white coffees and three cats.'

'Do they do lemon drizzle?' asked Olive.

'Oh for God's sake, Ol!' said Roz. 'Ven doesn't even know what "cake" is in Spanish. She's not going to be able to order "lemon drizzle", is she?'

'Chocolate then,' said Olive. 'Surely that's an international word.'

'Will you stop laughing, Frankie Carnevale, and help me out here? You're the language expert.' Ven play-thumped Frankie in the arm.

'*Tres tortas de chocolate, por favor,*' Frankie ordered smoothly as she wiped the tears from her eyes. 'Oh, that was the funniest thing I've seen in ages. I wouldn't have missed it for the world.'

When the pieces of chocolate cake arrived, they were embarrassingly huge. Sitting on the pavement, people were passing and looking at them. A Japanese tourist actually took a photograph.

'That was divine,' said Frankie, polishing off the last cherry on the top.

'I should have had something,' mused Roz. 'I'm a bit peckish now.'

'Have a soup and some steak,' Frankie twinkled. Roz always did bring out the imp in her.

'We're not all as adventurous as you,' replied Roz frostily.

'But there's so much on the ship menus. How come you won't even try anything else?' put in Ven. 'If you don't like what you order, you could always send it back and then get a steak.'

'I like a steak,' said Roz with more than a touch of exasperation.

'Yes, but you aren't going to have one for sixteen nights running, surely?' Olive got in on the argument now. 'I'm not exactly Mrs Exciting but soup and steak every night would drive me mental.'

'Will it make your holiday any better if I eat a bloody fish?' said Roz, expecting an obvious no to her question, but getting instead:

'Yes, it will,' from Ven. 'Because I know you'd enjoy it.' *If you let yourself*, she added to herself.

'All right, if it makes you happy, I'll order some sodding melon balls tonight,' sighed Roz. 'Now what shall we do? Mosey around the shops?'

'Sounds good to me,' said Olive, heaving herself to her feet and having a mental flash of Doreen getting up from her chair.

'Come on then, girlies,' said Ven, handing a twenty-euro note to the waiter and pocketing the receipt.

'Here, I'll get this,' said Frankie.

'No, you won't,' said Ven. 'I'll claim it back from the competition people. All expenses paid, remember. Come on, then.' She beckoned them to follow her out of the square. Blimey, it was hot. They'd only gone about forty yards and wanted to sit down again in the shade of another roadside café and have some icy Cokes. Ven didn't want to be a killjoy, but what she would have loved to do most at this moment was turn on her heel and head back to the ship. She missed it already.

'We could hit the beach,' said Roz. 'Although I haven't brought my towel or anything.'

'I'm boiled alive,' said Olive. 'And tired out.' How the heck had she ever managed her fourteen cleaning jobs when eating a slice of chocolate cake had just totally knackered her?

'Well, how about we go to the ship, get our cossies and towels and then come back out and head for the beach?' Ven suggested.

With no one having a better plan in mind, they set off towards the shuttle bus stop. Coming towards them were

Royston and Stella. Royston had a yellow vest on, black shorts and bright yellow sandals. He looked like an elongated bee. Stella wore a short cream sundress that showed a lot of her enhanced cleavage.

'Hello, girls. We're just off to take a few photos of the place,' Royston declared. 'Well, the boss is. My main purpose of walking in this heat is to build up a thirst so I can enjoy some San Miguels under an umbrella.'

Stella rolled her eyes. 'Come on, moaner,' she said and he seemed happy enough to be dragged along by 'the boss'.

As soon as they stepped on the ship, a wrap of deliciously cool air enveloped the four women, and they sighed collectively. To Ven, the idea of going back out again into the midday sun to sit on a beach lost its pull immediately. She looked at the faces of the three others and could see they were feeling exactly the same.

'Topaz pool and some cocktails?' she suggested.

'*Perfecto*,' said Olive.

It was true what Eric had said: with most of the passengers on shore, there was the pick of the sunbeds to be had, no queues for lunch and two empty Jacuzzis at the head of the Topaz pool. Ven, Olive and Roz sat in one whilst Frankie softly snored on a sunbed – in the shade, Roz noticed. No longer a hardline sun-bunny either, it seemed. Was this really the same Frankie? *The same Frankie who made her partner cheat . . .* Roz sliced off that thought before it spoiled yet another day.

'Are we right in the head?' asked Ven as the water bubbled and glugged around her. 'We're in Spain and we're sat on the ship. I feel like I should be out there studying architecture.'

'Well, I'm having a lovely time,' said Olive, raising her face to the sun. 'If I'm wasting the day, so what? I'm on holiday.'

'You're more relaxed than I've seen you in years,' said Ven.

With her face tilted up, Olive looked just like she did as a schoolgirl – all fresh skin and smiles.

Olive sighed, fighting an irritating thought: how many days was it now until she was back at home? She didn't want to count. She didn't want to know what day it was or what the news was back home or even what she was going to do next. She was savouring each moment. She suddenly had a rush of the munchies and fancied a pot of tea and a diddy cream scone.

As if her thoughts had filtered across the pool, Frankie jerked awake, looked around her, spotted her friends in the Jacuzzi and mimed drinking a cuppa over at them.

'That's my cue,' said Olive, hoisting herself out of the Jacuzzi. 'I'm off upstairs for a nibble in the Buttery. Coming?'

'Nope, I'm staying put right here,' said Roz.

'Ditto,' said Ven.

'See you in a bit then,' said Olive with a backward wave as she caught up with Frankie, slipped on a sarong and together they headed for the restaurant.

'Have you rung Manus?' asked Ven.

'No,' said Roz tightly. 'We agreed not to have any contact with each other so I'm sticking to that.' She didn't say that she had switched on her phone that morning to check if he had left her a message. If there had been one, she knew she would have rung him back. There wasn't and she had switched the phone off and almost thrown it into her safe.

'Oh Rozzy, don't split up with him. You'll never find another man as nice as Manus.' Ven thought he was lovely. Roz was lovely too, just so lost. She had a huge chance to be happy with Manus, if only she would let him love her. After the dysfunctional upbringing she'd had and all the crap luck with men, Ven knew that Roz had finally raised her guard after Robert ran off, and found it nigh on impossible to drop it again. Ven, herself, hadn't been that lucky on the man front either. Once upon a time she carried a little bubble of hope in her heart that someday her white knight would appear, and though she remained outwardly positive and laughed along with the others about being swept up by a handsome hunk and carried off into the sunset, inside she knew it would never happen.

'I didn't say we were definitely splitting up,' said Roz, some-what impatiently.

'Are you missing him?' Ven asked tentatively, not wanting to upset Roz. She knew that behind that hardened façade, her friend was a soft, mangled mess of hurt.

Am I missing him? Do I wish he was here in this Jacuzzi with me? Do I wish his clothes were sharing space in the wardrobe with mine? Was I disappointed when I switched on my phone to find the one solitary message from fucking Orange?

This was what Roz thought, but instead she answered, 'Ven, trust me, I'm not thinking about him at all.'

Chapter 30

Manus pulled himself from under the car, hearing a set of high heels tap into the garage.

'Excuse me, can you help me, please? I've broken down just around the corner and I didn't renew my recovery insurance. Four years I've had it and never used it, and two weeks after it's run out, this happens! I could scream.'

Manus wiped his hands on a cloth as he got to his feet. The rain-soaked, trembly-voiced gold-and-caramel-haired lady in front of him was petite, in a smart navy suit and matching coloured heels, carrying a laptop case and looking vaguely familiar.

Her narrow-eyed expression hinted that she'd seen him somewhere before too.

'Is it Manus?' she said. 'Manus Howard? Do you remember me? Jonie Spencer. We were at Holbank School together.'

'I thought I knew your face,' said Manus, breaking into a friendly smile. *Jonie Spencer!* He'd been in the same class as her for History and French and Maths. He'd had a real crush on her at school, then at sixth form college. But all the lads had a crush on Jonie Spencer. Her hair was always short in a cheeky pixie style, now it was long and woven in a loose plait, but her face was just the same. She had obviously aged after twenty-five years, but she had done it beautifully.

'How lovely to see you!' said Jonie. 'You look great.'

'So do you,' said Manus, suddenly bashful. 'Really well.'

'I'm twenty-five years older than the last time you saw me,' smiled Jonie as genuine delight sparkled in her eyes.

'You must have a portrait getting older in your attic,' Manus joked, although she could have had because there were no lines around her eyes at all. 'Come on, let's go and sort out your car,' he said, leading the way. Had he grown that much? He remembered being only a little taller than her, but he had a good foot and a half on her now.

She had a lovely silver CLK Mercedes. Classy. She suited a Mercedes. She flicked the bonnet open for him and he had a good look inside as she turned over the engine.

'Your battery is as flat as a pancake. I'll juice it up and have a look at it in the garage for you. You won't have it back today though.'

'That's okay, I can live without it for a couple of days,' said Jonie. 'Thanks so much. I know nothing about cars – I was beginning to panic.'

'You're a girl, that's why,' grinned Manus.

'I promise I'll go home and do some washing up and know my place, sir,' Jonie saluted him. Her smile was just the same as it had been at college. It lit her face up – and the street. It was a long time since he had managed to make a woman smile.

'What's the address of this place?' Jonie took her mobile out of her bag. 'So I can order a taxi.'

'I'll run you home.' Manus indicated that she put her phone away. 'So long as you don't live in Bournemouth.'

'Park Boulevard.' Again she smiled. 'Number seven.'

A spark of memory flared up. 'Didn't you live there when you were a kid?'

'Yes. I bought my mum and dad's house from them when they moved to France.' She smiled again. 'Apart from the years studying at Oxford, I never moved away.'

'Oxford? Wow. What did you study there then?'

'Law,' she replied. 'I'm a solicitor now.'

All those years living so close to each other and I never bumped into you once, thought Manus. He took his car keys out of his pocket and called to his assistant mechanic that he was nipping out for five minutes, then he turned to Jonie and indicated the black Audi behind her.

'Let's get you home and dry,' he said.

'Thank you so much,' she replied. 'I owe you big time for this, Manus. I'm even glad I broke down now – it was worth it to see you again.'

Manus took the business card she held out to him with her phone details on it. He was all too aware that old pleasant memories were being stirred up, too thick and fast for comfort.

Chapter 31

Roz surprised everyone that evening not only by having a duck starter, but an oriental noodles and seafood main, and grudgingly conceded that she enjoyed it better than the soup and steak.

'You'll be having a dessert next,' laughed Frankie.

'I don't think I will,' said Roz. She allowed herself one slice of cake every fortnight with Olive and Ven, then afterwards starved herself until the next day. Carbs were the devil's vomit.

The dress code was smart casual but it didn't stop Royston wearing a very large Rolex with his Ted Baker shirt.

'Look at the way that hand sweeps – beautiful.' He held out his wrist so Eric could admire the craftsmanship. 'Seventeen thousand pounds, that cost. If someone would have told my old dad that one day his son would be walking around with a watch that cost more than his house, he'd have had them thrown in the nearest loony bin . . .' And on he went.

Stella nudged Ven and whispered as she held out a bling-encrusted wrist, 'See that bracelet? Romford market. Three ninety-nine.'

Ven hadn't been expecting that and nearly choked on her Key Lime Pie. She wasn't sure she believed Stella, though. If she was loaded and had the pick of designer shops, why would she buy things from a market? Maybe she was just saying that to balance out Royston's bragging.

'Honestly, since the day his business took off, he's been a right royal pain in the bum with his designer this and designer that,' Stella went on in a low voice. 'If he could buy Armani loo roll, he would.'

'Well, he's just enjoying his good fortune,' said Ven. Royston was a terrible show-off, but there was something quite cheeky-cockney-chappie about him that just let him get away with most of it.

'Too much,' said Stella, tapping her temple. 'Went to his head a bit. A lot, in fact. And all that money changed my daughter as well.' She leaned in conspiratorially. 'My grandchildren are called Sonata and Arpeggio. What sort of bloody silly names are those, eh? They're not even musicians. She owns a beauty salon and her husband sells computers.'

'How can I comment, with a name like "Venice"?' said Ven.

'Ah, that's what Ven is short for, is it? Venice – that's a lovely name,' said Stella. 'Did your parents call you that for a reason?'

'It's where I was conceived,' explained Ven.

'There you go. But where's the story behind "Sonata" and "Arpeggio"? I get the evil eye if I call them Sonny and Pegs. Mind you, they go to this posh school where you have to be called something bloody silly before they'll even let you in the door. There's a Strawberry, a Water-Lily, a Nostradamus – silly sods, some of these people are. I bet I wouldn't have to look hard for a Ferrero Rocher either. They think they're bloody film stars.'

'Did the money change your family so much?' asked Ven, leaning forward with interest.

'My daughter disappeared up her own arse, as I said. My son – well, he lives on a big farm in the country but the lot of them are always in jeans and riding on ponies – he's the happi-est of the lot of us.' Stella pointed over at Royston. 'He used to be worse than this,' she said. 'He's calmed down a bit, reeled in his line. Three years ago, he ended up having it away with a woman in his office who did the books. Cheap bit of skirt, you know the type. Gave an old man a bit of attention in the hope he'd give her a bit of spend. It was prostitution all but in name. He thought his money made his paunch and varicose veins invisible. He was over five stone heavier then.'

'No!' gasped Ven.

'Oh yes,' said Stella, calmly with a wry smile. 'And it cost him a lot of jewellery, a boob job, tummy tuck, nose reconstruction, face-lift, Botox, the promise of two cruises a year at least and a villa in Florida to stop me divorcing him and taking half of everything.'

'Bloody hell,' said Ven. 'I thought you were really happy. I mean, you've been married thirty-nine years!'

'We are happy,' said Stella. 'I get to come on cruises whenever I ask, and he gets to keep his balls.'

'I can't believe it,' said Ven, genuinely stunned.

'Believe it, girl, it happened. He lost all the extra weight with stress when he thought I was going to walk out. He's looked after himself a lot better since, because I'm *facking* gorgeous now and what is sauce for the goose . . .' Stella grabbed Ven's hand and forced it on her stomach.

'Feel that. Tight as a drum. I didn't have a tum like this even when I was nineteen. And my tits' – For one horrible minute, Ven thought Stella might have made her feel those as well – 'are the best money can buy. You ever need some work doing, you tell me, darlin'. I have a surgeon in Turkey with a five-star, spotless hospital. Only thing real about me are my lips and my arse, and I'm having both of those done for Christmas.'

'Blimey!' was all Ven could manage, relieved that Stella had released her hand.

'He looks about twenty years younger today than he did

three years ago,' Stella concluded. 'I reckon that if he hadn't had that fling, he'd be dead of a heart-attack now.'

'So,' Ven tried to phrase this carefully because she was the queen of putting her feet in her mouth, 'she sort of did you a bit of a favour in the end.'

'Yeah, I suppose so,' mused Stella. 'Didn't stop me smashing her front teeth in though.'

'You didn't!' shrieked Ven. 'Did you get away with it?'

'Oh no,' grinned Stella. 'I ended up in court. "A woman of hitherto unstained character, driven to the edge of despair by a grasping, blackmailing, home-wrecker". Yes, my barrister was brilliant.'

'Blackmail?' probed Ven.

Stella moved in even more closely. 'She volunteered to drop the charges if I paid her five thousand pounds. Little tart met me at Royston's office to pick up the money. I just happened to have my hand pressed down on the Tannoy switch when I told her I wasn't paying up, after all. I had twelve witnesses to that conversation. Courts don't like blackmailers. I walked out of there a heroine.'

Ven grinned. 'How very delicious.'

'Before all this,' Stella gestured to her many surgical procedures, 'and before the money, I had to fight all my life for everything. You don't mess with East End women,' she winked.

'He must be worth clinging on to,' Ven decided.

'Ah, he's a bloody silly man but he's got a heart as big as his mouth. Very large. But I get more pleasure out of picking up a bargain like this,' she stroked her bracelet, 'than I ever could about having what I want out of Tiffany's window.'

'My husband ran off with another woman,' said Ven, surprised she was confessing this to a relative stranger, trading crap-men stories.

Stella drained her glass of Merlot and Angel appeared quick as a wisp to replenish it again. 'I hope you made him pay.'

'No, he ended up making *me* pay. He got fifty grand in cash and our house in the divorce. He took over the mortgage and is living in it with her now. He's fuelling a mid-life crisis and a twenty-four-year-old blonde's whims with it.'

'Bastard,' said Stella. 'Still, it won't last a long time with a tart to impress. That money will be gone before you know it, and she'll be off.' She put a comforting hand on top of Ven's. It had a diamond on the ring finger as big as a bull's eyeball. 'He'll get his comeuppance in the end. Just you wait and see, darling.'

That evening, they went to see the comedian who was performing in the theatre. He was great fun, but though Ven was laughing along with the rest, half of her was somewhere else. She was wondering if Stella was right. And what would happen when Ian's fifty-thousand-pound bonus booty ran out. And most of all, she wondered what her ex-husband would think *when he found out about her secret.*

Day 5: At Sea

Dress Code: Formal

Chapter 32

Ven didn't think she would sleep because so many things were whirling around in her head, but the ship's gentle motion worked its magic. She was up early the next morning and walked twice around the Prom deck, which constituted over a mile. Quite a few people were walking the same circuit, mainly pensioners, taking a leisurely stroll in the already warm air. She'd heard people over the years say they'd feel claustrophobic being stuck on a cruise ship. They obviously had no concept of how big these vessels were.

She had a coffee by herself in Café Parisienne and read her book, and one by one the others drifted to her. Café Parisienne, it seemed, had become 'their place'. Olive had bought handbags from the stalls outside Market Avenue, and Roz had been belly dancing again. Frankie arrived with very oily hair because she had gone for an Indian Head Massage in the spa.

'Now we're all here, let's book some trips,' announced Ven, reaching in her bag for an excursions book.

Over muffins and more coffee they looked at all the places they could visit at the next ports. Ven wanted to go dolphin spotting in Gibraltar, Roz wanted to see that underground lake in Cephalonia that Eric was talking about, Olive wanted to go on a gondola in Venice.

'I've had a fantasy about being on a gondola eating a Cornetto for as long as I can remember,' she said.

'We can discover Venice by ourselves though,' said Frankie. 'We'll get a waterboat over to Murano and watch some glass-blowing . . .'

'Wow,' cut in Roz sourly.

'I'm not saying we have to, I'm just saying we could do our own thing in Venice rather than be tied to a trip.'

Olive tapped the table with her fork to bring them all to order. 'It's Ven's birthday, I think she should decide what we do on that day.'

'I'd rather not go on an organised trip, if you're asking,' said Ven. 'I'd like to go on a gondola and then somewhere nice for lunch with you and then, if you don't mind, I'd like to wander around by myself for a while. I want to find the hotel where Mum and Dad stayed on their honeymoon.'

'Okay, whatever you want,' said Olive. 'It's your big day.'

Royston and Stella passed and waved.

'Did you see the dolphins this morning, girls? Hundreds of them, there were!' Royston called.

'Oh no!' said Ven. She was sure the dolphins were avoiding her. Everyone on the ship had seen them except her, apparently.

'He's looking extra bright today,' Olive remarked as Royston walked on. He had trunks on which were bright orange on one side, electric yellow on the other.

'Hope he removes his super-sweeping-hand watch before he goes in the pool,' said Roz.

'I've gone off him a bit,' said Olive. She had been really disappointed in Royston when Ven had told her about what Stella had said the previous night. 'I don't mind him being the world's biggest show-off because he's quite funny with it, but fancy cheating on poor Stella.'

'They all do, given the chance,' said Roz with a bitter tone.

'Right, who's for booking those trips, then a spot of sunbathing?' said Ven, cutting that line of conversation off straight away. 'Phoar, look at that – double whammy.'

Passing the front of the open-plan café area was that hunky officer in white talking to Dom Donaldson, who was wearing black shorts and a black muscle vest. Ven leaped off her chair like Zola Budd in hot pursuit of a gold Olympic medal. She might as well have some eye-candy to gaze upon whilst walking down to the trip-booking desk.

Chapter 33

Manus parked the Mercedes neatly outside 7, Park Boulevard. He saw the front curtain twitch as he clicked the lock on with the car remote, and Jonie had opened the door by the time he was halfway down the path.

'Come in, come in,' she greeted. 'Thank you so much, Manus. I am completely lost without my car.'

He had intended to put the key and the envelope with the invoice inside quietly through the letterbox and go, but she was halfway down the hallway expecting him to follow and it felt rude not to. He closed the door behind him.

'I've just this minute put a pot of coffee on,' she said, beckoning him into the kitchen at the end of the hallway. It was a lovely sunny square room looking out onto a long flowery garden which backed onto the park. He'd always wondered if these houses were as nice on the inside as they were on the outside – and now he could see that they were even better, if this one was anything to go by. Her home was a perfect reflection of the Jonie Spencer he remembered, trendy and neat and bright and stylish. And very girly. He didn't notice any men's shoes on the rack or male coats on the twirly white wire stand by the door.

'Coffee or tea?' she offered. 'It's no trouble to boil the kettle if you want tea.'

He was going to say 'neither' but she was getting him out a cup. 'Coffee, please. Black, no sugar. Thanks.'

As she stretched up to the cupboard he saw a flash of her tanned bare stomach. He averted his eyes. 'Not working today?' he asked.

'I'm working from home,' she said. 'I don't mind the odd day doing that, but it would drive me insane if I did it all the time. I like to talk too much.' She smiled and poured a coffee into the cup and topped up her own.

'Sit down,' she said.

'I can't stay long,' said Manus. 'I've got an MOT to do this afternoon.' He was lying, though; he didn't.

'You can stay for a thank-you coffee – I insist,' said Jonie. 'And tell me how much I owe you.'

He felt awkward asking her to pay, for a reason he didn't know. And yet what signals was he giving out if he let her off the bill? As it was, he'd settled for just charging her for the parts. The labour wasn't that much anyway.

'I don't expect any favours as far as the bill is concerned, you know,' Jonie said with a little pout that whisked Manus back twenty-five years, to being in the leavers' disco and wishing he was the one slow-dancing with her and kissing that pout and not that knob-head smooth-boy captain of the footie team, Michael Ashley.

'I've just invoiced you for what it cost me – honestly, that will be fine.' Manus handed over the envelope, and Jonie opened it immediately.

She made a gently-chiding sigh and pulled a chequebook out of a drawer behind her. She quickly wrote out a cheque, ripped it out, folded it and gave it to him. He slid it straight in his pocket.

'Aren't you going to check it?' she asked with a little smile and two perfectly arched eyebrows. 'I might have only made it out for fifty p.'

'I trust you,' said Manus.

'Thank you, you saved my life.'

'That's putting it a bit strong,' said Manus, taking a small sip because the coffee was too hot to shift quickly.

'Trust me, when a woman's car goes wrong, she is reduced to idiot level.'

'My other half says the same,' said Manus. He saw Jonie's head give a little twitch.

'Did you marry anyone I know from school?' she asked. 'I don't know about you, but I only kept in touch with a couple of people.'

'No, Roz didn't go to our school. And we just live together, we're not married.' He didn't know why he volunteered that. He felt immediately uncomfortable about it afterwards, as if he was making the point that he was legally available – which he wasn't.

'Any children?'

'No,' said Manus. 'You?'

'God no,' laughed Jonie. 'I'm a career girl. Single, no kids, not even a goldfish. That way, if I want to jet off to Paris for the weekend I can do so at the drop of a hat.'

'Roz is on a cruise at the moment,' said Manus, again wondering immediately afterwards if he should have said that.

'Oh? Alone?' Jonie asked, her interest sparked.

'No, one of her friends won a cruise for four. They've all gone together.'

'Oh, how lovely for them,' said Jonie. 'Although I've never fancied it myself. Maybe when I'm eighty.' She smiled. Her eyes were full on him. Big and blue. A warm blue though, not like Roz's which were a paler, icier shade.

'I better get a move on,' he said, abandoning the near-full coffee. She didn't try to stop him.

'Of course. You've got your MOT to do.' She stood. She was tiny next to him. Neat and cute and perfectly pocket-sized, he'd always thought so. And age hadn't diminished her appeal; if anything, it had added to it. 'Manus, thank you SO much for sorting my car out. I'll recommend you to everyone I know. I'll tell them to mention that Jonie sent them.'

'That's nice of you, thank you,' said Manus bashfully.

She rubbed the outside of his arm at the door in a joint gesture of goodbye and gratitude.

'Take care, Manus. It was lovely to see you. I can't wait to tell Layla and Tim. Do you remember Layla Baker and Tim Stott? They were always glued together at school. They still are – in holy matrimony!' She laughed. 'They're coming round for dinner soon. Tim's a barrister now.'

'I remember them well.' Manus had liked the lovebirds Layla and Tim. 'Well, it was great to see you too, Jonie,' he said.

'Oh, how will you get back to the garage?'

'I'll walk, it's not far.'

'Let me give you a lift. I insist. If you're in a rush to do that MOT.'

Damn, he'd cornered himself there.

'Besides, I can check that you've mended it properly,' she winked at him.

'Cheeky,' he smiled.

Five minutes later he was waving goodbye to Jonie after she had dropped him off. Her perfume was still in his nose. It was spicy and exotic and very like the one Roz wore. It made him ache inside. Even the cheque had the faintest whiff of scent on it. Unfortunately, when he unfolded it, it didn't have Jonie's signature on it. *Oh hell*.

Chapter 34

Dinner that night was another formal affair. Roz didn't even look at the steak option but went straight for the Lobster Thermidor, as did everyone else at the table. Buzz buzzed around them adjusting the cutlery, assisted by Elvis, Angel flitted expertly between them filling up everyone's glasses, and Supremo regally made sure, as he did every night, that all were happy, that diabetics were being sufficiently catered for, that the waiters were attentive, the wines were to taste – and that everyone felt a little special for his attention.

The Great Supremo ran a tight ship, and no one who worked for him ever wanted to get on his wrong side. He relished his role as Restaurant Manager. His great chest puffed out of his ever-immaculate uniform with pride because the Olympia was his kingdom. Supremo was the perfect title for him.

'Next stop Corfu,' announced Eric with glee. 'We love Corfu, don't we, Irene?'

He turned to Irene who was buttering a warm roll crusted with poppy seeds. It looked so nice that Roz's resistance to carbs crumbled and she took one from Buzz's basket when he proffered it. Not only that, when the menus came around, she had eyed up the desserts for later as well. Manus's favourite was on – Bailey's cheesecake. She started to wonder if he was

missing her, until Royston nudged her out of those thoughts
with a tale about how he had just booked a Caribbean cruise
for Christmas for the whole family. And obviously how much
it had cost. Stella hushed him halfway through the tale and
told him to stop showing off.

'I'm not showing off, am I?' he asked the table with genuine
shock that he could possibly be perceived that way.

'Which ship are you going on?' asked Eric. 'We're going on
the *Io* at Christmas.'

'Oh poor you,' said Stella. 'You'll be bumping into us lot
then. You can learn all about my daughter's Rolex as well.'

The table exploded in a splutter of giggles as Royston
remained blissfully unaware he was the butt of the joke. He
bought everyone at the table a port after coffee which they
enjoyed with some extra truffles which Buzz had sneaked to
them, and the subterfuge made them taste extra delicious.

'This really is the life,' said Frankie with a satisfied burp,
looking out at a big orange sun sinking into a sea that looked as
calm as glass.

'Isn't it?' dittoed Olive. That thought was bittersweet. She
wasn't sure she would ever be able to fit back into Land Lane
after this. She was acclimatised to a life in the sun already.

There was another show that evening by the theatre company – *Kings of Swing*. However did they learn all those lines
and song lyrics? Everyone worked so hard to make sure the passengers didn't have to do any work. It was a bit like Mrs
Crowther sitting there doing her nails whilst Olive wove her
Dyson around her legs. Olive felt slightly guilty to be on the
other side of things.

Ven went for a walk again up to the top deck after saying
goodnight to the others later. It was a lovely, balmy evening
with a slight ruffling breeze. Above her the sky was midnight
blue, the moon a gently curving smile, its dark side just visible
if you looked hard enough. She felt so beautifully calm and

chilled, as if the sea air had seeped through into her bones and soul and soothed the very essence of her. She was the only one on the top deck; the ship might have been deserted for how quiet it was. Considering how many people were on board it was odd.

'Lovely, isn't it?' said a sudden voice beside her, which made Ven jump because she had thought she was alone up there. The voice belonged to an elderly lady in a long black sequinned two-piece that shimmered where it caught the moonlight. She nudged back a white swoop of hair that fell across her eye. Ven decided she must have been a real beauty in her day.

'It certainly is,' said Ven. 'I could stand out here for hours.'

'Yes, it's rather strange, isn't it, the attraction that the sea can hold.' She had a voice that matched her quiet elegance: well-rounded vowels, the product of elocution lessons as a girl most likely. 'My husband Dennis spends a lot of time looking out to sea to spot dolphins and whales and seals. He's always saying "Look, Florence, there's one," but mostly it's the sea playing tricks on his old eyes.'

'Have you been on many cruises?' Ven asked, immediately thinking, Blimey, I'm turning into Eric!

'Quite a few. We were on the maiden voyage of the *Mermaidia* four years ago, you know. It's our favourite. We're celebrating our Diamond Wedding Anniversary onboard this time.'

'Oh how lovely,' said Ven. 'When's that then?'

'The second to last night. The Black-and-White Ball,' said Florence.

'So the waiters will be serenading you,' smiled Ven.

Florence laughed. 'Yes, we always enjoy the singing. Anyway, I must go and find Dennis. Oh, there he is.'

Further up the deck a man with a thick head of steel-grey hair and glasses was waving in their direction.

'Enjoy the rest of your evening, my dear. Goodnight.'

Florence walked towards him, a slight limp to her step, her sequins twinkling. Ven's attention was claimed then by a group of four teenage girls to the other side of her, loud and laughing and enjoying themselves. Were she and Ol and Frankie and Roz ever that young and wrinkle-free and full of energy? It seemed a lifetime ago and yet, in a different part of her head, it could have been only yesterday.

Ven yawned. It was just after eleven o'clock but the ship was like a giant cradle, in which they all slept like newborns. And in a few days, she would be a forty-year-old baby. Ven decided she'd better cram in some serious beauty sleep before then.

DAY 6: AT SEA

Dress Code: Semi-Formal

Chapter 35

Roz had built up a real sweat after that morning's belly-dancing class. Gwen made it look so easy, but they say the easier someone makes it look, the harder it is – certainly that was the case with belly dancing. She felt totally justified in heading up to the Buttery and having one of those almond croissants that Ven was always going on about.

Olive was having a look around the shops. Every day new stock was wheeled out. Today there was a soft-toy sale and children were clustered around cuddling teddy bears and begging their parents to buy them something. A sad little stab of pain nicked Olive's heart. She had never even had a sniff of pregnancy. She had hoped that getting pregnant would have made the whole family buck up their ideas, but it never happened for her to test the theory. Maybe it was a blessing – she couldn't have worked as she did and cared for Doreen and David and raised a child. But of course now she knew the truth – that she need not have given them all that assistance – and suddenly that sadness was replaced by a whopping great thump of anger.

Frankie bumped into Vaughan when she passed through the photo gallery on the way to find the others and grab some lunch. He was wearing a shorts-and-vest ensemble that made the best of his long, lean, muscular body – and showed off the stunning black Celtic tattoo on his shoulder that made him look very gladiatorial.

'Good morning, Friend of Dorothy,' he whispered.

Frankie laughed. 'I won't live that one down in a hurry, will I?'

'Enjoying yourself?'

'It's not bad,' sniffed Frankie. 'Although this weather isn't a patch on Skegness.'

'That's amazing.' Vaughan stepped back in amazement. 'I feel exactly the same.'

'Yeah, right!'

'Look at this.' He held up a photograph of his party at a table, taken last night at the Formal. 'If the lads at the bike club saw me in a bow tie, they'd die laughing.'

'Perfect blackmail material for the family then,' smiled Frankie.

'No more bouts of sea-sickness?'

'No, thank goodness. But I'll be down at the doc's for an injection if I do. How fabulous was that?'

'Dad!' Vaughan's daughter appeared with her young, handsome husband. She immediately recognised Frankie as the lady she had entrusted her father to in the sick bay.

'Hello again,' she said and smiled, looking just like her father when she did so – minus the facial hair. 'You're a bit less green in the gills than the last time I saw you.'

'This is Kim, my daughter, and Freddy her husband,' Vaughan said, introducing them.

'Hello,' replied Frankie. 'Yes, that injection worked wonders. I highly recommend it.'

'Ooh, I look a bit rough on that pic, Dad. You're not buying it, are you?' said Kim, catching sight of the family portrait. Frankie was stunned at how such a beautifully photogenic woman could see anything to complain about on the picture. She looked lovely on it – something her husband jumped in to say too.

'That's nice, that is, Kim. We're having that.' He had a real Wurzel voice which didn't match his slick, groomed exterior.

'No, we're not,' she returned.

'Yes, we are,' said Freddy, taking the picture from Vaughan and going over to the queue to purchase it, Kim following him and protesting.

'Wedded bliss,' tutted Vaughan, making Frankie laugh. 'We're going for lunch in the Ambrosia restaurant. It's a sit-down-and-be-served affair. You wouldn't starve on here, would you?'

'No, you wouldn't,' said Frankie, feeling the teeniest pang that their conversation was about to end.

'Mind you,' Vaughan leaned in close to her ear, 'some people on here take greed to an art form.'

'I don't know where some of them put it all,' Frankie replied.

'You're welcome to join us,' he said.

'Thanks,' Frankie told him, 'but I'm just on my way to meet up with my friends.' As soon as she had said it, she wished she hadn't. The others wouldn't have minded her going off and having lunch with Vaughan, just as long as she supplied any juicy details later. But it was too late to retract now.

'Well, see you around,' said Vaughan, turning to rejoin his daughter. And Frankie felt herself sighing in the manner of a teenage girl who had just caught the eye of the school rugby captain.

As Olive was heading up the stairs on her way to Café Parisienne, presuming the others would be there, she noticed a cruise card lying on the stairs. It was Dom Donaldson's and he was just ahead of her and about to walk into the lift. Olive ran up and tapped him on the shoulder.

'Excuse me . . .'

He whirled around. 'I'm on holiday,' he said, eyes and smile cold, palms spread out towards her.

'Sorry?'

'I'm on holiday – okay? Please respect that.' Then he moved forward into the lift, leaving Olive feeling really bemused. She looked down at her hand with the card in it, then realised that he had thought she wanted an autograph. Well, she hadn't and he'd been bloody rude. She turned on her heel and went down to Reception to hand in the card and leave him to sweat a bit. She just hoped his fake tan wouldn't slide off too much when he did.

Twenty minutes later, Olive was sitting in Café Parisienne, drinking ice wine and telling Frankie and Roz all about it, when Ven turned up.

'Where've you been?' asked Roz.

'I had a message to meet Andrew and do an interview.'

'Ah, the elusive Andrew,' said Roz. 'What's he like?'

'Nice, ordinary. Nothing special to look at.'

'Where did you go?'

'A sort of sitting-room area,' said Ven. 'Behind one of those doors that says Staff Only. He asked us if we could get some photographs done together for PR purposes.'

'No worries,' said Roz, taking a long sip of her ice wine. 'I don't mind posing around in posh frocks.'

'Sounds a bit odd for a high-profile competition though,' Frankie mused. 'Getting your own pictures done.'

'He said he didn't want to compromise our holiday. Anyway, I've given him an interview and he said that I'll see him again before the end of the cruise. They obviously know what they are doing.'

At that moment, Dom Donaldson passed by the open front of the restaurant. He was striding along with Tangerina, who was tottering in extremely high heels. 'Yes, of course I had it when I came out! I must have dropped it,' he was saying irritably.

Ven's shoulders dropped two feet with a sigh. 'Isn't he the most gorgeous man ever? Wonder what he's looking for.'

The rest of them kept schtum. None of them had any intention of smashing their friend's illusion with the sad reality that Dom Donaldson was actually a total plonker.

Chapter 36

Manus had just broken the news to an old couple that their beloved ancient Morris was past its last legs. They'd had it for over fifty years and Manus imagined they'd bought it as a young couple and ferried their children around in it and travelled on holiday with it. The old man was sniffing back tears as each option he suggested was greeted with a slow sideways shake of the head from Manus. The insurance company had declared it a write-off and, determined not to give up, the couple had invited various mechanics to see it, only to be told the same thing that Manus was telling them now.

As Manus got back in his van and drove away from them, his heart felt heavy in his chest. The words he had used about the car seemed to have a strange, deeper meaning: *It's scrap – you can't do anything with it but let it go. Whatever you try to do, it won't work any more.* It was as if he was talking about his life with Roz and not their car. If he and Roz split up, would she punish the next man for his sins as she had punished him for Robert's? He doubted it. He had not made a fraction of the impact upon her that her ex-husband had – that seemed more and more obvious to him with every passing day. He wondered often if she were punishing him because he was Manus and not Robert. Was having to deal with the old car some subliminal message from the Cosmos, guiding him to let their relationship go, because it was unsalvageable scrap?

As he parked up at the side of his garage, he saw Jonie outside it, big smile spreading across her face when she spotted him.

'Hello, Jonie,' he said, forcing up the corners of his mouth in greeting, although all he wanted to do was get back to work so he could concentrate on something that would stop him from thinking about the events of the morning and what they had stirred up inside his head. 'What brings you here? Come into the office.'

'Tell me I'm wrong,' she started after a deep breath, following him inside, 'but I have a stupid suspicion that I didn't sign that cheque I gave you yesterday. I may have done, but we were talking and I can't actually remember doing it – and I'm rather prone to that habit, alas. Always getting them sent back to me.'

'Ah,' said Manus. 'You didn't actually. It's not a big deal though. It wasn't exactly thousands.'

'You weren't going to leave me in blissful ignorance, were you?' Jonie gasped. 'Oh, you silly man, you'll never run a successful business letting stupid people off their debts. I am *so* sorry to have put you to this trouble.' She looked genuinely upset by her forgetfulness. 'Thank goodness you didn't get nasty about it like the window cleaner did last month.'

'No point in getting nasty about things like that,' said Manus. 'It's a mistake. No one's perfect.' He hoped it was an error on her part too and not some flirting manoeuvre. He didn't want any more complications in his life – not when his brain was still mashed potato from *that* talk with Roz about trial separations and his heart was so, so lonely and aching for a green light. Affairs could have the tiniest starting point – a spark to dry tinder – and suddenly they were forest fires and totally out of control; he had seen it happen to a few people over the years. Manus knew he was vulnerable and in real danger of snatching something that would comfort him. He handed over the unsigned cheque after taking it from a drawer.

'I had to check with you. I'm so glad I did now,' Jonie said. She scrabbled in her bag for a pen, took out a triple pack of sandwiches so she could hunt underneath it, and eventually retrieved a pretty white pen with gold lattice markings on it.

'Have you had lunch yet?' she asked.

'No,' he replied. *Ah, wrong answer!* It would probably lead to her saying, *Would you like to share mine?* Jonie clicked on her pen and scribbled her signature on the cheque. Then, to his surprise, she put the sandwich pack back into her bag.

'Sorry again, Manus,' she said. 'I'll let you get your lunch now and stop bothering you.'

'It's no trouble at all,' said Manus, a little taken aback, for he really had been expecting her to volunteer to share her lunch. That served him right for being a self-deluded prick. Then again, he was never very good at reading women – his relationship with Roz had driven that point home well enough.

'Thanks again,' said Jonie. 'See you again soon, I hope.' And she twirled and waved and was gone.

Chapter 37

There was an outdoor theatre performance that evening around the Topaz pool, which had been set up for the occasion with huge fake palm trees and pirate decorations. But the four of them were more in the mood for a quiet night in Beluga – the champagne-and-caviar bar on deck eight.

'Look at us old farts,' said Ven. 'We could be out raving and we're sitting here in big leather armchairs.'

'We're sitting here drinking champagne and eating chocolate truffles though,' corrected Frankie. 'And I, for one, have still got all my own teeth to bite into them. So less of the old, Venice Smith.'

'I've never had caviar,' said Olive, looking at the menu.

'Get some ordered,' said Ven.

'Are you kidding?' said Olive. 'After all I've eaten tonight? There's no room in here.' And she patted her tummy.

'Well, before the end of the cruise we'll come back and have some,' said Ven.

'On your birthday,' suggested Roz. 'Only three more sleeps!'

'Fab idea, Rozzy,' said Frankie, taking a long sip of her Kir Royale and wondering if Vaughan was at the pirate show.

Roz seethed quietly. *Rozzy*. How dare she be so bloody

familiar again? Frankie seemed to be under the impression they were all best buddies now, just because Roz was keeping a cork in it for Ven's sake. *The cow.*

Ven went for a walk up on the top deck before turning in. It was so easy not to think about anything beyond life on the ship – something else she would have found impossible to believe. She stood there for a while, looking out and letting her mind drift until she began to yawn. *Ah well, Corfu tomorrow. Bedtime*, she said to herself. As she headed back towards the door, she glanced over the balcony and saw an old couple dancing on the deserted deck at the back of the ship. It was Florence and Dennis. She recognised the black shimmery dress, or it could have been a similar one – goodness knows, her mother used to have forty variations on a theme for everything she wore. The old couple were waltzing slowly, smiling at each other and talking softly together. Ven waved but they didn't see her, they were too wrapped up in each other. Just like the way Ven's parents used to look at each other. They loved to dance too. Ven wondered if that would be her one day, dancing in the moonlight with a man she had grown old with. Or if she would simply be a lonely old lady hanging over a balcony looking at the rest of the world paired up in couples.

How lovely it must be, still to be dancing with each other at that age. They looked so in love. She had married Ian never doubting that they would grow old together too. She could never have imagined that he'd turn out to be such a greedy and selfish person. In the end, he was no longer recognisable as the sweet guy she had exchanged vows with ten years ago. Who would have thought that a change in career would have altered everything about him? He didn't even look like the same man she had married, with all those overstuffed muscles.

Revisiting it all started to stir up angry feelings inside her, then she remembered what had happened to her recently – *what she had told no one yet.* Maybe it was a case that, in life, some paths seemed hard to travel but they didn't half lead on to the best gardens.

DAY 7: CORFU

Dress Code: Smart Casual

Chapter 38

Corfu was a pretty and lush green island, and in the distance the hills looked like a Japanese watercolour painting. The sky was impossibly blue that day, as if God had decided it wasn't quite deep enough and added some extra pigment. It looked very, very hot – and it was. As soon as the four girlies stepped out of the ship, the heat smacked them full on.

'Blimey,' said Ven. 'I think I'd be overdressed if I was naked in this heat.'

'Don't test out the theory,' said Roz. 'You might give some of these old 'uns a heart-attack.'

Roz adjusted the tie on her shorts, loosening it a touch. She needed to throttle back on some calories or she'd be a dead ringer for Clive the bus driver by the time she got home. They walked to the bus terminal, passing a monster of a private yacht, apparently owned by a Russian oligarch.

It was even more boiling in the shuttle bus, until the driver switched on the engine and the aircon revved up. The whole bus sighed with such orgasmic relief that it was like being part of a giant orgy.

It was only about a twenty-minute journey to the edge of Corfu Town. On the road between the steeply rising city walls, motorcycles zipped and weaved around the buses and the grid-locked cars. Roz took a long drink from her bottle of water, fresh from the fridge in her room, to find that it was almost warm enough to make a cup of tea with.

The bus crawled along the road past fresh-fish markets and pastry shops, but eventually made it to the drop-off point. From there it was just a short walk to the thick of the shops. Roz saw one selling bottles of Limoncello. Manus loved it. She'd buy him a couple of bottles when they were heading back to the ship. Or should she?

'Anyone fancy an ice cream?' asked Olive, spotting a man by a Mr Whippy-type machine twisting out the biggest cornets she'd ever seen.

'What flavours does it say he sells?' asked Ven.

'Dunno, it's all Greek to me,' said Roz, laughing at her own joke.

'I don't care if it's tripe, shite and onion-flavoured – if it's cold, I'm having it,' said Frankie, who was on the verge of selling her soul for something to cool her down.

But she needn't have worried about making herself understood. The waiter spoke perfect English and soon the women were all walking off with four half-chocolate half-vanilla ice-cream turrets. Ven had to abandon hers halfway through – her stomach felt a bit unsettled that morning. She hoped to goodness she wasn't coming down with something. Not so close to her big day.

It was so hot the ice cream was melting all over their hands faster than they could eat it. They were in such a mess at the end that they went into a café and bought three lagers and a coffee for Ven, just so they could use the cloakroom.

'I'd forgotten the delights of a Greek bog,' said Roz, exiting with her fingers pegging her nose.

'Hope you remembered to put your toilet paper in the bin at the side and not flush it away,' reminded Olive.

'I did unfortunately,' said Roz. She took a long gulp of lager which made her gasp with delight as it splashed against the back of her throat. 'My, that's good. There's nothing like a pure German beer for hitting the spot.'

The Barnsley honeymooners passed holding hands and looking very young and golden. A few other people whom they recognised from the ship waved and shared a little witticism like, 'Terrible this global warming, isn't it?' or, 'It really makes you appreciate the British weather, being in a hellhole like this, doesn't it?'

Apparently back home today it was raining and chilly. No one managed to read news like that in the *Mermaidia Times* without a smug smile.

'Nothing urgent,' said Ven, trying to underplay things, 'but if you see a chemist, let me know, will you? Better to be safe than sorry.'

'Oh no, are you okay?' said Olive.

'I'm perfectly fine,' lied Ven with an attempt at breezy. 'But I think I'll get some stomach-settling stuff just in case.'

The Greek coffee was strong and tarry and Ven would probably have been better off having a beer with the others. When she went to pay the bill, she collared the ancient café-owner and asked him where the nearest pharmacy was. He didn't speak a lot of English and Ven wasn't particularly keen on playing out diarrhoea in charades. She did a mock-vomit instead, which the café-owner seemed to understand. He grabbed her by the shoulder and pointed up the steps of the alley outside.

'What was all that about?' said Frankie.

'I just asked him if there was a chemist nearby,' said Ven. She didn't want to spoil anyone's day by wimping out and going back to the ship; she knew her friends wouldn't have let her return by herself. But boy, her stomach really was starting to feel dodgy.

'Come on then, let's go and sort you out,' said Olive, pushing her gently out of the café.

They wouldn't have known it was a pharmacy, had there not been a big green cross outside a serving hatch set in the wall. In the absence of a door or a doorbell, Ven rapped tentatively on the wooden shutters. They snapped apart to reveal a very short woman with a scarily unsmiling demeanour.

'Er . . . I have stomach pain,' said Ven in her best staccato Granglais, rubbing an imaginary circle over her tum. 'I need medicine.' In a tourist town like this, how come she had met the only two people who didn't speak any English?

Frankie and Olive turned quickly away, on the brink of a fit of giggles. Frankie wasn't much help on the translating front in Greece, alas.

The woman came out with a flurry of Greek that Ven, with a totally blank expression, shook her head at. Then the woman rethought and mimed stuff coming out of her mouth.

'*Oui ja,*' said Ven enthusiastically. The woman appeared to understand. She disappeared for a moment, then came back with a white box which she proceeded to open and show Ven the brightly dual-coloured capsules. She pointed to one of them, then a second.

'She means take two,' said Roz.

'How often though?'

'HOW MANY TIME?' asked Roz, in loud fluent pidgin Greek, her palms tilted upwards in a gesture of questioning. Then she had a brainwave and tapped her watch.

The woman held up two fingers in V formation.

'I think she means every two hours,' said Roz.

'Either that or she's telling you to bugger off, you bladdy Eeenglish tourist,' said Frankie, giggling with Olive.

The woman feigned some more vomiting then clamped her hand over her mouth.

'I think she means that will stop any vomiting,' said Roz, pleased with herself. Who needed language?

Then the woman waved a slow warning hand in front of her

mouth and did the two-finger thing again. Then she held up four fingers and waved her hand back and forwards.

'What the heck does that bit mean?' asked Ven. 'It's like watching an old *Vision On* with the sound off!'

'Haven't a clue,' said Roz, deciding that maybe you did need language, after all.

Ven handed over a ten-euro note, hoping that was enough. The woman didn't volunteer any change.

'Veystron,' said the woman. She held up her two fingers again and tapped them with the other hand, making a definite point about the number two which Ven took as being that she needed to take two. Easy enough to understand.

'Veystron,' repeated Ven, presuming that was Greek for thank you.

As they turned back towards the town, Ven dry swallowed two of the capsules until Roz handed over her bottle of now horribly warm water. But Ven was only glad that she had medicine in her system now and was going to be all right.

They headed then for a handbag heaven shop. The leather smelled gorgeous and the shop-owner didn't pester them. He was rewarded with a sale of six handbags, four purses and two belts.

'Fancy a spot of lunch?' asked Olive, after they'd all bought cowboy hats to shield themselves from the sun.

'We can't come here and not have a Greek salad,' said Roz. Ven nodded, but knew she couldn't face any food. She would get something and poke around in it, hoping the others didn't notice that she wasn't eating much.

Around the corner, who should they see sitting at a pretty pavement table under a sheltering awning bearing the lettering *Restaurant Rex* but Royston and Stella, also wearing cowboy hats. Royston was in a bright purple vest, looking twelve degrees more tanned than he was the previous night – and knee-length flowery shorts.

'*Yassou*,' he called out. 'Hello, girls. Isn't this awful, all this sunshine?'

'Terrible,' said Roz. 'What's the food like here?'

'Let me tell you,' began Royston, 'this is the oldest restaurant in Corfu. We've been coming here for years. Beautiful. Best Dolmades in Greece and shrimp the size of lobsters. My Stella has the Greek salad and it's superb, isn't it, boss?'

'It's divine,' endorsed Stella, finishing off the last of her coffee before waving her immaculate golden nails at them. 'Just had these done in the spa. Ask for Roxanne, she's the best. Here, you have our table if you want. We're going to get a taxi now to Paleokastritsa. Lovely little bay to swim in.'

'Thanks, Stella,' said Roz, sitting in the seat which Stella had just vacated. An army of waiters arrived and began changing the tablecloth whilst Stella and Royston gathered up their bags.

They really were a sweet couple, Roz decided. Okay, he might have been a bit of a naughty boy once, but anyone could see they butted together like a dovetail joint. So he made a mistake once. The irony in her thinking bypassed her.

'Oh, and if you're going to buy any local liqueurs, turn left at the top of this street and you'll see a shop with a swinging sign saying "Yamas!" on it. Go there.'

'Thank you,' waved Roz.

'See you at dinner,' said Royston loudly. 'Casual tonight, I do believe. *Yassou*.'

'*Yassou!*' they all returned.

'Yannis,' called Royston to a rotund man with a huge moustache who came out to wave also, 'these ladies are friends of ours. Be nice to them.'

Royston was right about the fare in Restaurant Rex. Yannis brought out a basket of bread big enough to feed the five thousand – even without the fish – and a huge dish of fat oily black olives to nibble on whilst they perused the menu, but they couldn't find anything they wanted more than Greek salad. The tomatoes were big and beefy and tasted divine, the feta cheese was creamy and on the right side of salty. Ven ate because her mum always said she shouldn't take medication on an empty stomach but even she was surprised at how much she put away. Olive's huge burp at the end of it summed it up perfectly.

'How nice was that,' said Roz, popping the last of her feta cubes into her mouth and rolling it around to savour it.

'Very,' said Ven.

'I don't want to move,' said Roz. 'I want to sit here for ever and watch the world go by.'

So they didn't move for another half-hour. They ordered coffees which came with an accompaniment of sticky dates and cubes of nougat. Then Ven paid the bill, once again insisting she would claim it back, and after a visit to the loo, they set off for the 'Yamas!' shop.

They didn't want to venture into the new part of Corfu Town; the quaint labyrinth of shops in this quarter was enough for them. And they reckoned after exhausting every leather shop in the place, that they had built up enough appetite for a dainty cream tea back on the ship. Ven nodded along with the idea but was just glad that she would soon be on board again. The medicine had stopped her from throwing up, but the effect wouldn't last for ever.

Laden with bags, the four of them set off for the shuttle bus stop. The queue was long, but two buses turned up one after the other and they were soon being driven out of Corfu Town.

'Show me the way to the scones,' sang Frankie.

'And me,' chorused Roz.

Ven just smiled. There was no way she was going to do anything but have a lie-down for half an hour. She decided she would pick up a port and brandy from one of the bars to take to her cabin as well. Her dad always said that was a surefire way to settle a stomach.

'I'm going for a jog on the top deck first,' said Olive, as she loaded her shopping bags onto the ship's security X-ray machine.

'You are joking,' said Roz.

'Course I'm bloody joking!' Olive told her. 'I'm going for the full cream and jam shebang. Thank God for shorts with Lycra in them!'

When the others went up to the Buttery, Ven took a double port and brandy to her room. She felt a fabulous relief as she pushed open the door and found her cabin totally Jesus-ified. It was like coming home, with its big soft bed and non-Greek loo.

She ran a bath and sank into it whilst she sipped at half of her port and brandy. Minutes after she had got out of the water, she was asleep on top of her bed, naked and still damp. She was awoken an hour and a half later by the noise of children running down the corridor. There was three-quarters of an hour until dinner – she had better rouse herself, but boy, she really didn't feel 100 per cent at all. She drained the rest of the port and brandy whilst she got herself dressed in her favourite buy, a sweet blue dress with frothy cap sleeves. She didn't apply much make-up because her hand was a bit shaky. Her lipstick took three attempts to get right.

Thirty seconds before the others called for her, she threw a second lot of the Greek tablets into her mouth and washed them down with some mineral water. Hadn't the pharmacist said something about her needing four tablets – presumably for full effect? She felt quite spaced, slightly removed from herself. She obviously needed food, but she really didn't want any. She pasted on a smile of normality and opened the cabin door.

'Your eyes look a bit glassy, Ven – are you okay?' asked Frankie, as the bing-bong call to dinner sounded through the loudspeakers. '*Ladies and gentlemen, dinner is now being served in the Olympia and the Ambrosia restaurants. Do have an enjoyable evening.*'

'I'm fine,' insisted Ven, in a slightly slurry voice. 'I've not long woken up so I'm a bit groggy. I'll be great after I've had something to eat. I'm starving now,' she lied.

'Good, let's go and get some food inside you then,' said Olive, taking her arm. It was a good job she did too, because Ven was having difficulty seeing the ship as it was. The walls looked as if they were twisted out of shape and she doubted she could have negotiated the staircase. She made them take the lift down to the Olympia, then thought she had better go to the loo again before going to the table.

'I'll come with you,' said Olive. 'Roz, Frankie – we'll meet you inside.'

Eric, Irene, Royston and Stella were already at the table when Frankie and Roz reached it – they were all beaming. An extra place had been laid at the table.

'Apparently the Captain's dining with us,' said Royston proudly. 'I'm trusting you don't have any objections, ladies?'

'Ooh,' said Frankie. 'Let Ven sit next to him, seeing as this is her birthday cruise.'

By the time Olive and Ven arrived at the table, Captain Nigel O'Shaughnessy had already made his introductions to everyone. Olive was getting a bit worried about Ven. She wasn't too steady on her feet, and her speech was slurry, even though she insisted she was perfectly fine. The Captain stood as Elvis and Buzz pulled the chairs out for Ven and Olive. Ven found herself being seated next to the same tall, drop-dead gorgeously handsome officer in white who made her visibly melt whenever she saw him around the ship.

'Nice to meet you, ladies,' he said in a lovely soft Irish accent, shaking their hands in turn. 'I'm Nigel O'Shaughnessy.'

'Hello,' said Olive, answering for Ven who had her mouth open wide enough to catch a passing helicopter, never mind a fly. 'I'm Olive and this is Venice.'

'Venice? We'll be visiting your namesake in a couple of days. Were you named after it?'

'Yes,' said Ven, trying to sound sober and failing. 'I was concepted in Venice. My parents thought of it long before the Beckenhams . . . *Beckhams* did.'

Olive mouthed 'concepted?' at Frankie behind Ven's back. Frankie made a face that managed to say with one gesture 'Well, this is Ven we're talking about!'

'Ven's forty when we go to Venice,' said Roz, with a wink at her friend.

'I know,' said Nigel.

'Do you?' said Ven, deciding then that this man must be someone who looked after records.

Two bottles of wine arrived on the table, courtesy of Nigel. Ven decided to stick to water. She was becoming more spaced by the minute, and if she had a mere sip of anything alcoholic, she felt in danger of leaping up on a table, dancing to 'Knees Up, Mother Brown' and showing off her knickers. She took some speciality bread from the basket which Buzz was proffering – sage and onion – and buttered it, although her coordination wasn't spot on and she ended up buttering some of her hand as well.

'So, Mr Ocean Sea.' She considered the name as her mouth said it. The words sounded echoey as if they hadn't come from her but from someone at the side of her. 'Hey, what a great name for someone who works on a ship.'

'Mr Ocean Sea,' Nigel repeated with a very deep grin. 'I've never heard that pronunciation of my name before.'

Across the table, Royston, Stella, Eric and Irene seemed equally impressed and were nodding and smiling.

Frankie topped Ven's glass up with water and, with more than a gentle hint, held it up to her. Ven took a big glug and then said, 'This isn't wine, is it?'

'It's water,' whispered Frankie. 'I think you may be in need of some.'

'Is she all right?' mouthed Irene to Roz.

'I hope so,' whispered Roz, by way of explanation. 'She's been a bit poorly today and took some tablets. She hasn't been drinking, if that's what you think.' She pressed the point in case Irene thought Ven was tipsy.

'So, are you all having a good cruise?' said Nigel. 'Ship up to standard, is it?'

'Brilliant,' slurred Ven. 'We've even got Jesus cleaning our cabin. And Mary and Joseph doing room service.'

'Our cabin steward is called Jesus,' explained Frankie to the bemused sea of faces around the table. 'The Mary and Joseph bit is a joke.' Frankie gave Ven a puzzled stare.

Royston, Stella, Eric and Irene gave a little laugh. Nigel was smiling too as he turned his attention to his menu.

Buzz appeared at Ven's side to take down her order. The words she was reading kept swimming in and out of focus. She took a deep breath and tried to herd herself into line.

'I'll have the asparagus tits. Sorry, I mean tits not tips. Then the . . .' Crikey, she'd better get this one right. She took it slowly and carefully. 'Flambéed duck,' she said, and giggled. 'Good job I said that right. I nearly—'

'I'll have the same,' Olive cut in quickly. Bloody hell, what was wrong with Ven? She sounded pissed as a fart!

But in Ven's head everything was now lovely. Her body was buzzing from a nice mellow hum, her lovely friends were around her, there were four other lovely people on the table and Mr Drop-Dead Lovely-Gorgeous at her side. She couldn't remember why he was at her side. She hadn't pulled him, had she? She sat and listened to the lovely lovely lovely conversation happening around the table which sounded slightly muffled, as if a layer of cotton wool was wrapped around them all.

Eric was making some small talk about wine with Nigel and having a 'Have you tried the South African Merlot?' conversation.

'How come we have an officer at our table?' Olive quietly asked Frankie.

'They join passengers sometimes. And he's not just an officer, he's the Captain.'

Olive's eyes sprang open to their limit. 'No! I thought that short bloke posing for photos the other night was the Captain.'

'Apparently not – he's the Deputy Captain. This guy is the big cheese.'

The starter arrived. One thing about this cruise dining, thought Frankie, they didn't have to wait more than five minutes for the food to arrive.

Ven was very well-behaved through her starter. Her friends had just begun to relax when her mouth revved up again.

'I don't know why I ordered duck.' She nudged Nigel with unintended force and knocked a prawn off his fork. 'I think they look much better swimming about on a river than carved up on a plate.'

'Is she okay?' Roz mouthed at Olive.

Nigel gallantly humoured her. 'The same cannot be said for prawns. Ugly wee fellows.'

'They're blue, aren't they, in real life? So much better pretty pink.'

'I think we might have to take her out and upstairs for a sleep,' Roz whispered to Olive. 'She's going to die when she remembers this in the morning.'

'We had some lovely ice creams today in Cor-flu,' said Ven, trying to contribute something to the conversation which made her sound in control. 'I didn't eat much of mine, sadly,' she confided in Nigel. 'I didn't feel all that brilliant. And you know what Greek toilets are like.'

'Shut her up, will you!' Roz barked at Olive.

'I had to mime in the chemist,' Ven went on.

'Okay, that's it,' said Frankie, standing and grabbing Ven's handbag.

'Ven, how many of those tablets have you taken now?' said Roz.

'I took another couple before I came out tonight. The farmer said four, didn't she? So that's what I took.' Ven's eyelids were drooping now.

'I'm not so sure you should have taken any at all now,' said Roz, turning then to explain to Nigel about the Greek tablets and the non-English-speaking pharmacist.

Nigel prepared to stand. 'Let me help you take Venice to the sick bay. We'll get those tablets checked out with Pierre Floren.'

'It's okay, I'll take her,' said Frankie decisively. She was going for damage limitation now. Ven would be so embarrassed about this as it was; being helped out of the restaurant by the Captain might have her throwing herself overboard with shame.

'I'm not going anywhere before I've eaten my duck!' Ven protested, trying to sit down again, but being stopped by Frankie's short – but full – might.

'Yes, you are. Come on.' She turned to Olive and Roz. 'You two stay here and carry on with your evening. I'm okay. I'm tired anyway, after all that sun. It won't do me any harm to have an early night.'

Roz's lip curled. Who was she kidding? She was doing this for brownie points. Saint bloody Frankie of Barnsley. Miss 'Holier-Than-Thou', Miss Butter-Wouldn't-Melt! She threw a big mouthful of wine down her throat in anger.

'Sorry folks, excuse us,' said Frankie to the rest of the table, who were making lots of noises of concern. 'Have a lovely evening.'

'Where am I going, Frankie?' asked Ven.

'For a little lie-down, love,' said Frankie.

'Then goodnight, good people,' said Ven with a wide, sloppy arc of a smile. 'Goodnight, Mr Ocean Sea. *See* you around. Geddit – *see*!' She laughed at the pun. Frankie gave her a tug and steered her to the nearest exit with enough skill for anyone to think they were just two very sober ladies off to the loo.

'Oh dear,' said Irene. 'I do hope she's all right.'

'She will die tomorrow if she remembers this,' sighed Olive. 'Ven is just the loveliest quietest person. It has to be those tablets which have sent her loopy.'

'Poor girl,' said Irene softly.

'Well, she will be looked after in the capable hands of Dr Floren,' said Nigel.

'I know,' said Olive. 'Frankie had sea-sickness on day two. She met him and his magic needle then.'

'Terrible thing, sea-sickness,' said Nigel in his soft deep burr. 'I have only ever suffered from it once when I first started my career, and the sea wasn't even that rough. I sometimes think I was given that bout so I'd know how bad it was for my passengers in the future and be able to fully sympathise.'

The mains finished, it was time to pick sweets.

'Oh, Lord, look,' said Olive with a heavy sigh. 'What a shame. Coffee profiteroles, that's Ven's absolute favourite. She loves anything coffee-flavoured.'

'The waiters will get you a portion to take up to her,' said Nigel.

'I don't think she'll be in a fit state to eat it,' Olive replied. She was feeling guilty about picking out desserts whilst Frankie had the responsibility of sorting Ven out and said to Roz, 'I think I might skip pudding and go and see what's happening.'

'If Ven thinks she's ruined any more dinners, she'll be upset. We'll go later,' said Roz, stopping her. She wasn't being selfish; she knew how Ven's brain worked.

Olive was torn, but she accepted that Roz was right. So she picked a trio of chocolate desserts and a coffee to follow and remained at the table.

'How many times have you cruised then, Captain?' Eric was saying to Nigel. It seemed he just couldn't resist asking.

As soon as dinner was over, Olive made straight for one of the many phones around the ship and rang Ven's cabin.

Frankie's voice answered straight away and told them that Ven was sleeping like a baby.

'It was definitely that medication she bought in Corfu,' she went on. 'The doctor said that it's far stronger than would ever be allowed in the UK, and the side-effects can include severe confusion and even hallucinations. No more than two are supposed to be taken within twenty-four hours, and under no circumstance should they be mixed with any alcohol. Ven, however, had a large port and brandy when we were scoffing scones.'

'Oh God, will she be okay?'

'She just needs to sleep. She nodded off as the doctor was talking to her. She had to be wheeled to her cabin by one of the crew.' Frankie laughed. 'Oh poor old Ven. Listen – I'm going to stay with her this evening. I don't mind at all. I've got to a good bit in my book so I'm happy enough. You two go and have a nice evening.'

'I don't want to if you're stuck in a cabin all night,' said Olive.

'Don't be daft,' Frankie said. 'One early night on a dream cruise is no hardship. Go enjoy.'

So Roz and Olive went to see the comedian who was performing in Flamenco. He used to be on the television in the eighties and was always one of Olive's favourites. She only had to look at him and his daft hairstyle and his pained-with-life expression and she was laughing. Then Roz suggested going for a bit of fresh air out on deck. She was drinking her fourth large glass of wine which had only served to amplify her earlier feelings of annoyance with 'Saint Francesca'. As usual with Roz, her anger was mostly with herself, but warped to target someone else. Roz knew deep down that Frankie's motives in staying in to look after Ven were purely selfless because Frankie was always the most kind and considerate person. Roz hated that their friendship was over – at her own insistence. Not once had she let anyone try to explain to her what had happened that night; she had judged and damned and slammed her heart shut on her friend but more times than she cared to remember since, she had fought against swallowing her pride and asking what had led to the two people she loved most in the world falling from their pedestals.

Roz looked over the back of the ship and watched the sea churning and foaming. She imagined pushing Frankie and her stupid short white hair and big fake tits over into it. Then an annoying unbidden vision came to her of Frankie at school, laughing, jollying her out of every bad mood. They had been inseparable – *Froz* – and if Frankie ever died early, Roz had made her a solemn vow that she would somehow break into her house and throw away her Rampant Rabbit and furry handcuffs which she kept in her bedside cabinet before her mum and dad spotted them – a duty only the most intimate of friends could be trusted with. Roz took a fierce long drink from her glass to drown those thoughts.

'Gorgeous out here, isn't it?' said Olive. Really, there was nothing but dark to see. But pin-prick lights from small boats in the distance could have been stars for all they knew – giving the impression they were sailing in the sky rather than on water. 'Pity Ven's missing tonight. I really enjoyed that comedian. Mind you, he's doing another show in a few days so she'll catch him then. Frankie would have enjoyed him as well.'

'Saint Frankie, you mean,' huffed Roz.

Olive didn't dignify that with a reply. Instead, she said, 'Frankie looked a bit tired as well tonight, I thought. I don't think I've ever slept as hard or as long in my life. I wonder what they put in this sea air?'

But Roz was in the mood for some Frankie-assassination and wouldn't be dragged away from the subject. 'Frankie wasn't tired,' she scoffed with a bitter tone to her voice. 'She just wanted to look self-sacrificing. You watch – tomorrow there'll be a spring leaking out from where she sat at dinner. All the people in wheelchairs will come to it to be healed. Saint Frankie and the new Lourdes.'

'Give over, Roz,' said Olive tightly.

'Or rather "Whore-des".'

'Oh for God's sake, leave her alone,' snapped Olive. 'We're on holiday!'

But Roz was on a roll now. The alcohol was weakening the holds on all those thoughts and questions which she was constantly having to push back into their boxes – such as why were Olive and Ven even friends with someone who could do that to one of their own? And why did Roz always feel that *she* was in the wrong whenever she mentioned what Frankie had done behind her back? Wasn't she allowed to feel pissed off that her so-called best friend tried to shag her boyfriend?

'Well, I just find it funny how you're both on her side,' needled Roz.

'What do you mean?' said Olive, thinking that she really was fed up with the whole Roz and Frankie thing. Four years with no sign of a let-up. She decided on a diversionary tactic. 'Let's go down to Samovar and have a hot chocolate.'

'Why do you always want to shut me up whenever I talk about Frankie trying to cop off with Manus?'

'Because it's ancient history,' sighed Olive. 'And everything that could possibly have been said about it has been said.'

'Maybe in your book, but it hasn't in mine!' spat Roz. 'I tell you this: if Ven had tried it on with your David, I wouldn't have ever spoken to her again. It's called loyalty.'

Loyalty? Olive almost laughed, but it would have been a very hollow sound. If Roz only knew it was bloody *loyalty* that had got them all into this mess in the first place.

'Drop it, Roz. I'm going down to the Samovar; are you coming or not?'

'Actually no, for once, Ol, I won't drop it,' said Roz. She was like a heat-seeking missile. Once she trained her sights on something, she couldn't let up.

Olive tried to take Roz's arm to persuade her inside, but she pulled roughly back.

'Why is it that I always felt you sided with Frankie over me? Why didn't you have a go at her for being a total bitch to me?'

Olive chewed on her lip. This was getting dangerous now. And she'd had a couple of wines herself. 'Of course we said something to her,' she said crossly.

'Yeah, course you did. What did you say? That if she lost weight, got some false tits and dyed her hair blonde that she might have more chance with Manus because she'd look more like me then? Too bad she couldn't grow a foot taller as well, but you can't have everything, I suppose.'

'Roz, you're talking stupid,' said Olive. She was a gentle woman with vast reserves of patience, but after four long years of this, Roz had used them all up.

'You see, you still won't say anything against poor little Frankie who's lost her job and her boyfriend and sold her house to buy some new tits. Nice to know who your friends really are.'

'I'll see you in the morning,' said Olive, opening the door to the inside of the ship. But Roz slapped it shut again.

'There you go again. Avoiding the subject. Why can't anyone give me a fucking straight answer, because I don't get it?' Roz had lost volume control as well now. She was totally off the leash – wild, and incapable of reason – and Olive was trapped in a cage of so-called *loyalty* with the lock strained and on the brink of springing. 'What is it, Ol?' Roz's face was a rictus of frustrated smile. 'Just tell me, will you, what pretty, wonderful, fabulous, sweet little Frankie Carnevale had that made her so fucking precious to you?'

'Cancer, Roz. That's what Frankie had. That's what made her

reach out for someone – anyone – and it just happened to be Manus that she found first!' Olive screamed back in her face. There, it was out – that word that Frankie had forbidden them to mention, but it couldn't be snatched back and swallowed now.

'What?' said Roz, almost inaudibly with the hint of an unsure laugh in her voice.

'You heard,' said Olive with a rare vicious edge to her voice. 'Cancer. Frankie had breast cancer. No one gave Frankie a harder time than we did when she told us she'd kissed Manus. And yes, Ven and I did give her both barrels about it, for your information. She was disgusted with herself, didn't even try to give us an excuse; she didn't tell us she'd been diagnosed until a few days later. She rang us up and asked if we'd go and see her and that's when she told us why she fucked up with Manus. She went up to your house that day to tell you – YOU – that she'd just been told she had it, but you weren't in. Manus was, though, and she just wanted someone to put their arms around her.' Olive fought back the angry tears that were threatening to spill. This was a time for strength, an overdue time.

'Manus didn't know what was up with her, before you ask, and he still doesn't. He could see she was upset about something and he put his arms around her and you know the rest. He didn't know what was going on in her head, but he did know that kissing him wasn't the right way to sort out whatever it was. But Frankie was prepared to take everything you threw at her because she felt so shit about what she did.'

Roz was frozen, unable to move, unable to talk. That day forced its way to the front of her mind. She and Manus had had another row, something too stupid to even remember, but she knew she was the root cause of it. She had stormed off, had a coffee in a café then decided to go home and stop being so puerile. Manus had met her at the door, looking tortured about what had happened in her absence. And he had 'fessed up because he wanted to tell her that something was troubling Frankie, for her to act that way. But had she even considered that last point? No – she'd fixated on his fall from grace, enjoyed that it justified her behaviour and proved once and for all that no man was *ever* to be trusted. And boy, had she then run with it.

She closed her eyes against the truth as she now knew it. Her head felt light and buzzy. 'Why didn't you tell me? I'd have understood that,' she said breathlessly.

'No, you wouldn't,' said Olive, her voice uncharacteristically harsh. 'You haven't listened to anything we've said since you and Robert started going downhill. You treated that scumbag like a god and then Manus – lovely Manus that we'd all kill for – he copped for all the bile you should have given Robert. It's as if you were waiting for your chance to stick the boot into him because you never stuck it into Robert, and then Frankie gave you that perfect opportunity to let rip. It must have been like a gift for you, Roz. That bloke must love you a hell of a lot to put up with all you've dished out to him.'

Roz looked slapped. But for once, she was listening and it was Olive who couldn't stop herself.

'We wanted to tell you from the off about Frankie, but she made us swear not to. "It's not an excuse," she said. "I had no right to do what I did, whatever was going on in my life." She knew you'd never have done that to her. Jesus, we gave her a hard time when we found out, but that was nothing to the beating-up she gave herself. She then had her op and it was successful, and so Frankie reckoned that you need never know about her illness. She said that if you poured all your vitriol her way, you and Manus would get back on track. But it didn't work out as well as she planned it, did it? I can't tell you how many times I've been close to telling you, especially when you were moaning that we'd had to cancel a couple of our Saturday afternoons to go and help her. You'd say, "Ooh, the world stops when Frankie wants you", not knowing what was really going on. It wasn't fair on you, Ven and I argued that, but when Frankie realised she'd made a wrong call, she knew she'd left it too late to say anything because you'd never forgive yourself for hating her that much. She reckoned it was better that you carried on rather than learn the truth and hate yourself.'

Roz's eyes filled with tears that plopped silently down her cheeks. But Olive hadn't finished. There was no point in keeping anything back now. Roz might as well learn the lot.

'She had to have both breasts off and reconstructed, and she went for a bit extra to what she had before so she could get a little confidence back because she was rock bottom, Roz. And her hair, for your information, isn't dyed blonde. It fell out with the chemo and it's just started growing back that colour. She didn't want to risk dyeing it back to black in case it all fell out again. Plus, she says, it's easier to hide any patches when it's fair. So no, she *wasn't* trying to pretend to be more like you so Manus would fancy her. This ends tonight. I have to say this, Roz, you've been swimming in a lake of ME for so long I'm surprised you haven't grown a dorsal fin.'

Roz covered her face with her hands. The tears slipped in between her fingers onto the deck. 'Oh God,' she said, over and over again. She thought of all the horrible things she had said about Frankie. She felt the weight of her shame which all that hatred projecting outwards had masked. Roz saw herself through the eyes of others and it wasn't pretty.

'So now you know,' said Olive. God, she felt sick. Ven and Frankie were going to kill her – what had she done? She almost wished she could be transported back home to Land Lane in order to avoid them. Roz was crying hard now, but Olive couldn't bring herself to comfort her. She was spent and tired and fed up and angry that it had fallen to her to burst such a fetid balloon of secrets. Four long years of wasted energy and lies and bitterness which had taken its toll on every single one of them. She was done with it all. She opened up the door to the deck and left Roz alone.

Roz wiped her eyes, not caring that her mascara was probably down to her knees by now. She let her mind wander past its locked gates. She thought of Frankie coming to her house after being told she had cancer, seeking out Roz first before anyone because they were 'Froz'. She imagined how scared she must have been, head bursting with fear that she was probably going to die. But she didn't find Roz there, she found lovely, sweet, caring Manus instead. And she knew Manus would have put his arm around her and led her inside and asked her if she wanted a cup of tea, because he was like that. And Frankie would have just wanted a hug, because she was like that. And Roz would have been there to give her that hug, had she not been a total bitch and argued with Manus.

Chapter 39

Frankie was reading her book in the lounge area of Ven's room when she heard the gentle knocking at the door. She opened it to a bleary-eyed Roz.

'Hi Frankie, how's Ven?' she said, no trace of her usual aggression in her voice.

'She's sleeping,' said Frankie. 'She'll be okay.' She smiled. 'Roz, are you all right? What's up?'

Roz fell on Frankie, her arms tight around the small, thin-framed woman who had once been so solid-bodied.

'Frankie, I'm so sorry, forgive me. Please, I don't deserve it, I know I don't. Olive told me.'

'Oh shite. You'd better come in,' sighed Frankie. 'I'll put the kettle on.'

Roz sat on the sofa at the other side of the suite from the gently snoring Ven.

'Still milk no sugar?' Frankie asked.

'Please.'

Frankie delivered two cups of coffee to the table.

'You should have told me,' said Roz, suddenly angry. 'I didn't have a clue.'

'I did what I thought was right at the time,' said Frankie ruefully. 'Obviously I made a total bollocks of it. I did think, halfway through my treatment, that I should ring you and explain, but you'd have felt all mixed-up and guilty and in the wrong – and that felt worse.'

'You silly, stupid cow,' sobbed Roz. 'And are you . . . okay now?' She wasn't sure she wanted to hear the answer.

'So far,' nodded Frankie. 'The fags have gone, obviously, and I don't drink a quarter as much as I used to, unless you count this holiday. I put some decent things in my body – no joke intended – and try and look after myself a bit more than I did.'

'I just can't believe it,' said Roz. 'What if you hadn't been okay? What if you'd . . . you'd gone and I never got the chance to say sorry?'

'You hadn't anything to say sorry to me *for*,' Frankie told her. 'I was the one in the wrong. And if . . . if it hadn't gone well, I promised the others I'd tell you. They made me swear, just like I made them swear not to tell you.'

Roz sipped on coffee she didn't really want, but she badly needed to draw warmth from the heat coming from the cup. The cabin's air conditioning was too effective and she was shivering.

'I turned it up to max for Ven.' Frankie read her mind – they were always on the same wavelength, except on the Manus episode which had blindsided both of them. 'Hang on, I'll turn it down a bit.'

'No, leave it, I'm okay, it's not important,' said Roz. 'How did your mum and dad take it?'

Frankie shrugged her shoulders. 'Dad's Italian so he went all dramatic because that's what they do. He told me that Carnevales didn't die until they were in their nineties at least and forbade it. Dad drank a lot of grappa, sang to Rossini operas and cried a lot. He did the same when I was given the all-clear as well. Mum just cried a lot. I think Dad telling me I wasn't allowed to die helped me fight a bit harder. My family were fantastic.'

'Oh, Frankie . . .' *I wasn't there for you when I should have been.*

Roz couldn't get the words out past the massive lump in her throat.

'Roz, it's a part of my life that's over, touch wood.' Frankie reached her fingers out to touch the wood of the table hopefully as she said it. 'I just want to look forward and enjoy things.'

'Can I be your friend again?' Roz crumbled into a ball.

'Course you can, you daft mare,' said Frankie, putting her arm around her and pulling her into her shoulder. Roz could feel the hard bone against her ear and it turned the tap on her tears up to full flow.

In the background Ven gave a snort.

'Jesus, who let that pig in the room!' whispered Frankie, making Roz spurt out a pocket of laughter that she didn't think was in her.

'Dubrovnik tomorrow.' Frankie gently rocked, still holding Roz. 'Apparently it's very beautiful. I reckon it's going to be a lovely day if Sleeping Beauty is okay.'

'For all four of us,' said Roz. 'I'll make sure it is.'

Frankie stayed awake long after Roz had left the cabin, thinking back to that day, the beginning of the rift. She honestly didn't know what she would have done, had Manus not gently pushed her away. If he had tightened his hold on her and reciprocated the kiss she had given him, she wasn't sure she would have left his embrace. That was why she had taken the full brunt of Roz's hatred. But maybe now her debt was paid – maybe she had suffered enough.

Day 8: Dubrovnik

Dress Code: Formal

Chapter 40

Ven awoke to the noise of someone shifting next to her in the large double bed.

Oh hell, was her first thought. I've pulled and I can't remember who.

Her eyes focused on Frankie's spiky hair, just poking out from under a throw on top of the quilt. She wondered why Frankie was there, and what happened last night, and how the hell did she get to bed. She groaned, loud enough to wake up Frankie.

'Morning, druggie friend. How are you feeling?' Frankie smiled through a yawn then got up and headed for the kettle.

'Oh God!' sighed Ven. 'Tell me I didn't make a total arse of myself in front of the whole ship. What happened to me?' A picture loomed up in her mind of that handsome bloke in white sitting next to her at the dinner-table. She hoped that bit was a hallucination.

'You had some dodgy Greek medicine, remember?' said Frankie. 'And just for good measure, took far more than you should have done and mixed it with alcohol. Very sensible.'

'You didn't answer the first question,' said Ven, not wanting to hear the answer now.

'Don't be daft,' replied Frankie. 'You were fine – just a bit spaced. You didn't wet yourself or fart loudly at the table, if that's what you were wondering.'

Frankie's attempt to jolly Ven up, alas, put unbidden images in her brain and scared her half to death.

'Look, Ven, it wasn't your fault. Everyone was really concerned. Especially the doctor.'

The doctor. Ven's trail of memory ended with walking out of the restaurant. 'How did I get to bed?'

'One of the crew helped me.'

'Oh God, he didn't carry me, did he?'

'Nobody's that strong!' grinned Frankie. 'No, he ... er ... pushed you in a wheelchair.'

'Oh no!' Ven's head dropped into her hands. She wanted her hands to grow large enough to envelop the whole of her so she could hide in them.

'No one saw you. And even if they did, there are a few people in wheelchairs around the ship. It's not something to be ashamed of.'

'I bet they weren't singing "Show me the way to go home" though, were they?' said Ven.

'Oh, do you remember that bit?' said Frankie.

'Jesus Christ – I didn't, did I?' Ven gasped.

'No, of course not. Chillax, you silly thing.'

'Was ... was there an extra man at the table?'

'Yes. Nigel. You can remember him, surely?' Frankie busied herself putting coffee in the cups. 'He's the bloke you've been ogling for days.'

'Oh heck. So not only did I make a show of myself in front of my fellow passengers, I made a prat of myself in front of a member of staff as well!'

Frankie's mouth opened and then slammed shut again.

'What?' said Ven, alarmed. 'What were you going to say?'

'When?'

'Just then!'

'Nothing,' said Frankie.

'Yes, you were. We were talking about that officer bloke and you were just about to say something about him. What? *What?* What did I do?'

Frankie sighed. She could see that Ven was filling in the missing time blanks with ludicrous thoughts – like dancing on the table and showing Nigel her knickers. Ven really should have followed her earlier leanings towards a literary career – her imagination was a powerful, loaded tool.

'All I was going to say,' said Frankie, in her best under-playing voice, 'was that he was the Captain.'

Ocean Sea, Ocean Sea. Why am I thinking that? wondered Ven.

'Captain Nigel O'Shaughnessy?' Frankie tried to encourage Ven's brain to remember. Unfortunately, it all came flooding back. *I kept calling him Captain Ocean Sea, didn't I?*

Ven buried herself under her quilt and Frankie thought she heard some choice expletives of the Anglo-Saxon persuasion, although they were very muffled.

'Ven, you really didn't do anything wrong at all. You were sweet and funny and under the influence of very strong medication.'

Ven's head popped out from the sanctuary of the quilt a wee bit. 'Honestly? I didn't do anything that people will point to me for?'

'No, of course not. Do you think any of us would have let you make a cock of yourself?'

No, they wouldn't have. That Ven did believe.

'How's your stomach?' Frankie handed her a coffee.

'It feels absolutely fine. Now.'

'Brilliant. The doctor said you just needed to sleep it off. Now have that coffee and then let's go and get some breakfast,' suggested Frankie gently. 'You'll see that no one will stare at you as the on-ship entertainment. Then, if you feel well enough, we'll go out into Dubrovnik and see the sights. Okay?'

Ven's confidence slipped down a few notches when she stepped out into the corridor and heard the Irish Captain's voice boom over the Tannoy, warning passengers not to buy any foreign medicines from foreign pharmacies, and that trust-worthy help for stomach-aches and sea-sickness was available from the Emporium, or the sick bay if more severe.

'Just think,' put in Frankie, trying to help, 'you may have pre-vented lots of other people from falling down the same hole.'

Ven nodded, wanting to turn back and hide, but she knew that she couldn't stay in her cabin for the rest of the cruise. Best to face the world. And hope to God she didn't run into 'Captain Ocean Sea'.

Luck was not on Ven's side, as far as that was concerned, though. Halfway up the stairs, Frankie doubled back to the cabin for her watch, and Ven went on ahead up to the Buttery to find them a table. She took one step inside the restaurant, only to find Nigel striding towards her. She did such an obvi-ous about-turn that she almost toppled over. Her cheeks had raced from a shade of pale and interesting to burned tandoori by the time Nigel had caught up with her.

'Good morning,' he said, voice overflowing with gallant Gaelic concern. 'And how are you feeling today, Venice?' He looked freshly shaved and pristine and she caught a whiff of his aftershave which had a deliciously fresh tang.

'Oh, hello! Er . . . I'm fine, thank you, much much much better,' said Ven. Her cheeks were boiling hot. One of the chefs could have used her as a stand-in for a George Foreman grill.

'I am so glad,' said Nigel. 'I went down to the sick bay to find out what that medicine was you got from Corfu. Your friend kindly brought it down to Dr Floren. Very strong stuff. Best let us dispose of it safely, I think.'

'Yes, yes of course,' said Ven, trying hard not to get eye-con-tact.

Then Eric and Irene, complete with matching *Mermaidia*-logo-ed baseball hats and thick-soled walking boots on, appeared as well.

'Hello, my love,' said Irene, eyes full of sympathy. 'Are you all right this morning? Eric and I were so worried.'

'Yes, yes I'm fine,' said Ven, trying not to go any redder.

'No buying any foreign medicines today, young lady. If you need any sickness or diarrhoea medicine, come and find Irene or me,' said Eric far too loudly. 'We always bring lots of first aid with us for any eventuality.'

'That's right,' said Irene. 'And it's from Boots so we know it's okay.'

'Anyway, I must away to the bridge,' said Nigel. 'Glad you're fit and well. I shall see you all at dinner, if you'll permit me to join you again.'

'Lovely!' said Ven. At least that way she could be on her best behaviour and prove to the Captain that she was quite normal and not a drug addict really.

'So you all have a nice day now. Are you going ashore?' Nigel asked.

'We most certainly are,' said Eric. Ven nodded too, as Nigel looked for her answer also.

'Remember – plenty of suncream on. It's going to nudge the high nineties,' said Nigel, giving her a friendly salute and a smile warm enough to nudge the high hundreds.

'I will,' replied Ven. 'Bye, Captain Ocean-er . . . nessy.'

As he turned to go, Ven could have sworn she saw Nigel repeat the words 'Ocean Sea' and grin to himself.

Ven spotted Olive, chewing absently on a piece of toast at a table by the window. She was so absorbed in her thoughts that she didn't even notice Ven until she had sat down opposite to her at the table.

'What's up with you?' asked Ven.

'Nothing,' said Olive, too quickly. 'More to the point – how are you?'

'Right as rain. Thank goodness.'

'Good, I'm glad,' said Olive, her face a mask of stress.

'Come on, out with it,' prodded Ven.

And, without further prompting, out it all came. 'Oh Ven, Roz and I had words last night. Big ones and many of them. And I told her about Frankie. I couldn't help it. She was going on about her and Manus again, and I lost it and told her the lot and I walked off and left her. I've had a shit night's sleep because—'

'Ol, Ol, shhh,' Ven interrupted, squeezing her friend's hand. Olive was on the verge of tears. 'Do you know what? I'm glad.'

'Are you?' asked Olive, not convinced that Ven wasn't just being her nice, kind self.

'I am,' replied Ven. She didn't say any more because coming into the restaurant, behind Olive, were Frankie and Roz. Together. 'Bloody hell, Olive. What have you done?'

'What?' said Olive, turning to see what had made Ven go so wide-eyed.

'Morning, you two,' said Roz with a smile. 'How are you feeling, Ven?'

'I'm not well and hallucinating,' said Ven.

Olive couldn't meet Frankie's eyes. Frankie knew why and ruffled up her hair.

'I'm sorry I opened my big fat mouth,' said Olive. 'And I'm sorry to you as well, Roz. I was out of ord—'

'Ol, shush,' said Roz. 'I've been a bit of a twat, haven't I?'

'I think that honour goes to me,' said Frankie, speaking directly now to Ven and Olive. 'Ol, you did the right thing last night.'

'If only you stood up to the Hardcastles like that,' said Roz, and winked. 'I didn't know you had it in you.'

'Thank God it's all out in the open,' Ven sighed, feeling the weight of four long years fall from her shoulders.

'Anyway – less of that. Frankie and I had a mega talk while you were snoring, Ven,' said Roz.

'We had to have a half-time break and ordered chocolate fudge cake from room service at quarter to one,' laughed Frankie.

'We're sorted,' said Roz. 'We're all sorted, I hope.'

Ven burst into tears and threw her arms around Frankie, then around Roz.

'This is the best birthday present I could have wished for.'

'Oy, it's not your birthday till tomorrow,' said Roz. 'Anyway, how are you feeling, Amy Winehouse?'

Ven didn't care any more about what had happened last night. It faded into oblivion beside this. All she cared about was the here and now, Frankie and Roz friends again. *Froz* was once more an active term. And the Fabulous Four were reunited.

'I honestly and truthfully couldn't be better,' she replied.

Chapter 41

Dubrovnik promised to be very busy. There was a huge Italian ship berthed at the side of them, plus a Norwegian one and three massive American ships nearby. And another little vessel in the distance just sailing in which was probably huge but, when compared with the moored giants, looked diddy.

'Royston and Stella are off to a beach today,' announced Frankie, approaching the breakfast-table with her bowl of Granola and side order of two hash browns. 'Roz and I passed them on the stairs on our way up here. He's got nice sober navy-blue shorts on. I nearly didn't recognise him.'

'Don't swear,' said Ven. 'I'm declaring the word "stairs" illegal.' She had been determined to walk up and down them instead of taking the lift, but her resolve was getting weaker and weaker each day.

'What shall we do?' said Olive. 'We are getting off, aren't we? I'm dying to see the city.'

'Me too. Apparently it's lovely,' said Frankie.

'It's going to be heaving,' said Roz, calculating that if these ships had at least two thousand passengers each, then that was an awfully big influx on a port.

There was a shuttle bus at the portside to take them to the old city walls of Dubrovnik. It was a pretty drive there. The bus rose up a steep road flanked by lush green hills which were crowded with orange-roofed dwellings and shops. Narrow twisty lanes veered off at either side, crying out to be explored.

Fifteen minutes from the harbour, the bus deposited them alongside the old city walls, which looked remarkably intact and impenetrable. Ven would have liked to have dragged a certain firm of tradesmen out here to see what good craftsmanship meant after they made such a cock-up of her fireplace.

They walked over the slatted wooden drawbridge to one of the city entrances – the Pile Gate – where two brightly dressed sentries stood in ceremonial guard stance and silently withstood the photographs being taken of them. It was very busy with all nationalities of visitors: lots of Americans and Japanese tourists strung with cameras like comedy caricatures, and Italians with loud expressive gestures.

There were two parts to the Pile Gate, they discovered. After they had passed through the outer arch, there was an inner narrow gate which was very busy with people both entering and leaving. It took a frustratingly long time to step through as the crowds shuffled forwards, but it was worth it to see the city stretch out before them. Whilst Ven was appreciating the lovely Onofrio Fountain, Frankie and Roz were giggling at a waterspout-gargoyle set low into a nearby wall which looked the spitting image of Bruce Forsyth. There were no cars in the Old Town, which was just as well because there was no room on the road with the number of tourists who were sightseeing.

They wandered slowly down the main street – the arterial Stradun which was apparently under the sea until the Middle Ages, its stone cobbles polished by years of tourist-shoes to marble smoothness. To the left, a narrow road led off to a high bank of intriguing steps that Olive wanted to explore, but it was far too hot to climb up to scary heights. Olive said it looked like Harry Potter's Diagon Alley, but still no one volunteered to go with her and discover if there was a Flourish & Blotts present there.

The British tourists were obvious from their reticence to push their way through knots of crowds like the other nationalities. Two people shoved in front of Ven in the ice-cream queue and she was too soft to do her British, 'Excuse me, I think you'll find it's my turn.' Frankie, however, wasn't. She placed Ven out of the way first then claimed the shop assistant's attention with a very loud and impossible-to-ignore order. She was smiling when she came out of the shop with the four large cones.

'I'd forgotten how much fun it was to be bolshy,' she said. Events of the past few years had made her far meeker than she was ever put on earth to be with Italian blood flowing through her. A few spats with some rude tourists had awakened something dormant inside her.

They sat on the steps of St Blaise Church people-watching for five minutes, whilst they ate their enormous ice creams. Two bronze jacks in the form of soldiers struck the big bell in the clock-tower, resulting in a pretty peal, a lovely sound in the hot, clear air. Then they took photographs of each other outside the Sponza Palace – it took a few attempts as tourists kept walking in front of them. Thank goodness for digital cameras, thought Frankie, as she deleted two pictures of a portly Japanese man's bum which had got in front of her as she snapped away. They wandered around the labyrinth of alleyways and through a bustling market, where Frankie bought two bottles of grappa for her dad and a huge lavender bag into which she buried her nose. The scent took her back to school Christmases, sewing lavender pockets to take home for presents. She loved the smell – it was so reminiscent of happy times.

The sun was boiling in the sky; Ven half-expected to look

up and see it melting. Typically a load of British people she recognised from the ship passed and moaned about the heat, which made her laugh to herself. They came to places like this to be hot then couldn't stand it, but then went home and bragged about how fabulous the weather had been, and wished they were back here as soon as they sniffed winter.

It was difficult to find anywhere to eat as all the cafés seemed full. And the shops were bulging with visitors so it was hard to get in them and look around.

'Slow walk back to the shuttle bus, anyone?' suggested Roz, as she had seen everything she wanted to. She was greeted with a flurry of yeses.

They were strolling back to the Pile Gate entrance when a familiar, 'Hello,' halted them in front of a café. Under a bright stripy canopy, Eric and Irene were tucking into big plates of pasta and glasses of plum brandy.

'Drinking at this time, you two?' teased Frankie.

'We deserve it,' said Eric.

'We've just walked around the city walls,' added Irene, raising her glass and wishing them *Cheers*.

'What the hell for?' asked Roz, wiping the drips off her forehead. 'Are you mad?'

'We did it to prove that we could,' said Eric. 'See you later, girls. Formal tonight! Best frocks on, remember.'

They wandered off smiling, leaving Eric and Irene to enjoy their well-earned pasta. The nearer they got to the Onofrio Fountain, the thicker the throng of people became. They joined the queue of tourists trying to get out of the city through the inner Pile Gate. The trouble was, there were as many people wanting to come in – and suddenly the crowd became a crush where no one was moving any which way. Ven pushed back against some big bloke pressuring her forward where there was nowhere to go. Roz noticed Frankie's arms forming a protective cage over her breasts and tried to reach her. It was even scarier for Frankie being short and unable to see over people's heads. She yelped as someone stepped back and elbowed her in the chest.

'Roz, I can't move,' she cried out.

Roz stumbled and was pushed further away from Frankie by a large, wimpy bloke who was saying, 'I feel sick, I have to get out of here,' and flailing his arms like a big girl. Roz wanted to kick him, the selfish bastard. She couldn't see Frankie at all now but she heard Ven shout, 'Roz, are you there?' Thanks to Wimp Man, Roz was now nowhere near her friends. She caught a flash of Frankie swallowed up in the crowd and knew she'd be breathless and panicky. Polite English voices were saying 'This is ridiculous,' amongst louder ramblings in other languages.

In the worst of the crush, Frankie was crying. Everyone around her was at least a foot taller and too intent on getting themselves out of the city to acknowledge anyone else's vulnerability. She was pressed between two solidly-built men and she didn't have the strength to stop the one behind squashing her chest further into the one in front. Suddenly there was a very English, 'Whoa whoa whoa!' and three tall male figures cut between the crowd with determined and considerable force to move the outgoers to the left, the incomers to the right. Two Frankie recognised immediately as men in Vaughan's party – Freddy and his father. The other, head and shoulders above even the tall bloke in front of her who'd have the imprint of her boobs on his back for a few hours to come, had a cleanshaven face, give or take a thin line of beard at the jaw, gelled-back, shoulder-length fair hair – and a magnificent Celtic tattoo. It was Vaughan.

'We'll all move a lot quicker if you don't push,' Vaughan warned in a loud booming voice, his tone – if not his words – understandable in any language. He reached over to Frankie and hoisted her towards him, shielding her from people behind with an arm of iron. He didn't have enough time to say anything other than, 'You're okay now.' Suddenly Frankie felt space around her and Roz grabbing her arm at the other side of the arch. Frankie could breathe again; she stood against the wall trying to still her rasping chest. Then she saw Olive push herself out, followed by Ven deliberately elbowing past someone who'd just stood on her toe.

'You all right, kid?' said Ven, who knew that Frankie always hated being closed in, and anything near her chest area panicked her terribly these days.

'I am now,' said Frankie. 'I feel like I've just plopped out of a birth canal.'

Two policemen nudged into the crowd now to officially sort out the bottle-neck.

'I wish I knew the Croatian for "better late than never",' tutted Roz to their backs.

'Come on, let's get to the shuttle bus and go home,' said Ven. 'I need a big glass of ice wine after that.' Substituting the word 'home' for 'ship' was an unconscious slip of the tongue.

It seemed that some nations enjoyed a good crowd-push more than others. There was pandemonium as a shuttle bus arrived for one of the other ships and the ordered queue disintegrated as everyone ran for the door. Grown men were tugging at each other's shirts and gesticulating madly. Meanwhile the queue for the British *Mermaidia* stood ruler-straight and perfectly calm.

'I'd love to come back here when it was quiet,' said Roz.

'I bet it's lovely at night,' Ven agreed.

Frankie remained quiet. Roz looked at her and noticed how small she was, especially after such a weight loss. Now she was seeing her through different eyes, Roz saw the full extent of the changes in her and it made her ashamed that she had ever thought those changes were down to vanity rather than illness. She vowed to make it up to her – somehow.

The Figurehead shuttle bus pulled up and the *Mermaidia* passengers climbed on. The air conditioning hit them like a delicious cold shower. Every passenger seemed to collapse onto a seat and then begin twittering about the Pile Gate crush.

But the pay-off was that it was extra-restful to enjoy the journey back to the portside, viewing the mountains plunging straight into the sea, the big ships at anchor, the private yachts showing off their swanky presence in the harbour, the pale-stoned houses with their green gardens and bursts of bright purple blossom on the trees. And it really did feel like coming home when they presented their cruise cards at the ship's entrance and put their bags through the security machine.

After one glass of ice wine, all four of them stretched out on sunloungers and alternated between light snoozes and book-reading. Frankie was also giving Ven a crash course in Italian so she could find her way to the hotel she was looking for in Venice. Then, at five-fifteen, the ship set sail. Songs from the deck party around the nearby Neptune pool filtered over – 'La Bamba', 'Tequila'. They joined the people lined up at the sides to wave to passengers on the *Merry Cruises* ship next door. Ven leaned over and watched the Croatian pilot step off the *Mermaidia* onto a small boat. He looked like an elderly James Bond in his slacks and shirt. He waved goodbye to the ship too as his transport twisted sharply in the water and headed back to Dubrovnik. The *Mermaidia* blasted a polite farewell to the mainland, which sounded like a 'thank you for having us' to Ven. There was a real sense of happiness pervading, as if a fishing net of smiles had been cast over the ship. It was odd, but lovely.

Then Nigel's soft voice came over the Tannoy with the information that there was a whale on the portside. The four women stood and watched as something too far away to see jetted up a plume of water into the air and made yet another lovely memory for them all.

Chapter 42

That evening, as they took their places at the dinner-table, Ven asked if anyone else would like a turn at sitting next to Captain Nigel, but everyone seemed quite happy with the present seating arrangements. So Ven sat quietly next to the vacant seat, waiting for their guest to arrive and hoping she could get through the next two hours without making a total twerp of herself.

'Have you seen those blokes who helped us through the crowd in Dubrovnik yet?' Roz asked Frankie. 'We owe them a drink or twelve.'

'Nope,' came the reply. It wasn't for the want of trying though. Frankie had walked all round the ship a few times since they set sail trying to find Vaughan to say thank you for rescuing them. But she hadn't seen anything of him or his party at all. It seemed that she only bumped into him when she wasn't actively trying. She would meet up with him sooner rather than later, she hoped.

Royston was wearing a white shirt with frills down the centre. He looked like the offspring of the Queen's private bingo-caller and Shirley Bassey. Roz reckoned that shirt must have cost a fortune too.

Ven spotted Nigel coming in from the other side of the restaurant and her leg went immediately into a nervous spasm. He really was totally gorgeous. She reached out for her glass of water, knocked over the wine which Angel had just poured out for her and caused havoc yet again.

Oh dear noises came from Irene, even louder ones from Eric. Buzz ran over with a serviette to mop up the worst of it and Ven wanted to die. Captain Nigel arrived just in time to witness the chaos.

'Good evening, everyone,' he said. 'I'm sorry I'm late.' He looked at the red-wine stain spoiling the perfect table.

'My fault again, hey ho,' said Ven. 'Can't blame any medication this time, though.'

'Glad to hear it,' said Nigel.

Elvis whispered something to the Captain, probably about changing the cloth but Nigel waved him away with a, 'No, it's fine, Elvis. Really. There are worse things at sea.' He smiled and little crinkles appeared around his grey, grey eyes. Ven felt her heart boom against her ribcage.

'Have we all had a nice day?' Nigel addressed the table collectively.

A merry chorus of chirruping yeses came in response.

'I heard it was a bit of a crush getting in and out of the Pile Gate.'

'It was really scary,' said Olive. 'We were all caught up in it.'

'I tried to berth another day, because there were too many ships in, but it was impossible,' said Nigel.

'We didn't bother going into the city,' said Royston. 'We got a taxi to a lovely little beach, didn't we, boss?' He turned to his wife for confirmation. Stella had obviously collected quite a few more rays today – she was making Dom Donaldson and Tangerina look like Frosty the Snowman.

'Nice when we got through into the city though,' said Olive. 'Beautiful.'

'We walked around the city walls,' said Eric proudly. 'Marvellous view. I've never managed it before so we were determined this time, weren't we, Irene?'

'Absolutely,' said Irene, who was looking lovely that evening with a creamy light tan building nicely and her lovely brave-pink dress contrasting beautifully with her white hair, which had obviously been done in the salon for that evening.

'Do you ever get off with the passengers, Captain?' asked Ven, trying to contribute something sensible to the conversation and ending up doing quite the opposite. 'I mean, go off with them . . . leave . . . disembark.'

'Here, have a big roll, stuff it in your mouth and shut yourself up,' Roz whispered in Ven's ear as Buzz reached between them with the bread-basket.

'Sometimes I do,' said Nigel, crinkled eyes fully trained on Ven. Her cheeks could have given the red-wine patch on the tablecloth a run for its money. 'I'm getting off at Venice actually. I always try and "get off with the passengers" at Venice.'

Ooh, was that a hint of a flirt there, Olive, Roz and Frankie each asked themselves. Interesting.

'You must go on a gondola at Venice, Venice,' said Eric, chortling at himself.

'We fully intend to,' said Frankie.

'It's a beautiful name: Venice,' said Irene.

'She hates it,' Roz thumbed at Ven. 'She used to go mad at school if anyone called her anything but "Ven".'

'Hark at you – Rosalind!' said Frankie.

'Hark at you as well – Francesca!' returned Roz.

'Why would you all want to shorten such lovely names?' tutted Irene.

'Venice is okay if you're a film star,' said Ven. 'You need to have a fancy surname and parents with bags of money to carry it off. Venice Smith just sounded so wrong. Like Tatiana Riley or . . . or Fanny Sidebottom.'

Oh NO did I really say Fanny? Ven tried not to cringe, then Nigel said, 'I have a niece called Tatiana Riley.'

'Oh, please tell me you're joking,' said Ven with panic strain-
ing her voice.

'Yes, I'm joking,' Nigel grinned.

Ven's heart-rate had just about slowed down when the
starters arrived. She liked the sound of the Feuillête of Poached
Egg, but she wasn't going to show herself up trying to pro-
nounce it, so she plumped for the roasted beetroot and rocket
salad, followed by steamed lemon sole stuffed with a prawn
mousseline in a dill butter sauce. Roz was really going for it
tonight with loin of pork with rosemary and roasted pumpkin.
And for someone who was supposed to be watching her carbs,
she didn't half get stuck into the croquette potatoes when Buzz
expertly served them up.

'So what are you doing for your big day tomorrow then,
Venice?' asked Nigel over a dessert of rich chocolate rum slices
garnished with fruit coulis.

'Well, we're riding on a gondola, having lunch, then I'm
going to try and find the hotel where Mum and Dad had their
honeymoon and conceived me.'

'Ah, so you were a honeymoon baby?'

God, he said 'honeymoon' so beautifully, thought Ven. *Honi-
muin.*

'Yep,' said Ven. 'I'm leaving the others to their own devices
for a bit and wandering around by myself.'

'There's no nicer place to wander aimlessly,' said Royston.
'Get to Saint Mark's Square and just let yourself off the lead,
that's what I always say.'

'Then we're having caviar and champers!' put in Olive, who
really couldn't imagine what caviar tasted like. She hoped she
wouldn't be too disappointed – like she was when she first had
oysters. Yeurch. They didn't make her feel randy, only nauseous.

'You should get up about six o'clock tomorrow morning
and watch us sail into the Grand Canal,' added Eric. 'Stunning.'

'Six?' said Frankie. 'Sod that for a lark, Eric.'

Milly Johnson

'Well, maybe you'd all like to come up to the bridge tomorrow and watch us leave the Grand Canal instead,' Nigel offered.

'Ooh, could we?' twittered Irene. 'That would be marvellous.'

'Eeeh, it would that,' echoed Eric. 'Thank you very much, Captain. We'd like that.'

'Settled then,' said Nigel, dabbing at his lips with a serviette and making a move to stand. 'All of you meet me at Reception at half past four tomorrow. Now, if you'll excuse me, have a wonderful day tomorrow, won't you? Venice, have a very happy birthday.'

'Thank you, Mr . . . Captain O'Shaughnessy,' said Ven, thinking that even though she'd remembered his name correctly, she still pronounced it *Ocean Sea*.

'What a lovely man,' said Stella as she watched the Captain having a word with Supremo. 'Very handsome. Bet he's got a girl in every port.'

'Port, that's a good idea,' said Royston. 'Angel? Angel love, can we have a round of ports after the coffee.'

Eric protested immediately, brandishing his cruise card. 'My turn.'

'No, mate, I'm loaded,' said Royston. 'I insist.'

'Oh let him, Eric, he gets his pleasure from flashing his wad. Don't ruin his holiday.' Stella flapped her hand at him to shut up. And she had great intentions of letting her husband be very happy in some jewellery shops in Venice tomorrow.

After coffee and the most delicious home-made cherry fudge accompaniment, the four women headed off to the theatre to watch the Mermaidia Theatre Company perform *Rocket Man*, a tribute to Elton John. Roz, however, suddenly darted off, telling them to save her a place and that she'd be there in a moment because she needed the loo. She didn't; she had just spotted Dom Donaldson and Tangerina Orange Jelly having a drink in Darcy's – the bar next to the theatre. Darcy's was a plush-seated, non-children bar which allowed smoking. Roz pulled out the small birthday card she had bought from the Emporium a couple of days ago, and which she had been carrying around with her in the hope of bumping into him. You couldn't miss him tonight though, in a dark blue sequinned jacket that only someone very macho could pull off.

'Excuse me,' she said, quite meekly for Roz. 'I know it's an imposition but it's my friend's fortieth birthday tomorrow and she's such a fan of yours. It would absolutely make her day if you would just sign this card for her. Her name is Venice – as in the city.'

Dom Donaldson, so twinkly-eyed and smiley on the soap in which he acted, turned an ice-chipped gaze onto Roz who was holding out the card and a pen hopefully. He took them, without saying a word, and scribbled something on the card before closing it and thrusting it back to her.

'Thank you so much,' said Roz. 'She'll be thrilled. I'm so sorry to have interrupted you. Have a lovely evening. And thank you again.'

She mouthed, 'Miserable bastard,' to herself as she left the bar. Anyway, Ven would be thrilled and that's all that mattered. Outside the theatre, she stole a peek at what he'd written. There in angry capitals were the words GO AWAY I'M ON HOLLIDAY!

The rotten ... Roz turned on her heel and took two steps back to Darcy's to tell that jumped-up little turd a word or two of hard truth, then she stopped herself. What good would that do? It wasn't as if he'd apologise and say, 'Oh I am sorry, let me get you another card and do it properly for your friend.' He was just one of those smarmy actor types who'd got a bit of female attention and become a god in his own eyes. He made Russell Crowe look like Graham Norton, the bad-tempered cock. Plus he couldn't even spell 'holiday'! Why didn't these celebrities realise that all they had to do was be nice to the people who had given them their status in the first place? He just had to write *Happy Birthday* on a card, for God's sake, not donate a kidney.

Roz contemplated buying another card and faking his signature, but knowing Ven she would go up and thank him and then he'd take pleasure in putting her right and that would ruin her day. Better just to abort that surprise. Roz ripped up the card with a strength she would have liked to have exerted on Dom Donaldson's head and put it in the circular bin outside the theatre. Venice would have a brilliant birthday without that vain shite's contribution. They'd all make sure of that.

Roz took a deep composing breath outside the theatre before joining the others. She was standing with her back to the wall, opposite the staircase. Her breath had just about got back to normal when a man came down the stairs and her eyes fixed on his and could not tear themselves away. For there, in a magnificently cut black suit and bow-tie and the whitest shirt she had ever seen, was Raul Cruz. His eyes were locked onto Roz's with equal force. And though he did not say anything, but merely nodded his head to her, she almost slid down the wall and became a pool of drool.

Day 9: Venice

Dress Code: Semi-Formal

Chapter 43

For David Hardcastle, 24 August would forever after be known as 'the day when his life went totally tits up'. It was on this date that everything as he knew it was totally slaughtered with a wrecking ball and then immediately began to reconstruct itself in an entirely different way. Like the old Co-op on Newland Street, razed to the ground and quickly rebuilt as a gym. Although maybe that wasn't the wisest parallel, seeing as the gym developed a structural problem and had to be demolished within six months.

It started innocuously enough with a planned cooked breakfast. He hummed as he snipped at the sausage links and cut up tomatoes and mushrooms and thick slices of black pudding. As the lard in the frying pan began to melt and give its first limp spit, the phone rang. He heard his mother pick up and start talking to someone on it.

'Yes, this is Doreen Hardcastle . . . Oh, I am so sorry to hear that,' she was saying. Then her voice dropped to a low whisper and he didn't hear anything again until, 'Yes, yes . . . tomorrow. I'll be here . . . Yes, of course I still do – need you ask? . . . Till later then.'

The smoky breakfast smells snaked up David's nostrils and made his enormous stomach growl with anticipation. He reached for the egg box, deciding he'd cook three this morning –

two for himself and one for his mother – but he was to discover that the egg box had been sitting in the cupboard empty. It was one of Kevin's many annoying habits, putting empty packages back on shelves instead of throwing them in the bin.

'Bloody Kevin!' he growled. The only thing he didn't use and abuse in this house was toothpaste. There was no way David could have a cooked breakfast without fried eggs – it was illegal in the Hardcastle household. Angrily, he twisted the knob of the hob down to the lowest setting and felt in his pockets for some money. Apart from two pence and a ball of tissues that smelled vaguely of cheese, they were totally empty.

'Mum, have you any money for eggs?' he called. 'I'll have to nip to Warren Street shop and I've got no cash at all. Not a bean.'

He went into the lounge to find his mother deep in thought, staring into space.

'Mum? We haven't any eggs. Have you any change?'

Doreen shifted her attention to her son. He looked crest-fallen. She didn't see a man one step away from a monster cooked breakfast, only her little boy with a pushed-out lip of sadness. Doreen studied him. It was the same face he used to pull when he wanted a Curly Wurly and had spent all his pocket money. So like his father when he needed solace.

Yes, she decided, it was time now. The fates had stepped in this morning and told her as much. She reached into her cleavage for the key she wore as a pendant.

'I've got some change upstairs,' she said. 'In the trunk under my bed.'

'Oh heck, haven't we anything down here? I'm going to ruin the breakfast otherwise.'

'In the trunk under my bed upstairs,' Doreen said again, holding out the small key. It felt warm and sweaty in David's hand.

'Okay,' he sighed, taking the key and running upstairs as fast as his bulk would carry him.

His mother's bedroom was the biggest one in the house, a total waste seeing as she never slept in it. Olive kept it dust-free and as immaculate as the rest of the house, though. David got on his knees and reached under the bed for the trunk which he had always presumed his mother kept her 'treasures' in – the Mother's Day cards he'd made at school, photos, memorabilia, etc. He tugged it out but it took considerable effort.

'Blimey, Mum, what have you got in here? It weighs a bleeding ton,' he said to himself. He slid the key in the lock and the lid sprang open. Inside were indeed a scattering of photos and baby bootees and the Blue Peter badge he had found in the park but told everyone that he earned it for inventing a machine that turned vegetables into chocolate. Not exactly the sort of currency that the Warren Street shop would accept.

'Mum, there's nothing . . .' he began to shout.

'Lift the flap in the bottom, son!' Doreen's voice cut in and travelled upstairs.

David felt around and found a metal loop. He pulled it and a flap was released. He lifted it and stared down at what lay underneath. Wads and wads of paper money, neatly tied with elastic bands, and bags of two-pound coins. The box was so deep it seemed to go on for ever; it was like something out of *Treasure Island*. The sight trampled over all thoughts of his cooked breakfast on the floor below. Something not even pictures of Samantha Fox in her heyday could have done.

He was hallucinating through lack of food, obviously. He closed the lid and snapped it open again, but yes – the money was still there. He took out a single five-pound note, closed the lid again, locked it, slid it back under the bed and lumbered downstairs in a haze. Had his mother robbed a bank? It sounded incredible, but then again, she had a secret 'able-bodied' life he'd not known about until recently. Who was to say that masquerading as a poor disabled lady wasn't part of some bigger, stranger charade?

'What . . .where . . .' he blundered, pointing upstairs.

'It's a nest egg,' said Doreen. 'It's all yours.'

'Mine!' said David.

'I didn't put it in the bank because I don't trust banks. I turned out to be right as well, didn't I?' Doreen nodded smugly, although she had had more than a minor panic recently when she thought Olive had found her secret stash and run off with it. 'Plus I don't want any greedy council bastards taking it off me if I ever went in a home.'

'But where's it come from, Mum?'

'Your father,' said Doreen.

'Dad? *Dad?* Dad didn't have a pot to piss in!'

'Your father,' corrected Doreen, 'had a selection of pots to piss in. Plus I added to it by betting some of it on horses. I used to be very good at winning on the nags. I should have been a professional gambler, your father used to say.'

'Dad? He never gambled in his life!' Herbert Hardcastle was a non-drinking, non-smoking, non-gambling paragon of virtue.

'David,' said Doreen with a softness in her voice he hadn't heard for years, 'we're going to have a visitor later on today. I want you to tidy around a bit so it's nice, like Olive does it. All will become clear, son.'

'Who's coming?' David asked, scratching his head.

'Wait and see,' said Doreen, putting her hand over his and giving it a fond squeeze. 'Now, get out the Hoover, love, after you've been to the shop. There's a good lad.'

Chapter 44

Venice awoke to a none-too-gentle knock on the door. It was only eight o'clock, but when she opened it, her three friends pushed their way into her cabin bearing cards, presents, hugs, streamers and flowers.

'Happy fortieth birthday to you . . .' they sang.

'Fabulous day as well, weatherwise,' said Olive. 'I had a look on deck. It's so beautiful outside. Look,' and she pulled Ven's curtains open. The weather might have been lovely, but the view was disappointing – lots of tall industrial chimneys and scrappy-looking boats – even if they were bathed in early-morning misty sunlight.

A second later and there was another knock at the door.

'I'll get it,' said Roz, who knew who it was, because she had arranged it. Or at least some of it. In came Jesus trundling a trolley containing four long flutes of Bucks Fizz, a huge plate of handmade truffles, an arrangement of pink flowers and a pretty posy of yellow roses. Jesus was grinning and wished Ven a very happy birthday also before leaving the women to raise a toast to the birthday girl and dive on the choccies.

'Coffee truffles!' said Roz. 'We didn't order these – or the roses. I bet they're from the competition people.'

'Yes, I expect so,' said Ven, looking rather puzzled.

'Ooh,' said Olive, spotting a card under the posy and wolf-whistling. '"From Captain Ocean Sea and the crew." Ooohhhh! He's actually written "Ocean Sea" as well, not "O'Shaughnessy".'

'Oooh,' the others joined in the trill.

There was yet another knock on the door – more flowers. This time the card read *From Andrew and all at Figurehead Cruises*.

Then more flowers – from Royston and Stella.

'Bloody hell, it looks like Donny Road Crem in here!' laughed Roz. 'Here, open your presents.'

There was the beautiful, old-gold heart-shaped locket which Olive and Roz had bought. It had a tiny ring of red roses engraved on the front, circling a swirly letter V. From Frankie there was a huge showy diamanté necklace and matching earrings – Ven could never have enough jewellery, they'd always known that. Manus had sent a silver bracelet, the links all cats with tiny green eyes. Roz felt a dull ache when she saw it released from its clumsy wrapping. He had chosen that gift so carefully because it was perfectly suited to Ven. She gulped down a sudden tearful feeling and wished she could ring him.

Roz had switched on her phone that morning with the intention of texting *Missing you* to him. But then she thought: what if he didn't reply? How would that make her feel? So she didn't send it, after all. She clicked her phone shut and imagined that he was thinking the same, scared to get in contact for fear of rejection. This break had to be one of her most stupid suggestions ever, and boy, did she have some making-up to do. The damage would need much more than a couple of bottles of Limoncello to mend. Dragging her focus away from Frankie had made her realise the full picture of what a bitch she had been to him. She couldn't just turn on being nice again. Not at this distance. She needed to give him space too.

'Get dressed, Ven, and we'll have a sit-down breakfast in the

Ambrosia this morning instead of slumming it in the Buttery,' said Frankie, popping another truffle into her mouth.

'You can't "slum" it anywhere on here,' said Roz. 'It's impossible.'

'Give me five minutes then,' said Ven, jumping off the bed, gathering up some fresh clothes and disappearing into the bathroom.

'Roses from the Captain?' Frankie raised her eyebrows. 'I'm sure that doesn't happen to everyone who has a birthday on the ship.'

'It *is* her fortieth,' said Roz. 'And he *is* sitting next to her at the dinner-table.'

'Still . . .' said Frankie with a mischievous glint in her eye, 'that would be rather nice, wouldn't it – a little dalliance with a tall, dark, handsome man, especially one in a sexy white uniform? She's well overdue a snog.'

'Da-da!' Ven was ready in a flash and burst out of the bathroom clad in a white top with a pretty frill and a bright green short skirt. It showed off her tan to perfection. She put her birthday heart-shaped locket on, saving the diamanté one for that evening, applied a slick of lipstick, grabbed her bag and announced that she was ready. 'Oh, and my ears were burning in there. You were on about those flowers from the Captain, weren't you?'

'Course we were,' said Roz, following her out of the door. 'I'll be very interested to see what happens at dinner. Wonder if you'll get a gypsy violinist instead of the waiters' choir.'

'Oh God,' said Ven, visibly cringing. 'I'd forgotten about that ordeal.'

Chapter 45

In 15, Land Lane, David was dusting in preparation for the arrival of the mystery visitor. A grey film had landed everywhere since Olive had gone on holiday and it annoyed him. He had taken a clean house for granted and he now realised that muck didn't shift by itself. He flicked the cloth and sent the dust motes swirling in the air. They'd fly around a bit and then settle again so he wouldn't actually get rid of them, he thought. What a waste of time. How anyone could do cleaning for a living was beyond him.

At twelve, Kevin made lunch for everyone. Over the past couple of days he'd turned into Gordon Ramsay in the kitchen – or at least a cut-price version. He had poured boiling water over three chicken-and-mushroom pot noodles and stirred them. Then he had tipped them on a plate with some slices of turkey burgers and sprinkled the whole thing liberally with dried parsley and a dash of soy sauce. Sweet had been a slice of swiss roll each and squirty cream with a Cadbury's chocolate finger stuck in the middle of it like a totem pole. Then he made himself scarce for a couple of hours, as Doreen had asked, until the mystery man – or woman – had left. Now Doreen was sitting in her smartest dress and had even applied some make-up and curled her hair with her hotbrush. David couldn't remember ever seeing his mother in make-up. Her non-existent eyebrows were now two high brown arches, her eyelids seventies blue as if she was in Abba, and her lips had been extended by very pink lipstick that he was sure would have shown up in the dark. It was like some awful ventriloquist doll come to life.

'Put that duster down now and get the kettle on ready for our visitor, David.'

'Who is it, Mam?'

'Wait and see.'

Right on cue as the kettle heralded its boiling point with a shrill whistle, there was a sharp tattoo of raps on the front door. Doreen nodded at David to go and answer it whilst she straightened herself up and patted her curls.

At the door, David wasn't sure he dare open it because his imagination was going into overdrive about who he would find there. The police was one option – come to arrest his mother for her part in The Great Train Robbery. But when David did take a deep breath and open the door, his brain experienced the biggest anti-climax imaginable. For there stood Vernon Turbot, the owner of the local fish shop who definitely wasn't the some-one his mother had done herself up like Danny La Rue for.

Or maybe he was, because Vernon was dressed in a very sharp black suit, complete with a black band on one arm and holding a very nice and expensive bunch of tightly petalled vel-vety red roses.

'Hello lad,' said Vernon with that odd fondness in his voice that was present whenever he spoke to David in his shop. 'I've come to see your mother.'

'Come in,' called Doreen, in such a high voice that David wondered if she'd just sucked some helium out of a canister.

David stood aside to let in the man they'd always bought their fish and chips from. Just the ordinary man who lived a few streets away and who was hardly George Clooney. So why would his mother have got herself tarted up like that for him?

Vernon handed over the flowers to a very twittery Doreen, who coo-ed over them before telling David to get a vase to put them in.

'Add a bit of sugar to the water and they'll last a couple of extra days,' threw in Vernon. David obediently got a vase out of a kitchen cupboard, put in sugar and tapwater whilst shaking his head and muttering under his breath that he wished someone would tell him what the bloody hell was going on. Shrieks of delight from his mother and Mr Turbot were filtering through from the lounge.

'I was just saying, it's lonely being a widower,' said Vernon to David when he returned with the flowers in the vase.

'Oh, I'm sorry, I didn't know your wife had passed on, Mr Turbot,' said David, mustering up a bit of guilty sympathy then. 'When did that happen?'

'Friday,' said Vernon.

'Friday!' echoed David. It was only Monday now. Crikey, he didn't let the grass grow beneath his feet, did he?

'Aye, lad, but you can't afford to muck about wasting time at our age.'

'That's why we're getting married as soon as we can,' said Doreen, wiggling her left hand which was now sporting a serious diamond ring on the third finger.

'You're doing what?' said David, reaching a finger in his ear to unplug the wax that must have been distorting his hearing.

'Obviously we'll wait until after tomorrow's funeral,' said Vernon, stroking Doreen's knuckles and then placing a tender kiss on the back of her hand.

'Obviously,' said David. If he had thought today and all that trunk business didn't make any sense, that was nothing to all this!

'You see, lad, ours is no ordinary love story,' Vernon went on.

'Love story? Since Friday?' cried David. He was going mad. Sure as eggs were eggs. Maybe they weren't, though. Maybe eggs were bananas – anything was possible in this world in which he now found himself.

'No, silly boy,' Doreen giggled. 'Our story begins forty-one years ago.'

David opened his mouth to say, 'What?' but no words came out. They were glued to a big ball of shock that was stuck in his voicebox.

'I was married to the late Mrs Turbot then,' continued Vernon. 'Her parents wanted me to marry her and my parents wanted it as well, so we did. Like you did in those days. We were both virgins and didn't know owt about passion.'

'Or orgasms,' added Doreen.

Oh God, thought David, hoping another one of those sex speeches of his mother's wasn't going to start up. He'd been having nightmares ever since she revealed that his dad didn't know what foreplay was. He didn't have a part of his brain that was comfortable storing information about his parents swapping bodily fluids, however rare an occurrence that seemed to have been.

'Then one day, into my chip shop walked this slim, leggy, dark-haired beauty,' continued Vernon wistfully.

'Who was that then?' said David.

'Me, of course,' said Doreen, her laugh as tinkly as a crystal glass being gently rapped by a dainty silver spoon.

'I'll never forget what you ordered,' said Vernon. 'Fish and chips twice, scraps and a pickled egg.'

'And they say romance is dead,' said David to himself under his breath.

'I thought, She's ordered two fish, I bet she's married, and my heart sank,' said Vernon.

David wondered if he should be jotting this down and writing it up later as a Mills & Boon.

'I was married too, but I couldn't resist him,' said Doreen. 'Our passion knew no bounds. Pogley Top Woods in the summer, in the open air, we—'

'No, no!' said David. He didn't want to have Pogley Top Woods blighted with a picture of his mum and the local fish-and-chip magnate rolling around in them.

'. . . consummated our love,' said Doreen, unstoppable now.

'We were young and daft and in love,' said Vernon. 'I'd never felt owt like it. I was hook, line and sinker in.'

'I couldn't think about anything but him!' smiled Doreen.

'Obsession. That's what it was. We couldn't have fought it. Not even with a Sherman tank and two Foreign Legions. *In vino veritas* – I came, I saw, I conquered.'

'We never thought there would be consequences . . .'

A silence hung in the air then. A heavy one, full of secrets.

'What sort of consequences?' asked David suspiciously. He dreaded to think. He hoped the answer didn't involve the word 'crabs'.

'Pregnancy,' said Doreen in a very soft, warm voice.

David's mouth moved over the word, but his voice was gone. What the hell was she telling him? That he had an older brother and they were all going to meet up on *The Jeremy Kyle Show*?

'I didn't shirk my duties,' said Vernon, straightening his spine. 'I gave your mother a lump sum and have paid her something every week since. And you never went short of extra portions when you came to my shop. I always gave you large peas but charged you for small.'

'It was a travesty because your dad was a good man, David love, but he was crap in the bedroom. Alas, that's what you get for marrying a much older man,' sniffed Doreen. 'Ask him to put a shelf up and it would be perfect, ask him for cunnilingus and he'd disappear to his shed.'

David missed the last half of that sentence because he started to 'la la' loudly to drown out Doreen's voice.

'Mrs Turbot fell ill shortly after your mum got pregnant,' said Vernon. 'I wanted to leave her, but I couldn't. It wouldn't have been right. Eeh, Beryl was a creaking gate for forty long years.'

'We had to end the affair, we didn't want any scandal, but at least I had my little souvenir,' smiled Doreen, looking at her son fondly with lipstick all over her teeth.

'I used to see you walking past the chip shop to the bookies and sigh,' said Vernon, gazing deep into Doreen's eyes. 'I never fell out of love with you.'

'Or I with you, Vernon. We vowed that one day we'd be together, when it was right in the eyes of God.'

'When Herbert and Beryl had died.'

Jesus. Move over, Barbara Cartland.

'Where's this baby now?' asked David. He wished there was an inhaler handy because he was losing his breath. 'Did you have him adopted?'

Doreen held out her hand towards David. He took it and then felt his other hand being squeezed by the man who sold fish suppers on Lamb Street.

'That's why you're called D-A-V-I-D,' said Doreen, gazing alternately at him then Vernon with the look of someone who was in raptures – or on crack cocaine. Her eyes were almost pulsing out big cartoon hearts in Vernon Turbot's direction. It was quite sweet in a horrible, macabre way how they looked like a cover of a Mills & Boon for geriatrics.

'Eh?' said David. What the frig had his name got to do with anything?

'It stands for Doreen – And – Vernon – Immortally – Devoted.'

'You're my son, lad,' said Vernon. 'You are baby Turbot.'

Chapter 46

The phone in Manus's pocket rumbled and he snatched it out and quickly looked at it, then threw it angrily down on the desk. He didn't want a special offer on Domino's Pizzas. He wanted Roz to send him a text or ring – anything to let him know she was missing him. He had been on the brink of dialling her number so many times since she went on holiday, but had successfully fought the temptation. Roz was the one who had made the rule of non-contact so she must be the one to break it. She would only resent it if the first move came from him. He wondered if she was missing him. He didn't want to think about missing her, because he did and it hurt. He combatted those feelings by working hard until he was dog tired and then coming home and going straight to bed. He didn't know how much longer he would be doing that though, because it was no way to live. But then neither had the past four years been any better.

The phone rumbled again, this time an incoming call – an unknown number. He picked it up and pressed connect.

'Hello, Manus Howard.'

'Hello, Manus, it's me again. The pest.' Jonie. With immaculate timing and a voice as soft as velvet.

'Hello, Jonie.' Manus felt his frown smooth, his grimace soften.

'Listen, I've been thinking. I told you Layla and Tim were coming over for dinner soon. Well, we've fixed a date for Saturday – why don't you come too?'

Manus opened his mouth to refuse automatically, but no words came out.

'I know I'm putting you on the spot,' Jonie went on, 'so think about it and let me know. I was telling them that we'd met quite by chance and they said they'd love to see you again. And I'm a damned good cook!' She laughed. A nice sound that said she was happy to be talking to him and really hoped he'd join them. 'It's better than sitting in the house by yourself, surely? It'll give you a break from buying a Greggs pasty on the way home from work too. Please say you will come.'

'Cheeky!' replied Manus. 'I can look after myself, you know. I'm not an entirely useless man.'

'I never for one minute thought you were,' said Jonie. 'I don't want to hold you up or pressure you – but please come, please, please, please. It'll be fun, I promise. We'll have a laugh.'

And Manus, sick of his own company in the house, sick of eating by himself, sick of being constantly lonely, sick of having no one to laugh with, found himself saying, 'Thank you, Jonie. Yes, I would love to come and have dinner with you all on Saturday.'

Breakfast in the Ambrosia was a very relaxed affair. Instead of queueing with a tray and helping themselves, the four women sat at a table, perused a menu at their leisure whilst being served coffee and orange juice by waiters, then gave their order.

'Why don't we do this every morning?' said Roz, buttering a slice of toast.

'I kind of like the Buttery, though,' said Olive. 'The view is lovely up there. Plus I'm not sure I could eat this amount of food every morning.' She pointed to the plate of Full English which she had just been given. Admittedly the portion was a perfect dainty breakfast size, not too over-facing: two-pound-coin size black pudding, dinky sausage, but it was still far more than she was used to in the morning. 'Nice for a treat though,' she added with a sigh, as the waiter appeared from behind her to grind some black pepper over the plate for her.

After a quick teeth-brush and loo call in their cabins, the four women headed out of the ship and got on the launch boat that would take them from the portside directly to Saint Mark's Square. It turned left past a huge Italian cruise ship and bumped across the water, buffeted by a mischievous swell. Ven looked out of the window and her disappointment at the view changed to one of delight as things began to look a lot more 'Venicey' the nearer they got to the square. Buildings started to appear which were in pretty Saint Clement's colours: lemon and cream stone with earthy-orange roofs; domes and towers came into sight on the skyline, and on the water cheeky little boats moved to and fro next to the berths of luxurious private yachts.

Half an hour later and they were in the beautiful Venice of films and books. To the left, gondolas rocked in the water, gondoliers with hats and stripy tops balanced on the backs of them. To the right was the covered Bridge of Sighs, the intricate stone façade of the Doges Palace, and the pigeon-heavy Piazza San Marco. Bells were ringing, and even they sounded as if they had an Italian accent. They wouldn't have made the same sound anywhere else in the world.

'Of course we're going on a gondola first,' said Roz, joining the queue. 'Although if anyone tries to sing "Just One Cornetto" I will chuck that person overboard.'

'I'd take that red T-shirt off,' said Venice to Frankie. 'You look like that homicidal dwarf maniac in the film *Don't Look Now*. We've no chance of getting a gondolier to take us whilst you're wearing that.'

'Ha ha, very funny,' said Frankie. She had bought the red T-shirt in Market Avenue the previous evening after noticing how drab her wardrobe was looking these days. For the first time in ages, she felt brave enough to risk attracting attention to herself with a bright shade or two of her old favourite colour red.

'Isn't it gorgeous?' said Roz, rotating to take in the whole of Venice and shielding her eyes from the sun. 'It *is* just like a film set.'

'It's fish-shaped, look,' said Olive, holding out the complimentary map they had been given as they came off the ship. 'And did you know it was named after Venus, the Goddess of Love?'

'Mr Metaxas taught you well, my child,' scoffed Roz. 'I wonder what else he would have liked to have taught you.'

'Alone together, in the stationery cupboard,' added Ven, getting a good-humoured slap from Olive for that.

'That's Giudecca Island somewhere over there,' pointed Frankie. 'Where the Hotel Cipriani is. Look at those wooden boats with the hotel's name on the side. Anyone fancy a very expensive lunch?'

'I wish,' said Roz.

'And that's the island called San Servolo,' Frankie went on. 'Far more suited to us.'

'Cheaper restaurant?' asked Roz.

'Loony bin,' corrected Frankie. 'At least, it used to be.'

'Cheeky cow,' laughed Roz, moving forward down the queue. They were next now. Two gondoliers were heading towards them – a tall, hunky one with muscles bulging out of his blue and white top, and a little fat hairy one talking into his mobile.

'Bet you can guess which one we will get,' tutted Ven. But the gods were smiling down on them. Mr Hunky came in first and held out his hand to Ven because the water was quite bobbly and the boat was rising and sinking quite dramatically on the swell.

He signalled that Roz and Olive were to sit on the sides and Frankie on the front-facing seat with Ven.

'You're the ballast,' said Roz.

'And this is the Italian for "go arse" – *ma vai a quel paese!*' Frankie replied, with a shrug of Italian passion. God, she had missed the banter with Roz!

The gondolier guided them skilfully along the canals. There had been a rise in the water levels and the girls had to lean to one side under certain bridges to get them through. It was such a beautiful calm journey, although some berks in the gondola in front of them were singing 'Just One Cornetto' at full blast.

'Bet they haven't heard that one before,' said Roz. 'We English are so predictable.'

'We Italians have far more class,' sniffed Frankie. '"O Sole Mio" is perfectly acceptable to trill.'

'I thought the water would be smelly,' said Ven, pleasantly surprised that there was just the merest niff of stale water. If anything, there was a heavier scent of basil in the air – wafting from restaurants.

As the gondolier pushed his boat along the water channels, passing under the bridges gave them some cool relief from the damp-edged heat. Sightseers above them took aim and snapped photos, prompting Frankie to say that she felt like a film star.

It was so beautifully tranquil on the gondola ride, the only sound the slap of water against the boat and the occasional commentary from the gondolier. 'This pink house is where Mozart lived for a while . . . There are four hundred and thirty-six bridges in Venice, and one hundred and seventeen small islands . . .'

There were a lot of ships in the harbour which meant crowds of tourists, but there on the gondola, no one was pushing anyone or trying to get past with sharp elbows; it was blissful. Washing hung from windows, water swished over the bottom steps of hotel entrances, flowers grew everywhere; it was chocolate-box lovely.

And when their ride was over, they were all reluctant to get off – although Mr Hunky's hand on their arms and the other on their waists in assistance was a small consolation prize in reaching terra firma again.

'That was wonderful,' said Ven dreamily. 'I don't think anything can top that.'

'Oh? I would have thought flowers from Captain *Ocean Sea* might have been your highlight of the day,' teased Roz.

'We're just around the corner from the Rialto Bridge, come on,' urged Frankie, striding off.

'I am getting so hungry,' said Olive as her nostrils were

assaulted by all the food smells in the air: pastry, pizza, chocolate.

The Rialto Bridge was made up of inward-facing shops with
a line of stalls running up the middle. It was a feast of interest,
with lots of beautiful masks for sale. They all bought one, and
Ven got extra ones for Jen and her daughter and an Inter-Milan
football shirt for her nephew.

A man was selling slices of coconut in a shower of icy water
next to a woman trying to tempt tourists with cups of fresh
fruit slivers.

'I need food urgently now!' cried Olive. 'This sodding sea air
is going to make me put twelve stone on.'

'You didn't have all that much to eat for breakfast though,'
said Roz. 'The sausage was tiny.'

'That reminds me, wonder how your David is?' said Ven
with a nudge.

'Oh, don't say that! You'll set her off worrying that they've all
died without her there to wipe their bums,' admonished Roz.
But Olive was not going to let her thoughts travel back over the
sea to home. Whatever it was that was allowing her to enjoy
herself and not think about the occupants of 15, Land Lane
today, she was more than grateful to it.

'Let's head back to Saint Mark's Square and find a nice
restaurant for lunch,' suggested Ven.

'Isn't it really dear there?' asked Olive.

'Yes,' said Frankie. 'But at least you'll get a table. All the
cheap places are packed solid.'

'It'll cost a bomb,' said Olive. In saying that, she would have
sold her liver for a bread roll.

'It's my birthday, so let's do it,' said Ven, following Frankie
along the narrow streets and over some of the bridges under
which they had just travelled.

'What about here?' she said, as they drew level with the
almost entirely glass façade of a very grand-looking café with

pale swishy curtains tied back with generous swags of material. 'Gran Caffè Polo.'

'Ven, shhh,' said Roz. 'They've just charged you five quid for saying the name of the place out loud.'

But Ven ignored her and pushed open the door. As soon as they entered, they were in another world. A quiet, cool, dignified one of yesteryear.

'This is *so* not going to be cheap,' whispered Roz. 'The waiters are in frigging Armani!'

A tall smart Italian waiter, better dressed than a bridal groom, smiled a perfect-toothed smile and beckoned them past a glass cabinet filled with gift-cakes and biscuits, and into the downstairs restaurant. It was a beautiful room, with pale lemon and green walls, huge oval mirrors and old, dark portraits – everything exquisitely shabby-chic.

The waiter led them to a window table. Outside, crowds scurried and perspired, occasionally stopping to gawp through the glass to see what sort of people dined in places like this. He then produced menus for each of them with a practised flourish and a basket of bread and breadsticks.

'The water's eight euros a glass!' said Roz in a whisper so high it nearly shattered the huge crystal chandelier above their heads.

'*How* much?' shrieked Olive – it was the most commonly asked question by Yorkshiremen.

'Look,' said Ven sternly. 'I am tired and thirsty and hungry and just for once, I'm going to totally and utterly ignore what things cost and just have them. Today I'm going to live like a person who chooses what she wants from this menu instead of one who goes for the cheaper option. Anyway, the competition people will pick up the bill – so if I'm not worrying, neither should you be.'

'The competition people won't pick up this bill, surely,' objected Roz. 'They'll think we're taking the piss.'

'They said "everything" on the paperwork, which I do believe is legally binding. So shut up and choose something.'

'I can't stop looking at the prices,' whimpered Olive, after Ven had ordered a bottle of prosecco that cost more than Doreen Hardcastle's house.

'Force yourself,' said Frankie. 'Just for once, let's live like kings, whether Figurehead coughs up for this or not. It's not often your best mate is forty.'

'Sod it, you're right,' agreed Roz.

'Yes, you are,' added Olive, deciding she was going to be a Mrs Crowther rather than an Olive Hardcastle today.

The waiter left it the perfect length of time before he came to fetch the ladies' order. Roz ordered a lasagne, Frankie a spag bol, Olive and Ven grilled chicken.

'You'd have thought the menu would be fancier, wouldn't you?' Roz imparted quietly to the others. She had just ordered the most expensive common-dish in history.

'You don't pay just for the food in La Piazza San Marco,' said Frankie. 'You pay for the privilege of being here, listening to the band playing outside and for the ambience.'

'I hope this ambience comes with chips,' said Olive. 'I'm starving.'

They sat silently chewing bread, letting the cool calmness seep through their every pore, enjoying the sound of the orchestra playing outside in the square. It was a little touch of heaven in a very busy city.

The food, when it arrived, wasn't in huge portions and didn't come with chips – but it smelled divine and was perfect in its simplicity. Olive and Ven's grilled chicken came with crunchy lettuce, fat, salty black olives and thick, creamy home-made mayonnaise.

'Venice, happy birthday, kiddo.' Roz raised her glass of prosecco and clinked it against the birthday girl's. 'I am so glad you picked the Italian restaurant and didn't leave the choice to me this year.'

'Yes, well – when I say we're going to the Great Wall of China for *my* birthday, I mean the takeaway on Hill Street, not the real one,' put in Olive, touching her glass to Ven's.

'You never know, you might have won the lottery by then!' said Frankie.

'Or have written a slogan for their tourist board. "Have a ball, on the wall",' laughed Roz.

'"There's nothing finer, than the Great Wall of China",' Ven came back with. 'Leave all the competitions to me, you flaming amateurs.'

'This is the most divine meal I've had in years,' said Roz. 'It was nearly worth the heart-attack I had when I saw the price.'

Olive scooped up the last of her mayo with a swoop of bread. A small ladylike burp escaped her as she put her cutlery down in the centre of her plate, and she clamped her hands over her mouth.

'Don't burp in here, you scruff,' said Roz.

'Don't fart either,' said Frankie, making Olive giggle so much she worried she just might.

Ven got out her purse. The others did the same until Ven kicked up a fuss.

'Let's make a deal. If Figurehead come back to me and say "We're not paying for this" – which they won't – I'll tell you and we'll split it four ways. How's that?'

They were all too chilled out to argue, so Ven paid the waiter and tucked the bill into her handbag. Then they rejoined the heat and the madness outside.

'Are you off on your wander now?' said Roz.

'I am. Are you sure you don't mind?' said Ven.

'Don't be daft. This is your day, you do what you want to do. You unsociable cow,' replied Roz, adding quickly, 'joke.'

'You can have our company of course,' put in Frankie. 'But we perfectly understand that you need to be alone for a while.'

'Thanks,' said Ven. 'I do.' Frankie had taught her the Italian for 'Excuse me, can you direct me to the Hotel Ani,' and she had a crude map of where the hotel was – the best the internet had to offer, alas. She was as armed to find it as she could be.

'See you back at the ship then, birthday girl,' said Frankie, blowing her a kiss as they parted company in the square. '*Ciao, bellissima!*'

'*Arrivederci!*' called Ven.

As the others crossed the square for a nosy at the legendary Caffè Florian and the even more infamous menu prices, Ven cut down one of the little alleys to where she thought her map was directing her. It was a dead end. Not that it mattered, because Venice, she decided, was indeed the perfect place to get lost. She explored a couple of shops selling the most beautiful leather goods and furniture, and window-shopped in some famous designer stores. A couple holding hands passed her, and a sharp pang hit Venice from left field. Here she was in one of the most romantic cities of the world, alone. No, more than that, she suddenly felt lonely because all around her were couples, groups, families. She had a moment of panic and wanted to run back and find the others. She knew then that she had made a wrong call, wanting to wander around by herself.

Feeling a hard prickle of tears in her eyeballs, she made a pretence of ogling all the different ice-cream flavours in a shop. Then her eyes shifted focus to the reflection in the glass of a tall man standing behind her. It took her a few seconds to recognise him out of his uniform.

'Hello, Venice. And a very happy birthday to you,' the man said as she turned round to face him.

'Oh hello, Captain,' she said, stumped for words. 'You look so different in blue.'

He didn't look any less handsome though, in cut-off jeans and a cornflower shade of T-shirt, said her interested heart. 'Oh, and thank you for my lovely flowers. That was a lovely surprise.'

'A pleasure. Did the truffles arrive as well? They were coffee-flavoured, I hope. That's what I requested.'

'The truff . . . Oh, they were from you too?' Ven felt her face getting hot. She was sure this couldn't be normal birthday customer service for everyone on the ship. Was he flirting? Or was he just being nice? Oh God, she was so crap at reading signals.

'Yes, yes, I got those too,' she mumbled. 'Thank you. They were lovely.' *Do you know any other adjectives besides 'lovely'?* asked a snipy little voice in her head.

'Your friends told me coffee was your favourite,' Nigel went on.

'Yep,' nodded Ven, not able to think of anything else to say that didn't involve the word 'lovely'. Her head was whirling. 'Down, boy,' her brain was warning her heart.

'Are you all alone now?' Nigel asked.

Why don't we just call into this little hotel and let me give you your real birthday present . . .? Ven tried to ignore her vivid imagination and be sensible.

'Erm, yes. I've just had lunch with the others and now I'm off to find my hotel.'

'Don't forget to have your picture taken there so you can show your parents when you get home.'

Already closer to tears than normal, his words hit her with a whoosh. Just for a moment there, the tiniest moment, she had been about to say, 'Yes,' and do that for them. A delicious sliver of time had existed where that was a possibility, a second of smoke that clouded reality before lifting as quickly and letting truth smack her hard in the face with its full force. Ven struggled to hold down the tears and not make a show of herself in front of this gorgeous man, but they were too strong and pushed themselves out, down her cheeks, faster than she could wipe them away.

'My goodness, Venice, what did I say?' gasped Nigel, whilst Ven flapped her hands, unable to speak, and plundered her pockets and her handbag for a tissue but sod's law she didn't have one. And no amount of dropping her head could disguise the fact that she was crying. She felt his large, warm hand on her shoulder, his sympathy flooding out towards her and making the tears flow even faster.

Then Nigel pushed his handkerchief into her palm and she had no choice but to use it and sink her face into the soft man-fragrant linen.

'Sorry,' said Ven, trying to gain some composure and cough down her emotion. 'My parents are both gone, alas.'

'I'm so sorry,' said Nigel, his sing-songy voice both deep and calming. His hand was still on her shoulder.

'You weren't to know.' Ven attempted a smile but she predicted it wouldn't look that fabulous. The tears were crescendo-ing inside her again. She stamped her foot like a stroppy bull in a neurologically deficient way to stop them.

'Coffee, cappuccino, latte!' said Nigel suddenly, like a beverage form of Tourettes. The concerned hand on her shoulder slipped to her arm where it gripped her elbow and guided her around the corner to a quieter spot because he felt embarrassment coming off her in tidal waves.

'I'm so sorry,' said Ven again. 'God, look at me, what an idiot.'

'Can I take you for a coffee?' asked Nigel softly. 'I know you want to be by yourself and have things to do, but I'm afraid I'm not leaving you alone until you're all right.'

'Don't worry, honestly I'm fine,' said Ven bravely, but obviously she wasn't.

'You've got over three hours left in Venice,' said Nigel, taking a quick glance at his watch. 'I'm going to steal fifteen minutes of that and take you to my favourite place here – Caffè Angelo – if you'll let me. It's just two minutes away and I think you need a sit-down and a few wee quiet moments.'

Ven was going to protest, but he was right, that was exactly

what she did need, so she shut up and let him lead her down
the narrow street and over a tiny metal bridge.

'It's tucked away,' Nigel told her. 'Ah, here we are.' They
came to a pretty little coffee house. Inside, it was like a tiny version of Gran Caffè Polo – all beautiful mirrors and pastel walls.
But this one had the addition of the most enormous ice-cream
cabinets Ven had ever seen in her life.

'This is all home-made and trust me, it's the best gelato in the
world,' whispered Nigel.

A smiley bright-eyed man with thick grey hair welcomed
Nigel warmly with a man-hug and a flurry of Italian.

'Venice, this is my friend Angelo,' said Nigel as Angelo shook
Ven's hand so vigorously he nearly broke it off.

'Table for two for the capitano!' Angelo barked at a young
waiter who scurried to clear a space for them. 'Do you require
lunch, signorina?'

'No, I think just coffees and possibly ice cream,' Nigel replied
and looked to Ven for confirmation. She nodded and then
Nigel said something to Angelo in very fast and fluent Italian
which made the old guy chuckle.

'Wow,' said Ven, impressed. 'Was that gobbledegook or the
real thing?'

'I always found languages very easy to pick up,' said Nigel,
without sounding big-headed in the slightest. 'I speak fluent
Italian, French, Spanish, a little less German and Portuguese but
I'm working on it. And a smattering of English, of course,' he
added with a grin.

The waiter arrived and pushed two long menus into their
hands and asked Nigel what sort of coffees they wanted whilst
they were perusing.

'Latte grande for me. Venice, what sort of coffee do you want?'

'Same for me, thank you,' said Ven. She looked down at the
menu which was made up entirely of flavours of ice cream and
sundaes. It went on for pages.

'You have to try a sundae, especially on your birthday,' said Nigel, adding quickly, 'but only if you have time.'

'I've got time,' said Ven, enjoying the temporary respite from being lonely in this most beautiful of all the world's cities. She wasn't even going to try and protest as a waitress passed with two heavenly glasses of ice-cream scoops covered in cream and sauce and cherries. She studied the menu and eventually narrowed her choice down to fifteen. Then to five, then to the Cappuccino Fantastico sundae. Nigel had gone for the Midnight Mint Magnifico. Ven left it to him to give the waiter their order.

Through the window, Ven saw her three friends ogling the ice-cream cabinets. Then they noticed her, gossiped a bit and shot off. Subtle as a sledgehammer. Nigel saw them too and it seemed to tickle him.

'They've been a total embarrassment since we were at school,' Ven smiled. 'I don't know why I bother with them.'

'Ah, so you're all old friends,' said Nigel, as if he had been pondering about their relationship. Crikey – he didn't think they were two lesbian couples, did he?

'Yes, old friends,' sighed Ven. 'Two with partners – male partners – and two of us without male partners.' Aaargh! Did that make her sound as if she was making her single status too clear? 'Happily single, though,' she tagged on – but, hang on, that was worse. That made her sound as if she suspected he might be after her and she wasn't interested. The waiter came back with two coffees and rescued her before the hole she was digging herself into reached the centre of the earth.

'So, do you know where the hotel you're looking for is?' asked Nigel.

'Not really,' said Ven, 'but I'll find it. I have my trusty treasure map.' She foraged in her pocket and showed Nigel the child-like map she had printed off. 'Plus, Frankie taught me how to ask directions.'

'Go on then,' said Nigel, sipping his latte. 'Practise on me. Pretend I'm a Venetian.'

'Okay,' said Ven, clearing her throat in preparation. 'Are you ready? *Oggi compio quarant'anni, mi vuoi tastare le tette?*'

Nigel didn't so much cough on his mouthful of latte as choke on it. He turned aubergine purple and gasped. It was now Ven's turn to say, 'Are you all right?' and get up quickly to slap him on the back before he died and the ship was left captainless.

'Sorry,' he said through a gaspy rasp. 'It went down the wrong way.'

The ice creams arrived then. Nigel had never been as thankful for a diversion in his life.

Roz tried not to look at the fake Louis Vuitton handbags which the street-hawker was selling on the steps. They'd been told on the ship that if they were caught buying them, they, as well as the vendor, could be fined thousands of euros should the police see them. But they really were good copies. She tried to displace her thoughts of owning one by licking on her ice cream. They'd seen Ven and the Captain ensconced in the café and made a swift and, in their eyes, subtle exit to leave them alone, and bought their ice creams from another vendor instead.

'Wonder how Ven is getting on?' said Olive, snatching the thought directly from the brains of the others. 'With the Captain,' she added salaciously.

'She must have just bumped into him, because she wouldn't have kept it secret from us that she was meeting up with him,' said Roz, who couldn't wait for the gossip later, back on the ship.

'I hope she finds her hotel. If she does, it will just be the perfect day for her,' said Olive.

'Oh shit!' screamed Frankie. She and Roz both stared at each other in open-mouthed horror.

'You did tell her in the end, didn't you?' said Roz.

'I forgot,' said Frankie.

'Oh bloody hell,' said Roz now. Her eyes suddenly went all sparkly.

'What are you on about?' said Olive. She couldn't work out if the two staring gargoyles at either side of her were about to laugh or cry.

'That phrase I taught Ven to find her hotel ...' began Frankie.

'What about it?' said Olive.

'It wasn't "Where is the Hotel Ani?"'

'What was it then?' Olive asked.

'"I'm forty years old today. Do you want to feel my tits?"'

'Oh Frankie!'

'I feel sick and full,' said Ven, anchoring her spoon into the last scoop of coffee ice cream left in the bottom of the tall sundae glass. 'I can't finish it. I'll burst if I do.'

Nigel had no such trouble. 'That,' he announced, 'is the reason I take half a day off every time I come to Venice. I have my fix, then I walk for an hour afterwards to burn some of it off.'

'Do you get off at every port?' asked Ven, trying to let the burp building up inside her seep out unheard.

'No,' said Nigel, 'I'm usually too busy, but I always try and visit here.'

'I suppose you've seen everywhere twice and more,' realised Ven.

'Yes, but it's not that much fun wandering around by yourself,' said Nigel with a surprising note of sadness in his voice. 'However beautiful the places are.'

'You're not married then?' said Ven, flicking her eyes towards his empty ring finger.

'I was,' said Nigel. 'Alas, it didn't last very long. My wife hated being at sea, and I couldn't give it up – it was an impossible situation. She wouldn't come on board and so we hardly saw each other.'

'Didn't she realise what life would be like as a Captain's wife then?' asked Ven, confused, trying to hold back the 'stupid woman' comment. Then she wondered if she was being too nosy and was about to apologise for it when Nigel opened his mouth.

'She said she did, but she obviously didn't,' he replied.

'I thought you'd have women running all over you. Everyone seems to wet their . . . er . . . get all flustery when they know you're in the vicinity,' said Ven. 'Even men.'

'It's the romantic white uniform,' grinned Nigel. 'But if a wife isn't travelling with a Captain, it's a lonely life for both of them, with three-month stints at sea. And an even harder life if you have children. Which we didn't.'

'I suppose it must be,' said Ven.

'This job is my lottery win in life,' said Nigel with smiling passion. 'It's all I ever wanted to do and I love it.'

Ven gulped. 'That's wonderful,' she managed. 'It must take you years to become a Captain.'

'It's quite an apprenticeship, yes,' he affirmed. 'Twenty years in my case from cadet to Captain, via college and life aboard oil tankers and Navy vessels.'

'How long will you be on the *Mermaidia*?'

'We're usually assigned to a ship for two years, but obviously that can be longer or shorter depending on circumstances. I've only been on her for four months,' Nigel explained, before picking up an earlier thread of the conversation. 'Do you have any children, Venice?'

'Me? Nooo. Funnily enough, none of us have any,' replied Ven. 'Even though we all planned to have four each.'

'Have you been single long?'

'Since last year.'

'An amicable split?'

Ven sighed and wondered whether to elaborate on the slow shake of the head she gave by way of an answer.

'Nigel, if I told you, you wouldn't believe me.'

'Try me,' he said, his arms folding on the table and moving in to listen.

'We kind of started to fall apart about three years ago,' began Ven. 'Both my parents became ill at the same time and ... one of my friends was just recovering from a health problem too. Ian's work was slow so things were a bit rough. He was a self-employed electrician. Used to market himself as "Electric Ian" – Electric*ian*, get it? However, his main business rival was called Alec, who used to market himself as *Alec*-trician. Alec undercut him at every opportunity and he was a much slicker outfit than Ian, to be honest. So there was a lot of pressure on the marriage with illness all around us and not much work for him. Feel free to laugh at any point in this story, because this is where it gets really ridiculous,' said Ven, though Nigel did not look as though he found it funny. He was listening intently as Ven continued.

'Anyway, Ian was a good-looking guy, always preening himself, plus he was, well, how to put this delicately ...' flaming heck, why had she ever started this story? '... quite blessed in the trouser department, although there's a reason why I'm telling you that.' Ven gulped and felt herself growing pink and hot. 'Well, a few of his mates formed a sort of Chippendales tribute act and said he should join them because they were earning really good money. So he did. He started beefing himself up at the gym and having fake tans and bleaching his hair and having his chest waxed, and in the end he got to be so good at it that he went solo as a male stripper – calling himself ... Knobbie Williams.'

Still Nigel didn't laugh.

'I didn't recognise him any more. He used to be a nice,

decent bloke, but all the attention he got changed him. To cut
a long story short, he got himself an old open-topped sports
car and a bit on the side, so I found out later, and two weeks
after my dad died I came home from work to find he'd moved
out. I hadn't a clue he was having an affair. Mum and Dad left
me a little house and a nest-egg that they'd been saving for
me – I was so cross with them because I didn't want that sort
of money – I'd have rather they spent it on themselves. In the
end, I had to give Ian half of it in our divorce settlement.
Then not long after he'd cashed in the cheque, I was made
redundant.'

'That's awful,' said Nigel, eyes full of sympathy. 'Cruel. Did
you have to sell your home too?'

'Ian took over the mortgage and moved his girlfriend in. I
didn't want to live there anyway, especially after finding out
what those two used to do in it when I was out working. I
moved into Mum and Dad's place but there are too many sad
memories there for me.'

'What a shame,' said Nigel.

Ven plastered on a smile, suddenly panicky that Nigel
would think she was a drama queen. 'Oh, please don't let me
leave you with the impression that I'm a miserable old bat. I'm
a great believer in what is meant to be, will be. Mum and Dad
were always very positive people. They believed in karma,
although they didn't actually call it that in their day. And they
were right because ...' *She nearly told him!* '... because now
I'm in the middle of Venice and Ian is in the past. And life's
good.'

'And you are forty today and looking nothing like that age
and one man, at least, isn't going to take your money from
you.'

Before she had a chance to protest, Nigel swept up the bill
from the table and opened up his wallet. 'If you wait for me, I'll
help you find your hotel,' he said, disappearing to the rear of the

café, in the direction of the loo. He came back in time to see Ven in conversation with a bemused Angelo.

'... *quaranta anni, mi vuoi*—'

Nigel made a loud interrupting cough. 'It's fine, I think I know where the hotel is. *Grazie Angelo, y arrivederci.*'

'*Arrivederci, signorina, Capitano*. We will see you again soon, we hope.'

Nigel herded Ven quickly out of the café.

'You stopped me practising my Italian,' she protested.

'The thing is ...' began Nigel. *How to put this?* 'The Venetians have a different way of putting things to most of Italy,' he bluffed. 'It's a little like the difference between a Glaswegian accent and a Cornish one. What Frankie taught you ... er ...' he searched for the words 'doesn't translate properly here.'

To his relief, Ven appeared to buy that. 'Oh, I see. Well, that was a waste of time learning that then,' she sighed.

'Think it might be best if you let me do the talking,' said Nigel with Irish gallantry, leading the way out of the alley.

Olive stepped off the vaporetto water bus as it pulled in at the little island of Murano.

'I've always wanted to come here,' she said to the other two. 'Barnsley was famous for glass-blowing at one time, you know. That's why there is a glass-blower on the coat-of-arms.'

'You sound just like Mrs Euston,' said Roz, pulling a face at the mention of the horrible old form teacher in their school whom they had all hated. 'Just don't start growing a unibrow like she did.'

A tall, good-looking Italian man was welcoming the crowd who were disembarking and asking them to follow him.

'Wow, now I'm interested,' said Frankie.

'Where's he taking us?' Roz wanted to know.

'Heaven and back, I hope,' joked Frankie.

But she knew, as they all did, that they were being shep-
herded towards a glass-blowing demonstration and then on to
a shop in the hope they would be buying a Murano glass
souvenir – or even better, getting a huge mirror or chandelier shipped home. They followed Mr Handsome-Italian into
a workroom filled with benches and brutal-looking tools and
a fire-filled kiln. There, waiting for the crowd to assemble,
was a round old man with chimp-hairy arms, chequered shirt
and very tatty and baggy jeans. He looked more tramp than
artist as he was introduced as Enrique who was a master
craftsman. Apparently the glass-blowers of Murano were the
rock stars of history. Very greatly desired as husbands. Roz
hoped that in the Middle Ages they wore better-fitting
clothes than old Enrique. He made the Rolling Stones look
smooth.

Boring as Roz thought all this might be, and although she
had just come along because Olive wanted to, she found it as
fascinating as the others to see a blob of glass be heated and
rolled and pincered into a fragile Ferrari horse. Old Enrique
deserved the round of applause he got at the end. Not that his
sex appeal had changed any. He might have been brilliant at his
job but no one was throwing their knickers at him.

The girls wandered around the shop together, ooh-ing and
aah-ing at the magnificent mirrors and lamps and trying not to
bump into anything.

'I'm going to buy this for Ven,' said Olive, picking up a red
glass heart threaded onto a leather thong. 'Just a little extra present for her and a souvenir of Venice.'

'Get the matching earrings as well and I'll half you,' said
Roz. 'It'll serve as an apology later when we get back to the
ship. Unless she did get her tits felt and enjoyed it.'

'Add the bracelet and let's pay a third each,' put in Frankie,
fishing her purse out of her handbag. 'I really hope she found
that hotel without having to ask for it.' She gasped. 'Oh my, you

don't think she practised her Italian out on the Captain, do you?' The three women looked at each other and broke into a naughty fit of laughter. Even a Murano jewellery set wasn't going to fully make up for this one.

Ven and Nigel found the Hotel Ani, tucked into a corner at the side of a bridge. Big pots of red flowers flanked the door. It looked romantically shabby with its balconied windows above loaded with pink and white flowers. Ven could imagine Juliet leaning over there and having a conversation with Romeo below.

'Well, Lady Venice,' said Nigel, 'I shall now get back to my duties aboard the good ship.' He added politely, 'You'll be able to find your way back okay?'

'Thank you, Captain, I will,' said Ven, looking up at the crumbling façade. Nigel waited for her to go inside before he left her, but she wasn't making any move to.

'Aren't you going in?'

'No.' Ven shook her head. 'I'd never be able to gesticulate that I just want a look around.'

Nigel looked at his watch, then said, 'Come on, I'll take you in.'

'No, it's fine, really,' said Ven, although her face said otherwise and Nigel pushed open the door of the Hotel Ani and beckoned her to follow him.

'You can't come all this way and not go the last furlong.'

Ven followed him. It was so cool inside, painted cream walls with the slightest green tint and beautiful ancient furniture, all mismatched pieces but perfectly suiting their surroundings with their understated grandeur. Nigel approached the reception desk where a very slim woman in a black dress was standing and began to talk to her.

'*Chiedo scusa, sarebbe possibile se la mia amica desse un'occhiata in giro? Vede, i suoi genitori quarant'anni fa hanno speso la loro luna di miele in questo albergo, e siccome non ci sono più, la mia amica voleva vedere il luogo in cui era stata concepita . . . rimarrà solo pochi istanti.'*

'Ma ci mancherebbe, ci dia un'occhiata. Siete i benvenuti!' replied the lady with kind enthusiasm, beckoning Ven forwards.

'I asked her if you could look around for a few minutes,' explained Nigel. 'I told her that your parents honeymooned here and she said that you are very welcome.'

'Si, si,' waved the pretty young receptionist, throwing her arms open to gesture to Ven that she was free to wander at her leisure.

'Venice, I am going to leave you. I feel as if I've intruded enough on your plans,' said Nigel. 'Will you be all right? The water launch is—'

'Yes, yes, I know where to find it,' said Ven. 'Thank you so much, Nigel. You really haven't intruded at all.'

'Don't forget to meet me by Reception at half past four for your bridge visit,' he reminded her.

'Oh yes, we'll be there.' Ven smiled. 'We're all really looking forward to that.'

Nigel mock-saluted her and Ven waved as he left the hotel, then she shyly began to look around.

Her parents had been in this very room. She closed her eyes and tried to imagine them skipping down the staircase as new-lyweds. It was too easy and her eyes blurred with tears. What a lovely place to begin their married life, she thought. It was so calm and cool and beautiful, and the huge picture windows looked out onto the nearby canal and the gondolas rowing their passage along them. She knew her mum and dad had taken a gondola because they told her they had. How could they not? Who could come to Venice on honeymoon and not take a gondola ride? And in one of these rooms in this hotel, their child was made and they couldn't have called her anything else but Venice, however pretentious it might have sounded for a Barnsley council-estate couple.

Ven felt as if the hotel was 'hers' in some way. How nuts was that? Did that make her really part-Italian, being conceived in this lovely city? More Italian than Frankie who was actually born in Sheffield?

She sat down on one of the pale golden slipper chairs. The furniture looked terribly old but beautifully preserved. It all fitted so perfectly into its surroundings that she wondered if the hotel had been built around it. She suddenly shivered, because it was as if her world had sailed close to one in which her parents were now, and the thin skins between them had brushed. She gave her head a little shake to get rid of the rising emotion. It was a ridiculous thought, of course, because once you were dead you were dead. She wished she believed in a heaven, but she didn't. There were no ghosts, no after-life and so such thing as reincarnation. Anyway – every programme she'd seen about reincarnation involved someone who 'used to be' an Egyptian priestess. Oh, for the days when she couldn't get to sleep in anticipation of Father Christmas or the Tooth Fairy because Ven knew she had lost the ability to see magic, after all the events of the past few years. She badly needed to believe in some, but the luxury eluded her.

Venice took a final long look around the stucco walls, the dark portraits in their heavy gilt frames, the chairs and huge glass tables with the intricate legs, the beautiful kind receptionist, the views from the tall windows.

'*Grazie, signorina*,' she said.

'*Prego*,' the receptionist replied with a sweet smile.

Ven opened the front door to the sunshine, and the real world once again. Her memory was made and she would take it home and treasure it. More than one memory, in fact, because there was also the interlude with lovely Nigel who had rescued her from a sadness that she hadn't anticipated. She just wished that every time she felt lonely from now on, he would leap out from nowhere to treat her to ice cream and coffee. *Yeah, like that was going to happen to someone like you, Venice Smith!*

Now she had to get back to the ship and face a grilling from the others as to why she'd been spotted in an ice-cream parlour with a handsome Captain when they'd left her to go hotel hunting.

Chapter 48

Nigel was waiting for them when the four women arrived in Reception at half past four and he was back in his uniform. Ven had to suppress a low growl in her throat. It put the cheap fake uniform her ex-husband had in his 'stripper's closet' to shame. She had a sudden vision of Nigel stripping off to the *Full Monty* theme tune and had to pull herself to order. The dress code for that evening was semi-formal, but as it was Ven's birthday, they had upgraded it and were all in long evening dresses.

As Ven had anticipated, the others were gagging for details when she got back to the ship and Ven was forced to explain – right down to what flavour sauce she had on her ice cream.

'That Italian you taught me wouldn't have been understood, by the way,' said Ven, wondering why Frankie's eyes seemed to suddenly dilate. 'Apparently the Venetian dialect is different to the rest of Italy.'

'Oh, who told you that?' asked Frankie.

'Nigel,' said Ven. 'He said he'd do the talking for me when we were looking for the hotel. He can speak fluent Italian *and* Venetian.'

'Did you ... did you try your newly learned Italian out on him then?' Frankie asked, whilst doing her best to look innocent.

'I did,' said Ven proudly. 'And I think he was secretly impressed by my accent, you know.'

'Thank You, God,' said Frankie silently when Ven's back was turned. The gentlemanly Captain went up even further in her estimation.

Eric and Irene, Royston and Stella joined them five minutes later, also dressed for dinner as there wouldn't be a long time after sailing out of the Grand Canal before the restaurant bing-bong sounded. They brought cards for Ven, and Stella had bought her a gorgeous pink Venetian mask too. The group was twittering like kids on a school trip. It was a first for all of them, apparently, going on the bridge.

They went up to deck twelve in the forward lift, then through a Staff Only door and along a passage. Nigel drew back a curtained door and gave them all a glimpse into his office. Then they travelled up a steel set of steps, along a passage and cleared a security door. Then they were on the elusive bridge, which was nothing like any of them had imagined.

The space was remarkably clear, except for a concentrated bank of telephones and computers in a central console, where two officers sat with the Venetian pilot happily drinking tea. He was the man who would help guide the mighty ship out of the Grand Canal and into the open sea, without actually touching the controls himself. Nigel explained that there was less than three-foot clearance under the ship in the canal. It was a complicated manoeuvre getting out.

Aided by tugs, the *Mermaidia* began a long and laboured three-point turn in the shallow waters. The whole ship juddered as she struggled through the mud, but eventually, they were on their way. The pilot's job done, he headed downstairs to take the boat back to Venice, and the *Mermaidia* began a smooth cruise down the Grand Canal.

There was little conversation from the party who stood in true awe enjoying the scenery.

Ven could feel Nigel directly behind her, looking over her head. She imagined him leaning forwards, placing his lips on the side of her neck, his hands around her waist. Then Roz rudely awoke her from her fantasy with a sharp nudge to alert her to the last view of Saint Mark's Square.

'It's absolutely beautiful,' said Stella breathlessly.

'Stunning,' added Eric. 'What a treat.'

Ven gulped down a surprise of tears as the ship nosed into the open sea on course for the Croatian island of Korcula. It would have sounded daft had she said it aloud, but she felt that she had left something of herself in Venice – that part of her would be forever anchored there. Her mum and dad had been so lucky being there as lovers. Ven only hoped she would return to it with a lover of her own. She knew it would be too hard to come back to alone.

Then Eric's ecstasy levels went into overdrive as Nigel highlighted a small blob on one of the screens.

'That's actually the ship over there,' he said, pointing through the window to the real-life vessel ahead of them. All the details of the ship flashed up on screen – the name of it, how long it was, where it was destined for and that it contained some hazardous material – it was surprisingly fascinating stuff. Eric's questions for the Captain came thick and fast, and Nigel answered them all quite happily.

'Quick, look!' cried Irene, pointing to a pod of dolphins, lifting and diving into the sea as if trying to outwit the ship. However, by the time Ven had moved from the control bank to the window, all she saw was a slight splash in the water. She so wanted to see some dolphins in the wild and had been terribly unlucky so far on that score.

Olive too was standing, looking out to sea but her eyes were unfocused because she was quietly thinking. Her life with David and Doreen felt like a million light years away. And a million planets away. And from one of those planets the full picture of her marriage was clearly visible and it wasn't a pretty one. Looking at everything from a distance and gaining perspective was frightening. What she had wasn't a life – *this* was living. Having holidays, going out for meals, taking the time out to sit and read a book, having a laugh. She couldn't remember the last time she had laughed, or even smiled, in 15, Land Lane.

'Well, that was amazing,' said Royston. 'Thank you so much, Cap'n. That was special, truly special.'

'It's a pleasure,' returned Nigel before one of the officers claimed his attention again.

'We'd best go and leave them to it,' said Royston, checking his Rolex. 'We've only got just over twenty minutes to dinner.'

'I'll see you at the table very shortly, all being well,' called Nigel. 'Gilbert will show you the way out. Glad you enjoyed it.'

After thanking Nigel profusely, they all followed the junior officer Gilbert out of the bridge, down the passage and through the door which took them back into the main body of the ship.

'Would you like to join us for champagne?' Ven asked the two older couples. 'It's on me,' she added, because though Eric wasn't mean, she suspected he and his wallet wouldn't be too keen to get into rounds of champagne.

'That would be lovely,' said Stella.

They claimed some seats and a table in the Beluga bar, and Royston and Eric borrowed a couple more chairs so they could all sit together. The men ordered plain champagne, while Irene had her first ever Kir Royale, Ven had a Bellini and the others had champagne cocktails with brandy and brown sugar. Ven ordered a taster dish of caviar which came with tiny biscuits, and though it wasn't something she would have had every day, she enjoyed the idea that she was in the middle of the sea on a luxury ship drinking champagne and eating caviar.

'I sometimes ask myself, where did it all go wrong?' laughed Royston, shovelling a cracker and caviar into his mouth. 'Oh, isn't this the life?'

'It sure is,' said Olive, as a thought of the real life she would be returning to pushed through. How could she go back to scrubbing at Mr Tidy's toilet pan after this?

The dinner-table was covered in streamers and balloons with '40' on them bobbing above the middle of the table. Ven cast narrowed eyes onto her friends.

'You didn't have to announce my age to the whole world!' she growled with mock embarrassment.

'I wish I could announce that I was forty,' chuckled Stella. 'You're just a baby.'

They assumed their seats and looked at the menu. It was a beauty tonight:

Aromatic Salmon Confit Terrine
With a dill yoghurt dressing and toasted lemon brioche
Wholemeal Tartlet filled with Avocado, Tomatoes,
Quail Egg and Crispy Bacon
Vegetable Spring Rolls
With Thai salad and a sweet chilli dipping sauce

~

Scotch Broth
Chicken Consommé with Lentils and Herbs

~

Grilled Red Snapper with Wok Fried Rice
Served with sweet and sour sauce and prawn crackers
Confit of Duck Leg

Slow-braised duck leg served on a bed of creamed leeks and bacon
Pan-fried Herb-crumbed Escalope of Veal
Served with asparagus tips, crab and Hollandaise glaze
Prosciutto & Porcini Penne Pasta with Roasted Tomato Dressing
Served with chunky garlic bread
Bâtons of Root Vegetables Brussel Sprouts O'Brien Potatoes

~

Rum Tiramisu
Dark Chocolate Cake with Cappuccino Cream and
Cherry Brandy Sauce
Selection of Miniature Lemon Desserts
Lemon Cheesecake, Lemon Panna Cotta and Lemon Meringue Tart
Ice creams: Butterscotch, Melba, Madagascan Vanilla

Plus there was a cheeseboard to follow, with coffees, Italian Liqueur truffles and the special after-dinner drinks of the night – Tia Maria or grappa.

'Not much on there for me tonight,' sighed Roz.

'You're joking!' said Frankie.

'Of course I am, you fool.'

'I fancy having a red snapper,' Ven decided.

'I bet you wish the Captain would give you a red snapper,' Roz whispered, setting Ven off giggling.

'What's O'Brien Potatoes?' asked Irene.

'Don't know, but they sound very Irish,' replied Royston. 'Oh, look who's here – right on cue!'

'Evening, everyone,' said Nigel as Buzz dived forward to pull out his chair for him.

'Good evening, Captain,' everyone returned.

Buzz enlightened them on the O'Brien question – they were potatoes sautéed with pimiento and hot bell peppers.

Ostentatious, daftly generous Royston ordered two bottles of pink champagne for the table, but Nigel summoned over Angel and had a word in her ear.

'My treat,' he said, inspiring Royston to try and battle for the bill whilst Eric sipped quietly and hoped no one would expect him to make it a three-way contest.

Nigel won in the end. They toasted Ven yet again when everyone had a glass full. Irene was decidedly tipsy by the time her consommé had arrived. Then Olive made everyone nearly spit out their champagne with laughter when she excitedly told the table about 'the man they'd seen blowing a horse' in Murano. Even Nigel laughed like a drain at that. Ven decided that, out of his uniform, Captain Nigel O'Shaughnessy might be a very earthy man.

'What's Korcula like?' Ven asked him when the hilarity had died down and Olive had stopped hiding her head in her hands.

'Oh, it's a charming little island,' butted in Eric. 'And though it's spelled with a "c" it's actually pronounced *Kor-chew-la*. Isn't that right, Captain?'

'That's correct,' said Nigel, happy to let Eric take centre-stage with his knowledge.

'It's a brilliant place for fake designer sunglasses,' Stella informed them. 'Ten euros a pair, but barter. And walk off if they won't drop their prices – they'll chase you soon enough.'

'I got them down to five euros for my Golce and Dabbana ones,' said Irene, a little more loudly than she usually spoke. 'I mean Bolshy and Banana . . . Dolce and Gabbana. Oh dear, I'd better not have any more to drink, had I?' she giggled.

'Oh go on, live a bit.' Royston nudged her.

'Well, I might have just one more. If you insist.'

'It'll be a lot quieter than Dubrovnik. We're the only ship in port that day,' promised Nigel.

'Oh, that's good,' replied Ven, then turned to Frankie. 'Have you seen Vaughan yet – to thank him for us?'

'No, still not seen him,' said Frankie with a disappointed sigh.

She had fantasised more than once that day about sharing a gondola with him.

As coffee was served, waiters started to gather around the table.

'Oh God,' said Ven as Supremo led a terrible chorus of 'Happy Birthday' and the whole restaurant joined in with the clapping in the second verse.

'I hope they never release an album,' said Eric.

'Aw, it's sweet,' said Frankie. 'And you have to have a bit of ritual humiliation on your fortieth birthday as well as the nice stuff.'

'I'll remember that for your birthday,' said Ven. 'I'll book my ex-husband as your strippagram.'

That was the first time she had been able to joke about him, the others noticed with a smile inside their heads. It proved the very deep wounds that Ian Walsh had caused her were healing. At last.

'Grappa or Tia Maria, anyone?' asked Angel, bearing a tray full of liqueurs.

'I think I'd like to try a grappa, please,' trilled Irene, who was distinctly glassy-eyed by now.

'Nine grappas please, Angel,' said Eric, whipping out his cruise card. His eyes were as glassy as his wife's.

'Not for me, thank you, I'm on duty,' said Nigel. 'And sadly I must once again leave you and get back to the bridge.'

'Eight then, please, my lovely.'

'Dad's favourite,' said Frankie, smiling at the thought of her lovely mad Italian father. If there was a disaster, grappa was his essential salve. If there was something to celebrate, it couldn't be done without a toast of grappa.

'Enjoy Korcula,' said Nigel. 'And Venice, I sincerely hope you have had a lovely day.'

'Nigel, I think this has been one of my favourite days of my life,' Venice beamed.

Nigel's eyes lingered on her for a second longer than his goodbye merited, but it was enough to make Ven's heart jump in her chest. If only he'd given her a birthday snog. The day would have been upgraded from favourite to perfect. That, and the sight of a wild dolphin.

After dinner that night, Eric and Irene went to their cabin for a lie-down.

'That's the last we'll see of those two lightweights tonight,' laughed Royston, watching them wend a very weavy path towards the lift.

'I fancy a bit of a "lie-down" myself,' said Stella, with a saucy look in her eye.

'And the last you'll see of us two as well,' smiled Royston, rubbing his hands together. 'Have a lovely day in Korcula, girls. See you tomorrow. Happy birthday, gel!' And he leaned over, gave Ven a big sloppy kiss on her cheek then held out his arm for his lady to link.

'Randy old buggers,' said Frankie, envying them. 'I haven't had sex for nearly five years.'

'Five years? You?' said Roz. She was about to ask how come a man-eater like Frankie had been celibate for so long, then she remembered that sex hadn't exactly been a priority for her either.

'Well, I can't promise you a man, but I can at least help you get a handbag. Come on, they've got a sale on in Rodeo Drive. Ven, Olive? That sound like a plan?'

'That sounds good to me, Roz,' nodded Ven. In the event of not having her face snogged off by the Captain, there were worse compensation prizes than the prospect of a new birthday handbag.

Ven lay in bed that night, grinning inanely. She was thinking of Nigel's truffles, Nigel's legs in his cut-off trousers, Nigel's gentle lilting voice, Nigel's eyes on hers as he left the table. What a lovely day she'd had. It would have been a perfect time to tell her friends *the news* – whilst they were all happy. But something had stopped her, so maybe it wasn't meant to be today. Soon though. Ven giggled sleepily to herself.

Day 10: Korcula

Dress Code: Smart Casual

Chapter 49

They were at anchor for Korcula, which meant a ride on the tender boats from the ship to the island. Ven opened up the curtains on yet another sunshiney day. The vista was dominated by a huge mountain studded with cream-stone houses with cheerful orange roofs. She could see the tender boats full of early-rising eager passengers crossing from the ship to land.

Her cabin phone rang just as she was blotting her lipstick on a tissue.

'It's me,' said Roz's voice. 'We're up in the Buttery. Come and join us. We've saved you an almond croissant.'

'Go and get me another one, I'm starving,' said Ven, grabbing her handbag and sunglasses and wishing Jesus a cheerful 'Good morning,' on her way out.

Eric and Irene were just going up for breakfast as Ven and the others were heading off to get their tickets for the tender boats.

'We had a lie-in for once,' said Eric. 'My, I can't remember sleeping for that long in years.'

Irene looked a bit bashful, as if she'd been caught doing something she shouldn't.

'Do you think they . . .?' began Olive as the lift doors closed on the old couple.

'Course they did!' said Frankie. 'Nice to know someone's getting some.'

The tender boats were great fun. They bumped against the *Mermaidia* like rooting babies then, loaded with passengers, jiggled naughtily on the water, making a few passengers shriek. Not exactly a white-knuckle ride, but maybe a light-pink one. As instructed, they had 'familiarised themselves with the location of the life-jackets' although secretly Ven wanted to fall overboard and be rescued by a dolphin – it might be the only way she got to see one. A far too short (in her opinion) five minutes later, all the passengers were being helped onto the shore by the gallant crew taking their hands as they did a little leap from the bobbing tender boat onto the island. Behind them was a private yacht, sailing like a preening black swan and looking like something a James Bond villain would own. It had a sigh factor of at least an eight. In front of them was a huge round tower, part of the ancient defensive walls that surrounded the town. Ven thought she might just defy anyone not to fall in love with Korcula from the very first sight of it.

'Oh, this is pretty!' said Olive, echoing her thoughts. 'What a lovely place.' Café tables flanked the curving narrow road that led up to the main part of the town. Diners sat under the shade of umbrellas with large seafood platters and pizza, enjoying the view of the sea which was a sheet of blue and silver today. The grand ship was in the distance, and the orange tenders crossed in the water like playful goldfish. White cats slept in gardens, old fat dogs with collars on hovered near the café tables wagging their tails in anticipation of snack donations.

'I spy sunglasses,' said Ven, as they rounded the corner and strode over to the first of many stalls full to the gills with football shirts, sunglasses, hats, bags, watches, souvenirs.

'How much do you think the real thing would be worth?' asked Olive, picking up a huge pair of Jackie Onassis 'Dior' sunglasses with a white frame.

'In that case, about three hundred quid,' replied Roz.

'Blimey! I'd be scared of taking them on holiday and losing them,' said Olive. 'However rich I got, I don't think I'd spend three hundred quid on a pair of sunnies.'

'But at ten euros a pair, you could take them and not worry too much, couldn't you?'

Olive nodded, then suddenly wondered why she was even looking at more sunglasses. It wasn't as if she would be going on holiday for a few more years. Then again, at least she wouldn't be held back from booking one by her mother-in-law's poor health, seeing as she was probably fitter than Olive. Or David's claim that he didn't want to go away because he liked to sleep on his own firm mattress at home 'for his bad back'. There was nothing wrong with either of them that a good stretch and a few pounds off their bulk wouldn't cure.

'Isn't that your mate over there?' Roz nudged Frankie. Frankie turned round to look at where Roz was pointing and she felt her heart gallop a few strides down the road. There, in the near distance, looking at postcards like a touristy Viking, was Vaughan.

At last, she mouthed under her breath. Then to her friends she said, 'Do without me for a while, will you? I've got a big fat thank you to deliver.'

'Yeah, see you later,' they called. Olive added cheekily, 'Good luck.'

Frankie tried not to run towards the tall blond man with the much shorter hair now, but there was a definite skip in her step as she neared him.

'Hello,' she said, with a croak in her throat.

'Oh hi, Frankie!' He seemed genuinely pleased to see her. 'Where have you been hiding?'

'Where have *you* been hiding, you mean. I've ... we've all been looking for you to say thank you for helping us in Dubrovnik.'

'Oh, no worries at all,' said Vaughan. 'I was just glad we were there for you. It was pretty scary, wasn't it? Especially for the old people.' Then he added with a grin, 'And the short ones.'

'Yes,' she said, mirroring that grin. She hadn't a clue what to say now. All words were lost, however much she scrabbled around inside herself to find some. She was so out of flirting practice.

'I owe you a beer,' was the best she could manage. *Damn damn damn. How weak was that?*

So she was totally gobsmacked when he replied, 'Yep, I could go for that.'

'Oh, okay.'

'There's a place down here I was going to check out.'

'Lead the way. I might even throw in a pizza.'

'The way to an old rocker's heart. Pizza and beer.'

Frankie didn't answer that. She was too busy trying to stop herself salivating as she followed him towards a small taverna around the corner from the town square and alongside a narrow stretch of beach.

They sat under the awning of the café and he and Frankie ordered a pint and a half of lager, two giant slices of pizza and a salad. She hoped the café-owner would take his time delivering it so she could sit here and bask in the company of this drop-dead gorgeous Nordic-looking man.

'You cut your hair,' she said. 'If it hadn't been for your tattoo I wouldn't have recognised you in Dubrovnik.'

'I was so hot,' Vaughan replied. *You're telling me*, thought Frankie to herself.

'It suits you just having a thin line.' She swept her finger along her own jawline.

'I was worried I'd feel like Samson and lose all my strength,' he smiled. 'It's certainly a lot cooler with it all off.'

Frankie had a sudden flash in her head of him astride the prow of a ship, horned helmet on his head, sword aloft, ready to leap out on shore and plunder a village and seduce a maiden or two.

'Frankie?' he prompted, as she seemed suddenly a million miles away.

'Oh sorry,' she said. 'I was just thinking about Vi . . . violins.'

'Violins?'

'Yes.' *Oh help!* 'This place looks like the sort of café where a couple with gypsy violins would suddenly appear.' She cringed at how stupid that sounded, but Vaughan only smiled.

'Rustic, isn't it?' he said, looking up at the windows with their pretty white-painted shutters. He paused until the waiter had delivered their beer then pointed to the black yacht cruising in the water. 'Doesn't that boat look like Darth Vader's head?'

Frankie laughed and agreed with him, then took a sip of the cold, cold beer and wondered if this day could get any better. She doubted it.

'Are you all enjoying yourselves?' Vaughan asked, gasping with delight himself as the beer cooled his parched throat.

'Oh boy, are we!' said Frankie. 'Are you? Where are your family today?'

'They've gone off on a sailing trip,' replied Vaughan. 'I wanted to feel land under my feet today though, and have some time to myself.'

Frankie gulped. 'Oh I'm sorry, and here I am forcing you to have company.'

Vaughan raised protesting palms. 'No, I didn't mean you. This is lovely. I wanted to watch the world go by with a beer and not be part of a crowd for once. Two's much better.' He looked at her with unblinking blue eyes and she couldn't recall the last time someone had looked at her like that. She might have been out of practice with men, but she knew he liked what he saw and her whole insides responded. It was like a machine revving up after a long period of being rusty.

Over the beer, she learned that he lived in a small rural

village called Bucklow in Dorset. The thought of an ex-Hell's Angel biker transplanted into a Miss Marple setting of country cottages made her laugh out loud. Bikes were his true love and he mended them for a living. She discovered that he had married young, had his daughter Kim and been divorced before he was twenty. But it had been an amicable split and they had shared custody of Kim. His ex-wife had married again and had two sons, one of whom worked for Vaughan in his bike shop. How civilised was that for a wild man?

The pizza arrived, and it wasn't exactly brilliant, but it didn't matter, because Frankie wouldn't have swapped it for the best pizza in the world, nor would she have chosen to be anywhere else. The salad was fresh and green though, with peppers and oily olives and fat slices of herby scattered tomatoes.

'So where are the husbands then?' asked Vaughan, dipping some torn-off bread into his salad. Frankie prepared to give an answer that didn't sound too much of a come-on but at the same time made it perfectly clear that she was on the market. If he was the shopper anyway.

'Well, Roz has a partner and Olive is married, but Ven and I are both on the shelf swinging our legs.'

'Happily on the shelf?' Vaughan asked, his blue eyes sparkling as much as the sun-sprinkled sea.

'I'd like to see Ven with a nice man,' mused Frankie. 'She's such a lovely person and hasn't had a great deal of luck in the past. Her ex-husband didn't treat her very nicely and she deserves someone who'll take care of her.'

'And you?' Vaughan took a long swallow of beer and Frankie watched his Adam's apple bob slightly in his throat. He really had been an idiot to cover that handsome face up with a big silly beard.

'Well, if the right man came along, I might relinquish my place on the shelf for him,' Frankie replied with a straight face and a twinkle in her eye.

'You live in Barnsley?'

'The others do, I moved to Derbyshire.'

'Why?'

'Well, I followed Mum and Dad when they moved down there to be near to my brother and his children.' *And I needed to be with them when I got cancer.* 'I bought a beautiful old house in Bakewell.' *I thought I could manage it, but I was too ill and had to sell it and move back in with my parents for a while.* 'Then I sold it and found a tiny little cottage instead.' *When I got better. When I wanted to get back to normality again.*

'No children for you?' asked Vaughan. He was deliciously nosy, thought Frankie. Interested. That was a good sign then.

'God no,' she said. 'I've never had a partner that I could honestly say I thought I'd end up sharing my pension with. And if I couldn't visualise that longterm, there wouldn't have been any point having children with them. I was never very good at picking men. Out of all the ones I've gone out with, I'm not sure they've got a full set of balls between them. What about you then?'

Even before Vaughan had opened his mouth, Frankie felt a shift in the atmosphere as clearly as if a cold wind had blown between them.

'Happily single,' said Vaughan, biting down on his pizza crust and ripping it off hard. 'In fact, the reason I agreed to come on this cruise was that I thought it would be the sort of place where I definitely wouldn't meet anyone. A holiday romance is precisely not what I want or need.'

Frankie was knocked. *What the heck did I say to make him drop his smile like that?* The warmth had drained from his eyes. They were chips of blue ice now rather than tropical-ocean-coloured.

'Have you been single long?' Frankie asked in a soft voice, hoping to recover the ground they had lost somehow.

'Four years,' said Vaughan, tilting the beer glass and draining it.

'Four for me,' said Frankie. 'Give or take a couple of months.'

To her dismay, Vaughan then stood and reached in his back pocket for his wallet.

'No, I said this was on me,' protested Frankie.

'I couldn't let a woman pay for me,' said Vaughan, pulling out some kuna notes.

'No, I insist—'

But Vaughan had already hijacked a passing waiter and pushed the money into his hand, telling him to keep the change.

'Thanks for the company,' he said to Frankie, coolly polite. 'Listen, I'm going to get off and stretch my legs. Hope you enjoy the rest of your holiday, yeah?'

'Er yeah,' said Frankie as Vaughan waved, turned and strolled off. Just like that. One minute he had been gently flirting, the next he had pulled all the plugs out, things had gone very dark and he had gone. Frankie sat, heavy disappointment weighing her down, thinking back, dissecting her words to find the sharp pin in them which had burst the lovely atmosphere. Had she dissed men too much and come over like an 'all men are bastards' type? Had she insinuated that she had a string of lovers and was a bit of a slapper? Had she sounded desperate? A child-hater? A gold-digger? She hadn't a clue. All she knew was that she was sitting on a beautiful, beautiful island and felt more desperately alone and sad than she could remember being in years.

Later on, they watched the sailaway from Korcula from the top deck. The sea was bright shades of emerald and sapphire at the coastline, like something off an old Bounty advert. Churches sat on the huge mountainside, seemingly impossible to reach except by the extra-devoted with a sturdy set of crampons. The whole scene looked as if it had been painted with a limited palette of cream, green, light-blue and terracotta, but no other colours were needed to make the view any more perfect than it was. Frankie, however, couldn't appreciate it because her heart was drenched with too much sadness for even the warm sun of Korcula to dry up.

'I just can't understand men,' she said to the others as they headed down to the shops which opened when the ship had left the confines of the harbour. As it was Fiesta night, the on-sale specials were hair flowers, very loud Hawaiian shirts and bright shorts – the sort that Royston wore every day. 'I mean, we were getting on just fine and then he couldn't bolt away fast enough.'

'Well, don't ask me,' said Ven. 'I'm as much in the dark as you about them.'

'I don't even want to think about men,' said Olive, putting a huge red flower next to her ear and asking how it looked.

'Buy it,' said Roz. 'It looks gorgeous. You should wear more red.'

With a light mocha tan Olive's green eyes looked super shiny and all the sunshine had lightened the streaks in her hair. She felt fresh and pretty, and as if a light had been switched on inside her.

As luck would have it, just then Vaughan descended the big staircase that led to the shops. *If I'd been looking for him, I wouldn't have found him*, Frankie huffed to herself. Wasn't sod's law a marvellous thing. She wanted to turn and look at him, see if he waved or smiled, but she knew he wouldn't. She managed to keep her eyes forward, but in her peripheral vision she saw that he suddenly took an abrupt right where he made an obvious pretence of looking for his party. Then he moved totally out of sight. She had thought better of him than that. Another wanker to add to the long list of wankers she had been attracted to. The fact that she was drawn to him should have told her that he was a wanker. She grabbed a huge orange flower which matched the top she had bought for tonight. Something wildly bright and confident and everything she didn't feel at that moment.

'Sod him,' said Roz's surprisingly soft voice in her ear. 'We spend far too long looking backwards and trying to work out what went wrong.'

'Sod who?' said Frankie, getting out her cruise card to pay for the flower. It was something the old Frankie would have said, but then the old Frankie would have felt it too.

Chapter 50

Vernon Turbot walked into 15, Land Lane in a very smart black suit and tie. He walked straight over to Doreen and kissed her bull's-eye on her peach-painted lips.

'Thank goodness that's over,' he said with a heavy sigh. 'Now I can look forward to life with you.'

'Did you give her a good send-off?' asked Doreen as he sat down on the sofa next to her and held her hand possessively. 'David, put the kettle on.'

'No, I need something a bit stronger,' said Vernon, pulling a quarter bottle of Scotch out of his pocket. 'Have you got a couple of glasses, lad?'

When David handed him two tumblers, waving away the invitation to join in, Vernon poured two generous measures into them and handed one to Doreen.

'To Beryl, rest in peace,' he said, raising his glass and chinking it against Doreen's. 'And to us, may we enjoy whatever time we've got.'

'Hear, hear,' said Doreen. David noticed she had painted her nails as well. Prostitute red. That bottle of nail varnish must have been in the cupboard for twenty years.

'David, lad, I hope you don't mind, but I'm going to take your mother to live with me as soon as possible. I've got a huge house on Kerry Park Avenue, with a live-in housekeeper who is packing up Beryl's stuff as we speak to make way for yours, darling.' He turned to Doreen, then shifted his attention back to David. 'Your mum will want for nothing. I've got a villa in Cyprus and when I retire we'll spend weeks out there.'

'Ooh, that sounds wonderful, Vernon! When are you going to retire?' asked Doreen.

'Tomorrow morning,' replied Vernon.

Blimey, he's a fast worker, thought David, with a splash of admiration.

'I don't want to wait any longer,' said Vernon masterfully. 'Doreen, you are the love of my life and I want us to enjoy the chance that Beryl's death has given us. *Terra firma*, my love. Time flies – and we have wasted enough of it.'

'We have that,' chorused Doreen, and smiled.

Vernon let go of Doreen's hand and walked over to David, putting an arm around the man whom he could now openly call his son.

'David, lad. I'm handing over my empire to you. It's all yours. Ten fish-and-chip shops and a restaurant. It runs itself like clockwork because I've got good loyal staff working for me. All you have to do is show your face every so often and be a presence. It's all yours, son. Enjoy it. You're a rich man.'

David didn't know what to say. His first thought was, Damn, I'll have to sign off! to be replaced by the wider view that he would have to sign off because he would have more money than he knew what to do with. He and Olive could move into the big bedroom upstairs. He could buy a 50-inch plasma TV with Blu-ray and cinema surround. Not to mention have free fish and chips for life!

'I . . . I . . .' was all David managed, whilst his mother looked at him, tears of joy in her eyes.

'It's a lot to take in, David lad, I know. And the day after tomorrow, you and me are going around the empire and I'll introduce you as my son – and my heir.' Vernon Turbot was oozing pride as he spoke.

David found he was shaking. In the past ten days his wife had buggered off on a cruise ship, he had found out that the kind quiet man who used to skive off work to take him fishing wasn't his real dad, that his mother had a pirate's chest of loot under her bed and the bloke at the fish shop was his father and was handing over a fortune to him.

'I'm going to leave you to pack. Will you be all right, Doreen?' Vernon asked gently. 'I've just got a few "t"s to cross and "i"s to dot. I want everything to be perfect when you move in. Although I don't mind if you come as you are. You don't need to bring anything – I want you to have everything new. No expense spared for us, girl,' he said.

It was funny to hear his mum being called a girl, thought David. But in a way that's what she looked like, giggling and smiling and sighing and seeing Vernon Turbot through eyes so rose-coloured he must have looked like a giant strawberry to her.

'Till tomorrow,' said Vernon at the door, blowing Doreen a kiss, which she caught and clutched to her heart. He slapped his hand on his son's shoulder and announced, '*Corpus delicti*, as the Romans say – seize the day. Well, your mother and I are certainly going to seize our day, son.'

David saw him out, noticing the Rolls-Royce and driver waiting outside to whisk him home to his big house at the back of the park. Crikey, there was a lot of money in a few haddock and some sloppy peas then.

He stood at the door and waved off his new dad, thinking about all that had happened. And then he smiled, visualising Olive's face when she returned from her cruise and he told her that her cleaning days were over for ever.

Chapter 51

Frankie had cheered up considerably by the time dinner was announced. The ship had a very happy carnival feel that could-n't fail to nudge anyone from a dark mood. The sound of steel drums filtered through from the decks where bands were play-ing, and most people were dressed in loud clothes. Even the majority of the more staid guests in their traditional cocktail dresses had made some sort of an effort and were sporting bright earrings or flowers in their hair. All the waiters were wearing yellow Hawaiian shirts with patterns of palm trees, and the head waiters were in blue with pictures of bright orange suns on them.

'Supremo's trousers are a bit tight tonight,' Frankie told the others. 'I think I see why they call him Supremo now. A man of unhidden talents.'

'Don't be rude,' tutted Roz, who stole a look anyway.

'Good evening, ladies.' Supremo handed them all a floral lei to wear. 'How are you all?'

They twittered that they were all very well as Elvis and Buzz attended to them, draping the serviettes over their laps. The waiters were always so chirpy and smiley even though they never seemed to stop working.

'They're thinking of the tips at the end of the cruise,' explained Royston when he arrived at the table in a lime-green shirt decorated with pink flamingos that exceeded the legal decibel limit – and three leis draped around his neck. 'I'd smile at anyone like that as well if I thought they might give me a big tip,' he went on, flashing a Simon-Cowell-white grin.

'Don't be daft,' said Stella. 'There's a lot of mean swines on here who don't tip. Celebrities are the worst, apparently. 'Ere, did you know that actor from the telly is on board – Dom Donald?'

'Dom Donaldson,' corrected Eric, who had also joined in the dress code and was wearing a floral shirt but at the more sober end of the scale. 'Yes, we've seen him a few times around the ship.' He didn't sound that impressed. 'He's one of the brigade who reserve their sunbed in the morning then wander off until after lunch.'

He didn't absorb the lesson we gave him then, thought Frankie. She wasn't surprised really. Dom Donaldson was far too arrogant to think that other people's rules applied to him.

Nigel caused quite a stir when he made his arrival. He was wearing lots of bright leis around his neck and had one of the table party-blowers clenched in his teeth, which he blew loudly when he sat down. He explained that people were more likely to join in festivities if they saw him taking part. No one said anything aloud, but they all noticed how Ven puffed up visibly when Nigel took his seat next to her.

'And how was your day?' Nigel asked the table in general as he sat down.

'Awful!' said Royston. 'There was actually a cloud at one point. I nearly asked for a refund.'

'Gorgeous,' corrected Stella. 'Korcula is one of our favourite islands.'

Frankie stayed quiet. She couldn't have cared less if she never heard about the place again. It would be forever tainted with memories of being rejected by a drop-dead gorgeous hunk and not having a clue why.

The menu was very tropical that night – lots of coconut and banana scattered about the dishes. Ven just hoped she had enough room for the banoffee cheesecake. She suspected she might just squeeze a forkful or two in.

'Excuse me.' Nigel leaned across her for the butter pats and his arm brushed against her hand, which he immediately apologised for. Under the table her knees went ever so wobbly. There was a little cut on his neck where his razor must have nicked it. She wondered if his face was as smooth as it looked or whether she would feel stubble on her cheek if he kissed her.

'And what did you think of Korcula?' Nigel asked Ven, turning the full beam of his attention onto her for the first time that evening. 'She's a bit of a jewel, isn't she?'

'Lovely,' said Ven. 'Not quite as nice as Venice though.' She deliberately made that sound like a flirt, only to regret it immediately afterwards as he didn't react and a second later had turned and was talking to Royston. Annoyingly, Royston and Eric claimed most of his attention over the main course as well, talking about technical ship-things.

Any plans Ven had to engage him over dessert were thwarted as Nigel made his excuses when Buzz brought the menus back. He wished them all a good evening and hoped to see them up on deck for the party. He touched Ven on the shoulder as he did so. She felt a stupidly romantic sigh swell up inside her. He made her spirits feel like she was on an Alton Towers ride. She might have been forty on the outside but inside she was fourteen again, nursing her secret crush on Mr Lambert the English teacher, who was the Mr Rochester to her Jane Eyre.

'What are you doing tomorrow in Cephalonia then, girls?' asked Royston, ordering a round of banana liqueurs for everyone with their coffee and, as usual, allowing no one to stand in his way.

'We're going to the caves,' said Roz. 'Have you been?'

'Yes, we have,' said Irene. 'Wear sensible shoes because there's a lot of steps.'

'Yes, Olive told us,' Frankie replied. 'She lived in Cephalonia for a while.'

'A long time ago,' added Olive. *In another lifetime.*

After coffee, they all headed up en masse to the deck party. Frankie spotted Vaughan at the other side of the pool. He was wearing a shirt with bright orange giraffes on which complemented his ruffled blond hair. For such a big man he looked cute, but she didn't want to smile at him this time. The shadow of a very big scowl fell across her face until Olive saw it and nudged her back into their company and away from once again trying to work out what she had said whilst they were enjoying pizza and salad on that lovely Croatian island.

'Come on, let's go and embarrass ourselves by doing "Agadoo",' she said, pulling Frankie towards the dance floor.

'You're on,' replied Frankie with a firm nod of her chin, and threw herself into pushing pineapples and shaking trees, even though she felt as crushed as one of those pineapples in a piña colada. Then all four of them did a fully coordinated macarena. Roz found that her hips seemed to be very much more snaky since she had started belly dancing. Frankie threw everything she had into the 'Ketchup Song' then they joined a long conga that was going to python past Vaughan and his party in about twenty steps' time.

'Don't look at him,' Olive ordered sternly, only hoping that she had the same strength left for herself when they were on Cephalonia tomorrow. Because she had an awful feeling she wouldn't be able to practise what she had just preached.

DAY 11: CEPHALONIA

Dress Code: Formal

Chapter 52

'Another shitty day in paradise!' called Royston to the four of them as they passed in the Buttery, before Stella slapped him on the shoulder for swearing so loudly in public.

There had just been an announcement over the Tannoy, in Nigel's soft Irish brogue, that today the temperatures were tantamount to being in a furnace and please to make sure that passengers were carrying plenty of suncream and wearing hats and keeping hydrated.

'That goes especially for you two natural blondies,' said Frankie, giving Olive a poke in her back and Roz a wink.

'Don't worry,' said Olive. 'I'm slathered in factor forty.' She just wished there was something that could have protected her heart as well, because she could feel its vulnerability, every time her head turned towards the shore and her eyes landed on the lush green island of Cephalonia.

She pictured herself aged nineteen, sitting in the Greek sun and being handed the forecast of the life that was to come to her. Would she have upped and left so quickly then, knowing what was in store? Would she have left the arms of a kind, loving man and an island of blue seas and white pebble beaches for a fat, lazy husband and a life of cleaning other people's toilets? God, what an idiot.

*

In 1943 Cephalonia had been occupied by Italian troops for two years. There was a co-existence between occupiers and occupied, friendships and relationships had grown and there was much merriment on the island. But when Italy surrendered to the Allies, German forces arrived en masse to disarm the Italians. However, the latter did not trust that the Germans would allow them safe passage and they were worried for the safety of the Cephalonian people. The Italians and the Cephalonians joined arms against the Germans, but alas, the Italians were overcome. Five thousand soldiers were massacred in battles and coldly executed in groups. And of the four thousand surviving Italian soldiers who were loaded on ships destined for labour camps in Germany, three-quarters of them died when the vessels hit mines in the water.

Olive cried in class when Miss Walker taught them about the slaughter of the Acqui Division in fifth-form History. The teacher brought the island to life for Olive, with her stories of goats and rabbits whose teeth were gold because of the minerals in the ground, of underground lakes and the caves where the acoustics were so superb that the opera singer Maria Callas sang in them for an audience of hundreds. But it was this episode of history which would eventually lead Olive to visit this island, cursed by earthquakes but blessed with outstanding beauty. And it was on this island that Olive's heart first learned to beat for another.

Olive tuned out on the tour bus as the guide started talking about Captain Corelli and the history of the island. There wasn't anything about the history of Cephalonia that Olive didn't know.

The bus trundled down the main street in the capital Argostoli. Olive saw the dress shop, renamed now, where she had bought the flowing white sundress that she hoped would catch Atho's eye. She saw the restaurant where Atho had taken her for her first ever meal out with a suitor. She saw the path which led up to the small farm where Atho's brother lived. *Atho Atho Atho*.

Every minute was one step closer to the Bay of Sami and the small hamlet in the hills – Tanos – where the Lemon Tree bar and restaurant sat. And as the bus pulled in alongside the entrance to the Drogarati Cave, Olive felt breathless from a rush of memories.

'I'm glad I've got flatties on,' said Roz, after descending into the cool cave. 'How many steps have we just done?'

'I don't know, I stopped counting at five hundred,' puffed Frankie.

'There's about one hundred and twenty,' corrected Olive. 'Drama queens.'

'I just want to start singing very loudly and see what it sounds like,' said Ven.

'Well, if it's anything like how you used to sing in the school choir it'll sound bloody awful,' replied Frankie, before Ven gave her a thump on the arm.

'Look at those.' Olive pointed up at the stalactite spikes plunging down from the roof of the cave. 'Took thousands of years to form and the Nazis used them for target practice during the Second World War.'

'Isn't it stalagmite?' said Ven. 'I get mixed up.'

'"Mites go up and tites come down",' chorused the others in unison.

'Can't you remember Mr Harrison in Science telling us that?' added Roz. Mr Harrison was very young and handsome, and that lent extra sauce to his 'tites' coming down. Funny to think he'd be tearing towards retirement now.

The sun was waiting for them outside the cave to hit them full blast with its heat. They sat at a nearby café with bottles of ice-cold sparkling mineral water in front of them and sleepy ginger cats weaving underneath their seats looking for scraps.

Then they boarded the bus for the second part of the trip – to the Caves of Melissani.

When they got there, Olive's knees felt trembly as she retraced the steps she had made twenty summers ago down to that cave. It had been closed for maintenance purposes then, but Atho had persuaded/bribed the foreman to open it and let them be alone for an hour. She had packed that memory away in her head like a beloved keepsake, but now it had leaped out of its case and had taken over her brain.

As she walked down the cool stone tunnel and her eyes touched on the first sight of the impossibly blue lake, Olive was instantly transported back to the intensity of that afternoon.

'Oh God, look at the colour of that water!' gasped Roz. The Lake of Melissani was in a cave, but a small portion of the roof above had fallen in many years ago. Now, at midday, the sun was overhead, pouring into the roof and lending the water its light.

'Wait until you get on the boat and then look down,' advised Olive.

Soon they had climbed into one of the small rowing boats and set off across the lake. The water was turquoise, clear and deep, half-salt half-sweet, fed from water from the other side of the island that magically found its way through the rock.

'I want to dive in,' said Roz, mesmerised.

'It's colder than it looks,' Olive warned her. She and Atho had made love in the boat under the eye of the sunshine and then slid into the water to taste it upon their skin. Olive trailed her hand in the lake. It was named after the nymph Melissanthi who had loved the God Pan, but when she found out he did not feel the same way, she threw herself in the water and drowned.

Love was such a precious fragile thing, to be treasured – yet people didn't and were fools for it – herself the biggest one of all. She'd felt the force of Atho's love and had run from it. Here in this cave he had told her what he felt about her, how much he wanted her – body and soul. His emotion was raw, his passion for her honest and wild, yet his love-making had been gentle and selfless. She had been in five-sense heaven that day.

David didn't love her, she had learned the truth of that since she had come on this cruise. She was essential to the smooth running of his life and if she ever left him that's what he would miss – not her, not Olive. That was the biggest difference between the men. Atho had loved Olive with all his heart, but David could have married anyone and been satisfied. And yet which one had she picked to spend her life with?

When the boat moored at the side, Olive suddenly knew she had to go to Tanos.

'I'll find my own way back to the ship,' she announced to the others at the cave entrance, heading quickly for one of two taxis which were waiting by the buses. As she climbed into it, she heard a chorus of three voices behind her saying:

'About flaming time an' all!'

Chapter 53

In the hallway were two suitcases with everything that Doreen was going to take to her new home. A few clothes, photos, toiletries – that was all. She was waiting for Vernon and his Rolls-Royce and driver to pick her up.

An added bonus for David was that Kevin had announced he was moving back in with Wicked Wendy. Apparently she couldn't do without her 'sausage love' he announced that morning, just as David was about to bite into a Walls skinless pork. So that meant that David and Olive were going to have a house to themselves – at last.

'I'm sorry if this has all been a bit too much for you to take in so quickly,' said Doreen, as she sat on the chair in the hallway. There was a gentleness to her voice as she went on to talk about the man who had brought him up. 'Herbert was a good man, you know. I liked him a lot. Of course he was a lot older than me, but it was a nice marriage all the same.'

David felt a bit choked up, remembering his 'dad'. He'd been a kind man, totally under the thumb – but he seemed to like it that way. He wasn't exactly Mr Workaholic, but they'd lived happily without any fancy stuff or posh holidays. He would take young David fishing in the school holidays and they'd make a load of egg-and-cress sandwiches and big flasks of tea to sustain them through the day – and sometimes the night. David could never remember his mum and dad arguing, but then again, he couldn't remember them talking to each other much either. Doreen went to bingo a lot, his father spent a lot of time in his shed. They co-existed, 'rubbed along nicely' some might have said – like he and Olive did. At least, he presumed she was content enough in their marriage; she didn't moan about her lot, anyway.

But since Vernon Turbot had swept into their house two days ago, his mother had flowered like a long-dried seed that had suddenly found some water and a one-in-a-million chance to sprout at last. She had softened and blossomed and seemed to have dropped twenty years of her age. There was air under her feet when she walked across the room, and an uncreasing of the frownlines that had given her a grim look for longer than he cared to remember. Vernon Turbot was walking Botox for her.

'I'm not leaving because I don't love you,' Doreen said suddenly. 'I do, you know. I love you and Kevin very much, but especially you – because you're my lad.'

Whoof. David's eyes suddenly flooded and he coughed hard, trying to stamp firmly down on the rush of emotion.

Doreen went on, 'You see, there are two kinds of people in this world, son: those who can live quite happily without passion and those who were never meant to. I'm one of those people who need to feel their heart beat faster for someone, and so is Vernon. Now Herbert, he didn't. He was happy enough with his shed and his allotment and his fishing rod. My mum and dad were the same; she had her knitting, he had his spaniels. I think you must take after them.' She sighed. 'I don't know which I'd have picked, given the choice. It would have been so much easier, had I been able to settle for a life where the limit of my excitement was a new set of cable needles. But I've been thirsty for too long and now I'm going to drink my fill from Vernon's pool.'

Another lewd image flashed into David's mind which he

shook away before it became an ingrained memory. Listening to his mum, David was half-glad he took after his easily pleased grandparents. Who the hell wanted to have the complications of all those feelings and dormant passions? Thank goodness he and Olive could do without that sort of rubbish cluttering things up.

'You were a love-child in every sense of the word,' Doreen smiled. 'Not like these things on *Jeremy Kyle* where the mothers can't remember who they took their drawers off for. You were born from our love. Herbert couldn't have kids. He always knew you weren't his, especially because you're the image of Vernon as a young man, but it never stopped him loving you as his son. He never made mention of anyone else being your dad.'

'Mam, stop,' said David with a croak in his throat. Then he looked at her and noticed the tears glistening on her powdered cheeks. And big as he was, he went straight over to her and put his arms around her ample body. They squeezed each other affectionately, which segued into a slightly embarrassed patting on the back as they recovered their composure.

'Anyway,' sniffed Doreen, 'we'll see you tomorrow if Vernon is taking you around the shops. No doubt he'll be bringing you up to the house with a parcel of fish and chips to share with me. He was always the best at making them. That Harry Ramsden looks like a nowt, compared to him.'

'Aye, Mam, I'll see you tomorrow,' said David, nodding, barely able to speak. 'That'll be nice.'

A puppyishly excited car horn sounded outside the front door.

'Well, here we go,' smiled Doreen, her eyes shining like jewels as she picked up her handbag. Turning to her son, she said, 'One more thing – I haven't been the best mother-in-law to Olive either. I've taken a lot of my frustration and boredom out on her, more than I have you. Tell her I'm sorry, will you?

She's a good girl. Anyway, now you've some money you can take her off on a holiday and buy her some nice things. Treat her like a woman should be treated.'

'Yes, Mam, I will,' said David. And he meant it. He had plans forming in his brain for them both. Big plans.

Chapter 54

It was less than a ten-minute taxi ride to Tanos and yet it felt like for ever. Olive asked to be dropped by the first farmhouse on the Tanos road. It was still delicately shabby and white with orange shutters on the windows – in fact, it hadn't changed at all. It was just as if she had been transported back twenty years. Even the old sign pointing to the hamlet was still hanging off at an angle from the pole.

The taxi drove off and Olive had a moment of panic about the crazy thing she was about to do. Her legs were jelly by the time she rounded the corner. Two more steps and she would see the Lemon Tree. She took the steps – and there it was.

The sign had been repainted, that was the only difference she could spot. The outside tables were still square and wooden, the chairs rattan-backed. She could see, through the café window, that the juice-machine blades were stirring through lemonade on the counter. A few holidaymakers were drinking coffee and reading newspapers, and a young waitress was busying around clearing tables. Atho always kept the café immaculately clean, but he never chased away the tourist-friendly animals who came to try their luck. The old stray dog who had adopted the café had obviously long gone, but there was a contented scruffy grey cat lounging on a stool which seemed to have been positioned under the shade of an olive tree especially for him or her.

Olive's heart flooded with fondness for the place. Once upon a time she was that waitress flitting around customers, delivering the generous plates of dolmades and moussaka which Atho insisted should be a portion and a half of what other cafés were serving. He was a generous man in all aspects of his life.

Then she saw him. He was there, in the shadows of the café interior. Atho Petrakis. He hadn't become squat and bald and middle-aged, he was just as she remembered him – thick, black hair, straight-backed, his tanned strong arms pulling a coffee from a huge machine.

Olive's head went woozy and the feeling spread quickly around her, weakening her legs and making her reach for a chair, scraping it back against the ground so she could sit on it before she fell. The waitress heard the noise and called to the man as she saw the woman sink down.

'Atho,' she called. And Olive just saw the tall dark man's shape approaching before she slumped in a faint onto the café table.

Moments later, when Olive opened her eyes, she looked up to see it was not *her* Atho, after all, even if he did look extraordinarily like her old lover from a distance.

'Lady, are you well?' the man was asking, and his voice was different from Atho's too – not as smoky or deep. And the hand that was resting upon her shoulder was lighter. Her Atho had large strong farmer's hands.

'I'm so sorry,' excused Olive. 'I was looking for Atho Petrakis.'

'I am Atho Petrakis,' said the man. 'Or was it my father you are looking for?'

Yes, thought Olive, this must be his son. Atho has a son.

'The Atho I'm looking for owned this place twenty years ago.'

'Yes, that is my father.'

'Is . . . is he here?' she asked tentatively. She knew he would-n't be. When these things played out in real life, the sought-after person tended to have picked that day to be somewhere far away. Knowing her luck, he had probably gone on holiday to Barnsley.

'My father is not here any more.'

The words crushed Olive's heart. He was dead. She'd been a fool to leave, and a bigger fool to come back.

'Oh, I'm so sorry,' she said. 'How long ago?'

The waitress smiled, nudged Atho Junior and said something fast and Greek to him.

'Oh no, he's not dead,' said Atho, waving his hand. 'He's retired from the bar. He lives in the house at the back.'

'Where his parents used to live?' asked Olive. Her heart couldn't take this stopping and starting much longer.

'Yes. He is there now. You must be an old friend of his – yes?'

'Yes,' said Olive, her voice quavering.

Atho held out his hand to Olive and, when she took hold of it, he pulled her up from the chair. 'Come with me, lady. I will take you to him.'

He tucked the tea-towel he was carrying into the waistband of his apron and led Olive down the old familiar path at the side of the Lemon Tree to the house where Maria-Grazia and Theo Petrakis had once lived. Now there were changes to see. The little cottage was no more. In its place was a beautiful new double-fronted, two-storey villa painted pale mimosa. The door was split, the top part open, the bottom half closed.

'Papa,' the young man called. 'I have an old friend for you.'

And there, in the top half of the door, appeared a man. Atho. *Her* Atho. The same strong jaw, the same shock of hair, though flecked with far more white now, the same soft lips and dark, dark eyes. Those eyes were shock-wide now, the mouth drooped in disbelief.

'Olive?' he called. 'No, you can't be. It is a dream.'

Then Atho Senior threw open the bottom part of the door and lunged down the short path towards his son and the visitor. His big arms enclosed her, then he held her out at arm's length to look at her, as if he could not believe she was really here, then his arms came around her again and crushed her to him. Behind her, young Atho seemed to be telling his father to be careful and not handle his guest so roughly. If that was the case, Olive hoped her Atho would totally ignore him.

'This is Olive,' Atho announced to his son in a soft and tender voice. 'She is a very old friend of your papa. A dear and beautiful old friend.'

One arm stayed around Olive and he pulled her towards the house.

'Go, Atti,' he said to his son. 'I have a lady to entertain. A lady from England who I have not seen for twenty years.'

And Atho Junior laughed and waved and said, 'I am going, Papa. I am going back to be your slave in the café.'

'Come, Olive, come into my house. Are you all right? Atti says I have to be gentle with you.'

'I'm fine. I just felt a bit faint when I saw him. I thought he was you.'

'How nice you think I am seventeen,' said Atho, taking Olive's hand now and turning to face her. His other hand came upwards as a gentle cup to her cheek and his brown eyes bored deep into her.

'I can't believe it. I can't believe it is you. Twenty years and you are here. How long are you staying with me? Are you here for ever?'

'I'm on a cruise. I'm just on the island for a few hours,' said Olive, unable to stop herself pushing her cheek deeper into his hand. His skin smelled the same – soap-clean with the merest hint of sweet herb. She closed her eyes and the years between now and their last meeting disappeared.

'Come inside,' he said, his voice soft and low. 'This is much different to the last time you were here, isn't it? Probably the only thing in Tanos that is.'

Inside the house was a large open space – a sparkling white kitchen to the right, to the left cream sofas and thick rugs. A long table with eight chairs separated the two areas.

'It's lovely, Atho,' said Olive.

'I had it built for the family,' he said. 'Sit, sit.' He reached for two glasses and a large jug on the worksurface and poured out two wines.

The family. It was a large house so he obviously had married and had sons and daughters and one day grandchildren – if not already. It was stupid to think he had waited on ice for her to return.

'Do you have a big family?' Olive asked, taking a sip of the wine.

'Just my son. One day this will be his, but I don't think he will want it. He prefers to stay at the room in the Lemon Tree. You remember it?' He smiled intently at her. The little room above the bar with the thickly plastered white walls and the tiny windows. And the very creaky bed.

'So this is just for you,' Olive tried not to blush, '. . . and your wife?'

Atho's hand came out and stroked a stray strand of hair back which had fallen across Olive's face.

'My wife died two months after Atho was born. She was a lovely girl but she had problems with her heart. We did not know this until she died.'

'Oh Atho, I'm so sorry.' Olive took his hand into her own. It felt so big and manly and firm.

'It was a long time ago,' said Atho. 'Now tell me about you.'

'I'm married, no children,' replied Olive.

'You are happy?'

Olive's lips manufactured themselves into a smile, but it was a very poor effort. Atho lifted her chin with his finger and he saw the unspoken sadness in her eyes.

'We will eat and you will tell me about the past twenty years,' he said. He stood and dashed around the kitchen gathering plates and food with celebrity-chef-like gusto. Olive smiled, properly this time. She remembered how he always moved with such energy and purpose, every gesture expansive. It was not only Greek blood that flowed through his veins, but Italian. His grandfather was one of the unfortunate soldiers of the Acqui Division slaughtered by the Nazis. His Greek grandmother, Ariadne, was pregnant with her daughter Maria-Grazia when he was killed in 1943. Ariadne gave her daughter the name of her lover's mother in honour of him.

Atho threw a loaf of bread at Olive to catch and slice. He tore salad leaves into a bowl, splashed them with oil and garlic which he crushed under the heel of his hand then added to it sun-dried tomatoes from a pot. He crumbled goat's cheese, sliced meat deftly with an ancient but deathly sharp knife. He squeezed fresh lemon over a bowl of shiny plump olives and delivered it to the table with a flourish.

Over that rustic, delicious lunch, they talked. Olive told him about her friends and the cruise and what she did for a living. And Atho told her how over the years he had bought up lots of property and was a man of means, and that his mother and father had retired to Fiskardo in the north of the island to be near to their daughter, but only when Atho Junior had grown up. He told her that he had not married again after his wife had died. He had not been an angel – there had been women, but no one with whom he wanted to share his bed for more than a night or two.

'I thought that maybe God was telling me I was meant to be alone,' he said, taking a sweet baklava and sweeping up some honey with it.

'You sound less alone than I am,' said Olive sadly. Atho stopped eating and poured more wine.

'I wrote to your mayor to try and find you,' he said. 'I didn't get a reply.'

'Did you?'

'Of course. He probably thought I was some crazy Greek after an English passport. Now tell me about your husband.'

Olive sighed. Where to begin? She hadn't a clue, so Atho prompted her.

'Does he look after you? Has he built you a nice house?'

'We live with his mum.'

'Does he work hard for you?'

'Er . . . he has a sore back.'

'Do you love him?'

Olive opened her mouth to answer and found that she couldn't. To say 'no' would have been disloyal, unfair. But equally, neither could she say 'yes' to someone she had loved as she had loved Atho Petrakis. How could she compare the 'love' of her husband and his big hot-air promises to the love of a man with whom she had eaten picnics on the beach, made love in olive groves, kissed in the sea and sailed on the blue, blue waters of a magical lake? She had flowered in that one Cephalonian summer, quickened by the kisses of a man who knew that love was all about giving. Olive too knew all about 'giving'; she had been hard-wired into caring for others from an early age, with her own wants and needs taking a rude second place. She didn't know how to accept someone doing things for her without it feeling uncomfortable, without feeling that she wasn't worthy of their efforts. With two people giving each other all they had, life could have been so good.

Atho's voice was heartbreakingly tender as he asked her, 'Olive, why did you leave me? I thought we were happy.'

'I was. That was the problem – I was too happy.'

'How can you be "too happy"?' His fists were clenched on the table.

Olive shook her head slowly from side to side. 'I've asked

myself this so many times, you know,' she said. 'Coming here was only ever meant to be one summer – for me. One summer when I knew my parents were well and I could get away. I never expected to fall in love with life so much here. I never expected to fall in love with you.'

'So you did love me?'

'Oh GOD, you're joking!' Olive laughed, but there was a spray of tears in that laughter too. 'I thought . . . I thought that girls like me didn't leave their families and move to Greece. *Shirley Valentine* was a story, a dream, it wasn't what happened in reality.'

It sounded so weak and pathetic, but that's exactly how it had been. Olive's mum had been in her mid-forties when she had given birth to her, her father nearly sixty, and with her dad in poor health, her mother had relied on her far too much. And they hadn't exactly been the type to encourage their daughter to spread her wings.

'And so who looks after you now, Olive?'

It was such a simple question, but wounding in its aim. People like Olive did the caring, they weren't cared for.

Atho reached across the table, took Olive's hand gently and tugged her to her feet. 'Come,' he said. 'I want to show you something.'

He led her out of the back door of the villa and swept his hand across the sight there. Olive gasped as her eyes focused on pots and pots of white roses.

'They don't grow well in the ground, but here in the pots, they bloom. Year after year they get bigger and stronger with more scent. Yorkshire roses. I planted them to remind me always of you.'

'No, you didn't,' scoffed Olive. But Atho had never been a man with a line in false seduction. He didn't need to. He only had to look at Olive and her knickers fell off. 'Did you?'

'Althea, my wife, she was a sweet girl,' said Atho, as he wove his fingers into Olive's. 'We would have been content to live together if she had survived. But my heart never beat as strong for anyone as it did for you.'

Olive wanted to laugh a little. As if she could inspire *that* sort of passion! But she looked up at this big strong man and saw the truth in his eyes.

Atho stroked her hair. His fingers came to it and left it as if he wanted to touch her, but felt it was wrong. But after twenty years and a crap marriage, Olive wasn't so sure she could hold herself back from all she had missed.

'I want to kiss you, Olive,' he said, his lips dangerously close to hers. She could taste the honey on his lips from the baklava he had just eaten.

'Atho . . .' His lips landed hard on hers and she didn't want to push him away. So she didn't. She savoured the fierceness of his kiss like a woman who was trying to cram twenty years' worth of all she had missed into a few seconds.

'I don't think you have been kissed for a long time, Olive,' he said in hushed tones, his chest panting with desire.

'I haven't been kissed like that since you last kissed me,' said Olive, and meant it. She had been so stupid. She had presumed her passion for Atho was a freak flame, a huge explosion then it would die out and leave her cold and alone in a strange country. So she had chosen instead a small flame that was too weak to warm her. And all the while the huge flame had kept burning and living – and hoping.

'What time do you need to go back to the ship?' asked Atho, his lips now on Olive's neck.

'I've got to be back on board for h...haaalf past four. At the latest.'

'I will make sure you are safe on your ship,' he said, pushing Olive against the tree of her namesake. 'I want to make love to you.'

Olive gasped.

'But I won't.'

Olive gasped even harder.

'You will come back to me this time, Olive. I will make sure of that.' His lips brushed against her collarbone, the black stubble quickening every erogenous zone within a five-mile radius. 'My God, you will be begging to come back to me.'

Atho Petrakis kept his promise and did not make love to Olive. His hard groin pressed into her as he kissed her against the olive tree and made it perfectly plain that he could have taken her at any moment – and been ready. His fingers undid one single button on her shirt, then his tongue dipped into the space it uncovered and no further. He kissed her till her lips were swollen, her neck raw, her legs barely strong enough to support her. Her nerves were screaming for him to finish what he had started when his thumb made a single fleeting brush across her nipple – then he rang his son, told him to send a taxi for his friend and he buttoned Olive's shirt up again as they waited for it to arrive. Annoyingly, it took only a few minutes before they heard a car horn toot its arrival.

He picked off the fattest white rose and kissed it before he handed it to Olive. He smoothed down her hair because it was wilder than a haystack in a tumble-dryer and kissed her – fleetingly this time – on her throbbing lips. He smiled knowingly into her eyes which were as green as the olives he grew, shining with the light that only a woman who was desired and loved gave out.

'Now you will return,' he said. 'We have twenty years to make up for. I can wait a few more weeks. Olive, you are a woman who needs to be loved and I know you still love me. Come back to me this time and stay and flower in my care like my white roses.'

As she waved goodbye to him, Olive was shivering from the strength of her reignited feelings. How could they still be there after all this time, dormant, waiting? She had not expected that at all. Atho Petrakis had known exactly what he was doing by not making love to her and merely flicking drops of water at her newly awakened thirst. Olive's brain was scrambled by the time the taxi reached the port.

Chapter 55

Ven, Roz and Frankie were thrown into panic when the Tannoy call sounded.

'Would a Mrs Olive Hardcastle of cabin C160 please contact Reception.'

'That means she hasn't come back on board!' said Roz, bursting into Frankie's cabin, with Ven at her heels.

'Oh hell!'

'I knew we shouldn't have left her,' said Roz, who had been saying every hour something to the effect of 'I'm not sure we should have let her go. It's been twenty years since she's seen Captain Corelli. He's probably a fat old sweaty bloke constantly pissed on ouzo now with twelve kids and a kebab van.'

Frankie dived for her handbag. 'Has anyone rung her mobile?'

'Tried it and it's switched off,' said Ven.

'Oh buggeration. What do we do?'

Their panic was further compounded by Roz's observation that the ship was pushing away from the portside. 'We're setting off!' she shrieked.

'I'm off to Reception!' yelled Ven, bombing out of the door and behind her, in quick pursuit, were the others. They took the stairs like Charlie's Angels chasing a felon. There was a queue waiting for assistance.

'This is no time to be British,' said Ven, preparing to muscle in on a pensioner questioning her interim room statement. She had just got to the 'excuse me' part when Roz pulled her back. Because there, above them on the gallery of the next floor, they could see Olive looking at a carousel of books outside the Emporium. She was standing next to the huge wall sculpture which stretched up through three floors of the beautiful mermaid 'Mermaidia' and – but for the size – looking like her twin. Both women had long, flowing pale hair and a dreamy, beatific look on their faces. As if they'd just had one hell of a shag, thought Frankie to herself.

'Where've you been?' Ven asked, when they caught up with her. 'We've been worried sick. We thought you hadn't got back.' She patted her heart, trying to persuade it to slow to a nice steady rhythm.

'Chillax,' said Olive, beaming. 'What's the matter with you all?'

'They've been calling you on the Tannoy!'

'Oh, my card didn't register correctly that I was on board. I just went to Reception to tell them I was here – end of.'

'We thought you'd done a *Shirley Valentine*,' said Roz.

'As if!' said Olive, who was the most unlikely person ever to have done one of those.

'Did you see Charlie Cairoli and his mandolin then?' asked Ven, allowing herself to destress a bit now that all was well.

'Was it in tune?' added Roz.

'Bang and Olufsen quality,' grinned Olive. She was about to elaborate when she remembered this was Roz she was talking to so she bit back on any extra-marital detail. 'Yes, he was there and made me lunch and we talked. I had a lovely afternoon. What did you lot do?'

'Well, we had some free time during the trip so we moseyed around some shops, went for some nosebag and ice cream then came back here and vegged out in the sun,' said Ven, still not fully recovered yet from thinking that the ship was sailing off without Olive. 'Well, Frankie and I did. Roz hit the gym.'

'I am getting *so* fat,' said Roz, patting her tummy and feeling a hint of a wobble. 'Belly dancing tomorrow. That'll burn off a few more calories.'

As they wandered back to their cabins to freshen up for dinner, Nigel's gorgeous voice announced over the Tannoy that they were now on course for Gibraltar and there were two lovely relaxing days at sea to look forward to. And that the forecast for those two days promised even more sunshine and calm seas.

Olive put on her green evening dress and studied herself in the mirror, trying to see herself through Atho's eyes. Did he really want her to return to him? The mirror threw back the image of a slim woman with a decent chest and green, green eyes that were shining from a fire burning inside her. She didn't look like Olive the cleaning woman. And she sure as hell didn't feel like Olive the cleaning woman. There was a swagger in her step as she joined the others in Beluga for a pre-dinner gin and tonic and a nosy at other women's formal frocks.

Frankie was wearing a dress she had bought that afternoon in Gallery Mermaidia – a stunning, bright red diamanté number that showed off her beautiful shoulders and fabulous chest to best effect. It was so nice to see her back in bright colours, they all thought. She wasn't built for dowdy.

It was funny how a bit of tanning affected everyone's bravery levels. Women who had huddled up in pashminas on the first few nights to hide away their pale bingo-wings, now couldn't give a toss who saw them. All sizes were showing off their bronzed bits with confidence, and heels were strutting all over the ship. It was lovely and liberating to see. The four of them could have sat in Beluga all night just people-watching.

But the call came for dinner and they wended their way down to the restaurant where they were greeted by the friendly smiling face of Supremo in a shirt so white it could have caused them serious snow-blindness. Eric relayed the apologies of Royston and Stella that evening. Apparently they had decided, last minute, to attend the Indian buffet that was being held in the Buttery. And Nigel didn't attend either, which pulled Ven's spirits right down. She was almost back at the college disco, waiting in vain for her then heartthrob to turn up. Feelings just didn't get any more refined with age, she had to accept. Her disappointment was just as raw now as then.

The menu was Greek-themed tonight.

'I'll have a stifado,' announced Olive confidently.

'Haven't you had enough of that this afternoon?' said Roz, with a cheeky nudge.

'Oy, he only kissed me goodbye!' replied Olive. She did not add that the kiss had lasted over an hour and stolen her breath for most of it. Especially not to Roz, who despite her teasing, would most categorically not have approved of a married woman being subject to the sort of erotic pre-foreplay that made *Debbie Does Dallas* look like an episode of *Dora the Explorer*.

At the other side of Olive, Ven whispered so that Roz couldn't hear, 'Was he as nice as you remembered?'

'Oh Ven, he was gorgeous. He wants me to go back and make up for lost time.'

'And much as you want to, you never will,' said Ven, with impatience. 'Fool.'

'You don't have to tell me what I am,' Olive answered with a smile, but one totally devoid of humour. She had felt brave – strong – on the island, but every second that passed was taking her further away from him, to a weaker place where sense and duty had a stronger pull than her own desires and needs.

The entertainment in the Broadway Theatre was Mikey 'Fingers' Lee, a camp old pianist who had been half his present width when, aged nineteen, he had won *Opportunity Knocks*.

He'd obviously tried to hang on to his youthful good looks with so much Botox that he made Stella look like Mr Bean. But it didn't matter an iota because he was cheesy-fab. Roz groaned a bit about being dragged along to it but she was cheering the loudest for Fingers to do an encore when he took his curtain bow.

'That was bloody brilliant,' she said. 'More. More!'

'What's come over her?' said Ven.

'She's loosened her corsets so much this holiday they'll ping totally off by the end,' giggled Frankie. Then she realised how close the 'end' of the cruise was getting and it made a sour little splash in her laughter.

Ven too heard that spoiling word 'end'. But at least she had something to tell her friends that would considerably soften that particular blow.

Day 12: At Sea
Dress Code: Semi-Formal

Chapter 56

Roz studied the tattoo on Frankie's shoulder as they sunbathed around the Topaz pool the next morning. She had to admit that, as a piece of art, the little angel was beautifully drawn.

'Did it hurt – the tattoo?' she asked.

Frankie stopped reading. 'It scratched a lot,' she said. 'In an annoying way.'

'What made you have it done?'

'I thought an angel on my shoulder might look after me. I would touch it and ask it to help me. Daft, I know, but you'll try anything when you're desperate.'

'Like buy beige clothes to blend in,' Roz teased.

'And hope Death wouldn't notice me,' added Frankie, but she laughed loudly to offset the dark words. 'Aye, well, they're going in the bin.' Her bosom sat proudly inside the new bright orange swimsuit she had bought in Cephalonia. She didn't want to hide away in dull colours any more.

'You never used to wear anything that didn't give me a migraine. It wasn't right seeing you in beige that first day on board. It felt wrong. Even though I hated your guts.' Roz smiled and nudged her.

'Yeah well, with you not around to wind up and spat with, I kind of lost my way a bit. You would have bullied me out of wearing anything less than psychedelic.'

A rush of emotion blindsided Roz and she volunteered to go and get some drinks and settle herself. God, she had been an evil cow. A blinkered, nasty, selfish old bat. How had Manus put up with her? She just hoped it wasn't too late to put things right.

Dom Donaldson pushed right in front of Roz at the bar. She noticed he lacked any ability to say the words 'Please' or 'Thank you'. As usual Tangerina was two paces behind him chewing one arm of her sunglasses as if simulating giving a blow job and positioning herself in a pose that made the best of her perfect figure. Roz wondered what they talked about at home: Einstein's theory of relativity? Darwin's theory of evolution? The vision of the actor in a smoking jacket and leather slippers holding court in a posh house with fellow luvvies came to her and made her burst out in an involuntary giggle. Dom Donaldson gave her a dirty look, recognising her as the woman who had had the effrontery to ask him to sign a common birthday card. If only his adoring public knew he was an arrogant arse. Ven, thankfully, was still in blissful ignorance about him. *Never meet your idols*, that's what they said, wasn't it?

Frankie spotted Vaughan passing in front of her before he saw her, and her heart jumped a massive beat. He turned his head towards her, as if he had heard it, and she didn't have time to avert her eyes and pretend she hadn't seen him. He gave her a small wave because it would have been too rude not to acknowledge her at all, but he didn't break his stride. Frankie tore her eyes away from his long, lean, tanned back but they quickly returned to it again. His sudden coldness hurt her more than she cared to admit to herself. The old Frankie would have raised two fingers to him and yelled, 'NEXT!' The new Frankie worried more about what people thought of her. There had been a lot of time for self-analysis when she was hiding in the shadows with her beige clothes on.

She forced a smile onto her face when Roz came back with

Chocolate Banana cocktails. It was a whole dessert in a glass, but also an essential part of their 'five-a-day', Roz argued.

'I can't believe it's nearly lunchtime,' said Olive, sitting up to receive her cocktail and glancing at her watch. Half past eleven in the morning and she was drinking alcohol. How deliciously naughty. But then she felt incredibly rebellious at the moment. Her dreams last night had been full of Atho Petrakis; in them he had carried on where he had left off yesterday, and she woke up feeling so horny she almost dragged Jesus in from the corridor to sort her out. She was under no illusions: she knew that if she were to return to Cephalonia, she would be in for the love-making of her life. He had always been incredibly attentive, inventive and superlative in that department. How the hell had she ever settled for David and his fumbling, selfish sexual 'technique'? And with Doreen on the floor directly underneath them, Olive could never shake off the fear that they were being overheard, which didn't make for abandon in the bedroom. Not that David was that sexually driven. He 'scratched an itch' in the same way every time, and if Olive got anything out of it, it was a mere byproduct. But then again, she hadn't exactly tried to change the way things were by dragging him off to Pogley Top Woods, which were about as near to an olive grove as was available in Barnsley, or guided his hands to where she wanted him to touch her. She had just let him carry on in his own merry way, thinking everything in his garden was lovely. She was partly to blame for her own frustrations.

She thought of 'this time next week'. She would be back in Land Lane, gathering her stuff together to do Mr Padgett's upstairs. The old man gave her the creeps, always taking any excuse to squeeze past her or touch her and make it look like an accident. Ugh. Maybe she would have had 'welcome home sex' with David by then. He would roll over in the middle of the night and she would lie there and let him enter her and grunt out his orgasm, whilst her imagination roamed to various film stars and Greek café-owners. It would be a poor substitute for the real-life man whom she knew would be patiently waiting for her in a garden full of white roses. Oh GOD – why had she gone back to the Lemon Tree? Life was so much easier without choices to make.

Ven sipped her Chocolate Banana and nearly choked on it when Nigel came into her vision, striding purposefully past at the other side of the swimming pool. She watched as a woman in a pink sarong halted him with a perfectly manicured hand and engaged him in conversation. She was swishing her hair about flirtatiously, sticking her boobs out whilst sucking in her stomach. She couldn't have been more obvious if she'd had *shag me* tattooed on her forehead.

Ven felt a stab of jealousy, unable to stem it even though she was quite aware it was a puerile emotion to feel. She had no claim on Nigel. He was a man paid to be nice to passengers; a man who wouldn't even remember her name in a week because he would be sitting with another group of people at dinner making small – if lovely and friendly – talk.

He was smiling at Pouty-Knockers who was using her hands a lot as she spoke – another flirty gesture. Then his eyes swept to the side and Ven thought they fell on her; she was just about to wave when he turned back to Pouty-Knockers and they strolled off together out of sight.

The sun was bright and high and shining its heart out, but that morning, there was a glum little cloud above four particular sunbeds on the ship.

Chapter 57

Roz was first in the room for her belly-dancing lesson that afternoon. Fifteen of the original recruits were still stalwarts, Roz the youngest by at least ten years. After a hip-swirling warm-up, she beat down all her self-tormenting thoughts by following Gwen's moves.

A woman aware of her sexual power was lit from within, something which Roz had never allowed herself to be. Despite her long legs, flawless figure and beautiful face with her to-die-for cheekbones, her insecurities had always distorted any image she had of her own attractiveness. She could not have been more desired by Manus, yet most of her self-confidence had been knocked out of her as a kid. She couldn't remember ever getting praise or warmth at home, only criticism and slaps, and the little remaining self-worth she had managed to carry into adulthood had been driven deep underground after Robert's betrayal. But during these belly-dancing sessions Roz – at last – was inching towards becoming in touch with her inner sexuality. The hip undulations and belly rolls were working her pelvic muscles, soothing away her tensions and increasing bloodflow to areas of her body that had been thirsty for a long time. They also gave a rude awakening poke to her libido. She was dangerously close to feeling horny.

She was flushed and breathless after this session. As was

Phyllis, a seventy-seven-year-old, who summed up everything Roz was thinking by saying, 'My goodness, I didn't even move that much down below on my wedding night.' Roz wished Manus were nearby. She had a flash of desire for him, to tear at his shirt like an animal, to be pulled down on the bed and pinned underneath him to do to her whatever he chose. But he wasn't there and a cold shower would probably be wise, so she headed off down to her cabin to get one. But as she was passing by the Restaurant Cruz, the striking figure of Raul Cruz himself rushed out from it and collided with her.

Now Roz had always been a more private person than her friends. Whilst they had shared their crushes, Roz had always been more reserved on that front. What the others didn't know was that Roz had a major torch burning for Raul Cruz. She always watched him whenever he appeared on TV, and everything stopped for *The Devilled Chef* where ten people competed to win his approval, probably more than they coveted the ten thousand pounds first prize.

Raul Cruz was a tall, big-shouldered Spaniard with wild black hair, huge sexy Bournville-chocolate eyes and the arrogant stance of a bullfighter. And here he was in the corridor, steadying Roz with his Michelin-starred hands and looking into her eyes as if he was about to devour her. Slowly – with relish.

'Do forgive me,' he said, his voice heavy and delicious as Rioja.

'It's fine,' croaked Roz, feeling even more blood flow to her pelvic region because he wasn't letting her go so quickly.

'I wonder . . .' he mused. 'Do you think you could help me?'

Roz would no more have answered that with a 'no' than she would have pulled her own nose off.

'Of course.'

'Come, come.' Raul Cruz took Roz's hand and led her into his restaurant. She didn't know why, nor did she care. If the others had seen her now, they wouldn't have recognised the trembling, breathless jelly she had suddenly become.

'Please sit down.' Raul Cruz pushed Roz down on a puffily upholstered chair, his hands firm on her shoulders. Then he tucked her masterfully under the table and asked her to wait for a few moments. He disappeared through a swing door and Roz heard him crashing about behind it.

Roz looked around as she waited. It was a beautiful restaurant, very sumptuously decorated in rich reds and deep purples. Low-volume Spanish guitar music was playing from a sound system and she imagined that at night, with the red candles lit on the tables, it would be a wonderfully intimate atmosphere in which to dine – especially with a lover.

The view from the windows was equally stunning. Before the cruise, she hadn't really thought how a stretch of water could be classed as 'romantic', but now she got it. The sea swept you away, soothed you with its gentle motion, but – like a passionate lover – could never quite be trusted, which gave it a thrillingly dangerous edge. Blimey, she thought, she really was getting affected by the erotic qualities of belly dancing.

The swing door opened with force and Raul Cruz appeared carrying a canapé-laden oval silver platter with one hand and two bottles of wine with the other. He put them down in front of Roz, upturned two glasses, which were already on the table, and poured into one a black-red wine so rich it came with its own Coutts bank account. The second was pink red – a much lighter affair.

'Tell me, please . . .' He gave a hand gesture that encouraged her to fill in the gap of her name.

'Rosalind,' she whispered smokily, aware that she was giving it a bit of a sexy edge with her rolling 'r' pronunciation. The others weren't here to snigger at her using her Sunday name, which was a very rare occurrence.

'Rosalind,' Raul repeated. The name sounded exotic on his

tongue. 'Which is the better wine for this food?' He picked up a piece of thin meat from the platter which had been marinaded in something oily with spices. He rolled it expertly between his thumb and finger and lifted it to Roz's lips. Then he watched her with intensity as she chewed as delicately as she could. On the television Raul Cruz was a dreamboat; close up enough to see his stubble and the tiny space between his eyebrows, he was pant-meltingly god-like.

'Now drink,' he said, seeing the small swallow in Roz's throat. She lifted the first glass and perched her lips upon the rim as if she were kissing it. Her nerves were on fire; this felt more like sex than sex did. She drank. She, of course, hadn't a clue if this wine was a good accompaniment for the food or not. She never paid more than a fiver a bottle for wine and, quite honestly, preferred a lager. But 'Rosalind' was not going to spoil this moment by admitting that.

He then picked up a small wafer and scooped up some caviar with it. He had beautiful long fingers, Roz noticed. No ring on the wedding finger either. She opened her mouth and allowed him to place the wafer on her tongue, like a sexy 'stuff-of-fantasies' priest. Then she tasted the second wine. They were both okay, but she pretended to think about it.

Raul next picked up a fat garlicky prawn and held it so that Roz had to bite into it. Her lips nudged his finger as she did so. She sipped the wine. He raised a small square of pastry with a strong tomato centre which made Roz purr in her throat. The pastry was so light she thought if she spoke it might come out squeaky as if from a post-helium inhalation.

'Good?' he asked.

'Oh yes,' she said, blowing out a bit of pastry onto her lip. But before she could remove it, Raul Cruz lifted his finger and dabbed it off. This was unreal – in fact, it was all more like a scene from a Hollywood film. Actually it was better because she'd watched *that* scene in *9½ Weeks* and couldn't understand

what all the fuss was about. But in real life, being fed by a man –
and no ordinary man but the Raul Cruz – her head was in
danger of blowing off into orbit. This man cooked for A-list
stars and had slept with Supermodels, although in saying that,
she doubted any woman would want to go to bed with him
and get any sleeping done.

Roz was only taking small sips of wine, but her heart-rate
was so fast, the alcohol was rocketing around her system. She
became aware that her body was entering serious flirt mode
for the first time in God knows how long. Her back was
straightening, pushing out her breasts, she was licking her lips,
keeping them moist; her own eye-contact with his was pro-
longed.

A cube of soft bread followed with oyster pâté, a flake of
seared fish, a plump black olive stuffed with lemon, a sticky
date pocket of crushed salty walnut cream, a roll of chorizo,
enveloped in melted manchego cheese in a light batter
case . . . Orgasmic. Then, after the crisp square of thin toast
with the curry butter, Raul's hand did not return to the tray.
Roz chewed slowly, not wanting this very strange episode to
end. Raul lifted the heavy wine to her lips, then when Roz
had drunk from it, he lifted it to his own and placed his soft
red mouth exactly on the rim where hers had been. He
might as well have snogged her face off, she felt as ravaged as
if he had. This bloke didn't need a chat-up line. He could
have had any woman twelve ways just by offering her a
Laughing Cow cheese triangle and looking at her with those
big, beautiful cocoa-coloured eyes. Roz was panting like a
racehorse which had just run the Derby with a forty-stone
jockey on its back.

'Well?' he asked. 'What is your verdict?'

'Gorgeous!' Roz sighed. She was looking directly at him and
talking more about him than the food.

Raul smiled. A sex-filled, white-toothed, Latin smile.

Roz gave herself a mental kick before she was totally hypnotised like Mowgli had been by the spiral-eyed lisping snake Kaa in *The Jungle Book*.

'I think the lighter wine,' she said, trying to sound detached and professional and as if she knew what she was talking about.

'I do too,' he half-whispered, half-growled. 'Thank you. You have told me everything I needed to know.'

The interlude was at a natural end now. Raul took Roz's hand to help her to her feet – luckily, because her legs were decidedly weaker than they had been fifteen minutes ago.

'You must come and dine at one of my restaurants in London,' Raul Cruz said at the door. 'And you must ask for me and say it is "Rosalind with the ice-blue eyes". And I will know immediately that it is you.'

'I will,' gulped Roz, at that moment fully intending to make her booking as soon as her moby had a signal.

He edged closer to her and smiled. 'You have the most beautiful mouth,' he said, studying it. 'If only I were a free man . . .' and he sighed.

Roz couldn't speak because her heart was clogging up her throat.

'Thank you again, *Rosalind.*' He imbued her name with the erotic qualities of Bridget Bardot and Sophia Loren both naked and covered in chocolate.

'It was an absolute pleasure,' sighed Roz, as Raul Cruz's lips landed butterfly soft on her cheek, but covered the corner of her mouth also, causing her to do the biggest gulp in her own personal history.

Raul Cruz closed the door after the woman with the Snow-Queen eyes had floated out of his restaurant. In truth, he *was* a free man. By the time the cruise ended, the tabloid papers would be flooded with stories of his young, fourth, soon-to-be ex-wife slagging him off for being a workaholic and forcing her to take up with an even younger lover who could perform seven times a night. She intended to hit Raul exactly where it hurt – in the reputation. She would reveal how, despite his hot-blooded Latin background, he was sadly lacking in the bedroom department.

Raul Cruz knew that men like him got more physically attractive with age – to a certain point – then the process sadly began to reverse, and over the years he had prepared for that. He was vain, an artiste, a genius who needed adoration and a team of masseurs working on his ego. But he was also a man with a good heart, and he knew there were ways and means to make himself shine without crushing women, but actually doing quite the opposite. There was presently an army of females out there whom he had locked into an intimate bubble or two for a short time. Women he had met on social occasions, reporters, fans, ladies he had pulled into his restaurants and asked their advice about wines pairing with food – only to agree with whatever they decided.

He loved to see women melt before his eyes: it reaffirmed his sexual power. He knew they would be smiling for the rest of the day because the great Raul Cruz had turned his light upon them. He had the support of the masses – a network of heaving bosoms out there who *knew* that no one could look at a woman in the way he did and be rubbish in bed. It was a win-win situation for them both.

Ice maidens were his favourite challenge – women like Rosalind, whom he had seen around the ship with her glacial good looks. He had defrosted her like an industrial microwave. Yep, he still had it! And he had added to his numbers yet another woman who would read what his ex would write in the gutter-press and *know* it was *mierda*.

On the way back to her cabin Roz's heart was like a big flapping bird trapped in her chest. What the heck had happened there? She had never believed that emotionally-charged moments like that could happen in real life; instead they were just excuses made by people who had behaved badly and needed a bigger entity to blame. Now, she had just learned that that was wrong. But, for all that, she didn't want to jump on Raul's bones. It was a sweet but isolated episode, not one meant to lead to more.

She thought of the situation reversed. What would she have done if Manus had told her that he had just been alone in a restaurant and fed delicacies by a woman who had made his heart-rate increase enough to do a three-minute mile? Roz knew she would have gone off in a strop for another hundred years. My God, they were all living breathing things, not dead inside, and perfectly capable of getting shots of desire without it meaning they were about to fall on the floor and fornicate with the person who had just poked at the primal urge within them; not everyone was a potential Jeremy Kyle contestant! In fact, wasn't it good to feel a flame inside? She ached to see Manus so much and tell him she was the Queen of getting things out of proportion. A few canapés and sips of wine had just proved that to her. Manus and Frankie's kiss suddenly seemed to shrink in importance to the size of an atom.

When she got back to the cabin, she decided to make her shower an extra cold one.

Chapter 58

It was so nice to have Royston and Stella back on the dinner-table that night. Royston was wearing a particularly colourful waistcoat that looked like a prop from *Joseph and the Amazing Technicolor Dreamcoat*. He was obviously rather proud of his terrible taste.

It was even nicer to have Nigel back. Ven found herself trying to stem the grin that rose up from the depths of her when she saw him entering the restaurant and making his way over to them.

'Did you get ashore?' asked Eric, happy to have made the joke again after being in port for so many days. Everyone shook their head, played the game and said that they'd forgone that particular pleasure today.

'One more stop to go,' said Irene with a sad little smile. 'This has been such a lovely friendly cruise.'

'Oh, we've still three full days yet, so don't talk about it all ending,' said Olive, who couldn't bear the thought of packing.

'Do you think you'll ever come on another cruise?' Nigel asked Ven, handing her the pepper-grinder. Her hand touched his as she received it and that tiny sensation of skin-to-skin contact spread inside her like hot melted butter.

'I'd like to very much,' quivered Ven.

'What about you girls?' Nigel directed the question to the others in Ven's party.

'It would be lovely,' smiled Olive, knowing that she never would again. Not on her cleaner's wages.

Roz nodded. At the beginning, she wouldn't have been able to picture Manus on board; he would have looked as out of place as Vaughan. But after living on a ship for over a week now, she knew he would have loved it. He looked gorgeous in a suit, on the very rare occasions he ever had to wear one. The last time had been his uncle's funeral. Roz hadn't told him how much he turned her on wearing it, because a) it would have been inappropriate and b) she was an icy-knickered cow who now felt as if she were defrosting by the hour in the Mediterranean sunshine.

'It's been different to how I imagined,' said Frankie. 'In a good way.'

'Like how?' Royston asked, pausing mid-way through ordering another bottle of Châteauneuf-du-Pape from Angel.

'It feels so safe. Before I came I had visions of me staying away from the sides in case the wind blew me overboard. And I thought it would be crowded everywhere I went. And I would have put money on me being bored. But I haven't been bored once. Or felt claustrophobic, or felt unsafe. It's been fabulous.'

Royston, Irene, Eric and Stella were a chorus of the Churchill nodding dogs.

'Yes, I'd come back in a breath. Not that I'll be able to afford it for a long time. If ever,' Frankie sighed.

'There are always deals to be had though, so don't write it off,' said Royston. 'I mean, you wouldn't believe what we got our suite for. It was an unbeatable deal.'

'You couldn't beat what we paid for this,' laughed Roz. 'Ven . . . arrghh!'

She shut up as Ven's high heel made contact with her shin

and Ven flashed her a very clear 'shut up' message with her eyes.

'I got a good last-minute offer,' Ven said quickly, to stem further inquisitions. 'But I bet we didn't get as good a bargain as you super-cruisers.'

Royston then launched into details of his mega-deal, and he and the others traded information on the best travel agents whilst Roz rubbed her shin and whispered to Ven,

'What the hell did you kick me for?'

'I don't want them knowing I won a trip,' said Ven through clenched teeth.

'Whyever not?' asked Roz. 'It's not exactly something to be ashamed of.'

'Shhh. I'll be answering questions all night if you tell them that!'

Which was a fair point, thought Roz. Although Ven's reluctance to tell anyone about her win made her feel, and not for the first time, that there was something she wasn't telling them.

'I don't think I'll be dining with you tomorrow,' said Nigel. 'I'm going to Cruz.'

'Oh, that's a shame,' said Frankie, adding pointedly and rather loudly too, 'Isn't it, Ven?'

'Oh yes, yes,' said Ven, wishing she were near enough to kick Frankie as well.

'Lucky you,' sighed Roz absently. 'What that man can't do with a chorizo isn't worth talking about.'

'And how would you know?' Frankie nudged her.

'I watch his programmes, of course.' Roz snapped back into herself. 'I imagine he's very good at what he does.' *In and out of bed*, she smirked to herself.

'What's all this I hear about the three ships, Captain?' asked Royston, diving into his passion fruit Pavlova like a starving man.

'The Cruise of the Grandes Dames, you mean?' said Nigel.

The others leaned in to listen because they didn't know what Nigel and Royston were talking about. Ven noticed he had missed a line of stubble on his cheek. She wished she could put her lips against it.

'The *Duchess Alexandra*, the *Lady Beatrice* and the *Dowager Mary* – the three Grandes Dames of the cruise world – are making their final journeys at the same time. They're sailing in formation for the Suez Canal. It'll be quite emotional. The *Duchess* was my first captaincy. We should cross paths with them tomorrow morning.'

'Liners!' declared Eric with gusto. 'They'd withstand anything the Atlantic had to chuck at them. Fabulous old girls. We've been on all three, haven't we, Irene?'

Irene nodded meekly in the background.

'What'll happen to them?' asked Eric.

'The *Lady Beatrice* will sail to the States to be a floating hotel, the *Dowager* will be a museum in Scotland and I think they'll break up the *Duchess*.' Nigel sighed, rather sadly.

'Bloody criminal, that,' said Eric with feeling. 'That ship has the most beautiful towering atrium I have ever seen.'

'Why do they always call ships by women's names?' asked Ven.

'Not all countries do,' said Eric, keen to jump in and show off his knowledge as always. 'Most, but not all. I believe the original reasons for that have been lost in history, isn't that right, Captain O'Shaughnessy?'

'Perfectly right,' agreed Nigel.

'It's because they'll give you a hell of a ride if you stump up enough money,' Royston guffawed until Stella slapped him, but she was laughing along with the others as she administered corporal punishment.

'I imagine,' began Nigel, 'it's because once upon a time men spent so long at sea they might as well have been married to it.

Calling their vessel by a female name made them feel close to some form of female entity. Some sailors called their boats after their mothers in the hope that she would protect them. Whatever the truth, it's a very intimate relationship between sailor and craft.'

Ven melted a little more. Nigel might as well have been reciting poetry. For a moment there she had a glimpse into how men could form emotional attachments with the things they drove – more so than with their partners, sometimes. She remembered how Ian had nearly cried when he'd bumped his sports car and knackered the door. She only wished he'd been as affected by knackering her heart.

'I like to think it's like a marriage,' Royston went on. 'The man thinks he's in charge, but it's really the woman who's controlling whether he sinks or swims.'

Stella's jaw dropped open, and she looked as shocked as anyone with three ton of Botox freezing her face could.

'That was lovely,' she gasped. 'I didn't know you had it in you.'

Royston winked at her. 'You see, gel, you still don't know everything about me.'

It seemed that poets' souls were all over the ship today. Ven had noticed in the *Mermaidia Today* that a poet she really liked – Rik Jones-Knight – was on board and doing a virtuoso performance that evening. She knew it wouldn't be the others' cup of tea, especially as there was a comedian from Liverpool on in the Broadway Theatre who got rave reviews from Royston and Eric, and so she was quite prepared to go there alone.

When Nigel stood to go and wished them goodnight, Ven wondered if she were being paranoid because he seemed to say it to everyone but her. His eyes glazed over her as if he was trying to pretend she wasn't there. It was just a shadow of a feeling, but slightly upsetting all the same, especially as the older she got, the more she knew she was in touch with her intuition. She ought to get a grip, though – really. She had as much chance of having a romantic interlude with the Captain as . . . well, as Roz had with Raul Cruz!

Chapter 59

If ever a man looked like a tortured genius, it was the poet Rik Jones-Knight. He had that shabby chic-ness about him that smacked of a man who belonged in a tuxedo but couldn't afford to buy a new one and had to rely on his very rich friends to give him their cast-offs. His hair was romantically unkempt and fell in long seventeenth-century raven-and-white curls to his black-suited shoulders. Frankie had the fancy that if he shook his head, a cloud of wig powder would escape.

'I never did "get" poetry,' she confessed. 'And this looks even more like pretentious bollocks than most.'

'He's a literary cult,' said Venice.

'That's very similar to what I was thinking about him,' scoffed Frankie.

'Stop it,' Ven warned her. 'You should have gone off to Broadway with the others if you felt like that.'

'Naw,' smirked Frankie. 'I volunteered to come with you because I find I'm in the mood for a bit of culture.'

'You're what?'

'Okay then, I was intrigued. Plus I reckon this bloke might be more hilarious than the Scouse comedian.'

'He's not funny, he's a maverick. He writes a complete poem then strips away every single word which isn't needed. It can take him a couple of years to complete a single one. So actually, yes, you're right to be intrigued,' Ven sniffed.

'I am,' Frankie admitted. 'Though probably not for the same reasons you are.'

Ven smiled. She knew Frankie wouldn't be converted, but she appreciated that her friend had come along with her to give her some company.

As Rik Jones-Knight climbed onto the stage, the applause revved up for him and he milked it with grateful nods and bows.

'Thank you, everyone,' he said, with an effeminate flick of his hair. There was a magnificent pause whilst he waited for silence to fall.

'In a world where poetry, to the masses, means unintelligible, copiousness, superabundance, my work is unique,' he launched into his speech modestly – not. 'I believe in using only the most everyday and thus perfect words for my Opera. I begin with "Rain".'

You could have heard a pin drop as Rik Jones-Knight collected himself and opened up his book of poems from which he read.

'Rain.'

There was enough time after the title had been announced for a small shower. He was certainly hell-bent on drawing out the anticipation.

'Rain
Hard
Fast
Wet.'

Then his voice broke into an orgasmic cry: 'IT COMES!'

The echo of his words faded in the room then rapturous applause exploded into the air.

'Why am I clapping?' said Frankie. 'Because he's made a shower sound like a shag?'

'More or less,' said Ven with high amusement.

'Here's some poetry,' Frankie tutted. 'Rik Jones-Knight, is totally sh—'

'Shush!' said Ven, drowning out her expletive.

Rik Jones-Knight waited patiently for the clapping to subside.

'My next poem is called "Myra".'

There were a few shocked, 'Oohs,' from the audience. Surely not Myra Hindley, it was thinking as a collective mass. Blimey, that was brave!

'Myra,' he repeated. Then his voice dropped to a despairing whisper.

'Why?'

He dropped his head as if in prayer and waited once again for the clapping to begin, which it eventually did.

'Genius,' said the woman next to Frankie, who was staring at Rik Jones–Knight as if he were the Second Coming of Christ. 'What more does anyone want to know about her?'

Frankie opened her mouth to reply but, quite honestly, the woman had a point.

'I almost understood that one,' whispered Frankie to Ven. 'I'm not sure if that means I should be shot for being a pretentious twat.'

'I'll have you writing limericks by the end of this hour,' winked Ven.

Poetry readings followed on various subjects. The Sun, Love ('Born. To die'), Footprints, Gin, Coal (Men. Mining. Crushed bodies. Adding. Layers. of Crushed Bodies), to name but a few. The woman next to Frankie almost needed a cigarette after Rik Jones-Knight's final crescendo; or a dunk in an ice-cold bath to dampen down her ardour. She was first in the queue to buy his book of poetry, priced at £30. There weren't many words in it, but a hell of a lot of black and white photos of the 'genius' in various poses of unsmiling intensity. They were either very old portraits or heavily Photoshopped.

'Not minimalistic on his pricing, is he?' said Frankie as she waited in the queue with Ven.

'Admit it, you enjoyed it just a bit, didn't you?'

'Absolutely. I'm going to my cabin now to write a book.'

'You would have thought so differently if you'd had Miss Tanner as your English teacher,' laughed Ven. 'She was the one who opened my eyes to how lovely poetry was.'

'Yes, well, we couldn't all be in the top set,' sniffed Frankie. 'Some of us had to put up with Mrs Euston, who was as bored teaching us as we were bored of being taught by that old cow. Wonder if she's dead yet. Or if she's still living part-time in Loch Ness.'

'Frankie, don't be rotten.'

'Mind you, I thought she was dead back then. I've seen more life in a cooked crab.'

'She was pretty awful,' Ven consented, as Frankie shivered at the thought of Mrs Euston. As Ven knew only too well, a good teacher could turn around lives. Frankie had been far too clever to be pushed into the bottom set for English Literature. But once trapped there, any interest that remained for the subject dug a grave and jumped in it. Ven, though, had flourished in her class under the tutelage of Miss Tanner. The rich language of Keats had first got her hooked, but she absorbed everything she read.

She was always going to become a writer, and Miss Tanner said she certainly had the ability. Ven hadn't written anything for a long time, though. Ian didn't like her working on her manuscript in the evenings – said it was rude of her to be so self-absorbed. And though Ven preferred the sumptuousness of word-rich poetry, Rik Jones-Knight had stirred something inside her tonight, however much Frankie might have scoffed. He had reignited her love of putting words together so expertly that a finished piece of poetry or prose was like a perfect jigsaw picture. She really must pick up a pen and a pad and see if she still had it in her.

They were now at the front of the queue. Close up, Rik Jones-Knight was wearing a lot of make-up which still didn't make him look anything like as young as his publicity picture. To Frankie, he looked a bit embalmed. Maybe he was related to Mrs Euston.

'Shall I personalise this book for you?' he asked Ven, who had gone a bit fluttery and girly.

'Yes, please,' she replied. '"To Venice".'

'Venice. Venice.' He mused over the name as if searching each letter of it for a hidden meaning. 'That is going to be the title of my next poem.'

Ven's excitement fluttered all the way down the queue. He wrote on the title page of the book with an exaggerated flourish and then turned to Frankie as one of the crew took Ven's cruise-card details so the book could be charged to her account.

'Shall I personalise this book to you, also?'

Frankie opened her mouth to say no, she didn't want to buy one – but put on the spot, she ended up saying,

'That would be lovely. Thank you – I really enjoyed you. Frankie – my name is Frankie.'

'Books are worth a lot more when they are signed by the author but not personalised to the reader, did you know?' said Rik Jones-Knight, with all the confidence of one who knew his autographed tomes would be battled for in Sotheby's auctions in years to come. Then again, he also appreciated that his public wanted his books made special for them, so he asked Frankie to spell out her name.

'You two-faced sod,' laughed Ven when they stepped into the lift.

'Aw, what the heck, I made him feel good,' Frankie smiled, then positioned herself into a grand Rik Jones-Knight pose. '"Venice. Captain-Shagger. The End".'

'Bugger off.'

'No really, I wanted to buy this book,' winked Frankie. 'It's the perfect size to prop up my wobbly coffee table at home.'

Ven went up to the top deck before she retired for the night. She passed by a crocodile of sleepy but smiley children coming from a late magic show and holding home-made wands and saw, en route, the deliciously gorgeous Dom Donaldson holding court with the young dancers and singers from the Mermaidia Theatre Group. Tangerina was seated next to him in a very short ra ra skirt showing off her impossibly long legs, which probably took up a whole tube of fake tan in one sitting. Each.

Ven wondered if Florence and Dennis would be up on deck again. She had never seen them around the ship during the day. She imagined they would frequent one of the more sedate bars or maybe preferred to plod around their cabin instead. Some of the plusher cabins had a grand piano in them, and an upstairs. And a magazine rack. Alas, she was out of luck as there was no sighting of them. There were quite a few people up there that evening, enjoying the stars and the lovely smiling moon. Ven joined them, sipping at her Tia Maria nightcap and enjoying the salving breeze. Just as she was about to call it a night, she thought she had seen Florence out of the corner of her eye, but when she turned with a smile, ready to say, 'There you are again!' there was no one there, after all. It was just a trick of the moonlight.

DAY 13: AT SEA

Dress Code: Formal

Chapter 60

The four of them were up early the next morning, determined to squeeze as much enjoyment as they could out of the precious last days, so they went down to be served posh breakfast in the Ambrosia restaurant. Elvis was their waiter, fresh-faced and smiling a 'Good morning,' as he delivered their order.

'I am never going to fit back into normal life,' said Frankie, who had got very used to being called 'ma'am' and having her meals made, her room cleaned, and the most taxing thing about her day being to decide what she should wear to dinner.

Ven opened her mouth to speak then stopped herself. *No, not yet.* She glugged down some orange juice and watched Dom Donaldson and Tangerina being led to the next-but-one table. 'I must get his autograph before I leave,' she said. 'I wonder if he'd sign this serviette . . .'

Roz stopped her quickly. 'No, not now,' she advised. 'He's having his breakfast. I bet he gets interrupted all the time. Ask at the end of the cruise.'

'Yeah, you're right,' Ven agreed, to Roz's relief.

But Ven did notice, as they stood up to leave, how Dom Donaldson clicked his fingers at Elvis for attention, and gave his order without a nod to the word 'please'.

Olive went off for her fourth massage of the cruise. She hadn't been able to get Leo and his strong hands this time, but still she hoped that 'Romana' would have a firm grip on deep-tissue massage. She didn't want a drippy kneading that made her feel she was merely being wiped down with a tea-towel.

Despite having enough dresses to wear, there was always time for more shopping, and rails of gorgeous gowns and suits had been wheeled out that day and were drawing a crowd. A long stall with perfumes and aftershaves had been set up as well and the girls were squirting themselves liberally with fragrances that they liked the sound of but had never tried.

'Isn't this just a slice of heaven,' said Frankie, before wincing at the pong she had just released from a beautiful-looking bottle. 'I smell like a sweet shop. Christ! Who'd wear that?'

'The youth of today,' said Roz. 'Put it down and pick up something more suited to your age. Here, look, there's a fragrance called "Cardigan".'

'Very funny,' ha-ha-ed Frankie, her chuckle drying up as once again Vaughan crept into her vision. She tried not to watch him wander over to the aftershave counter and sample something from a bottle that was the glass equivalent of himself – long, strong shoulders and a lean waist.

'What do you think?' Ven came over holding against herself a glittering gold dress in one hand and a silver one in the other.

'Wow!' whistled Frankie. 'They would look gorgeous on you.'

'I meant for you,' Ven told her.

'They would be too long for short-arse me,' said Frankie.

'You can get alterations done on board. You could choose one and have it sorted for tonight if you hurry up and buy it. Go on – treat yourself,' urged Ven.

'You mean "go on, let the poor sods paying your bill treat me",' smiled Frankie.

'Okay, yes, that's what I mean,' Ven said. 'They've got matching accessories in the shop – handbag, shoes. Get yourself totally gelded up for tonight and feel a million dollars.'

'Gelded? Gilded, isn't it?'

'Whatever,' sniffed Ven, inclining her head sharply in Vaughan's direction. 'You show *him* what he's missing out on.'

Frankie stole a glance towards Vaughan. He still looked like a big blond Viking who had been teleported a thousand-plus years into the future. Her heart made a lurch in his direction and to counter the feeling she grabbed a coat-hanger from Ven.

'Let's go gold then,' she said, heading towards the fitting room. 'No one remembers silver.'

They had arranged to meet Olive by the small Neptune pool. The area they were sailing through was renowned for its many dolphin pods and Ven, Roz and Frankie hoped to spot some. They were richly rewarded. Lots of teenage dolphins joined the passage of the ship, showing off by playing in the froth of the bow wave – alas, just when Ven had disappeared to the toilet and missed the lot.

Olive hobbled towards them like a crippled old woman.

'I have never been as manhandled in my life,' she explained, sinking gratefully onto a sunbed. 'Romana turned out to be a Hungarian sadist with thumbs like corkscrews. I feel like I've been run over by a combine harvester.'

'But did you enjoy it?' enquired Ven.

'It was bloody marvellous,' said Olive, with a cringe of pain. 'But I need a gin and tonic and quick.'

'Hello, ma'am, can I get you something to drink?' said the friendly voice of Buzz doing deck duty.

'Four gin and tonics, please,' said Ven, checking that was okay with everyone.

'And those are just for me,' groaned Olive. She could still feel Romana's thumbs pressing under her shoulderblades. Olive wondered if she was slightly masochistic to have derived so much pleasure from being battered for an hour. Then a nasty little voice reminded her that she must indeed be very masochistic for putting up with a lot more than one Hungarian masseuse subjected her to, namely years of drudgery from the Hardcastle clan.

'Ice and lemon?' asked Buzz.

'Oh yes please, my love,' said Ven, as Buzz buzzed off to get them.

Then up the stairs came Eric and Irene, dressed like twins in blue shorts and white tops.

'Hello, ladies,' Eric waved. 'I thought you might be ashore today.'

'Ah, we thought we'd give it a miss,' said Roz with good humour. Eric wouldn't be Eric without that stupid joke following him around.

'Look at that mist rolling in.' Olive nudged Ven. It was the weirdest sight. They were sailing into a low-sitting dry-ice of a mist that clung to the almost-smooth glassy surface of a very calm sea. Coupled with the silence, it was spooky to say the least. Like something out of a *Tales from the Crypt* Hammer Horror film.

'Not sure I like this,' shivered Roz. 'It's a bit weird.' Then she started to 'der-der' the theme tune to 'The Twilight Zone'.

'Ah look, here come the girls!' Eric pointed out into the distance. Three shapes were forming, becoming more defined with every passing second. 'Look, Irene, the *Duchess Alexandra*. There she is, bless her.' His voice crumbled and to everyone's surprise, Eric pulled a handkerchief out of his pocket and blew his nose loudly on it. He was man-crying. Coughing and shaking his head trying to disguise it, but there were glittery water traces on his cheeks.

Olive noticed how he then reached for Irene's hand and held it tightly.

'We met on that ship forty-six years ago,' Irene explained in her whispery soft voice. 'It has some lovely memories for us.'

A loud blast from the *Mermaidia*'s horn scared them all to death. Then, when it was answered by the deep mellow sirens from the three old swans swimming ever more closely, it felt incredibly touching, as if they were all benign sea-creatures calling to each other.

'It's like they're saying hello,' said Olive.

'Or goodbye,' sniffed Eric. 'What a lovely old girl the *Duchess* is. Solid as a rock. Never budged in a force twelve. Beautiful, beautiful. God bless her.'

By now the decks were crowded, everyone watching the hypnotic sight of the huge black-and-white painted *Duchess* with the bright orange funnels, flanked by the two smaller ships, like ladies-in-waiting. They looked as if they were gliding on the strange mist like ghosts. People on the decks weren't cheering, but stood in a silent reverence reserved for the graveside.

The three old Grandes Dames of the sea, laden with their passengers, sailed alongside the *Mermaidia* for a short while, then they turned again into the mist and plunged onwards at a speed that the much bulkier *Mermaidia* could not hope to emulate. Their horns called an echoey farewell, to which the young cruise ship eagerly responded. No one on the deck moved until the three old sea queens were totally out of sight. Some people were waving goodbye, Eric included. His hand made a slow, sad arc in the air. Reactions ranged from the awestruck to the tearful. Even Roz was seen wiping at her eyes.

'Well, if someone had told me that I'd be upset because I've just seen a few old ships, I would have laughed them out of town,' Olive said, also dabbing at her tear ducts.

'Come on, love,' said Irene, taking Eric's arm. 'Let's go and have a stiffening brandy.'

'Aye,' sighed Eric, sniffling into his giant hankie.

Venice wanted to hug him. 'Make sure you each get a double,' she called after Irene.

Half an hour later, the girls wandered up to the side of the

Topaz pool to watch the ice-carving demonstration. A member of the galley crew, armed with what looked like a big chisel, hacked away at a huge slab of ice and revealed the most beautiful detailed sculpture of a mermaid. He made it look as easy as peeling a banana. This was carried downstairs to form the magnificent centrepiece for the Mermaid's Sea Food Buffet in the Ambrosia restaurant that lunchtime, which the four girls felt delightfully obliged to attend. There was the most amazing display of fruits de mer – plump prawns and flaky salmon, squid, scallops and hot seared slabs of white fish and accompanying salads to die for. Ronnie and Reggie Tray were there, obviously, their plates piled as high as the Eiffel Tower. It was gluttony's finest hour.

Olive pushed her fork into the baked cod. Turbot's fish-and-chip shop would never have the same appeal after this feast, she thought, then quickly threw out all thoughts of home before they spoiled her day. She tried not to acknowledge how easy that was to do.

Amazingly, when they returned to the Topaz, they found four free sunbeds right by the pool with a great view of the giant sea-screen. *Mamma Mia* was about to start showing on it in ten minutes. And they were at the side nearest to the bar. The downside was they were very near to a loud man with a Brummie accent.

Frankie slathered on her factor forty whilst Roz, Olive and Ven dripped on their factor thirty that smelled of coconuts. They had bronzed beautifully and sensibly, unlike some of the daft teenagers who were sporting very red shoulders.

Nigel's voice came over the Tannoy warning people that the sun was much stronger at sea and that people should take extra care.

The Brummie was talking to a couple behind him. 'I don't need suntan lotion, me. I could cover myself in vegetable oil, me, and I wouldn't burn. I'm a Sun God, me.'

Buzz waved hello to the ladies. He had obviously done his stint on the top deck and was on 'shade' duty for a while. He wended over with his usual big boyish smile that suggested he was genuinely pleased to see them yet again.

'You following us, Buzz?' teased Ven.

'Of course,' replied Buzz. 'I am your devoted servant.'

'That's what we like to hear,' smiled Roz. 'I think that calls for a champagne cocktail.'

'Make that two,' said Ven.

'Three!' put in Olive.

'Oh, go on then – four. I was going to have a healthy sparkling water but you've twisted me around to your way of thinking,' Frankie laughed.

'Champagne *is* a sparkling water,' said Buzz. 'But special grape water.'

He didn't need to see Ven's cruise card because by now he knew the cabin number to charge it to.

'He's a lovely boy,' sighed Ven as he scooted off. She adjusted her head on her towel pillow so she was comfortable. Her brain emptied of everything but the sounds of children splashing, teenagers shrieking, the clink of glasses. Then, just as she was drifting off to a sleepy place, she heard an irate voice to her immediate right.

'I said, if you'd listened correctly, this is not a Mai Tai!'

She opened her eyes but it took a few seconds of adjusting to the light before she could make out that Dom Donaldson and Tangerina were standing nearby holding out their cocktails to Buzz with stiff aggression.

'A Mai Tai is vodka-based, not rum,' Dom Donaldson was saying, none too quietly either.

'No, no,' Buzz was protesting quietly. 'Mai Tai is rum and orange—'

'I know what a Mai Tai is, for God's sake. And this *isn't* a MAI TAI. Take. It. Back. Do you people understand English?'

Venice felt a bolt of adrenaline rush through her. How dare he talk to lovely Buzz like that? Then she saw Dom Donaldson, her heart-throb, stick out his finger and poke Buzz in the chest, repeating the words: 'Take. It. Back.'

Mild, sweet Ven flew off her sunbed and pushed in between Dom Donaldson and Buzz.

'Don't you dare talk to him like that!' she snarled at the actor.

Dom Donaldson was stunned that anyone would challenge him. And so it took him a few moments to find his voice.

'And who the hell are you?'

'Never mind who the hell I am!' said Ven, not cowed at all by his height or perfect, fit physique. 'Don't talk to Buzz like that!'

Dom Donaldson did not know how to react in this situation, because he was too used to people bending to his will and agreeing with him and fetching him whatever he wanted. So he reverted to the last time he had been countered and threw his toys out of the cot. Or rather batted Buzz's loaded tray to the side. The glasses narrowly missed a small child trotting by, and the ones that didn't land straight in the pool with their contents, shattered on the tiles at the side of it, the shards bouncing into the water. Not that Dom Donaldson cared, for he was too busy towering above Ven and turning purple. When his finger came out ready to poke her as he had done Buzz, Frankie leaped up from the sunbed ready to do what was necessary to stop him laying a hand on her friend, but she was still steps away when a large white sleeve dropped as a barrier between Ven and the irate actor.

'I think it would be a good idea if you came with me, sir,' said Nigel, calmly and politely.

'Yes, I most certainly will, thank you, Captain,' said Dom Donaldson with a sneer, following Nigel away from the pool area with a haughty swagger to his walk because now he was with the Master of *Mermaidia* and a company apology of the highest order was surely in the offing. And possibly a free holiday.

At the pool, crew were now shepherding everyone out and throwing a secure net over the top. The water would need to be drained to get rid of the glass. Dom bloody Donaldson and his hissy fit had ruined the fun for everyone. Luckily there were other pools, but that one seemed to be rather a favourite with everyone because of the film screen above it and the generous paddling area surrounding it.

'Was that my fault?' asked Ven, feeling a spot guilty as the crew guys busied around. She was shaking. Confrontation didn't come easy to her at all.

'No, it most certainly *wasn't* your fault,' said Olive, giving her a hug. 'It was that horrible actor's fault. I hope Nigel doesn't schmooze around him just because he's been in a couple of films and a soap.'

Buzz arrived with a tray of four cocktails just at the right time.

'Do you still want these?' he asked. He seemed a bit shaken up too. 'I would like to buy—'

'Oy, don't you even think about it, sonny, or *I'll* start poking you in the chest,' said Roz. Champagne on his wages – bless him.

'Thank you,' said Buzz. 'Tonight I will make sure you get extra truffles with your coffee.' He tapped the side of his nose. 'My girlfriend makes them in the kitchen.'

'That'll do us,' said Olive, taking a champagne glass and putting it in Ven's trembling hands. 'That'll do us all very nicely.'

Later on, when Frankie went back to her cabin to get ready for dinner, she found her new dress hemmed and hanging up for her. She showered, dried her hair, spiking it up with strong gel, and went to town on her make-up. After slipping on the dress and shoes and a magnificent chunky gold necklace which

she had found in Market Avenue for twenty quid, she stood
back to appraise herself in the mirror. If this didn't show that
bloody Viking what he was missing, nothing would.

Ven had a shower, wrapped herself up in her complimentary
white towelling robe and took a cup of coffee out onto the balcony. It was a beautiful late afternoon. The sea had barely a
ripple in it and the sky was full of ice-cream colours on the
horizon – vanilla and strawberry. It had been a hell of a day.
First there was that Dom Donaldson incident, then at afternoon
tea in the Buttery, they had shared a table with a gentle, elderly
couple from Southport. He'd had a stroke and hadn't really
done any of the port visits, but his wife explained for him that
it didn't matter because the ship itself was holiday enough.

'Enjoy it while you can, love,' the lady had said, helping her
husband to his feet when they were ready to go. Then she
nodded towards him. 'You never know what's around the
corner.'

She smiled, taking his hand and threading it around her arm
so she could lead him away.

'Take good care of yourselves,' Ven gulped.

'Oh I do,' the old lady replied chirpily. 'Fifty-five years we've
been together. We were eighteen when we married. They all
said it wouldn't last.'

And she walked off slowly, in time with her man's shuffling.

Frankie handed Ven a tissue just before she burst into tears,
because she knew what she was like.

And as Ven now leaned over the balcony, she knew she had
to take a lesson from that little interlude. She was going to suck
the juice out of her life when she got home, and make sure the
others did the same.

Then she saw it – a black arc of dolphin back curve out of
the water and nose-dive back in again. And another. Then two
more. Four beautiful dolphins in the distance, effortlessly rising

from the glass-like sea, four times – then no more. Ven raised a hand in triumph. At last she'd seen some – and boy, were they worth waiting for! She wondered if it was possible to watch them without smiling. Four beautiful shapes in the water. And four, she smiled to herself, had always been her lucky number.

'Wow!' said Roz when Frankie emerged from her cabin for pre-dinner drinkies. 'You look like ... well ... Frankie. Full-throttle Frankie Carnevale.'

'Is that a compliment?' Frankie asked sceptically, eyes narrowed.

'Course it is,' said Roz. 'And a very big one.'

Olive emerged in her long red dress and matching stole, Roz in a sleek black gown which fishtailed out at the bottom into a sea of ruffles, Ven in a chocolate-brown heavily sequinned two-piece which went perfectly with her glossy auburn hair. She looked like a princess. But Frankie, that evening, was the queen in that gold dress and sod-blond-Viking-type-men attitude.

'Oh Frankie, you look gorgeous,' sighed Ven. 'Let's go and get our formal pictures taken for the competition people before we eat.'

And they all swaggered off, feeling like four million dollars, in the direction of the grand staircase at the side of the *Mermaidia* wall sculpture.

They couldn't have timed it better. As the four of them were posing for the photographer, Vaughan and his party appeared looking over the balcony from above.

'Don't look up,' said Roz out of the corner of her mouth, like a really crap ventriloquist. 'Vaughan at twelve o'clock. He'll have a cracking view of your tits in that dress.'

Frankie couldn't resist looking up though. Her eyes locked with Vaughan's in his black tux, then she pulled them haughtily away and back to focus on the camera lens. That small rejection of him salved her ego a tiny bit but she was still feeling a heavy weight of sadness lodged inside her and wished it would bugger off. She knew it wouldn't wholly shift until there was time and distance between them, so she was stuck with it for now. She made sure there was an extra Mae West sashay to her bottom as she followed the others up the staircase to the restaurant floor.

They were slightly late going to dinner that night and Ven was delighted to see that Nigel had not gone to Cruz after all but was sitting in his usual seat at the table. He stood gallantly when the ladies approached but Ven noticed that he seemed to be having difficulty making eye-contact with her. Again.

The conversation at the table inevitably touched on the glass in the Topaz pool and the gossip flying around the ship about it. Royston and Stella had heard that a fight between some teenagers had broken out and a whole tray of cocktails had been tipped over but the girls put them straight with the real story. Nigel was very wishy-washy on what had happened with Dom Donaldson afterwards, avoiding giving any detail. All he would say on the subject was that 'it had all been sorted out now'. He tapped light feet around the subject like Michael Flatley in ballet pumps.

Ven decided that meant Nigel had taken Dom Donaldson to his office, apologised to him profusely and massaged his ego back up to its fully inflated volume. Why else would he be so evasive? She found herself being really disappointed in him. He had toppled from his pedestal, just like Dom Donaldson had that day. She didn't even get a raise in pulse when Nigel leaned over during the main course to reach for the pepper and his leg knocked against hers. And when he returned to the bridge before coffee, for the first time Ven didn't watch his back as he crossed the dining room with a sigh lodged in her heart. The only man who hadn't been a disappointment in her life was her dad. She'd grown up with him as her benchmark, and not one of the others had come up to the mark.

As the two older couples wended off to Flamenco to listen

to a jazz band, the four girls made a slow stroll over to Broadway to watch yet another production by the Mermaidia Theatre Company, who must have had brains the size of major planets to remember all those lines and song lyrics. The offering tonight was *For Your Eyes Only* – a tribute to the James Bond themes. Then, afterwards, laughing that they were really getting to be old farts, they sat in Café Parisienne with cups of Horlicks watching all the teenagers filing past on their way to Harlequins nightclub on the floor below.

When the others went to bed, Ven took her usual trip to the top deck again – her 'constitutional' as the others laughingly referred to it – to get some fresh air. Her head was full of Nigel and Dom Donaldson. *What did you expect a Captain to do?* asked a voice in her head that seemed to be insinuating she was being slightly unfair. *Crunch his fist into Dom Donaldson's nose and send him flying into the swimming pool? This is Captain Nigel, not Chuck chuffing Norris.*

'Hello, there,' said a cheery voice to her side, knocking her right out of her reverie. Florence in black sparkles and her familiar pearls. 'Ooh, was I interrupting you? You were very deep in thought, my dear.'

'Sorry,' Ven smiled. 'How lovely to see you again. How are you?'

'Oh, we're very well, thank you,' said Florence, holding up her arms in an expansive gesture towards the sea and the star-filled sky. 'How can you be anything else here?'

Ven nodded, looking out over the view. 'There's nothing to see, so why do I think it's so lovely?'

'A little glimpse of heaven, maybe?' smiled Florence.

Ven didn't comment. It maybe wasn't the thing to say to an elderly lady – that she believed in nothing beyond the final breath. But she gave a sigh that she wasn't conscious of, which prompted Florence to ask again if she was all right.

'Yes, I'm fine,' said Ven. 'Just had a bit of a strange day, that's all. Someone knocked a tray full of glasses into the pool and it all had to be drained. It was awful.'

'Still, the Captain dealt with it superbly,' said Florence.

'Do you think?' asked Ven, not convinced by any means.

'Oh yes,' said Florence. 'He can't have people like that on his ship.'

Ven's ears pricked up. 'What do you mean? What did he do?'

'That actor chap – he'll be off at Gibraltar tomorrow.' Then she was suddenly distracted and shouted in response to a sound Ven hadn't heard, 'Coming, dear. That's Dennis calling me. I'm attuned to the slightest sound of his voice after all these years. I'll have to go. If he can't find me he starts to panic. Have a lovely day tomorrow in Gibraltar, won't you?'

'Wait,' said Ven, as Florence turned. 'I have a card for you for your anniversary. Where do I deliver it to?'

'Oh, that's very kind,' said Florence with a wide smile. 'We're on table one in the Ambrosia restaurant. First sitting.'

'Let me write that down,' said Ven, getting a pen out of her bag and writing down the details on the back of a bar chitty. 'Table one, did you say? And before you go, what was that you said about the Capt . . .' She looked up but the door to the ship's interior was just creaking shut. The old lady had gone back inside to find her husband.

DAY 14: GIBRALTAR

Dress Code: Smart Casual

Chapter 61

When Ven drew her curtains it was to see the mighty sight of Gibraltar. She didn't realise that the rock *was* Gibraltar. She had thought it might have been a discernible bump on the landscape, not the huge steep mountain it was. She quickly washed and dressed because three of them were going on a dolphin-watching trip that morning. Roz was having a meander around Gibraltar by herself. She wasn't a fan of the unpredictability of little bobbly boats.

'Wakey wakey, are you uppee?' came Olive's voice and knock through her door. 'Got something to tell you – open up!'

When Ven opened her door, Olive was beaming. 'Guess who I saw in Reception this morning with bags packed?'

'Brad Pitt?'

'Not even close, although he might disagree with you. Only that Donaldson prat and Tangerina Orange Jelly. Seems the Captain told them to leave the ship after yesterday's performance.'

'You're joking?' gasped Ven. So what Florence had said was true.

'I am not,' said Olive, as Frankie's cabin opened and she joined in the gossip as they wandered up to the Buttery for a quick bite.

Ven had two almond croissants that morning. Suddenly her appetite, and her smile, were restored to full power.

Whilst Ven, Frankie and Olive were leaning over the side of a small boat, screaming like kids whenever they spotted the dolphins that leaped up to within touching distance, Roz was walking towards Gibraltar's long busy main street full of tourists buying cheap booze and cigarettes and kids looking for the latest console games at a snip. Roz suspected the prices were a lot cheaper when there wasn't a ship in town. Signs in shop windows promised the 'Best prices for *Mermaidia* Passengers'.

The last time she had visited Gibraltar, it hadn't been so busy. There had been no cruise ships in the harbour. She and Robert had travelled down from Benalmadena for the day. Roz drew level with a jewellery shop and went cold as the memory flooded back over her like a frozen wash of ice. She had been buying perfume in the pharmacy across the street and caught up with Robert here and found him looking at rings.

'I've got one already.' Roz had nudged him teasingly.

'It's not for you,' Robert had replied. It had just slipped out. He could have made a joke out of it but he had been as surprised as she was with what he had said. And once out, it was too big to fold back in and forget.

'What do you mean?' Roz looked into his face, smiling nervously, but she knew exactly what he meant. Two minutes ago she had been so happy, on holiday, feeling a rare semblance of security. Now she felt as if someone were quickly disassembling her from the inside, brick by brick, each one bringing her closer to her last total collapse.

'Not here, Roz,' Robert said, head held high, looking around him, trying to rise above the scene he hoped his wife wasn't going to cause.

He didn't say, 'Don't be silly, Roz. Don't exaggerate, Roz,' He said, *Not here, Roz.* He had something to tell her but *not here.*

Roz had wanted to scream. Her whole body was vibrating with tension, fear, panic. It had happened again. Another affair. Another cheap tart. Except that this time it wasn't, was it? Because this time he was looking to buy a ring for the 'someone'. In front of his wife, he was looking at rings for another woman. It was beyond the cruellest thing he had ever done to her, and he really had ground her nose into the mud over the years. Roz was too distraught to explode; she imploded instead. There on the street outside that jewellers, she began to cry. Fat, salty, full-of-pain tears began to slide down her face and she heard Robert's loaded sigh of embarrassment.

'Is it Kay?' she asked. She had suspected his PA for some time.

'No,' he said. 'Not any more.'

What the fuck? So it had been Kay and now it was someone else?

'Don't cause a scene.' He had grabbed her arm firmly and led her up a side street. She was so numb; her fingers were tingling as if the blood was racing around in confusion in her system, forgetting which direction to flow in. Her breath was short and staccato – nothing in her body seemed to know what to do.

'I was going to tell you when we got home,' he said. 'I'm sorry it came out now. Don't cry, for God's sake, Roz.' His plea was not concern for her well-being but more a warning growl that she shouldn't show him up in public. Roz tried to gulp down the tears and stop them but they kept coming.

'Who . . . who is it?' she hiccuped.

'You don't know her. Look, let's do this back at the hotel.' And then he delivered the killer line. 'I need to buy a camera before we go.'

And ludicrous as it seemed, Roz, her heart breaking, trailed behind Robert whilst he wove from side to side of the main street in Gibraltar comparing prices of SLRs.

'That's ten quid cheaper down the road,' he said, voicing his annoyance to her, as if she cared. The tears streamed down her face and she kept having to take off her sunglasses to wipe them away. She heard a little girl say, 'Mummy, why is that lady crying?' and Roz wanted to sink down onto her knees in the middle of that long road and just sob. And when Robert had bought his camera, she had followed him to the car, let him drive her silently back to the hotel and then packed for the next day's journey home.

He had moved out immediately when they landed back in Barnsley. It tortured her that he wouldn't tell her the name of the woman he was having the affair with. It tortured her even more when he admitted it was her Cousin Tina and she was pregnant. Then Robert came back home three weeks later saying it was all over, then moved out again two days later to be with Tina once more. Roz was at nervous-breakdown point. It had been Frankie who chucked all his stuff out onto the lawn and rang him to tell him to pick it up and feck off. Frankie had got the locks changed for her and made the appointment with the divorce solicitor. Roz had forgotten all that strength Frankie had shown for her when she couldn't find it within herself.

It had taken Manus years of patience to make her trust a man again. She wished he were here, to take away those awful vibes from this town. To walk up the street with her and imprint himself over every bad memory and make new, lovely, fresh ones for them to treasure. He was such a beautiful man. She felt her eyes filling. She would never have hurt Ven's feelings by saying this to her, but she was desperate to go home now. She wanted to fall at Manus's feet and tell him how much she loved him. She wanted to take back every rotten insecure barb she had ever thrown at him. From now on, she was going to love her man like he deserved. If he would let her. If it wasn't too late.

*

Frankie had had enough sun for a while. She had loved the couple of hours on the jaunty little Dolphin Safari boat, squealing long and hard with kids and pensioners alike at the sight of the darling creatures. She just wanted to dive off the side of the boat and live out a dream. Apparently, though, the Straits were renowned for violent undercurrents and it wouldn't have been one of her wiser moves. Still, it had been a magical morning.

She had got to a good bit in her book and wanted to read it in the shade. So whilst Ven and Olive were having a swim, she went down to the lovely coffee-and-cake shop on the fifth floor – the Samovar. She settled into the sofa seat in the corner by the porthole window and finished off a caramel latte and a slice of soft, creamy Victoria sponge beautifully presented with a sprinkle of icing sugar and a spoonful of raspberries on the side. The big-mouthed Brummie Sun God who yesterday insisted he wouldn't even burn if he basted himself in vegetable oil hobbled past walking like a crippled lobster, brimmed hat pulled right down over a very puffy face which was showing pain with every step. Apparently, like mere mortals, it seems he did burn and he should have listened to Nigel's warning about the sun being very strong for passengers sunbathing at sea. Poor bloke, but she couldn't resist a little smirk as she thought it.

Frankie looked up momentarily as she turned the fifth page and there *he* was again, just outside the Samovar area. Viking Vaughan. Looking gorgeous in long sloppy shorts and a faded black AC/DC T-shirt. Bloody man. Frankie dropped her head quickly and tried to get back into her book, but though her eyes were following the words, nothing was computing and she started the page another three times before a single word sank in.

She presumed the presence she felt at the table was the waiter asking her if she wanted anything else to drink, but when she looked up, it was to see Vaughan, staring down at her with his fjord-blue eyes.

'Can I have a word?' he asked quietly.

'No, you can't, you switchy-on-and-off loser, bugger off,' said Frankie. Well, at least, that's what she wanted to blast at him, but her perfidious mouth betrayed her.

'If you want.'

Vaughan sat down on the chair at the other side of the table, hands on his long, strong legs. 'I owe you an apology,' he said cautiously, as if expecting her to throw the sugar container at him.

'Do you?' sniffed Frankie. 'What for?'

Vaughan could see the annoyance in her eyes. Of course she knew she was owed an apology, but she deserved to see him crawl a little after his ungentlemanly behaviour.

'For running out on you in Korcula,' said Vaughan. 'I was rude and stupid, and I'm sorry.'

'Well, thank you,' said Frankie, returning to her book. He'd said his piece and now he could go. What else was there to say? That self-betraying part of her was hoping that he had plenty more to say – nice things.

He didn't go. Instead, with anguish bursting out of his low voice he said, 'Frankie. I felt a total shit the minute I got up from the table in Korcula. I was having a lovely time with you.'

'I could tell,' said Frankie, a hard edge to her voice. 'Men always run off as if their arse was on fire when they're having a good time with me.'

Vaughan sighed and rubbed his forehead with the flat of his hand. 'You won't understand unless I tell you, but it's difficult for me. I really like you. Really, *really* like you, Frankie. And I wasn't expecting to find anyone I liked that much again. Especially not on a cruise ship.'

In her chest, Frankie's heart started leaping up and down. She didn't know how to respond. Stupidly, she kept her eyes on the print in her book – but it might as well have been written in hieroglyphics for all the sense it was making.

Vaughan's hand came out, gently lifted the book from her hands, and he put it pages-down on the table between them.

'Hitler and I have a lot in common, apparently,' he said. Which at least made her look right at him. Had he really just said that?

'Probably not the best way to start,' Vaughan said, scratching the back of his head. Whatever it was he was trying to say wasn't coming easy.

'You mean you have a girlfriend called Eva Braun and a secret bunker in your house?' Frankie answered dryly, which made him smile gently.

'Not quite. You know that song about Hitler and Goebbels and Himmler?'

Frankie shook her head slowly from side to side. 'I'm sorry, I haven't a frigging clue what you are talking about.'

Vaughan puffed out his cheeks, took a deep breath and dived in.

'About how many balls they've got.'

This was random, Frankie thought. One minute she was reading a nice romance, the next she was talking about the quantity of bollocks that members of the SS had.

He waited then for Frankie to work it out. She was just about to say again that she didn't know what he meant, then the fog began to clear. 'You mean the one that goes, "Hitler had only got one ball. Goering had two, but they were small . . ."'

'Yes, that one.'

Frankie scratched her head this time. Surely all this wasn't just because . . .

'You haven't got two balls?'

'Shhh!' From the way Vaughan crunched himself low and looked around him, Frankie appeared to have guessed correctly – if rather loudly.

'So bloody what?' She laughed incredulously. 'What's that got to do with anything?'

'Oh Frankie, it's not just that,' said Vaughan, his eyes not meeting hers. 'A few years ago I had, you know, the big C . . . down there. My partner left me afterwards. She said she was scared of catching it.'

'You can't catch cancer!' Frankie barked back.

'I know, I know.' Vaughan held his open palms out. 'But, nevertheless, whatever was going through her head – well, that's why she said she was leaving. I'm okay now, touch wood. But I haven't been with another woman since. I'd always been the hard man – you know, bikes and tattoos . . .'

For a split second it crossed Frankie's mind that this was a line of seduction. Some men seemed to think it wasn't a well-known ploy to tell a woman they 'couldn't get it up' only for the silly cow to try and heal them by taking them to bed where – lo and behold – she found *with her* he was all man again. Four times. But Vaughan wasn't faking it. Any idiot could see he was reducing himself to base level by confessing this.

'I grew my hair long to hide behind. I didn't feel like a proper man any more with just one ball. Much better to be alone than risk getting rejected.'

Gary Barlow was right when he said it only takes a minute to fall in love, because Frankie looked at the pain in big Vaughan's eyes and knew she was one shove away from falling in love with him.

'You're the first woman I've reached out towards,' he said.

'But what did I say to you that put you off?' asked Frankie, reaching forwards herself and touching his arm.

'About your exes not having any balls. It was like balls equals man, no balls equals prick, if you know what I mean.'

'Oh God, I never even thought!' Frankie gasped. Then a laugh of shock spurted out of her, breaking an intolerable bubble of tension. 'I'm sorry for laughing, Vaughan. You've got more balls than all of them put together. You silly, stupid man! Just don't ever become a maths teacher!' God, he was gorgeous, vulnerable, hunky and she wanted to grab him and eat him all up.

'It doesn't put you off?' His eyes were full of the weight of disbelief.

Frankie stood up and held out her hand.

'Come to my cabin, big boy,' she said, her dark Italian eyes glittering mischievously. 'I'll show you how much it puts me off.'

'Because you feel sorry for me?' He didn't take her hand.

'No, because I want to restore a bit of faith in you. Plus I have a little story to tell you about hiding away from the world and why it's a bloody stupid thing to do,' she said.

Vaughan took her hand.

Chapter 62

When Frankie met the others later in the Vista lounge for pre-dinner drinks, she was smiling so much it looked like she had a coat-hanger caught in her gob.

'Ay ay, and what have *you* been doing this afternoon?' asked Ven.

'Vaughan,' sighed Frankie.

'You haven't!' squealed Roz.

'I have so!'

Over gin and tonics and the complimentary Japanese crackers, she filled in the others on how Vaughan, like her, was a cancer survivor. Because she understood what he had gone through, and because they had both lost parts of their body associated so closely with their sexuality, they'd found a safe harbour within each other.

'Actually he found it a few times,' winked Frankie. 'I haven't had sex for so long, I'd forgotten how damned good it is. When it's done properly, of course.'

'Spare us the details,' said Roz.

'Oy, don't spare me any,' put in Olive. 'I want to hear it all.'

It turned out that lying in bed and talking after long-overdue sex was something to be recommended. Olive wasn't quite convinced she would be wearing a mask of ecstasy like the one on Frankie's face after bonking David when she got home. She had a sudden rush of panic about the prospect of sleeping with him again, imagining he was Atho Petrakis and then opening her eyes to find he wasn't and never would be. She took a hard swig of her gin and tonic to splash it away.

And Roz was thinking that she would ask Manus if they could save up and come on a cruise together. She wanted to let the sea air sink into his soul and soothe him. She wanted to make love to him as the boat rocked. She wanted him to lie by the pool and find some peace. He never relaxed. If he wasn't working, she was stressing him out.

Ven let herself have a glimpse into another life where she was in bed watching Nigel O'Shaughnessy slowly stripping off to climb into the cabin bed with her. It would have made things less complicated if she'd thought he'd schmoozed around Dom Donaldson, because then he wouldn't have been the man for her after all and she could easily have forgotten him. As it was, he was back up to full neon-bright-light status, which was going to make it very hard to leave him. Like the holiday romance in Malta when she was fifteen and fell in love with Victor the barman with the black hair and doe eyes. She cried all through the flight home and thought she'd never heal. Weren't you supposed to grow out of that idiocy?

There were balloons on the table again when they went in to dinner.

'Is it your competition people?' asked Frankie.

'Er . . . I don't know,' replied Ven.

'What's going on here?' said Royston, when he arrived in a pink shirt with golfers embroidered on it. 'One of you girls not telling us something?'

'Is it your twenty-first birthday, Royston?' asked Olive.

'They're not because it's my first shag in five years, are they?' Frankie whispered to Roz.

Ven's heart started a drum solo as she saw Nigel enter the

restaurant. Hero Nigel who didn't take any crap – even from celebrities – on his boat. *The Nigel-ator*. Sigh.

'Good evening, everyone,' he said. 'Balloons again, I see?'

'These look like the guilty parties,' said Royston, as Eric and Irene approached the table – he in a suit and she in a coffee-coloured cocktail dress and a corsage of yellow flowers pinned to it. She'd had a hairdo and her make-up done too.

'It's our anniversary,' explained Eric bashfully. 'We didn't want a fuss. I bet this is my son's doing – I told him not to.'

'Why didn't you say, you silly bugger?' said Royston. 'Angel? Angel, come here, love!'

Sensing that he was going to go mad again and buy champagne, Eric shushed him gently. 'You're not buying drinks. We're going to get some prosecco for everyone, if that's all right. We prefer that.'

'Your anniversary,' conceded Royston for once. 'You're the bosses. So which anniversary is it then?'

'It's our first,' replied Irene, and from the looks around the table no one was expecting that.

'First?' repeated Stella.

'Yes, our first,' stated Eric.

That was confusing because they didn't look the type to have been living in sin for donkeys' years. And didn't they say they had met on one of the Grandes Dames, forty-odd years ago?

'Yes, it's our first, but we met on the *Duchess Alexandra*,' Eric began to explain after they had ordered starters. 'I was married to my first wife Mary then and Irene was married to Johnny and we had our kids with us. As couples we got seated together and we all hit it off so well, didn't we, Irene?'

'We did,' confirmed Irene.

'Johnny had his own building firm, like I did. Mary and Irene were in the WI. We had so much in common, so much to talk about,' said Eric.

'We went on holiday every year together after that,' Irene

continued. 'We were all such great friends. For forty-six lovely years. The children were all of an age and relished each other's company. In fact, Eric's son married my daughter in the end.'

'Then, alas, my Mary took ill and died three years ago. And we'd just buried her when Johnny suddenly passed over. Awful time for both families, wasn't it, Irene? Awful, it was.'

'We were both a bit lost,' whispered Irene. 'Our partners and best friends had gone in such a short time. We had so many lovely memories from our holidays.'

'We kept in touch, didn't we, Irene?'

'Yes, we did.'

'We thought we'd go on holiday as friends at first – you know, separate cabins, all above board.'

'It was a nice way to remember our partners, you see,' added Irene.

'We can still feel them with us,' smiled Eric. 'We knew they'd approve when we got married. Even the children said we should.'

'It was daft, the pair of us being lonely,' said Irene in her soft voice. 'We don't have to explain to each other that we're still a four really.'

Ven burst into tears. 'God, I'm sorry, that's so sad but lovely.'

'Aye,' said Eric. It was all he said in response to that, and all he needed to say.

Ven was panicking now because she didn't have a tissue and imagined her mascara sliding down her cheeks. Her friends were busy hunting in their evening bags for one. Ven was such a softy, she should never have been outside a range of five metres of a hankie.

'Here you are,' said Nigel, pulling a soft square of material out of his pocket. 'I think you're building up a collection of my handkerchiefs as souvenirs, Venice,' he smiled.

Ven was too choked up to answer. She just nodded. Soon

that's all she would have left of this cruise – a bucketful of memories and two of Nigel's hankies.

The prosecco arrived and Royston had sneakily ordered pink champagne. 'For the girls,' he winked. The man was incorrigible, in the sweetest possible way.

'Don't you meet some lovely people on ships?' Ven gushed to Nigel. She was still feeling quite emotional when her sea bass main course arrived. She decided not to drink much that evening. She didn't trust herself not to burst into tears again. 'How do you let them go, knowing you won't see them again?'

'It's my job,' replied Nigel. 'Alas, I can't possibly keep in contact with everyone I meet. I enjoy their company, then we part.'

Ven wished she hadn't asked.

'Dom Donaldson didn't look very happy at Gibraltar,' Roz said mischievously, spearing a tiny buttery potato and popping it into her mouth.

'I have to think of the safety of my passengers,' said Nigel, answering her but still giving away no detail. 'And I'm afraid that Mr Donaldson was already on a yellow card. Luckily, it is a very rare occurrence but he isn't the first public figure I've had to ask to leave the ship, nor will he be the last.'

'Ooh, who else have you chucked off?' Roz leaned over with a salacious grin.

'I couldn't possibly say,' Nigel said with courteous diplomacy. 'But some were much bigger names than Mr Donaldson.'

'Spoilsport!' said Roz.

Chapter 63

Manus had just had a shave and had splashed some aftershave on his hands ready to slap onto his face. He studied himself in the mirror and wondered if he was dressed appropriately. T-shirt and Diesel jeans – was that okay? This was new ground to him – going out for a meal without Roz. And it *was* just a meal with old friends, so why did he feel as if he were doing something slightly illegal?

He had bought wine, and that had been a nightmare too. He didn't want to take the three-bottles-for-a-tenner stuff they sold in the supermarket, nor be too flash with top-shelf stuff. The thought zipped through his head that if he and Roz did split up and he ended up back in the dating game, he wasn't sure he'd survive the tightrope of decisions which would have to be made for going out on a date. He couldn't remember things being that difficult when he'd asked Roz out. At least that side of things had been easy with her.

But, of course, this wasn't a date, he reminded himself. It was a four at dinner, two men and two women. And one of the women just happened to be the girl he had fancied like mad once upon a time.

Manus grabbed his car keys. He decided he would drive to Jonie's house and not drink anything. Alcohol was a key to a door that he couldn't risk opening.

*

Manus saw a shadow of disappointment pass over Jonie's face when she noticed his car parked outside her house. Then it was quickly gone and she kissed him on the cheek and pulled him over the threshold. He followed her down the hallway, noticing how even her long caramel-blonde hair seemed to sashay as she walked. She was wearing a simply cut leaf-green dress, a matching belt around her tiny waist. Manus couldn't believe that anyone as good-looking as Jonie Spencer could possibly be happily single. He could hear laughter coming from down the hallway and he recognised that chuckle immediately, even after twenty-five years.

'Manus Howard, as I live and breathe! How are you, mate?' Tim leaped up from the dining table to shake Manus's hand. Tim looked exactly the same as he did at school, give or take a four-stone weight gain and a big reduction in hair. Layla stood up to give him a hug. She still wore the hippy clothes she was renowned for and, though she had been quite plump at college, now she was super-slim.

'I run a lot these days,' she explained as they all parried stories about their physical changes. 'Tim doesn't, as you can tell.'

'It's so great to see you,' said Tim again, smile wide and genuine. 'Here, have a glass of wine and tell me everything you've been doing in the past quarter of a century.'

Manus was about to refuse the drink and say he was driving, but decided not to be a party-pooper. He could have one – and make it last.

Jonie had gone to considerable effort, Manus noticed, as his eyes roved over the table: cloth serviettes tied with ribbon, table confetti, place-cards. Although he rather thought she might be the sort of person who held a lot of dinner parties and had an appropriate stash of impressive decorations. He nibbled on some olives stuffed with almonds whilst he filled in a few details for Tim and Layla about the missing years, and they returned the favour with children's names, pet names and job positions. Once rebellious, Tim was now a barrister. Layla taught adults how to read.

'So how did you two meet up again?' asked Tim as Jonie put a plate of asparagus in front of him, wrapped in wafer-thin crispy rolls of prosciutto with a curl of hollandaise sauce on the side. The presentation was restaurant-standard; the taste matched it.

'He rescued me when my car broke down,' cut in Jonie. 'My knight in shining armour. All these years I've lived in this town and never knew he had that garage. Crazy.'

'Absolutely,' said Layla. 'I mean, I have never once seen you since we left college. And odds are we must have been in the town centre at the same time at some point.'

'We move in deeply grooved orbits,' decided Tim, eating a warm crusty bread roll. 'It's the only answer.'

Jonie topped up Manus's glass quickly; his protest came too late.

'Don't tell me you're driving!' Tim guffawed. 'Get a bloody taxi, man. I haven't seen you since we were kids. We can't catch up properly over a pot of tea!'

'Hand over the keys, come on,' said Layla. 'For once I agree with my husband. It's a rare occurrence and therefore must be documented for posterity.'

Manus half-sighed, half-grinned. He pulled his phone out of his back pocket first to get to his keys. Layla scooped up both and deposited them in the kitchen.

'There,' she said. 'No driving and no interrupting phones. Now where were we?'

Manus lifted the glass to his lips. The one thing he could be sure of was he wouldn't be missing any calls from Roz.

Chapter 64

'Oh God, the King's Singers are back!' said Royston as the waiters began to gravitate towards the table. Then Supremo arrived to count them in.

'Congratulaaations and celebraaations . . .'

Eric was clearly uncomfortable with the attention but the whole restaurant seemed to be joining in singing and clapping with abandon.

'Poor Eric,' said Ven, using Nigel's handkerchief now to wipe tears of laughter out of her eyes. 'He hated that, didn't he?'

'I think he did, but then again I suspect he wouldn't have missed it for the world,' Nigel returned in a conspiratorial whisper. Roz took a picture of Eric and Irene with a cluster of waiters around them and the square bulk of Supremo smiling in the middle. Eric, despite his humiliation, was grinning to the limits of his lips.

'I'll wash your hankies and get them back to you,' said Ven.

'Please don't worry about it,' said Nigel. 'I have quite a few for such occasions.'

Ven didn't want to hear that he had a stash of them ready to hand over to weeping women, as if it were a regular occurrence.

'Someone mention washing?' butted in Royston. 'You'd better get in early if you're washing tomorrow. The laundries will be full.'

'And woe betide you if the machine stops spinning and you aren't there to take your smalls straight out,' added Stella. 'The laundries on ships turn some people into Hannibal Lecter. That's why I can't abide washing on holiday. I always bring enough clothes with me so I don't have to. Once I brought twenty-three white shirts when we did a leg of the World Cruise.'

'I'm just the opposite. I do a few washes when I'm on board,' said Irene. 'Then I don't have much to do when we get home.'

'Neither do I,' laughed Stella. 'My housekeeper unpacks and does it.' She leaned into Roz and gave her a hearty nudge. 'She was part of the not-divorcing-Royston deal.' Roz did a quick calculation. Stella had made Royston stump up for a house-keeper, Botox, jewellery, cruises, new boobs, liposuction and a nose job at least. And that was cheaper than a divorce? Boy, he must be minted!

'Must be nice,' sighed Roz to Olive. 'Stella's got a house-keeper.'

Olive nodded. She wished *she* had a cleaner instead of being one. How lovely it must be, to walk into a house that was polished and shining. She didn't know how one old lady and a layabout husband could make such a mess between them in Land Lane. It must be wonderful to come in from a day cleaning someone else's house without having to start on your own. Olive loved cleaning – she took such a pride in seeing things sparkle, but occasionally it would be nice to sit down and rest in the rooms she had made so tidy. She coughed down the lift full of tears that had zoomed at warp speed up to her eyes. Last night she had had a nightmare about the state of the house she would be going back to. It was full of open cans and poo neatly parcelled up and bottles full of urine, like she had once seen on a grime documentary. And as she cleared it up and took it to the bin, by the time she got back, more had appeared. And she could only use one hand to clean because the other was holding a Willy-Wonka-type golden ticket that allowed her to fly to Cephalonia, but every time she looked down, the writing on it had faded a little more.

This was the downside of a holiday – it had to end and normal life had to resume once again, and the better the holiday, the harder the fall. Olive lifted her glass and swallowed a throatful of the pink champagne as she forced thoughts of Land Lane to the back of her mind. She would be there soon enough, so she was determined to squeeze the last delicious drops of juice from her holiday until it was wrung dry.

'When is this Andrew bloke going to meet us lot then, Ven?' asked Roz.

'I don't know if he needs to. I'll ask him tomorrow – I'm supposed to be seeing him first thing,' came the quick reply. 'Did you look at the desserts? What choices are there tonight?'

Funny that, thought Roz. She had asked that question as a test. Every time anyone mentioned the competition, she had noticed how Ven changed the subject. And she had just done it again. Hmmm . . .

'Can't believe we've only got two nights left after this,' said Irene, after giving an order for butterscotch ice cream to Buzz. 'It's just been so lovely.'

'Lemon cheesecake for me,' said Ven. 'A *small* one, Buzz, please.' Buzz seemed to be trying to thank Ven for sticking up for him, with food. He had just given her a portion of *patatas bravas* that could have sustained a small emergent nation during a three-week siege.

Nigel made his excuses before dessert, and as he got up from the table, briefly touched Ven on the shoulder in a parting shot. As St John Hite would describe him in wine form: *this is the one I'd want to be marooned on a desert island with*. She knew it was pathetic, how she puffed up from the slightest attention he gave her. She didn't even want to think about three nights' time when she would be sitting in her old kitchen eating a bacon sarnie for tea with only Ethel the cat for company.

Through the window Roz saw the fading vista of the Rock of Gibraltar. She was on her way home, and not just in the sailing sense of the word. Nigel and Eric were in deep discussion about the military history of the place.

'Sod it, I'm going to break my own rule and ring Manus later,' Roz whispered to Ven.

'Thank Christ for that,' said Frankie, with a very wide smile. 'So miracles do happen in life.'

Chapter 65

'So, Manus, how come you're not married then?' Layla braved after her fourth glass of Sav Blanc. 'We always thought you and Jonie would have got it together. It was always very obvious that you fancied her and she fancied you.'

'Oh shut up, Layla!' laughed Jonie. 'You're pissed already.'

Manus's mouth opened with a small involuntary gasp. *Jonie had fancied him?* He hadn't known that. He wondered how history would have changed if he had. It had never crossed his mind that someone like pretty Jonie Spencer could have ever fancied a grungy leather-clad rocker like him.

'I have a girlfriend,' said Manus. 'She's on holiday with her friends at the moment.'

'Oh, do you?' said Layla. 'I just presumed . . .' She trailed off, but it was fairly obvious to Manus what Layla had thought: that tonight was a date of sorts between them. Had Jonie let her think that?

'You got kids, Manus?' asked Tim.

'Nope,' he replied.

'Was that by design?' Layla topped up her glass.

Manus shrugged. 'We just never got round to it.'

'What – having sex?' Tim guffawed.

Manus smiled along with him. 'We're happy as we are, just the two of us.' *Happy?* As soon as the words were out he felt as if a giant sign was going to appear from nowhere and point him out as a liar.

'Having a load of kids isn't on everyone's agenda, Tim,' Jonie admonished him. 'Look at me. I'm more than happy without a house full of smelly nappies, thank you.'

'You're never with a man long enough to get pregnant,' Tim laughed. 'I reckon in a previous life, you were a Black Widow spider, Jonie! Somewhere in this house I bet there is a cupboard full of men who have served their purpose – and then you've bitten their heads off.'

Spider. The word unburied something Manus remembered about Jonie. Someone – who was it now? – at college had likened Jonie Spencer to a spider. The memory pulled the edge of another with it, like tissues from a box. It was Michael . . . Michael Shea. And as if Tim could read his mind he said, 'Hey, Jonie, remember Michael Shea? Ooh, he had it bad for you, didn't he?'

'Oh God, Michael Shea!' shrieked Jonie before she shuddered. 'Wasn't he awful?'

'Didn't stop you giving him one though, did it?' Tim nudged her.

'Oh, please don't remind me.' Jonie's hands covered her face with shame.

Layla gasped with recognition. 'Was that the bloke who stalked you? Sent you flowers and presents and those bloody awful poems?'

Jonie's head, still covered by her hands, nodded.

Layla was almost hysterical with laughter as details rolled back to her.

'And a ring! He bought you a ring as well, didn't he, and said that it was up to you what finger you put it on. Total nutter!'

Manus's memory was clearing too. Michael hadn't been a nutter, from what he remembered. Just some kid who Jonie had set her sights on, eaten alive and spat out – merely because she could. Jonie had easily seduced him away from the nice girl he had been seeing when she realised she wanted to bend his attention to her. She had always been very aware of her sexual power, Manus recalled. Michael Shea had been so distraught about it all that he abandoned his studies and left the sixth-form college. He had been crying when he told Manus that Jonie Spencer should have been born a spider.

'Enough,' said Jonie, aware that Manus wasn't joining in with the dissection of her fling with Michael Shea. 'Let's have dessert. Give me a hand, will you, Manus?'

Manus followed her into the kitchen. He had only drunk two glasses of wine but realised he was quite light-headed. He wasn't used to wine – he preferred a lager really.

'It all seems so long ago, doesn't it?' sighed Jonie, opening the fridge door. 'I bet you anything Michael Shea is a total hunk now and I'd wish I'd never turned down. Oh bugger.'

'What's up?'

'I was going to put some coffee on but I've run out of milk.'

'Where's the nearest shop?' asked Manus, feeling that a breath of fresh air might be a good thing. 'I'll go and get you some.'

Jonie smiled gratefully. 'Oh, would you? Thanks, Manus. It's only round the corner. There's a mini-Tesco first left. Semi-skimmed, please. Hang on, where's my purse?'

'I think I can afford a couple of pints of milk, Jonie, after the meal you've put on,' Manus protested as he headed out.

'Thanks, babe,' said Jonie.

He had been gone less than a minute when his phone, lying on the work surface where Layla had put it, tinkled. Curious, Jonie picked it up. A text from Roz. She opened it.

Manus, against the rules I know, but I can't tell you how much I've missed you. I've been such an idiot. I love you so much and I can't wait to see you again. Things are going to be different – I promise. Roz xxxx

The phone rumbled in her hand. Another text from Roz –

a repeat of the first. Jonie waited for a third. If Roz was abroad, she might send the message three times to make sure it got through – she would, if she were Roz. She was right. A third message appeared on the screen.

Jonie quickly deleted all three. 'Whoops!' she said to herself.

Chapter 66

'Look, stop worrying, will you? There could be all sorts of possible explanations why Manus hasn't texted you back,' said Frankie firmly. 'For a start, I know it says you had a signal and it seemed to go through okay, but I wouldn't entirely trust that any text you send has landed. The reception is hit and miss at sea – usually miss.'

Roz wanted to believe that, she really did. But the truth of it was that she imagined Manus had got her text and thrown the phone down in disgust. Too little too late. It was no less than she deserved really.

'Come on, let's go and play on some slot machines.' Frankie tugged at her arm.

'Do you really think that message didn't get through?' said Roz. 'I sent it three times.'

'Three times in the same area though, so if the first didn't go through, neither would the others,' her friend reasoned. 'Manus would have replied if he'd received it – you know he would have. He's a pillock for loving you like he does, but there you go.'

'Come on, you two,' Olive prompted. She was on 'bucking-up' duty tonight, what with Roz panicking that Manus had left her and Ven strangely quiet.

'Okay,' said Roz, plastering on a smile. There was nothing

more she could do for now. She had to hope that the texts were floating around in the stratosphere somewhere and that they would land in the next few hours. She knew they did that sometimes. Things were in the lap of the gods. She just had to hope and pray those gods were nice friendly ones who liked a happy ending.

Chapter 67

Manus had intended to leave at the same time as Layla and Tim. He didn't quite know how Jonie managed to convince him to stay for a nightcap coffee. She had made him feel that it would have been churlish to turn it down. It was only a coffee, after all.

He went to the loo and returned feeling that the lights had been dimmed a notch. Jonie was opening a box of Godiva chocolates.

'I got these as a gift from a client,' she said, smoothing her hair back over her shoulder. The candlelights on the table picked out the golden strands and made it shimmer. 'Come and rescue me from eating them all by myself and putting loads of weight on.'

He doubted Jonie Spencer would have qualified as even an amateur glutton with her figure. He chose a dark oval one with a flick of icing on the top.

'So when is Roz home?' Jonie asked, delicately licking the tops of her fingers where her chocolate had melted.

'Tuesday,' replied Manus. 'She was in Gibraltar today, then she has two days at sea, then she's home.'

'Do you always take separate holidays?'

'No, this is the one and only time. We don't take holidays, to be honest.' As soon as he had tagged that onto the end he knew it opened up the ground for further questioning.

'Oh, why's that?' Jonie leaned in slightly with interest.

'We're both too busy, I guess,' he replied coolly, taking another chocolate.

'You guess?' prodded Jonie with more than a touch of disbelief.

Manus opened his mouth to elaborate that neither of them felt they were missing anything by not escaping to the sun together once in a while, but nothing came out, because it would have been a lie.

'Manus.' Jonie put her hand on his and squeezed it. 'Look, I'm not stupid. Half of you has been somewhere else tonight. What's wrong? Talk to me. I'm good at listening. I'm a woman, in case you haven't noticed.'

She laughed because she knew that men noticed she was a woman very much. She had no fear about that not happening.

Manus sipped his coffee. Was it so obvious that his head was spinning with what was going to happen when Roz returned? He really couldn't see that things were going to change and he couldn't carry on as he was. So that meant only one thing – in three days the words would be said by one or both of them that would begin their splitting-up process.

Jonie's eyes were full of soft concern.

'It's you and Roz, isn't it? This holiday is a trial separation.' She was nodding as she said it because she knew she was right. She saw Manus's shoulders tighten as she hit the nail on the head.

'Yes,' was all he said, like a man tired from carrying a great burden. He let out a long breath and those shoulders slumped.

'Oh boy,' said Jonie. She reached behind her to a stash of alcohol, grabbed a half-bottle of brandy and poured a hearty slosh into their coffee cups. 'This calls for reinforcements.'

Manus didn't protest. 'Thanks.'

'How bad are things?' she asked.

'Oooh ... pretty bad,' said Manus. He smiled but there was no mirth whatsoever in it.

'What's the problem? Money? Someone else?'

Manus felt the ground crumbling beneath his feet. He shouldn't talk about this with anyone. Especially not Jonie. Why had the fates conspired to reunite their paths again? Were they trying to tell Manus that they made a mistake long ago? Was his destiny Jonie Spencer and not Roz Lynch? Jonie wanted him, that was obvious. Roz didn't.

'I should say goodnight,' said Manus, standing, not liking where his head was starting to go.

'Manus, don't.' Jonie's hand pressed onto his. 'Sit down and talk to me.'

And Manus found that he wanted to sit down and let it all out because he didn't know what to do any more. A future without Roz seemed cold and frightening, even though he knew that's probably what he would have to face very shortly. From the very start of their relationship, he'd *known* without a doubt that they fitted together. When she gave herself wholly to him in bed, he felt sublime. Never in all his life had he imagined finding someone so perfect who slotted exactly into the waiting part in his heart, which is why he had continued to hang on in there.

Everything spilled out to Jonie and she listened intently, her hand still on his, conducting her warmth and concern. Warmth he so badly craved.

When he had finished talking, Jonie sighed.

'Oh Manus. No one deserves to be constantly punished for one kiss. You shouldn't have let her get away with it for so long. You're only human, for God's sake.'

Jonie couldn't have said anything that Manus wanted to hear more. She had a dangerous aptitude for it. Manus's eyes glittered with tears and he wiped them away with the heel of his hand, embarrassed. Then Jonie leaned forward and he felt her arms close around him.

'Hey, come on.' Her soft voice was in his ear, her perfume in his nose. Then she pulled away and held him at arm's length. Her fingers were in his hair now, pushing it back from his eyes. 'You've obviously struggled with all this for too long, babe. It's time to stop. It's time to stop hurting, Manus.' She sighed and smiled. Her teeth were white and perfect, her lips soft and shiny. 'I just wish I could snap my fingers and we could go back to college. I should have claimed you then. Why didn't I? I always liked you so much.'

Her blue, blue eyes were giving him a green, green light.

Jonie's hands were on his cheeks – soft and warm and gently stroking. 'Oh Manus.' Those big blue eyes locked with his. Her mouth edged closer.

Day 15: At Sea

Dress Code: Formal

Chapter 68

Roz did not have a very good night's sleep. She dreamed that Raul Cruz had sent a letter to Manus telling him that they had had wild sex on a dining table and Manus did not believe her, however much she told him it was lies. He was so cold to her, and the feelings in her dream were too real for comfort. It was torture for however long the dream lasted – probably only minutes – and yet she had put Manus through the same thing for years. She was glad when she woke up. She bounced out of bed, dressed for another hot, sunny lazy day and went up to the Buttery for a strong coffee and carbs.

She spotted Olive and Frankie sitting at a window table.

'You've just this minute missed Ven,' said Frankie. 'She's gone for a meeting with that Andrew from the competition. Do you want a coffee, Roz? I'm just going for a refill.'

'Yes, please,' replied Roz. 'Oh sod, I've forgotten my beach bag. Get me a coffee and I'll be back in a minute.' She dug her cruise card out of her shorts pocket. If she didn't hurry up, Jesus would be cleaning up her room and she hated to interrupt him. Luckily for her though, when she got back to her cabin he was standing outside Ven's cabin, listening at the door.

'Is she in there?' Roz mouthed to him.

'Yes, she just came back,' said Jesus softly.

'I've just forgotten my beach bag,' said Roz. 'Then I'm out

of your way at least.' Ven must have done the same thing as her – forgotten something or other and had to go back for it before her meeting. This sea air was turning them all into cabbage-heads.

'Thank you, ma'am.'

But Ven still hadn't emerged by the time Roz had gathered her book and towel and glasses together because Jesus was still waiting to get into her cabin to clean it. And something made Roz hang around the corridor because this Andrew and the cruise-winning story had always seemed a bit fishy to her.

Ven came out of the room twenty minutes later. Roz tailed her, unseen, up the stairs to the Topaz pool where she found Frankie and Olive on the sunbeds. Roz arrived just in time to hear her tell the others about the face-to-face interview she had just given Andrew for a future *Figurehead* magazine, but she stayed silent about it. For now.

Chapter 69

David hung up the three dresses over the mirrored wardrobe door in what was to be his and Olive's new bedroom – his mother's old room. He'd had the dresses made by the seamstresses in Lamb Street at considerable expense too. He'd paid right over the odds so they would be done extra quickly. He had taken the measurements from a winter dress that Olive had in her wardrobe, so he knew they would fit. She would especially like the green one, he knew. Green looked so nice on her, brought out the colour in her eyes. He was very proud of himself for what he considered was his finest romantic gesture. Olive would be over the moon.

The house was spick and span as well, in readiness for her return. He had found a cleaner in the *Yellow Pages* – Dolly Braithwaite – who was available at short notice, and she had tidied up the downstairs and changed the sheets on his mother's old bed. Dolly smelled of cigarette smoke and strong coffee, and was someone who didn't find the overflowing ashtrays in the kitchen revolting at all. In fact, all the time she was working, a lit Benson & Hedges was perched on her lip.

Olive would be home in approximately forty-eight hours now. He couldn't wait to tell her about everything that had happened in the past two weeks. She was going to worship the ground he walked upon after he explained what their new life was going to be like. David Hardcastle hadn't been this excited since Charlesworth's had opened their new pork-pie shop just around the corner.

Chapter 70

Olive had a little break from the sun and went to stretch her legs inside the ship. She watched a couple who had just got married on board posing for photos on the Grand Staircase. She recognised the party – they'd got on at Barnsley too. The bride was tall and slim, mid-fifties, with beautiful thick white hair. She wore a simple sleeveless ivory satin dress and carried a posy of bright yellow flowers which coordinated both with the flower the beaming groom was wearing in his buttonhole and the Matron of Honour's fifties-style dress in the brightest shade of sunshine. The Matron of Honour had the same twinkly eyes as the tall, smiley groom, suggesting they were closely related. They were accompanied by two younger couples – a black man, his wife and a little boy, and two men, both dressed in 'his and his' grey suits, also with yellow ties. There was obviously a lot of affection zinging between them all, and the happy vibes were radiating outwards from them and filling the whole atrium.

Olive wandered around the shops for a while, perusing the stalls of duty-free goods, then moved up to look at the gallery of photographs. Hearing the noise of children coming from nearby Flamencos, Olive peeped in to see a fancy-dress competition just starting. Most of the costumes had been hand-made, by the looks of things. There was a little girl having a bit of a tantrum as her mother tried to staple her into a crepe-paper hula hula skirt.

'Chloe,' the mother was saying wearily, 'it's taken me hours to make this costume, please put it on.' But young Chloe wasn't having any of it.

'Kids,' the mother sighed at Olive. 'I got up at the crack of dawn today to make this for her and we still didn't get the pick of the materials.' Her head nudged to the side where the Tray Twins were standing with a small boy whose whole body was completely encased in a cardboard lighthouse. His face was bright orange to indicate the lamp, and waves of blue and green and white fronds of crepe were swaying two feet past the floor to indicate the sea. There was a rainforest of paper in that one costume. It seemed Ronnie and Reggie claimed a lion's share of anything that wasn't nailed down.

Olive slid into the theatre and took one of the back seats, slightly worried that she would be asked to leave if she didn't have a participating child. But then she saw Eric and Irene sitting near the front and relaxed.

The youth director led on the contestants one by one – a lot of pirates, a cat, and the lighthouse who was hardly able to walk in the confines of his straitjacket costume. The little hula-hooper not only continued to reject the wearing of her skirt but also refused to go into the stage arena. Then she was tempted by her appearance prize of a small teddy bear, so ran on, grabbed it and leaped back to her mother. The lighthouse's parents looked ungracious in defeat when their son didn't win, but a bee, in a very simple but incredibly cute costume, did. Olive laughed as the bee buzzed across the stage to be photographed, but the tears that started to slip from her eyes weren't happy ones. She wiped them away secretly, glad that she was at the back of the theatre and unseen. Where had her childbearing years gone? This fortnight was the first time she had looked up and seen that they had disappeared and she was almost forty now with nothing to show for her life. No house of her own, no babies to love, not even a decent bloody mobile phone. Suddenly the sight of that little bee was too much to bear. She couldn't go back to her sad existence in Land Lane – not after the sun had shone on her life and highlighted every empty corner.

The four of them had fajita wraps and chips from the Terrace Grill by the still closed-off Topaz pool and watched an episode of *Only Fools and Horses* on the giant sea-screen. A waiter called Relish brought them four glasses of sparkling mineral water and lots of chinking ice.

'So how was your meeting with Andrew then?' asked Roz, who had been waiting for the right moment to bring this one to the boil.

'Oh, it was okay. I just did an interview with him.'

'Where did you meet?'

'The Samovar.'

'What sorts of things did he ask you?' Roz pressed.

'Well, you know, have we had a good time et cetera, all low-key stuff. Anyone want anything stronger to drink?'

But Roz wasn't letting her change the subject this time. 'Doesn't he want to meet us?'

'He hasn't said.'

'Have you showed him the picture we had taken at the bottom of the staircase the night before last?'

'Yes, he's going to use it in the magazine.' Ven was trying to end the conversation but Roz wasn't letting her.

'Isn't he going to introduce himself to us before we leave?'

'I . . . don't—'

'Bloody hell, Roz,' put in Frankie. 'Are you practising for entry into the Gestapo?'

'Ven,' said Roz calmly. 'Come on, 'fess up. What's going on? You're telling us a load of old pump.'

'What do you mean?' said Ven, but she was jittery now and very red-faced. Deception didn't sit easily with her.

'Yes, what do you mean, "what's going on?"' said Olive. Now the others were sitting up and wondering what Roz was talking about.

'Ven, I know you didn't have a meeting with "Andrew" this morning. I don't think the bloody bloke even exists. What are you playing at?'

Ven growled in frustration and buried her head in her hands.

'Ven?' said Olive, not getting any of this at all.

'All right, all right,' said Ven, shaking her palms wildly at them to fend off any further questioning. 'I lied. I didn't win a cruise in a competition. I won some money to take us on a cruise. But I knew that if I told you that, you'd start being stupid and not let me pay for everything for you.'

'You silly generous cow!' exclaimed Frankie. 'You need that money. You shouldn't have spent it on us.'

'Yes, well, I *wanted* to spend it on us for this holiday and I didn't want you telling me that I shouldn't and getting all silly. Now you know, you'll not let me buy everything. Just great.' Ven gave a giant sigh of disappointment.

Roz felt awfully guilty now that she had spoiled her friend's generous surprise. When would she ever learn that she didn't know best at all?

'Oh Ven!' Olive leaned over and gave her a big hug. 'You are the loveliest person ever. But Frankie is right, you are also a silly cow.'

'Was it the lottery?' asked Roz, subdued now.

'Yes, Roz, it was the lottery,' said Ven. She leaned back on her sunbed and the others followed suit.

'I'm sorry, Ven, I didn't realise I was spoiling a surprise.' Roz gave her friend's arm a gentle butt.

'Well, it was going to happen today or tomorrow anyway. I was just waiting for the right moment. Seems it's here now.'

'How much did you win, Ven?' said Olive, hoping that Ven wasn't going to be out of pocket herself with her stupid generosity. They all really had bought a lot from the shops.

'Let me start at the beginning,' said Ven. 'On the sixth of June I saw Ian and his floozy out in a flash car and he gave me a really smug wave when he passed. I was pig sick about it.'

'As you would be,' added Olive. 'Bastard.'

'Some blokes should never be in sole charge of a penis,' added Roz.

'Well, I was so angry I went to the post office.'

'Steady on, Ven,' laughed Frankie. 'I'd hate to get on the wrong side of you, mate. What did you do? Buy some first-class stamps and rip them up?'

'No, I bought a lottery ticket,' said Ven when the laughter had subsided. 'A EuroMillions one. I picked the numbers based on how angry I was. Forty-one – for Ian's age, twenty-four – because that's how old his bit on the side is, fifteen – because that's the number of my old house which they're now living in, three – because that's how many letters there are in "Ian", and six – because it was that day's date: the sixth of June. And his bloody birthday. But for the star numbers I picked four – because we're a four and two because that's the square root of four and four is my lucky number. And I won. And the first thing I did was book this cruise for us. The second thing I was going to do at the end of the cruise, and that was to share out the rest of the winnings.'

'You've got some left?' said Olive. 'After buying all this, you've still got some left?'

Ven opened up her handbag and pulled out three envelopes bearing their names. She'd been carrying them around with her all holiday – waiting for the opportune moment.

They all lazily sat up. Frankie was the first to open hers and she laughed.

'My Aunt Rosa did this,' she said. 'She left fourteen of us in the family a cheque for fifty thousand quid each, but she only had seven hundred pounds in her bank account – total. Bless her.'

'God, Ven, you're a silly sod,' said Olive, looking at the cheque. *To Olive Hardcastle, the sum of four hundred and forty-four thousand, four hundred and forty-four pounds. Only.* She sank back onto her sunbed.

Only Roz was trembling, because she was looking intently at Ven and she knew Ven wasn't joking.

'I won just over four million quid,' said Ven quietly. 'I'm going to give Jen the same as you and donate a lump sum to the Macmillan nurses who looked after Mum and Dad. I won't have any arguments about this – I want you to share it with me, in accordance with four being our lucky number.'

Olive sat up again, her back straight and unbending and giving the impression she was rising from a grave – which she could easily have been, given the sudden pallor of her face. 'You are joking?'

'I'm not.'

'You won *four million quid*?'

'Yep. Just over.'

Maybe if Ven had said she had won ten thousand they would have whooped for her, but this figure was too much to take in, in one sitting. As it was, they decided to go and have a coffee. In the Buttery – because it was always free there.

'I was worried,' said Ven. 'You hear all these stories about people getting loads of money and it wrecking their lives. I was so excited that you wouldn't have to struggle financially any more, then I kept dreaming awful things – that we bought high-speed cars and died in crashes, and stuff like that.'

'Aye, well, trust you to look on the bright side of a four-mil-lion-pound lottery win.' Frankie laughed but her hand was shaking as she lifted the cup to her lips.

'I wanted Manus to have his big garage and you, Roz, to be able to tell that Mrs Hutchinson to stick her job up her bum. I wanted you, Frank, to buy a nice house and never have to worry about money again, and you, Olive, to give up cleaning and—' She didn't say that she wanted Olive to leave David and get a life; the money gave her no right to play God. 'Just don't cash the cheque until you're sure no one will take half of it from you like Ian did with me.' She said this to no one in particular, but Olive knew the warning was meant for her.

'I can't take this in,' said Frankie. 'I cannot take this in.'

'Think how *I* felt!' said Ven. 'I couldn't even tell anyone because I wanted this holiday to happen so much. And I didn't want anyone else to know before you all did.'

'Ven, that is a hell of a lot of money to give away,' said Frankie.

'Do you think I'd enjoy it, keeping it to myself?' said Ven. 'All for one and one for all. The Fabulous Four reunited again. Some things are worth more than money.'

'Nice to have both though,' winked Frankie. They all grabbed each other's hands as if about to embark upon a séance and squeezed. Because some joy just had to be let out slowly and carefully.

Roz attended her last belly-dancing class that afternoon. She would definitely have to find a class and continue lessons when she got home. She wondered if she dare do a dance for Manus? He looked at her with desire in his eyes when she was in her old dressing-gown, he'd blow up if she started gyrating in jingly scarves, enticing him to whisk her to bed.

As she practised moving her hips from side to side whilst keeping the top half of her body totally still, she tried to think of the last time she and Manus had made love. It brought her shame to think how she wanted to abandon herself to him, and could feel him willing her to love him with the same intensity that he loved her. He did turn her on, she did adore the feel of his skin next to hers. Stupid, stupid pride. She was going to love him to death when she got home and make up for every little rejection she had ever given him.

Chapter 71

'How do I look?' asked Frankie, head to foot in white shimmering sequins.

'Like a million-dollar glamorous snowman,' laughed Roz in black silk. The others were also in black: a long figure-hugging crushed velvet number for Olive, a black strapless taffeta gown with a feather boa draped around the shoulders for Ven.

It was Black-and-White Night and, with a few exceptions, most people had stuck religiously to the monochrome theme.

'Champagne, darlings?' asked Ven, gliding into the Vista lounge.

'No, let's have some ice wine,' purred Frankie, answering the disapproving look Ven gave her by adding, 'not because it's cheaper, just because I like it as much, if not more.'

She waved at Vaughan, pulling at his white collar, trying to find some space for his neck. He waved back shyly and made to come over.

'We'll meet you by the window,' grinned Ven, and the three of them moved away to give the couple some space.

'You look lovely,' said Vaughan.

'So do you,' replied Frankie, trying not to sigh like a schoolgirl.

'Didn't you get my answering machine messages?'

'Answering machine?' said Frankie, puzzled.

'I rang your cabin and left a message. Wasn't there a flashing light on your phone?'

'I never thought to look at it. Oh God, sorry.'

Vaughan looked visibly relieved. 'Phew, I thought you were avoiding me,' he said.

'Why would I do that?' said Frankie, giving him a wide grin.

'Frankie, I know it's hard on board . . .'

'Well, it was in Gibraltar,' she winked.

'Let me finish, you minx,' he said. 'I know it's *hard to meet* on board because you're with your friends and I've got my family, but what do you think about . . . would you like . . . Okay, here it is.' He coughed. 'How would you like to come back home with me after the cruise? I want to get to know you.'

'Yes,' she said immediately. 'That would be wonderful.'

'Wow, that was easier than I thought it was going to be,' said Vaughan, almost sweating with relief.

'For an ex-Hell's Angel, you aren't half a wuss,' Frankie told him. 'So, what did you say on your answering machine message?'

'Message-*s*,' amended Vaughan. 'You'll have to listen to them.' He waved them away bashfully.

'No, tell me,' said Frankie.

Vaughan started pulling at his collar again. 'I said I really enjoyed myself with you – not just the sex,' he said, 'although that was pretty hot, if I'm honest. I just asked if you'd meet up with me for a coffee or something. I wanted to see you again.'

He was so adorably uncomfortable saying all this to her face that she wanted to grab him and start snogging him.

'I can do better than coffee, Vaughan,' said Frankie. 'If you fancy some more wild rampant sex come to my cabin at eleven tonight. And wear those clothes, because I want to rip them right off you.'

Vaughan grabbed her, tilted her back Hollywood-style and kissed her full on the mouth.

'There, that was me not being a wuss – happy now?'

'Very,' Frankie said through a breathless grin.

'See you later then, Brown Eyes,' imitating Humphrey Bogart. Both his party and Frankie's were cheering in the background. Frankie joined the girls at the bar table wearing a smile as wide as the Straits of Gibraltar.

Five minutes before the call to dinner, Ven went to deliver her anniversary card to the Ambrosia restaurant for Florence and Dennis. She located tables five and four so she was in the right quarter, but when she looked around there were no tables with any balloons on them. She hailed a passing head waiter.

'Could you tell me where table one is, please?' she asked.

'Table one? There is no table one, ma'am,' he replied. 'Table two is the first number. Who are you looking for?'

'An old couple – Florence and Dennis. I don't know their surname. She has white hair, if that helps.' It obviously didn't because the head waiter was shaking his head.

'Not in first or second sitting in this restaurant, ma'am. Are you sure it is not the Olympia restaurant where these people are eating?'

'Maybe,' replied Ven, although she was sure that she hadn't got her facts mixed up. She took a slow walk through the restaurant hoping to spot Florence taking her seat. Maybe the old lady had got her table numbers mixed up. Oh damn.

There was a table one in the Olympia, but it was for eight people and the head waiter in that quarter also shook his head as Ven described the old couple. As she weaved her way through the tables to their own, she could see Frankie's grin a mile off. She envied her friend that look on her face and her budding relationship with Vaughan, who really was a bit of top totty now he had got all that hair off his face. He had kind eyes, like Nigel's. *Nigel*. She should have grown out of all this holiday-romance stuff at her age. It didn't get any better and she knew she was in for a rough ride when she got home, dreaming about what snogging Nigel would have been like and knowing she would never find out. Okay, so life would be fun looking for a new house, but it wouldn't make her knees go weak like a whiff of Nigel's aftershave did. Money didn't keep you warm at nights or make your heart gallop.

Nigel pulled the chair out for her and tucked her underneath the table.

'What a beautiful dress,' he said over her shoulder. She felt the heat of his breath on her skin and gave a delighted little shudder.

'Thank you,' said Ven. 'It's out of the shit shop, Ship Shot . . . SHIP SHOP!' Bang goes my class act yet again, she thought, cringing inwardly.

'Bit of a tongue-twister, "ship shop",' said Irene kindly, although she managed to say it without making a total prat of herself.

'Good job your dress sense is better than your control of the English language, gel,' said Royston. 'Doesn't our Ven look lovely tonight, Captain?' And he gave a big juicy wink to Ven.

'Indeed,' said Nigel diplomatically. 'As do all the ladies on this table.'

Ven turned to Frankie and whispered through gritted teeth, 'I hope none of you lot told Royston I fancied Nigel.'

'Don't be daft,' she replied. 'Although I might have let it slip out to Stella.'

'Great!' said Ven. As if things weren't bad enough with her verbal Tourettes, now she was going to have to endure Royston's amateur matchmaking. He was about as subtle as a sledgehammer with a self-playing vuvuzela attached.

'This is my favourite night,' said Stella. 'I love to see all the variations on black and white.' Then she cast an exasperated glance at her husband, who was wearing a white jacket, matching white trousers and shoes, black shirt and piano tie. With his tan in full bloom he looked like a photo-negative.

Ven was still blushing and shaking her head at herself. She was looking at the menu but not reading it because her brain was too busy calling her a total berk. Nigel gave her a gentle nudge to alert her to the fact that Buzz was waiting to take her order.

'The ham then the halibut, please,' said Ven. At least there was nothing to mispronounce with those two.

'Are you all right tonight, Venice?' asked Nigel. 'You seem a little . . . distracted.'

Too right she was distracted. The way Nigel said her name echoed in her head. 'Venice . . . Venice . . . Venice. *Come to bed, Venice, I have things to do to you . . .*'

She coughed. 'Yes, I'm fine,' she said. 'I'm just not looking forward to going home. I think I've enjoyed myself too much.'

'Join the club,' said Stella. 'You want to book yourself another holiday at the future-cruise desk by Reception. You'll get some on-board spending money included if you do.'

'I just might,' said Ven, trying to gee herself up to be a bit more cheerful. After all, she could afford it now – she was a millionairess. *A very lonely millionairess with a major crush on the guy sitting next to her.* If that wasn't a mix of emotions, then she didn't know what was.

'I did most of our packing today,' said Irene, as if Ven wasn't depressed enough that she'd have to pack tomorrow as well.

'Oh no.' Stella waved a perfectly manicured hand to dismiss that thought. 'Last-minute for us. I don't even want to think about packing.'

'What are your plans when you get home?' Nigel asked Ven.

'House hunting,' said Ven with a loaded sigh. At the moment, all the hassle of moving wasn't thrilling her. *Not even with all that money in the bank to spend on a country pile.*

'Sometimes they have spare cabins on following cruises and you can pay and just stay on,' said Royston. 'We've done that a couple of times, haven't we, Stell?'

'Alas, not on the next cruise on this ship,' announced Nigel. 'We're docking for a few days for some decorating before we head up to Iceland.'

'Will you stop off at Morrisons?' Eric quipped, proud that everyone joined in with his laughter.

'Are you staying aboard, Captain?' asked Royston.

'I'm making a flying visit up to Ayr to see my mother and stepfather actually,' replied Nigel. 'I haven't seen them for over six months and I'll be in trouble if I leave it any longer.'

As dessert was served, the waiters began to gather at a table of eight nearby and sang 'Congratulations'. Olive noticed they were serenading the couple who had got married earlier on. The snow-haired bride was in the most beautiful white suit, the groom in a white tuxedo. Even the little boy had a mini-tuxedo on.

'Did you marry that couple this morning?' Ven asked.

'Yes, indeed I did,' replied Nigel. 'Lovely people. Actually, they're from Yorkshire too. He's a dentist.'

'Do you do lots of weddings, Captain?' asked Irene.

'It's becoming very popular,' said Nigel.

'There you go, Venice,' began Royston, and Ven closed her eyes against what embarrassing thing he was going to come out with next. He didn't disappoint. 'Any chance of getting you married off before we dock? You married, Captain?'

Oh God, I am going to kill my friends and their big mouths, thought Venice and leaped in to change the course of the conversation before Nigel ended up as red-faced as she was becoming.

'Is there any way of trying to find a pair of passengers just by their first names, Nigel?'

Nigel asked her to elaborate and Ven explained about Florence and Dennis and being unable to find table one in the Ambrosia restaurant.

'There is no table one – the head waiter wasn't making it up,' said Nigel. 'It was considered unlucky after what happened.'

Eric was nodding, looking like a little kid in class with his arm raised to breaking-point, desperate to tell Teacher the answer.

'We were on the maiden voyage of this ship, weren't we, Irene?'

'Yes, we were,' affirmed Irene. 'And in the Ambrosia restaurant, first sitting.'

'The couple on table one were both dead before we got to Gibraltar, which was the first port of call on that cruise.'

'Such a shame. They were due to celebrate their Diamond Wedding on the Black-and-White Ball night, but she had a stroke on the first night.'

'And he had a heart-attack when they told him she'd died,' continued Irene.

'Ships are fraught with superstition,' said Eric. 'Which is why there's no thirteenth floor on a lot of them. The powers-that-be decided that table one would be unlucky so they don't have one in that restaurant. Because of what happened to that poor old couple.'

Ven was confused now. 'What were they called?'

'Haven't a clue,' said Eric. 'I dare say there will be a record of it somewhere. Internet maybe?'

'Someone's spinning you a yarn, girl,' Royston grinned at Ven. 'Either that or you've been talking to ghosts.'

'I don't believe in ghosts,' said Ven. She took a loaded spoonful of her ice cream, but it wasn't that which made her shiver.

The ship's photographers then approached and announced they were doing table shots.

'Oh yes, we'll have one of those!' Royston spoke for them all. The girls were expertly arranged behind the two couples, Nigel standing in the middle, his arms around Ven and Olive. Soon that's all she would have left to remind her of him – a wispy memory of his arm around her and this photograph and two handkerchiefs that she kept promising to return to him.

Chuffing hell, Ven, cheer up, will you? said a voice inside. *You aren't half a miserable cow, considering you're on a cruise ship with a couple of million quid in the bank!* She drew a little comfort from the fact that the posed party seemed in no rush to disassemble. Nigel's arm stayed around her for seconds longer than it did around Olive, though it felt much longer. *God, you're a saddo, analysing everything like this, Ven Smith!*

During coffee, Royston asked, 'Will you be dining with us tomorrow night, Captain?' Ven waited for the answer, heart in her mouth.

'I very much hope so,' replied Nigel. 'I can never say for definite, alas. It all depends what is happening up on the bridge.'

'Oh, it would be a shame not to see you on the last night,' said Irene.

'It most certainly would, wouldn't it, girls?' said Royston, giving Ven a big juicy wink. It was like having an embarrassing uncle hell-bent on trying to make her blush.

Nigel stood to go. 'Well, have a very enjoyable evening, everyone. I hear the theatre company's production tonight is very, very good.'

'Aren't they all?' said Royston. 'That little gay-boy dancer is an absolute star. I could watch him all night.'

'You can't say "gay-boy dancer"!' shrieked Stella. 'You don't even know he's gay for a start!'

'Oh, come on, love,' said Royston. 'Poncing about on stage like that, he makes Larry Grayson look like Bruce Willis.'

Everyone was laughing – even Nigel, though he was trying not to. Royston was a dear maverick both in his speech and dress. Ven, especially, found that she was going to miss him very much, despite his rubbish attempts at matchmaking.

'Come on.' Frankie nudged Ven, watching her watching Nigel leave the restaurant. Her friend had it bad and Frankie wished she could do what they did when they were younger – tell the boy in question that 'my mate fancies you' and force the

issue out into the open. But all the money in the world could-
n't take them back into the past.

They all trooped down to the theatre together to watch a musical extravaganza based on *West Side Story*. How the actors
changed so quickly was anyone's guess. One minute they were
in everyday fifties-style gear, the next in flamenco costumes.
Roz thought she might try flamenco dancing next. It was so
fluidly beautiful and passionate. She would never have believed
that a bit of dancing could have awoken her from the inside so
much. Then again, Manus still had not returned her text.
Maybe there would be no one to be passionate for when she
got home.

Frankie left them straight after the show to meet Vaughan.
She moved so fast up the Grand Staircase she looked as if she
were flying. Ven tried not to think that she would have moved
as fast, if she knew Nigel was waiting for her outside her cabin.

'Packing tomorrow,' said Ven, sticking out her tongue as she
flumped on one of three plump upholstered stripy seats in
Beluga.

'Aye,' sighed Olive. 'Ven, I have to say, this has been the most
wonderful two weeks of my life. Thank you.'

'It's a pleasure, my love,' said Ven. She smiled at Olive, who
looked a totally different woman to the one whom she had
picked up crying the night before they set off. Her hair was
shimmery and golden, her lovely face tanned, her eyes shining
like green gems in a mine. She had blossomed on board,
watered with rest and fed with some Greek attention. But she
worried for Olive because she knew what was in store for her.
She would go home, buy a big house with her money, and all
the bloody Hardcastles would move in with her. She would
give up her day job and instead have to pander to them 24/7.
Nothing would change for her except the number of bedrooms
she had to clean.

'Olive, I think you should bugger off to Greece,' said Roz, mirroring Ven's thoughts. 'I know I'm hardly Mrs-I'm-So-Great-at-Relationships, but if you go back home, I'll kick your arse from Barnsley bus station to Bridlington beach.'

Olive laughed. Roz giving out reckless advice was just too funny. Boy, she had changed during this holiday.

'Let's not even think about life beyond the ship,' chirped Ven, clapping her hands. 'We've got a full day left yet. And I want an Irish coffee and some chocolates. And I want them now.' Right on cue a waiter arrived and took their order. And the three of them snuggled back in the chairs, chilled out to the pianist, and watched a beautiful black-and-white world go by.

DAY 16: AT SEA

Dress Code: Smart Casual

Chapter 72

Frankie stretched awake, opened her eyes and saw that she was being stared at. By a naked Viking with a tattooed shoulder.

'Morning,' he drawled, with a cheeky grin. 'You slept well.' The emphasis on his words inferred that she'd been snoring.

'You tired me out,' she grinned. 'It's your fault if I made noises or dribbled.'

He pulled her towards him tightly and kissed her. The sea was choppier this morning and the boat was rocking a little more wildly. They lay back, not saying anything, just letting the sea buffet them along, enjoying the closeness, the feeling of being held.

'Do you ever worry it will come back?' Vaughan suddenly asked.

'It crosses my mind occasionally, but I try not to dwell on it,' replied Frankie. 'If I thought about all the bad things that could happen to me, I'd never get up in the morning. Vaughan, I hid myself away for too long. I got too scared to live and make plans because death cast this massive black shadow over everything. This past couple of weeks have really done wonders for me. I'm going to live until I die and look forward to the lovely things that might happen to me. Like going to your house.'

'Not changed your mind about coming back with me then?'

'Why would I?' Frankie snuggled into his chest, the fine blond hairs tickling her cheek.

'I still can't believe you're not put off.'

Frankie pulled away. 'You're not defined by one missing bollock, Vaughan.' She snuggled back into him as he shushed her, in case they heard next door through the wall.

'You have such a way with words,' he laughed. 'Honestly, you should have been a poet.'

'Are you put off by the fact these are replacements for ones I lost?' She nudged her breasts into him.

'Not in the slightest,' he replied.

'Do you feel you're going to catch cancer off me if you touch them?'

'Don't be daft.'

Frankie grabbed his hands. 'Then touch them, you stupid man. Can't you take a hint?'

Ven had packed most of her things before breakfast. She made as short a job of it as possible then called for Olive and Roz, who were both up early doing the same. They pushed a note under Frankie's door. She had a Do Not Disturb sign in her key slot which they all grinned at. They were in time to go to the Ambrosia for a waiter-served full *Mermaidia* breakfast and lots of coffee.

Then it was up to the now-open Topaz pool where people were swimming, lying on the sunbeds and watching *Moulin Rouge* on the big sea-screen, determined to enjoy every last second of their holiday. There was a definite increase in the number of clouds in the sky, but they were white and wispy and didn't take much of the heat away when they drifted across the face of the sun.

Frankie joined them at half past eleven, looking as if she had just bathed in a fountain of youth.

'You had an injection from some rejuvenating spring?' asked Roz.

'Yeah, and you should have seen the size of the needle!' snorted Frankie, throwing herself down on the sunbed next to her. She had a bright green bikini on which could have been seen from a space station. She ordered a Brandy Alexander from the waiter when the others were ordering mineral waters.

'Sod it, I'm on holiday,' she explained. 'And I haven't had any breakfast, so I'm going for the biggest burger I can find as soon as the clock strikes twelve.'

Ven grunted and sat up. 'This new costume is far too big around the boobs,' she said, adjusting it. 'I'm sure the label is showing the wrong size.'

'I'm going in for a swim,' said Frankie. 'Coming anyone?'

The four of them slid into the waters of the pool and sighed with pleasure.

'We'll have to do this again,' said Ven. 'Caribbean next time?'

'In your dreams!' laughed Olive. 'How will I be able to afford—?' She stopped herself mid-flow and looked gobsmacked at the others. 'I still can't take it in.'

'I could quite happily do this again,' gushed Roz. 'It's been brilliant, Ven. Forget the money thing for now, I mean the holiday. Getting us all together again, especially me and Frankie. You've made it all so special – it's been a dream come true.'

'Roz, you're starting to worry me,' said Frankie. 'Have you been taken over by an alien?'

'Bugger off, Carnevale.'

'Much better,' said Frankie, submerging herself.

'Totty alert!' said Olive, giving Ven an underwater kick. Captain Nigel was making a slow friendly walk towards the pool.

'Morning, ladies,' he saluted. 'Are you coming along to the Chocolate Factory this afternoon in the Olympia? Chocolate as far as the eye can see. I do hear it's every woman's dream.'

'Some women have different dreams, Captain,' said Frankie, smiling sweetly and kicking Ven from the other side.

'Yes, we'll be there,' said Ven, pulling herself up to rest her arms on the side of the pool. She saw Nigel twitch slightly and turn his head from her.

'Ok-ay,' he said quickly. 'See you all at dinner if not before.' And he strolled off in the direction of mid-ship.

'So he *will* be at dinner!' gasped Ven aloud, though she meant to say it to herself.

'Er . . . no wonder, Ven,' said Olive with a pained look on her face. 'I think you just made him an offer he couldn't refuse.'

Ven followed to where Olive was pointing. Her breasts had escaped from her costume, her nipples were bobbing on the surface of the pool. Ven sank to the bottom of the pool in shame. Was there anything left for her to embarrass herself with?

They bought four copies of the photograph taken of them all at the dinner-table the previous night. Nine smiling people in black and white captured in a happy bubble of time. It was a lovely picture. Nigel looked impossibly handsome with his smiling grey eyes and military-cut hair. Ven wasn't sure she would ever meet a man who could live up to that complete package of gorgeous voice, kind heart, fabulous body, brilliant uniform and discretion in the face of her Ronnie Biggs tits. Her head dropped into her hands at the thought of it.

'Stop thinking about Nigel seeing your knockers,' said Frankie, hitting the nail right on the head. 'Let's go and eat chocolate and be total pigs.'

The Tray Twins and young Lighthouse were at the front of the very long queue waiting for the restaurant doors to open.

'I hope they leave us some,' sniggered Olive. But she had nothing to worry about because when the Olympia opened, there were tables with chocolate cakes, truffles and gloopy fountains as far as the eye could see. The only thing missing was Willy Wonka and a couple of Oompa Loompas. There was a huge mermaid made out of chocolate and a cake replica of the ship. The Tray Twins family were in orgasmic delight, transporting two heaving plates each back to a table within reaching distance of one of the chocolate fountains.

Eric and Irene waved over. They had a shared plate of four tiny cakes and a pot of tea.

'Ah, bless them,' said Olive. 'I'm so going to miss those two. Aren't they a lovely couple?' As soon as she said it, she realised that no one had ever called her and David 'a lovely couple'. Where did it all go wrong? Once upon a time he was going to build them a big house with an indoor pool. She had been lonely when she met him and ripe for being seduced by big talk and the slightest bit of affection. She watched as Eric pulled out the chair so that Irene could sit down and gave her the first choice of cake. *That* small action showed her the difference between a true relationship and the sham she had.

As they lumbered out of the restaurant, stuffed as teddy bears in an over-generous kapok factory, they spotted a very happy Stella who had just won the snowball prize on the bingo.

'I was determined,' she said through her trout pout. 'Some of these bleeders only turn up on the last day and I wasn't going to let them win. Come and have a drink with me, girls!'

They drank Bellini cocktails and Frankie made them all laugh by reliving the story of Ven's mischievous bathing costume. People were coming in from the outside decks now for cardigans. Clouds were thickening in the skies and the sun was switching down a few gas marks with every passing hour.

The afternoon seemed to whiz unfairly past. Children had to leave the pools because the water was sloshing violently from side to side now, and safety nets had been cast over them. All over the ship people were packing or doing last-minute laundry. Cases were appearing outside cabins to be taken away by the crew for transportation to the Southampton terminal building. The girls changed into casual wear for dinner and walked down to Café Parisienne for their last ice wines.

There was a strange serenity about the ship as they sat there in silence, just watching the *Mermaidia* forge her way towards England. It was as if they were all cygnets on a mother swan's back who had made a safe and warm crossing over the water and would be delivered gently home.

'Got your tip envelopes for Elvis and Buzz?' asked Ven.

'Safe in my handbag,' replied Roz. 'Eric says we don't have to tip the wine waiters because they get a commission from everything we order.'

'Chuffing hell,' said Frankie. 'Angel will be richer than you, Ven.'

'Well, I'm still giving her something,' put in Ven. 'She's looked after us something rotten. I'll give Jesus his tip in the morning before we go.'

'Are you giving the Captain anything?' Frankie winked.

'I think he got enough this morning,' laughed Ven, although she knew her cheeks would start to smoulder as soon as she saw Nigel at dinner.

The dinner gong sounded and they wended their way down to the restaurant where the large square body and wide grin of Supremo was waiting to wish them a good evening.

'How can it be good, Supremo?' said Ven. 'It's our last dinner.'

'Then you have to come again, ma'am,' said Supremo. Which made perfect sense really. Ven wondered if she would ever be able to go back to a one-destination holiday again and airport luggage restrictions. In fact, Ven wondered if she could ever go back to dry land full stop!

Royston had saved his best until last: a Hawaiian shirt totally covered in banana patterns.

'Hello, girls. Have you seen that photo we had taken last

night? How lovely do we look?' he said as he approached the table.

'Fabulous shirt, Royston,' said Frankie.

'Thank you, darlin'. I've got matching underpants on – do you want to see?' Royston chuckled.

'No, she bloody doesn't!' Stella warned. 'Sit down and behave.'

'Yes, boss,' Royston saluted his wife.

The menu that night was full of traditional English dishes – presumably to acclimatise the passengers for the imminent return to Blighty. Not that any of them at the table wanted to be acclimatised until they reached the dock of Southampton – they wanted a reverse thrust to moussaka and stuffed vine leaves, carbonaras and paella.

Nigel still hadn't arrived by the time the bread had been distributed, much to Ven's disappointment.

'Might as well order,' said Stella. 'Doesn't look as if the Captain is coming. What a shame.'

Ven tried to look nonchalant, but a definite fat grey cloud had fallen over the evening for her. She buried her nose in the menu.

'My goodness, sorry I'm late,' came a breezy Irish voice from the side of her. 'Have you ordered?'

Royston cheered. 'Naw, we were just killing time until you came, Captain.'

Ven knew that if she had a tail, it would be wagging fifteen to the dozen now. 'Ooh look, Ven,' said Stella, glancing down the menu and then winking at her. 'Raspberry Ripple's for dessert.'

Ven cast her a warning glance. God, she hoped Stella hadn't told Royston about Ven showing off her raspberry ripples to Nigel.

'Did you tell Stella about my costume!' Ven whispered to Roz.

'No, I did not,' replied Roz indignantly. 'Frankie did.'

'I'm going to kill her,' growled Ven.

'Frankie told her to keep it to herself.'

'Oh, well that's all right, then,' huffed Ven.

'It was a pearler,' Roz giggled. 'We had to share it with her.'

'Everyone okay?' said Nigel, taking the menu from Buzz. He quickly perused it and ordered corn fritters and then a fillet steak stuffed with Stilton to follow. 'So everyone had a good time today?' he asked.

Variations of the word 'lovely' twittered to him in response.

'Let's hope this is the first of many more cruises for you all.'

'I think it's impossible to just go on one cruise,' announced Eric, reiterating, 'impossible. You have to come back, once you've experienced it.'

'Yep, I'll go along with that,' said Frankie. 'Finances allowing, I think we'll all be back.'

'Would you really come back, Venice?' asked Nigel, turning a beam of attention on her. It was so intense, it virtually burned her. At least, that's what was happening to her cheeks.

'I'd love to,' she whispered, shifting her eyes from his before he fried her retinas off.

'Frankie met a man,' smiled Roz. 'She's going back home with him to "get to know him better".' Then she started singing the theme tune to *The Love Boat*.

'Grass!' grinned Frankie.

'Yes, it's terrible when your *pals* tell everyone your business, isn't it?' said Ven.

But Frankie was too taken up with the opportunity which Roz had just handed to her. She was going to get Nigel and Ven closer tonight if it killed her.

'I didn't expect to find romance, I'll be perfectly honest, but it's bound to happen sometimes – ON BOARD – isn't it, Captain?'

Oh God, here we go again, thought Ven. She could smell a conspiracy just as sure as if a sewer had opened nearby.

'Indeed,' said Nigel. 'A few of my officers have met their partners that way.'

'There you go, Ven,' laughed Royston. 'You've got,' he checked his Rolex, 'just over twelve hours to hook a man in uniform.'

'I think I'm going to die,' said Ven through clenched teeth. She said it to herself, but from Nigel's fleeting glance sideways, Ven was almost sure he overheard.

'So how are you getting up to Ayr, Nigel?' asked Frankie.

'In my car,' said Nigel.

'That's quite a drive.' Royston stroked his chin in thought. 'You should play it safe and take a long coffee break halfway. That would be Yorkshire, wouldn't it?'

Poor Ven just wanted the floor of the ship to open up and allow her to drop straight down to the engine room. Or even beyond the keel of the ship where she could be eaten by sharks. It couldn't have been more uncomfortable than the conversation at the table.

After the starters were eaten, the main courses arrived. Ven had chosen the same as Nigel. She spied on his hands as he cut up his steak – even they were perfect too. She tried to bat down thoughts of those hands smoothing over her skin, kneading into her shoulders, unfastening her bra. She knew she was just tormenting herself by doing that.

Buzz brought desserts, and over coffee and delicious coffee truffles, Royston gave everyone his business card and Irene wrote down her address for Stella and Roz, who promised to copy it for the others. Eric and Irene weren't going back on the Easy Rider bus to Barnsley because they were staying for a few days in Southampton with friends whom they had met on a previous cruise. It was at that point that Nigel stood to go and Royston stood with him and shook his hand.

Oh bloody hell, thought Frankie. There was nothing she could do now to push Nigel and Ven that teensy-weensy bit closer – short of luring them both to a cabin and locking them in from the outside. She just wished Ven could have had a bit of romance – she was so overdue for some. She knew she spoke for the others in wanting Ven to be loved up with a nice decent man.

'Thank you for being such wonderful company,' Nigel said, shaking Eric's hand. He gave Stella and Irene a kiss on the cheek, then Roz, then Olive, then Frankie. Lastly, he said a very simple, 'Bye, Venice,' but as she moved towards him, her lips fell short and landed smack on his white collar, planting there a perfect red tattoo.

'Oh my God, I am so sorry. That lipstick isn't supposed to come off!'

'Please don't worry about it,' said Nigel.

But for Venice it was the final straw. All that money in the bank and she was still a bloody useless klutz. She was wrong in thinking there was nothing left to embarrass herself with in front of the most gorgeous man she had ever clapped eyes on. She didn't look up at him as she said, 'Bye.' She didn't want to see the cast of controlled annoyance she knew would be there.

The next few moments were blurred. Ven couldn't remember if he said goodbye again; all she would recall in future was the sight of his back leaving the restaurant.

'He's going to have to go and change now because of me,' sniffed Venice. 'He can't walk around the ship with lipstick all over his collar.'

'Ven, shut up and eat your truffle,' said Roz sternly. 'It won't be the first time he's had lipstick on his whites.'

Which didn't exactly do much to disperse Ven's cloud of despair, which was growing blacker and uglier by the second.

After the coffee had been quaffed and the table of eight stood to go en masse to Broadway for the last time, Buzz and Elvis presented each of them with a pack of souvenir menus. Ven didn't cock up the goodbye hug she gave either of them, she noted. In fact, both hugs were expertly executed, as were the ones she gave Angel and the Great Supremo standing at the door wishing everyone a pleasant trip home. Yep, it seemed that she only made an arse of herself in front of people wearing easily stained suits and whom she fancied the pants off.

The Mermaidia Theatre Company put on a rousing performance of a play called *Land of Hope and Glory*. There was much Britishness to be had – and waving of complimentary Union Jack flags – and it was a very spirited exit for the entertainment.

'Anyone fancy the nightclub?' asked Royston, executing a few steps of dad-dancing on the spot.

'Oh, why not.' Stella shrugged her shoulders. 'Might as well go out with a bang.'

'We're going to turn in now,' said Eric. 'It's been wonderful to meet you all, hasn't it, Irene?'

'It's been lovely,' said Irene with a very teary smile. Eric and Irene made gentle huggy goodbyes, Royston did big bear hugs and Stella suffocated everyone with perfume.

'Oh, by the way,' Eric said, doubling back. 'Venice, I looked it up on the net for you. Florence and Dennis Thompson. Those were the names of the old couple who died on the maiden voyage.'

Ven shivered. Someone was having a laugh, surely.

'Fancy a Horlicks in Café Parisienne?' Olive asked.

'Rock 'n' roll!' said Roz, leading the way.

'I wonder if the Captain got that lipstick off,' mumbled Ven.

Roz linked her arm and hurried her along. 'If he didn't, he'll have a constant reminder of you. Think of it that way.'

They sat in the elegant surroundings of Café Parisienne, nibbling on tiny muffins and having their cups of creamy Horlicks constantly refilled whilst watching the cruise world go by.

Teenagers walked past, tearful and clinging to their new friends and promising to keep in touch for ever; little children were carrying stacks of artwork and goody bags – souvenirs from their play clubs; lovers were braving the now very breezy decks for a long, last romantic look at the sea. The waiters were pulling the shutters down on the bars, Café Parisienne was accepting no more customers.

Finally Olive yawned and after tipping the last of her drink into her mouth, she said, 'That's me done for tonight. I'm off to bed, guys.'

'Me too,' said Roz.

'And me,' said Frankie. 'I've got a lot of bonking to do tomorrow. I need a good night's sleep.'

'Lucky cow,' said Roz. Then she let out a long breath. 'I hope I have.'

'Are we going down for breakfast together? Shall we synchronise our watches for seven?'

'Why – there's only four of us,' said Olive, cracking a joke, though she was feeling less and less jolly by the minute.

'Ho ho,' came the chorused reply.

'I'm going out for a bit of fresh air first,' said Ven. She hugged her friends goodnight and caught the lift up to the top deck, then opened the door and went out into the quiet, breezy dark.

She made sure she was quite alone before she dared to call, 'Florence! Dennis!' She knew it was ridiculous. She knew she hadn't seen ghost-people. There was no such thing as ghosts.

There was no response. Then again, she didn't expect there to be. She wasn't Derek Acorah. She had no explanation for the Florence and Dennis she had met up there. But Florence's words came back to her as a faint echo in her head: *A little glimpse of heaven, maybe?* And Ven knew then that if such a place existed, it would be a ship sailing through sea mists full of other jolly ghosts. Maybe somewhere in Venice her parents' souls were wandering unnoticed amongst the tourists there, in their own heaven.

'Time for bed,' she told herself as a wave of tiredness overcame her. She opened the deck door just as the faintest movement caught the corner of her eye. A single twirl of a dancing couple, a flash of black sparkly sequins – then it was gone.

Frankie dragged her suitcases outside the cabin to be taken ashore, stripped off and then knelt by her bedside. She spoke to God every night asking Him to look after her loved ones, but tonight she felt she needed the full big guns position of kneeling, hands clasped together like a portrait of a child at prayer.

'Dear God. Thank You for this lovely life and please keep my family and my friends safe,' she began as she always did, then added the 'special of the day'. 'God, You gave me the best gift You could have – my health back again. If it's not too much trouble, will You give me three more miracles as well? Please help Olive break away from those bloody Hardcastles – excuse the language – and please, please give Roz a chance to make it right with Manus. And PLEASE, is there anything You can do to bring Ven some love from a good man? And if You can make that good man Captain Nigel I'll go to confession every week. Well, every month. Not that I'll have anything to confess because I'll be so good You won't believe. Amen.' And she crossed herself and added yet another 'please'.

SOUTHAMPTON

Chapter 73

The ship was sickeningly still the next morning. Ven drew her curtains back to a view of grumpy skies and a dull grey sea. The sun hadn't even gotten out of bed, from the looks of it. It had opened one eye, thought 'sod that for a lark', and pulled the covers back over itself.

She was doing her fourteenth check around the cabin, making sure she hadn't forgotten anything when the others called for her. Together they wended down to the Ambrosia in long sleeves and jeans, and ordered their last monster breakfasts on board. Out of the restaurant window they could see people leaving the ship and entering the terminal to pick up their suitcases.

After breakfast, they went back to their cabins to pick up their hand luggage and say goodbye to Jesus. Ven checked the cabin phone, trying not to hope that Nigel had rung and left a message. He hadn't. Within the hour they were all queueing at the ship's exit, handing in their cruise cards, taking a last backward look at the opulent ship which they were about to abandon for a cold, depressing building in Southampton docks.

'I'd hoped Nigel would come leaping down the stairs for you,' said Frankie, giving her a comforting squeeze. 'At least to say "keep in touch – here's my mobile number". I'm sure he fancied you.'

Ven tried to look unconcerned. 'Don't be daft,' she said. 'How many women must fall in love with him every single cruise. And if he did fancy me, which he didn't, he should have said something.' And she meant it. There was no way that Ven would ever again settle for anything less than being claimed masterfully and firmly. She wanted a man next time, not a wimp. Only her own Richard Gere would do.

'Oh God, it's Clive again and his amazing pea repartee!' Roz noticed as they approached the buses. 'I might as well slit my wrists now.' She, Olive and Ven pulled their cases to the side of the Easy Rider coach heading to Barnsley and Leeds and York, whilst Frankie told the Derby bus driver that she wouldn't be coming back with him. Vaughan was waiting by the trolleys for her in black leather and looking back in his fashion comfort zone.

'Ring me,' said Frankie to Roz.

'Course I will,' said Roz, filling up.

'You'll be okay with Manus, I've got a feeling,' said Frankie, hugging her tightly. 'See you soon.'

'Promise,' said Roz. The tears were out now and flowing fast.

'Don't wear him out too quickly,' said Ven, giving Frankie a big kiss.

'I won't,' grinned Frankie. 'I want this one to last for a while.' Then she threw her arms around Olive. Oh, how she wanted to nag Olive, but the intensity of that hug said it all. She didn't need to say a single word.

Then the bus set off to Barnsley whilst Frankie and Vaughan waved it off, their arms entwined around each other's waists.

Chapter 74

The house looked deserted when Roz got out of the taxi. The door was locked when she tried it and her heart sank. She pushed the key in, turned it and just hoped she wouldn't find the place emptied of Manus's things.

The front room was tidy with a hint of furniture polish in the air. To her relief, Manus's denim jacket was hanging on the coat-rack – he would never have left without that. His work boots were lined up beneath it.

'Hello?' she called.

'Here,' said a small voice from upstairs so faintly that she almost doubted she had heard it.

Roz dumped her bags and climbed the stairs. Their bedroom door was shut. She pushed it open and found Manus sitting on the bed, a suitcase at the side of him, and she gasped. The room was full of flowers; everywhere she looked were bouquets of every colour, every kind, and the bed was covered in rose petals.

'I know you think they're a waste of money,' he said.

'No ... no, they're gorgeous.' Tears started to course down her face and when she wiped them away, she saw that his eyes were full of water too.

'Roz, I don't want us to split up, but I'm ready to go, if that's what you want.'

'Oh Manus,' she croaked in a tiny voice, 'I don't want you to leave.' The sight of that suitcase was breaking her heart. 'I've missed you. I wish I could tell you how much.'

The foreign tenderness in her voice forced Manus's tears to spill over and Roz's heart lurched towards him.

'Sod it,' she cried, 'I'm going to tell you how much: loads and loads and loads. I love you, Manus Howard.'

'Come here,' gulped Manus, holding out his arms. And Roz moved into them and let them close around her and she felt safe and warm and back home in every sense of the word.

There had been a mischievous little thought in Manus's mind that night of Jonie's dinner party. It was: 'What sort of man turns it down when it's on a plate?' because Jonie had made it very clear that no-strings sex was on the menu after coffee and her seductive Godiva chocolates. But Manus also knew that the answer was, 'A man in love with his woman,' because there was no other girl for him who would do. Not until he had pushed it far beyond the boundaries, not until he had more proof that his relationship was dead and gone and buried; whilst there was the hint of a breath left in it, he was determined to fight for it.

And then he had suddenly remembered how Jonie always tended to home in on boys who were with someone she could steal them away from. Probably the reason she had never been truly interested in young single Manus at college.

He had drawn away before her lips touched his skin and thanked her for a lovely evening. Then he had walked home.

Olive had a moment of bravery as the taxi drew up outside 15, Land Lane. She almost told the taxi driver to 'carry on'. But carry on to where? *Turn left at the bottom of the street and straight on until you reach Cephalonia.* Yeah, right.

She paid the taxi driver and stood outside the front door. She had a cheque for nearly half a million pounds in her handbag which would allow her to abandon everything she had in that house and make a fresh start, so why was she back here? She knew now that she didn't love David and she didn't know when she had stopped. If he met her at the door with a bouquet of red roses, would she stay with him because she daren't say the words 'I don't love you and I'm leaving'?

She hardly dared walk inside, because if Doreen was in a pickle and David was incapacitated, she knew her stupid ingrained sense of guilt and duty that bound her to them would tighten and hold her, however many digits there were on that cheque.

She pushed the door open, expecting the smell of smoke and dirty, sweaty clothes to engulf her, but was shocked to find her nasal senses being assailed by the floral tones of Shake 'n' Vac. Shoes were in pairs by the door – only David's shoes, she noted; the telephone table in the hall polished, the mirror above it free of dust, the carpet runner devoid of white bits. Likewise the lounge was perfectly tidy, the dining table clear, except for a beautiful display of perfect-petalled red roses in a vase in the middle of it. Doreen's chair was now in the back corner of the room by the sideboard. There was absolutely no sign of her at all.

'Hello, stranger!' said David, popping his head out of the kitchen. He looked remarkably calm for a husband whose wife had buggered off sixteen days ago without a word. He came forwards and they gave each other an awkward hug, because they didn't usually do demonstrative affection.

'Had a nice time?' he asked, wiping his hands nervously on his trousers. Clean trousers as well, she noticed. He'd never learned to use the washing machine, had he?

'Lovely,' said Olive.

'You look well.'

'Thanks.'

They were talking to each other like strangers on a first date. And that, Olive realised then, was because they *were* strangers.

They had lived in the same house, slept in the same bed, but they didn't *know* each other. The David she did know was long gone. This man in front of her might have had a bad back or not, she didn't know what he spent his slyly-earned money on or what he did whilst she was working. He might have known his mother was as big a health-charlatan as he was, or he might have been in ignorance. All questions and no answers, which wasn't the sign of a healthy relationship.

'Where's Doreen?' asked Olive, nodding towards the chair.

'She's left,' smiled David. 'And so has Kevin. The house is ours and ours alone.' He thumbed towards the kitchen. 'I'll just brew us some tea.'

Brew us some tea? She remained in a state of shock whilst he faffed about in the kitchen humming 'If I Were a Rich Man'.

'You'll never believe this,' he said, eventually appearing with a teapot, a carton of milk and a sugar bowl on a tray. *Am I in the right house?* said Olive to herself. She didn't even think he could pick out a teapot in an identity parade of that, a mop and an Alsatian!

'Well . . .' he began, pouring the tea straight out. It must have only brewed for seconds and was as weak as witch pee. Then he sloshed milk into both cups and two sugars into each. He didn't even know she liked it strong, black and sugarless. After thirteen years of marriage. 'It turns out that Vernon Turbot at the fish shop is my real dad. And his wife died. And it turns out – this is the funny bit – that he and Mum have been waiting for over forty years – *forty years* – to be together! He's moved her into his big house in Kerry Park Avenue. She's springing around like an Easter lamb.'

He took a huge slurp of tea and Olive shuddered at the noise. David was incapable of taking a drink without sounding as if it was being sucked down a drain.

'And guess what . . . he's handed over his fish empire. To me! We. Are. Rich!'

Olive shook her head to test she was still conscious and not in a coma somewhere, dreaming this.

'Your cleaning days are over, love. We're the ones with a cleaner now!' He spread his hand out towards the front room. Ah, so he hadn't done it himself. He'd got a woman in.

David put his tea on the table, next to the vase of flowers that she now saw were made of cheap plastic. 'Come upstairs, I've got more things to show you.'

For a fat lad with a documented back problem he didn't half leap up the stairs. Olive followed, wondering what other revelations he had in store. A helipad on the roof? A Juliet balcony built showing a view of a newly dug moat in the back yard?

'Da da!' He pushed open his mother's bedroom door and she walked in to see her cream duvet set on Doreen's bed. The door of Doreen's old wardrobe was peeping open and Olive could see her own clothes hanging up there.

'We've got the big bedroom!' said David, as excitedly as if he'd just announced he'd won *Britain's Got Talent*. 'And look.' He opened the wardrobe door fully and pulled out the three dresses he'd had made for her.

'Olive – you're going to manage the fish shops! It gets a bit hot in there, so the girls wear these dresses and an apron. The white ones are for during the week, the green one for weekends.'

He looked so thrilled by the present that, instinctively, Olive tried to arrange her features into a semblance of gratitude. But even she, nice person as she was, had a bit of difficulty with that. The result was a pained rictus expression, seen only on deranged clowns in low-budget horror movies.

'Two minutes. I need a crap,' David then said, throwing the dresses onto the bed for her to coo over and bouncing to the bathroom next door. Somewhere in the back of Olive's mind, a lone snapshot of Atho Petrakis arose to torture her. He would never have fanfared his intention to defecate.

'Can you believe Mum, eh? Forty years she's waited,' laughed David, talking above a staccato farting salvo that sounded as if a *Rocky* movie was about to start. 'She said that some people can't live properly without passion and how lucky we are that we can.'

Olive turned to the window. Someone from Ketherwood Club was just putting out two wheelie bins, the dossers from the social security flats were sitting outside clustered around a portable television watching a football match and drinking cans of cider. There wasn't a patch of green, a single tree, a hint of the sea, a hillside with a goat on it, a pot of white roses . . .

'I've been thinking, maybe we could have a little holiday before you start work. There's a lovely three-star hotel in Bridlington. And what do you think about a really big telly?' David flushed the toilet and scurried back into his mum's bedroom.

'I'd definitely leave it longer than five minutes before you go in there . . . Olive?'

Olive was not there. And when he went downstairs, he found the suitcases she had deposited by the door had also gone.

Chapter 75

Ven had just poured herself a cup of tea. Her eyes fell on the clock and she noted that it was the time for going up for afternoon scones and diddy sandwiches in the Buttery. As it was, she would have to satisfy herself with a couple of Jammie Dodgers. But she wasn't hungry.

She had just come off the phone from Jen to let her know she was home, only to find that Ethel had died whilst she was away. Fell to sleep in the sunshine and never woke up, poor old soul. They'd buried her in the meadow at the side of the farm and hoped Ven didn't mind. She didn't – she knew Ethel loved it there. And she wondered if the ghost of Ethel would wander happily around the farm sometimes, nosying in the barns for the fat mice she was too old and well-fed to chase – she hoped so. Heaven seemed a more believable prospect since she had been on the ship.

She forced some jollity into her voice as she shared the news of her lottery win with Jen. Only when she was off the phone did Ven let the façade fall and sob into her hands.

Ironically, the theme tune for *An Officer and a Gentleman* came on the radio and Ven sipped her tea and wondered whether men in white uniforms really did strut into workplaces, whisk women off their feet and carry them off into the sunset? She closed her eyes as Joe Cocker and Jennifer Warnes sang about love lifting people up to where they belonged and fantasised that Nigel was opening her gate, striding up the path and getting his thumb ready to press her doorbell.

She nearly fainted with shock when it then rang.

Ven poured out an extra cup of tea.

'I know it's a bloody cheek me asking this,' said Olive, 'but can you give me a sub on that cheque you gave me?'

'Only if you're going to spend it on a plane ticket,' said Ven.

'I am. I'm doing a *Shirley Valentine*.'

'What happened to make you change your mind?' Ven tipped a newly opened packet of Jammie Dodgers onto a plate.

'God, where to start!' said Olive. But start she did and told Ven all about the changes in Land Lane. '. . . I don't want to be in limbo for forty years like Doreen was,' she ended. 'She took her chance and I'm taking mine.'

'Bloody good for you!' said Ven. 'You're staying here with me, presumably, until you get a flight? You're not going to chicken out and go back?'

Olive thought of Land Lane, full of farty smells, a life of luxury managing fish shops and a long weekend in Bridlington on the horizon. 'I will, if you don't mind,' she smiled.

Ven's heart didn't jump when the doorbell went again. But it didn't half begin to pound when she saw who was on her doorstep.

Chapter 76

'Nigel?' she gulped. This was a bit random, to say the least. Especially because he was dressed in whites and looking so handsome that he made Richard Gere look like Quasimodo.

'Venice.' He sighed. From the way his hands were fidgeting and his lips moving soundlessly over words, it seemed he had something to say but couldn't find the beginning of the thread.

Olive came to the door behind Ven, then slipped back discreetly into the kitchen, where she scrunched herself up into a ball to stop herself screaming aloud with joy. She knew he hadn't turned up because her friend had inadvertently left behind a pair of tights in her cabin.

'Venice,' Nigel said again. He took a deep breath and launched in. 'I really enjoyed your company on board and I did think you were one of those guests who I'd be a little bit sadder about saying goodbye to. I also thought I was getting too involved and tried to distance myself some nights, but I found that was impossible. I just couldn't get you out of my mind.'

'Couldn't you?' squealed Venice. Mind you, that was no surprise really. He'd be having nightmares about her floating nipples for years to come.

'No, I couldn't,' he said softly. 'I'm going to the Fjords and Iceland, as you know, in three days. Would you like me to pick you up on the way back down from Ayr so you can join me on the *Mermaidia* again? See where we go from there?'

'*Me?*' said Ven, which even by her standards was a ridiculous thing to say. She heard Olive groan in frustration behind the door.

'Oh yes, most definitely you. I'll put you in your own cabin, obviously, I wouldn't want to presume . . . Plus if we don't get on, you can ignore me for the duration of the cruise.'

Then he moved forward and his hands came out and cradled her face. 'It was the lipstick on my collar that decided it all.'

'Oh God!' cringed Ven. 'Couldn't you get it off? I've got some Vanish—'

'Never mind that,' Nigel cut her off. 'I thought, This woman just can't get things quite right. The asparagus, the medicine, the Italian . . .'

What did he mean by 'the Italian'?

'. . . the shop, the swimsuit – then you stood up for the waiter and I thought you were amazing. But Ven – Venice Smith – when you put that lipstick on my collar, I just wanted to pick you up and kiss you.'

'Er . . . did you?' She couldn't work out the connection at all. Why would this big gorgeous officer and gentleman want to kiss a total twerp like herself who ruined his uniform?

'Oh yes,' said Nigel. His eyes were now fixed on hers. 'Everything in my life has always been so . . . precise. And you are –' he grinned a knicker-meltingly sexy grin '– a magnificent oasis of chaos. Would you allow me to kiss you, ma'am?'

'Kiss *me*? Do you really want to?'

'Oh, for God's sake,' rang out Olive's voice from behind the door. 'Don't bloody ask her, Nigel! Sometimes you can be too much of an officer and a gentleman.'

'Oooh!' Venice yelped with shocked delight as Nigel hooked his arm behind her legs and swooped her up. Then his soft mouth fell bull's-eye, with no mistakes, precisely and fabulously onto her own.

Epilogue

The Bahamas, Boxing Day, fifteen months later

'"Another shitty day in paradise", as Royston used to say,' sighed Frankie, stretching fully out on the sunbed, just as Roz flopped onto the next one.

'Have you checked on the boys?' asked Olive. 'Are they happy?'

'Well,' began Roz, reaching over to steal some of Ven's mineral water, 'I'd say the word is more *merry* than happy. Salvatore is introducing Manus to the joys of getting pissed on grappa.'

'Good old Dad,' smiled Frankie. 'Any excuse with him. So where's my lovely groom?'

'Vaughan, Freddy and Atho are on the ouzo,' said Roz.

'I don't know, marry a bloke on Christmas Eve and two days later he's deserted you to bond with the lads,' tutted Frankie with mock exasperation.

'Atho gets very frisky when he's had a few ouzos. I'd brace yourself later, Frankie. Vaughan will be hot to trot.' The six-months-pregnant Olive grinned. She was tanned and glowing and the picture of happiness. She was now Mrs Petrakis with a baby boy and baby girl twin Petrakises growing plump and beautiful inside her. She looked more Greek goddess than ex-

Barnsley housewife with her white-blonde hair wet and her olive-green eyes lit with loved-up, contented joy.

Frankie smiled at her. 'Do you ever think you did the wrong thing, leaving David?' They all burst into laughter at that.

'He's doing all right, trust me,' she said. 'I hear Dolly Braithwaite does his downstairs at least twice a week.' Which raised a chorus of 'oohs'.

David had been terrified that Olive would claim half his chip-shop fortune, but had been pleasantly amazed that she had promised – as the deserting party – to walk away with nothing from him if he settled for a quickie divorce. David and Dolly would be happy with a comfortable passion-free life, content within the confines of weekends in Bridlington, and with fish suppers on permanent tap.

'That's a nice tankini, by the way, Ven,' said Olive. 'Where did you get that?'

'Primark,' grinned Ven. 'And I'll tell you what, it doesn't half do the proper job in keeping my boobs in place, unlike that expensive designer one I brought with me on that first cruise.'

'You can take a bird out of Barnsley, but you can't take Barnsley out of the bird,' winked Roz.

'Bet Nigel is gutted,' said Frankie. 'I think he liked the old cossy just fine.'

The money hadn't changed them one iota. Not where it counted. Ven still liked to poke around 'Primarni' for her bargains, Roz was now working with Manus in his newly extended garage. She was now Mrs Howard, after Manus whisked her up to Gretna Green on Valentine's Day. Olive had bought property in Cephalonia, which she had scrubbed till it shone, and land at the back of the villa on which to grow more olives. She and Atho had a lot of fun in their olive groves. As for Frankie, she and Vaughan lived totally stress-free in the most beautiful olde-worlde cottage. She now taught 'baby Italian' at the local school and Vaughan tinkered around rebuilding bikes and wearing his old leathers. They were, in Yorkshire terms, 'happy as pigs in muck'.

'My little honeymoon babies,' sighed Olive fondly, her hand rubbing over her rounded tum. 'Though I'm not sure about following your parents' example, Ven, and calling them after the possible places of their conception.'

'Which are what?' asked Ven.

'"Kitchen table" and "against an olive tree".'

Venice laughed. 'You minx! Well, choose carefully, my darling, because their names could change their lives one day.' As she knew only too well. If she hadn't been called Venice, she might never have booked that birthday cruise to go there and met the dashing Nigel O'Shaughnessy. Or been lifted up where she belonged into his uniformed arms on her own doorstep. Or travelled to the Fjords with him, and the Canaries, or been proposed to in a storm of fireworks in Madeira as the New Year blasted in, or married him in – well, Venice of course. Her three bridesmaids flew in with Jen and her family for the weekend and devoured twelve-million-calories'-worth of ice cream in Angelo's. And she would never have had her interest in writing rejuvenated by Rik Knight-Jones enough to write a book about four friends on a ship, which was due to be published in the spring. It was part of a three-book deal – a series of stories about different people finding love on board.

And now the four of them were all married and Olive was having babies. And they were on the *Mermaidia* once again, but this time on a twenty-two-nighter, sailing around the Bahamas.

'So how many cruises have you been on now?' smirked Ven in a pompous tone. 'I'll have you know, this is my fifteenth on the *Mermaidia*. We did have to slum it for a little while on the new ship *Selina*. Absolute hell. Only five swimming pools.'

'Cocky cow!' laughed Frankie. 'Have Eric and Irene been on recently?'

'They were on the Saint Petersburg cruise. Royston and Stella went on the New Orleans one. He and his wardrobe are as loud as ever, I'm happy to report.'

'Look at that cloud – it looks like a flamenco dancer,' said Frankie.

Roz put on her sunglasses and looked up. 'That's a hell of an imagination you've got there, Frank. How in the name of cock does that look like a flamenco dancer?'

'Look.' Frankie drew into the air. 'That's her skirt and that's her arm up and there's that comb thing on her head.'

'Mantequilla,' clarified Ven.

'Mantilla, you fart,' laughed Frankie. 'Mantequilla is Spanish for butter.'

'Oy you, don't you dare start flashing your language skills about on my husband's ship!' Ven shook her finger at her friend. 'Do you know, it took Nigel over six months to 'fess up to me how you'd taught me to ask for directions in Venice.'

'Whoops,' laughed Frankie. 'Still, I like to think it endeared you to him a little bit more. And I bet you've said it again to him since,' she added with a wink.

'You still dancing, Roz?' asked Olive.

'Yep: belly, bhangra and I've just started flamenco.' She leaned forward to the others and whispered, 'Manus likes the costumes, if you know what I mean. I only have to pick up my castanets and he's got that look in his eye.' But Roz didn't seem to be complaining.

Ven could see the dancer in the sky along with Roz. But she had never seen Florence and Dennis Thompson again, however many times she had been up on the top deck at night. Not even a shimmer of sequins in the shadows. Maybe they really had just been there to show her a little taste of the heaven she was now certain existed.

'Eeh, you can't buy this, can you?' said Olive, with a contented yawn. 'Well, you can buy the big houses and the nice cars and the olive groves and the cruises, but you can't buy the babies or the lovely men or friendships, can you? You can't buy *us*.'

'No,' sighed Mrs Ocean Sea with smiley dimples as deep as the Adriatic sea and a grin that couldn't be bought. Not even on worldwide eBay. Not even for a billion pounds. 'No, Mrs Petrakis, you most definitely can't.'

Acknowledgements

There is a host of fabulous people I have to wave thanks to for both inspiring and helping me to write this book.

Firstly the P & O Cruises posse: to my lovely friend the angelic Michele Andjel who introduced me to ice wine – just when I thought life couldn't get any better. And to Lorraine Sadowski, who looked after me so beautifully on board the *Azura*. To Captain Paul Brown who answered all my daft questions with generous patience and Captain Hamish Reid who is quite simply unforgettable. And members of their wonderful crew: 'Ice-cream Jonathan', Pete Diaz, Neil Lopez, Marshall, Malone, the 'supreme' Frankie, the charming Vincent in '17', Bombay Bertie, Jerry, George, Rebecca, Brooke, 'John the Perfume' and the fabulous Neil Oliver – the presence of these people makes going on ships such an added joy for my family and me.

And to all the lovely friends I've met and made on my travels abroad including: the generous and mad Baister family – Wayne, Liz and Elle, Ian and Liz Barry, David and Sylvia Williams, Pete and Jean McCormack, Brian and Catherine Stevenson, 'The Royle Family' – Olive and Don, Margaret and Paul Richards, Pat, Sam and Keith Richards (not 'that one' but he's still a damned good musician!), Julie, John and Will Hopcroft, Terry and Dave Wigham and the press pack on my last 'essential research' holiday who were such fun to break bread with – Peter and Joan Charlton, Richard and Emma Gaisford, Gerard Greaves and Lisa Sewards. Keith and Eileen Hamilton, Gary Buchanan – and so many others who have been a joy to mingle with.

To the sublimely talented James Nash at www.james nash.co.uk. An amazing poet, a sweet man and my friend.

To the bellissima Franca Martella at BBC Radio Sheffield who sorts out my Italian, however embarrassing the task! To the adorable Carnevale family who lent me their magnificent name. And to the wonderful Restaurant Rex in Corfu for converting me to olives.

To my cruise-buddy – the fabulous Jill Mansell who wrote my header quote and with whom it will always be a pleasure to drink a glass of bubbly on the high seas.

To 'my team' – my gorgeous agent and amigo Lizzy Kremer and all at David Higham and to EVERYONE at my publishers who have been such a constant support and a dream to work with, especially the superlative Suzanne Baboneau, Libby Yevtushenko, Max Hitchcock, Amanda Shipp and Grainne Reidy. You are the BEST and I am blessed to have you.

Last but by no means least – the biggest, fattest thank-you imaginable to my publicist par excellence Nigel Stoneman. He knows what for.